PEGASUS IN SPACE

Anne McCaffrey's books can be read individually or as series.
However, for greatest enjoyment the following sequences are recommended:

The Dragon Books
DRAGONFLIGHT
DRAGONQUEST
DRAGONSONG
DRAGONSINGER: HARPER OF PERN
THE WHITE DRAGON
DRAGONDRUMS
MORETA: DRAGONLADY OF PERN
NERILKA'S STORY & THE COELURA
DRAGONSDAWN
THE RENEGADES OF PERN
ALL THE WEYRS OF PERN
THE CHRONICLES OF PERN: FIRST FALL
THE DOLPHINS OF PERN
RED STAR RISING: THE SECOND CHRONICLES OF PERN (US publish as DRAGONSEYE)
THE MASTERHARPER OF PERN

Crystal Singer Books
THE CRYSTAL SINGER
KILLASHANDRA
CRYSTAL LINE

Talent Series
TO RIDE PEGASUS
PEGASUS IN FLIGHT

Tower and the Hive Sequence
THE ROWAN
DAMIA
DAMIA'S CHILDREN
LYON'S PRIDE
THE TOWER AND THE HIVE

Catteni Sequence
FREEDOM'S LANDING
FREEDOM'S CHOICE
FREEDOM'S CHALLENGE

The Acorna Series (written in collaboration with Margaret Ball)
ACORNA
ACORNA'S QUEST

Individual Titles
RESTOREE
DECISION AT DOONA
THE SHIP WHO SANG
GET OFF THE UNICORN
THE GIRL WHO HEARD DRAGONS
NIMISHA'S SHIP

Written in collaboration with Elizabeth Ann Scarborough
POWERS THAT BE
POWER LINES
POWER PLAY

PEGASUS IN SPACE

Anne McCaffrey

BANTAM PRESS

LONDON · NEW YORK · TORONTO · SYDNEY · AUCKLAND

TRANSWORLD PUBLISHERS
61–63 Uxbridge Road, London W5 5SA
a division of The Random House Group Ltd

RANDOM HOUSE AUSTRALIA (PTY) LTD
20 Alfred Street, Milsons Point, Sydney
New South Wales 2061, Australia

RANDOM HOUSE NEW ZEALAND
18 Poland Road, Glenfield, Auckland 10, New Zealand

RANDOM HOUSE SOUTH AFRICA (PTY) LTD
Endulini, 5a Jubilee Road, Parktown 2193, South Africa

Published 2000 by Bantam Press
a division of Transworld Publishers

A catalogue record for this book is available from the British Library
ISBN 0593 043278

Typeset in 11/12pt Times by Kestrel Data, Exeter, Devon

Printed in Great Britain by
Mackays of Chatham plc, Chatham, Kent

1 3 5 7 9 10 8 6 4 2

This book is respectfully dedicated to
Christopher Reeve
With the devout hope that he realizes his ambition – to
stand on his own two feet once again in 2002!

Acknowledgements

Foremost on my list of 'thank-yous' for this novel is Dr Steven Beard of the UK Astronomy Technological Centre, Royal Observatory in Edinburgh. I asked for help and he gave me a large measure of valuable information, so that I had more than enough for this part of the *Pegasus* universe. Not only is he a marvellous punster but also a dedicated researcher, leading me to many previously unexplored paths of stargazing and suggesting useful websites where my basic reference texts were out of date. He patiently went over drafts, and consequently the relevant characters are well informed. I would like to thank Elizabeth Kerner, author of *Song in the Silence*, for introducing me to Dr Beard.

Dr Brian Kane of the Lowell Observatory website also responded to my specific queries for which I am indeed grateful.

Mark Finkelstein, DO, FAOCR of Du Pont Hospital for Children, who dropped by Dragonhold for tea one afternoon with his friend, Michael Zeik, and offered assistance to me, found me taking him up on his kind offer.

Dr Donald L. Henninger of JSC NASA was somewhat surprised by my phone call asking to confirm some specific information on CELSS – controlled ecological life-support systems. He gave me what I needed to know and for that I am indebted to him. I hadn't realized so much had changed from what we SF writers used to use in hydroponic gardens on space ships and stations.

Books on Bangladesh, its geography, culture and language, published in Australia, were accessed from Amazon.com and Amazon.co.uk. The names will be different from those current in many American-printed atlases, especially as the major rivers change their beds and names to whatever the local people choose. I am deeply indebted for the help of Dr S. Farid Ahmed from Dhaka, currently Registrar at the Borders Hospital, Scotland, for his assistance that has prevented me from making several glaring misrepresentations.

My son, Todd McCaffrey, came forward magnificently with suggestions and solutions for the limo (lunar insertion moon orbit) scenes, and the quantum mechanical explanation of the parapsychic. Jenna Scott McCaffrey read with her copy-editor's eyes on the text. So have my daughter, Richard Woods, Georgeanne Kennedy, Lea Day, and Mary Jean Holmes.

I am happy to acknowledge the continued assistance and support of Shelly Shapiro, my editor at Del Rey, Diane Pearson, my editor at Transworld-Corgi, and Martha Trachtenberg, the copy editor who was able to joggle my short-term memory about names and relationships.

One other point: since the genesis of the *Pegasus* books (and indeed the *Rowan/Tower and Hive* series) is the short story I wrote back in 1959, I have been constrained to keep to the people and places mentioned so long ago. Forty years later, we understand science and ourselves more clearly and in greater detail. I have kept to the original premises and places in *The Lady in the Tower*, while moving along with such advances as are possible and extrapolating as has seemed logical.

A man's reach should exceed his grasp
Or what's a heaven for?

ROBERT BROWNING (1855)

CHAPTER ONE

As Peter Reidinger was teleporting in gestalt with the huge Jerhattan Power Station to bring the kinetics down from Padrugoi Space Station to Dhaka, an exhausted group of men and women were trying to reach the shelter of the nearest *shomiti*. With the bundles they had snatched from their homes before escaping the breached levees, they staggered to higher ground along the muddy banks of the Jamuna River. They had to scramble to bridge the gaps in the levee mounds that, in places, were sliding into the Jamuna's torrent. Despite Herculean efforts by the government and the local administrators in the Rajshahi Division, the levees had not supplied the longed-for protection to those living along its bank.

Anger at the 'authorities' consumed Zahid Idris Miah and sustained him as he slogged at the head of the group from his *bari*, flashing the long-life light ahead of him. In the gloom of this monsoon, the tool at least kept them from slithering into places where the Jamuna had chewed ravines into the levee bank in its rush to the sea. He devoutly mumbled prayers to Iswah that this tool was truly a 'long-life' torch. He half expected it to fade out now, when it was most needed, like so many other items that came to his small *bari* south of

11

Sirajganj as Rajshahi Division tried to – what was the *ingraji* word? – 'upgrade' him and the other jute farmers.

They should have kept a close watch on the levees in this storm. *They* should have worked more diligently to re-inforce the collecting lakes along the Jamuna River. *They* had promised to do so, to keep more of Bangladesh from sliding beneath the Bay. He vaguely knew that a great new engineering process that had kept some city in Italia from drowning had been adapted to keep the Bay of Bengal from inundating the coastal regions near the mouth of the Ganges. Much land had been lost along the sea coast in spite of the efforts of many very gifted engineers. The once inland city of Khulna was now protected by the Great Dyke, which had been erected three decades ago. Barisal City was also ringed south and east by the Ocean Dykes, invented by yet other westerners who had been determined to keep their land from drowning. Those islands that had once dotted the Bay of Bengal, Bhola, Hatiya, and Sondwip – where the Meghna River flowed into the Bay – had been inundated and the people saved only by the massive efforts of the World Relief Organization.

He had heard that the islands of Kutubdia and Maheskhali, near Cox's Bazar, were also gone, and the tip of Chittagong. Never having been farther from his *bari* than Sirajganj, these places might as well have been in Great India or Meriki. What had happened to those who had helped before? Had they, like so many others, deserted the Bangla in their hour of need? He wiped the sudden spurt of wind-driven rain from his face. Were they tired of rescuing poor Bangladeshi? He wasn't surprised: who cared, but Iswah, what happened to the poor? The wind smacked at his lean, work-honed frame again and he slid on the mud, the light briefly aimed to his right.

Was that debris now bobbing along on the swift-flowing current the plants he had struggled so to keep watered during the dry winter season? There was always too much of everything, Iswah be praised, he added quickly when it wasn't needed. The Jamuna had irrigated his fields but *this* was overdoing it.

'Where be those who aid? Where be they when we have great need of them? Curses be on their names and every generation of them!' Zahid roared above the wind, waving about both hands, making the torchlight stab about the darkness.

Behind him, Jamila wailed, berating her husband. 'Do not wave our light about so! How am I seeing where to put my feet? If it falls from your hand, how will we be seeing where dry land is?' She had hiked up her sari, its sodden, muddy hem banging against her thin calves. He had already reprimanded her several times for her immodesty.

'Hush, woman. Rafiq and Rahim have torches. Watch your sari that you do not tempt Ayud Bondha.' To emphasize his displeasure in her demeanour, he lengthened his stride, sweeping the ray of light in front of him to see where he was going. This disgruntled him more, for it might appear to her that he was heeding her complaint.

'How far to go now, Zahid?' Salma, Ayud Bondha's young wife, cried in ragged gasps. She had to shout above the wind's noise. She was many months pregnant with her first-born, and clumsy. Ayud was half carrying her, both of them slipping about in the thick mud.

Zahid didn't like Salma. As a young girl, she had been chosen from her village to go to the school to learn to read and write and do sums. Because of that, she did not efface herself, as a proper woman should, speaking out often in the *shomiti* with unseemly disregard of custom. Ayud Bondha always indulged her, smiling and doing nothing to discipline her, as a husband should.

'We will be seeing *shomiti* lights soon,' Zahid said, and sent his beam ahead of them, squinting to see any glimmer from their destination. *Shomiti* were still built on heavy concrete pillars, thanks be to Iswah, so their shelter remained above the flooded lands. There would be light cylinders – also of the long-life variety – hung on the corners of the covered veranda, to show refugees their way through the day's darkness, wind and rain.

'Aiyeee!' screamed his wife, sliding her length in the mud, face down. The fall both amused and irritated Zahid.

13

Sputtering curses, he caught hold of her arm with his free hand, the arc of the light he held going every which way again. Ayud Bondha grasped her other flailing arm and, between them, they managed to lift her out of the mud. Solicitously, Salma used the long end of her already sodden sari to clear Jamila's mud-smeared face while she gasped for breath and spat out the grit in her mouth.

'Aiyeee!' Jamila screamed again, wildly pointing at the rushing water. 'Something in the river!' She grabbed her husband's hand with her muddied ones and steadied the broad beam of the flashlight on what she had glimpsed when the beam was erratically flashing about.

'Nothing alive,' Zahid retorted, trying to wrest control of the torch from her.

'I see something, too,' Salma said, and Zahid snarled under his breath. That was all he needed. For her to side with the thin stick who was his wife.

'There is something,' Ayud agreed, and by then the rest of their group had caught up to them.

Rafiq and Rahim added their lights to his reluctant one and even he had to admit that there was something, a small child perhaps, clinging to the fork of two branches. Zahid was stunned. A tree of such size had to have floated down all the way from the Terai region. Even as he watched, he saw movement, a wide-open mouth in a white face, probably calling for help. Suddenly, the current of the Jamuna whimsically pushed the tree closer to the levee.

'*Joldi!*' cried Salma, pushing at Zahid. '*Sahajyo!* Quick! Help!'

'*Ki kore?* How?' Zahid demanded, one hand gesturing his helplessness, while with the other he stubbornly followed the slowly spinning mass with his light.

'Dig your feet in!' Rahim cried, leaping forward. 'We make a chain. Grab my hand, Rafiq. You too, Jabbar, Khaliq. Make a chain. Zahid, light us.'

Rahim barely got a firm grip on Rafiq's hand before Zahid pushed Jabbar and Khaliq into place, making himself the end of the human rescue line. He was as heavy as Rahim, and could be the anchor despite the slippery mud. His wife wailed and moaned that surely they would not be in time, that they would all fall in the water and drown, and then what would become of them? Then Salma grabbed the light from Zahid's hand as he was pulled forward, closer to the edge of the levee. Frantically he dug his heels into the slippery soil, determined to stop his forward movement. Khaliq also dug his feet in. Then Rahim, living up to his name of 'mighty soldier', caught hold of the nearest branch of the tree fork and hauled it closer. He stretched the human chain to its full length as he made his first grab at the child. It let out a shriek that could be heard above the wind's screech and lay limp across the bole. Rahim made a second grab and got a firm grip on one leg.

'*Tana!*' cried Rahim, struggling to shift his balance back to the levee.

Pull the others did, Jabbar going down on his knees in the mud to keep from sliding farther. As Rahim teetered backward, Khaliq dropped Jabbar's hand and rushed to grab Rahim's shirt to draw him and his burden to the relative safety of higher bank. Salma focused the light on the tree which, its passenger now safely ashore, was caught by an eddy and swirled away.

'Light, woman!' Zahid shouted, angrily snatching it back and shining it on the child.

Rain slanted down on the unconscious face and the open mouth. Suddenly Rahim jerked the tattered shirt down, glancing warily at Jamila who had bent to examine the human flotsam.

'A girl child,' she said. Then she saw and touched the limp left arm that dangled at an unnatural angle. 'Broken.'

'Give Iswah thanks for preserving the child,' murmured Zahid.

'Did I do that?' asked Rahim, panting from his exertions and reaching out to the injured limb.

'Iswah knows,' Jamila said with pious absolution. 'Young bones heal easily.'

'You were holding the other arm, Rahim Ali,' Salma said, flinging a sodden braid over her shoulder.

15

'How could you see?' Zahid demanded.

'I was holding the light,' she replied, but now Ayud Bondha tapped her shoulder in tacit reprimand. 'I did see,' she said defensively. Then she fumbled in the bundle she had over her shoulder and brought out a smoothed stick, the wood oiled by long usage in cooking. 'Jamila, this for a splint. Tie with this.' Dragging the end of a piece of fabric out, she gnawed a cut in the hem and then, with a strong gesture, tore off the end. She handed the strip and the utensil to Jamila.

With the experienced deftness of those accustomed to dealing with minor injuries, Jamila and Rahim straightened the thin arm against the smooth wooden stirrer and deftly wound the makeshift bandage around it. The fabric was already sodden from the persistent rain, but it would hold the tiny limb to the splint.

'*Joldi! Joldi!* Be quick,' Zahid said, irritated by the hold-up. He flashed his light towards the Jamuna, and everyone could see that the water had risen against the levee in the short time since the child had been rescued.

Jamila cradled the child in one arm and, with a toss of her head at the scowling Zahid, started off again. Zahid, imperiously waving his light, took a few running steps to take up his forward position.

'*Ami neta*,' he said in a fierce tone. 'I am leading.'

They had gone no more than fifteen paces when he saw the bobbing of lights coming towards them.

'Are you all right?' someone shouted.

'HA!' Zahid yelled back, cupping his free hand to his mouth.

'We were seeing you stop,' the someone said as half a dozen men came into the beam of his torch.

'We are all right but our women are tired,' Zahid called back. He did not wish to explain that, at great peril to their lives, they had rescued only a girl child. The saving of a boy would have been worth bragging about.

'We have saved an injured child,' Salma shouted.

Then the contingent from the *shomiti* converged on them, and assisted the weary travellers the rest of the way up

16

the slight but muddy incline to the welcome shelter of the community centre. The greedy waters of the Jamuna were still below the levee on this stretch, not yet washing at the sturdy columns that held up the building.

Salma had gone to school in this *shomiti*, so she called out to one of the teachers in the largest room where a huge pot was simmering on a brazier.

'Rupoti Apa,' she cried, and the woman looked up from stirring the rice mixture. 'We found a child.'

'A girl child,' Zahid said.

'We are all precious to Iswah,' the *shikkhika* said, giving Zahid a mildly reproving glance as she rose and came forward to see the limp figure Jamila held out.

'With a broken arm. Is the *daktar* here?' Jamila asked.

Shaking her head, Rupoti Apa peered at the limp body, noting the splinted arm, the many scratches and bruises and a skin wrinkled from a long immersion. 'He is not here. The child is not too badly hurt. Bring her and yourself, Salma, to the fire and be warm. Jamila, take bowls. We have rice and fish to eat. Hot and good.' She waved towards the stack of rough pottery bowls on the far side of the brazier.

When Salma had eased herself to a sitting position by the fire, Jamila transferred the child to her and set about serving the piled bowls to those from her *bari*.

Salma was glad of the excuse of the child and a position by the fire. When Rupoti Apa handed her a bowl of the rice, she made a cradle of her damp sari and put the child in it while she fingered the rice into her mouth. It was hot and burned a little as it went down, but the heat was welcome. So were the pieces of *mach* she was delighted to find liberally sprinkled in the rice. She tried not to eat too quickly but hunger was on her. Out of the corner of her eye, she saw Ayud, Rafiq and Jabbar in the corridor, eating as quickly as she. It was a generous portion and filled the empty places in her.

She was dozing, her chin on her chest, when the child – older than a babe or it would not have survived in the flood – finally roused. Its thin pained squall roused others in the room. Before Salma could orient herself and remember why she had a child in her lap, Rupoti Apa lifted the little girl out of her improvised cradle.

'*Daktar* Mohammed is here and will tend her. Do you know whose child she is?'

Salma shook her head and went back to sleep, not willing to relinquish her place near the fire, now embers of red charcoal. She never saw the child again.

When the telekinetics that Peter Reidinger had carefully 'ported at Dhaka's Zia Airport got to work, they managed to stem and control the flood's crest before the Buriganga River could inundate the sprawling city of Dhaka.

They could not repair all the levees that had collapsed along the four main rivers, which shifted their beds as often as they changed their names – Ganges/Padma, Brahmaputra/ Jamuna – along with the tributaries they acquired on their journey down to the Bay of Bengal. Those who lived in Dhaka called what flowed past them the Buriganga River. From the east came the less ferocious Meghna and Sitalakhya Rivers. It was feat enough at first to reinforce the levees protecting a city of twelve million souls, spread out in the apex of the river already enlarged by its tributaries. Lance Baden set up his headquarters in a quickly evacuated building in Motijheel, the financial district of the city. There he directed the operations, quickly organizing and sorting out the problems of the divisions most affected: Rajshahi, Dhaka itself, Barisal and finally Chittagong which had its own special problems stemming from Kaptai Lake. Whenever district engineers could make contact with Lance's personnel, he directed his telekinetics to send stopgap material to be rammed into place.

He brought Bangladeshi workers in from the drier divisions, Sylhet, the upper Rajshahi and Khulna. His kinetics managed to seal the worst levee collapses until reinforcing materials could be set into place along the Buriganga. A special team was making certain that the raging Jamuna would not undermine the Great Jamuna Bridge. That renowned structure was a source of great pride to all

Bangladeshi, built as it was by their labour and their hard-earned *takas*.

Four days later, when the weather satellites reported the abatement of the monsoon, additional relief, personnel and supplies were airlifted in and the work of mopping up began. Despite urgent entreaties from their section bosses on the Padrugoi Station, and outright threats and rantings from Commissioner Ludmilla Barchenka, the team did not rush back.

The injured were cared for, the homeless were sheltered, the hungry fed and the bedraggled clothed. The most needy towns were supplied with food, fresh water and seed. Fortunately the extremely fertile soil of Bangladesh could produce two crops a year – with any luck – so there might still be a harvest later in the year. While the weather had certainly been unlucky around the world, it was late October and perhaps the monsoons were over.

Among the homeless, the orphans were assigned to the various facilities, examined, registered and, depending on their ages and abilities, given such community tasks in the centre as their age suggested.

The child who had been rescued from the Jamuna was sent to an orphanage just south of Bogra. The local industry of hat-making made use of the nimble fingers of the older children and their employment was carefully monitored by a telepath, Bahadur Ali Shan. He came as often as he could, when the press of duties permitted, but, as he had never seen any abuse nor a shadow of it in the minds of the industrious and generally happy children, he did not worry too much when the floods enlarged the orphanage complement considerably.

The orphan girl from a small *shomiti* outside Sirajganj was judged to be four or five years of age. The broken arm that was mentioned on the tag carefully written by Shikkhika Rupoti at the *shomiti* did not appear on the X-ray taken at the Bogra medical centre during the routine examination. A green-stick fracture of the ulna was visible, but the injury so well healed that the splint and bandage were superfluous. If anyone noticed that the little girl kept stroking her left arm over the site of the old break, they did not mention it. The tag stated that the child was unknown to anyone in the *shomiti*. The examining physician found her uncommonly well grown and well nourished, but noted that she did not speak.

Possibly this is due to the trauma of her recent experience in the flood waters. But attempts should be made to encourage her to speak. She hasn't got a cleft palate, she's not speech impaired and there is no physiological reason why she is incapable of speech, read the medical report.

The nuns at the orphanage gently tried to wheedle her name out of her but she only regarded them with wide eyes. A child of four or five should remember its own name.

'They're a deep blue, you know,' Sister Epiphania said. 'Not brown.'

'Oh dear,' said Sister Kathleen. A child of mixed race by no means shocked her for all they had both thought her Bangladeshi. She peered at the delicate features – so many Bangladeshi children were beautiful. Some subtlety of feature and physique made her feel that, whatever she was, the child was not half-caste. 'Well, she's a child of God. We'd better give her a name.'

Sister 'Phania considered this, laying a calloused forefinger athwart her lips in thought. 'Zada? That means lucky.'

'You're assuming she is Bengali?'

'Well, yes. The report says that the bandage around her arm had been torn from a sari. And look at her black hair!'

Sister Kathleen held a strand out before tucking it back over the child's shoulder. 'What about Jamuna as a name? She was plucked from it, after all.'

'Not at all,' 'Phania said, pressing her lips together.

'Kalinda? Because she came from the river?'

'Hmmm.' That didn't seem appropriate to 'Phania either.

'If we go to a floral name, remember we already have two Lilas. You wouldn't like Kusa for grass? After all,' and Kathleen pointed to the little patch of ground, neatly fenced off with twigs, which had absorbed the little girl once she had finished helping to weed the kitchen garden, 'she's clearly interested in growing things. Maybe a farmer's child?'

20

'Ruchi?' 'Phania suggested, 'since that means taste?'

'Hmmm.' Kathleen deliberated a moment, then shook her head.

'Rudra? That, I think, is for the rudrakha plant.'

'I want something that's *her*,' and Kathleen smoothed the girl's hair back and smiled with success. 'Shaila,' she said emphatically.

Kathleen squatted down beside the newly named child. 'Say Shaila, dear. That's your name.' The deep blue eyes regarded her calmly. 'Let me hear you say Shaila, dear?'

'Shy . . . la.' The light voice stumbled.

'Shaila,' Kathleen repeated the syllables. 'You are Shaila.'

'Dida?' the child asked, smiling at the nun.

'I do believe that's the first time she's smiled,' 'Phania said, pleased.

'No,' Kathleen said to the little girl, 'Shai . . . lah,' and Kathleen repeated it, accenting no syllable and poking the child lightly in the chest. 'You are Shaila. I am Sister Kathleen.' She pointed to herself. 'Sister Kathleen.'

'Sss-er,' was the response. 'Kaaa.'

'She's old enough,' 'Phania said with marked patience. 'She should be able to handle three syllables.'

'The report says there's no physiological reason for her not to speak.' Kathleen sounded dubious even to herself. She hadn't heard a single word from the child, even to one of the other babbling children. Bangladeshi loved to talk, and the children chattered all the time among themselves. Except this one.

'The trauma of nearly drowning,' 'Phania stated.

'Shaila!' Kathleen repeated, determined to succeed in getting the child to speak her new name if she did nothing else that day. They had neglected this little waif long enough, getting the others settled in. She put a finger on the small chest, repeating the name once again.

The child shook her head solemnly, and poking her chest with a muddy thumb said distinctly, 'Ama*ree*yah!'

'Amariyah?' The two nuns were flabbergasted and looked at each other. Sister Kathleen looked back at the girl. 'Amariyah is your name?'

21

'Amariyah!' Then the child turned back to her endless gardening, crooning softly at her seedlings.

Sister Epiphania smiled. 'Amariyah is a lovely name.' She did not add, 'better than Shaila', because that would have been unkind.

'I don't recognize that as a Bengali name,' Kathleen murmured.

'It could be,' 'Phania said. 'But she's definite that it's her name.'

When Father Salih arrived, he was somewhat doubtful about the propriety of baptizing an orphan who might yet be claimed by a Muslim family. He did write *Amariyah* down in his diary. Uncles or grandfathers had now taken away all of the older boys who had been lodged at the Holy Innocents Orphanage after the flood. Even though traditional Hindi thinking was giving way to modern pressures, girls were not so quickly claimed. Still, he sided with Sister Kathleen that Amariyah had a more European cast of countenance and physique.

'She might even be younger than the doctor thought. She's well grown, which might be due more to her ethnic background than to her chronological age. Look at her bone structure and compare it with the more fragile-looking Muslim girls.'

The three of them did, watching Amariyah, her hair neatly braided down her back, as she squatted by her 'garden', carefully hoeing the ground with her fingers. As usual she was crooning to her sprouting vegetables.

'What is she singing?' Father Salih asked the two European nuns.

Sister Kathleen, who had a strong alto voice, shrugged. 'Nothing I ever heard. Surely nothing remotely Bangla. But she's no trouble. And she's very good about weeding her rows. If she's younger, are we asking too much of her?' she finished with a worried frown.

'If she is doing it, let her,' was Father Salih's advice.

'Would you also tell them in the diocese office that we may have a European cygnet among our Bangladeshi chicks?' 'Phania asked.

'I will be doing that,' the priest replied, but he didn't make a note of it when he should have. Later, he could not remember exactly what it was he should have entered into his report of the visit to that area.

In Dhaka, Lance Baden had continued to hoist in supplies. The heavy concrete curves that could be sunk in the torrents to prevent more levee breaches were vitally needed if they were to keep any more of Bangladesh from flooding into the Bay of Bengal. The Australian kinetic and his teams worked round the clock. He never thought he would yearn for the six-hour shifts of Padrugoi Space Station. But he wasn't working under the tactless, stifling personality of Barchenka, and that made a difference. Kayankira, the head of the Delhi Parapsychic Centre, had managed to get through by four-wheel-drive truck and now handled the emergency telepathic traffic.

The third day after they had controlled the worst of the flooding, local non-Talented relief personnel approached him to locate some of those listed as missing. That list was by no means complete. The drowned or fatally injured bodies – quickly buried or cremated – were slowly being registered. Among the missing were a civil engineer, Tony Bantam, his wife Nadezhda and their five-year-old daughter. They had not reached their destination, Nawabganj, where Bantam had been assigned to survey the Tajhat Palace for possible restoration before the beautiful building disintegrated. Nadezhda was a qualified architect and team-mate. Their last known stop was Sirajganj, located at the confluence of the Tista and Jamuna Rivers. They had purchased petrol at the station there: Bantam had signed a Division chit the evening before the monsoon hit. He had probably heard the weather report, since he was prudent enough to fill his tank and several reserve containers, but what had happened the next day was anyone's guess. Bantam had a sturdy four-wheel-drive vehicle with flotation capabilities – if he had to ford rivers – so they should have been safe enough even in monsoon conditions. Tony was known to be a competent driver. His wife was equally able for most contingencies.

There was no sign of the vehicle anywhere along the logical route they should have taken to reach Nawabganj. Nor was the chassis number reported when the flooding receded sufficiently to disclose abandoned cars and trucks.

'Look, if you have anything of theirs to give my "finder", Bahadur Rafi,' Kayankira asked hopefully of Bantam's Bangladeshi supervisor. The man had come to the improvised office to find out if the missing family had been found. Kayan's large eyes and expressive mouth conveyed the urgency of her request.

Lance only had one man in his group, Fred Kiersey, who had some 'finding' ability in his mainly kinetic Talent. Kayankira, unfortunately, had no one stronger at her Centre. Fred was already working longer than normal hours, shifting material kinetically to where it was urgently needed. In his 'spare' time, he tried, using the possessions of the missing, to find them. He was inordinately pleased with his success rate, even if he was only finding those still alive.

'In Engineer Bantam's office will be items he has been handling,' replied the man who had authorized Tony Bantam's expedition. The Bahadur bowed humbly, hand to his forehead, and with great sadness in his large brown eyes. 'I will be sending them to you as soon as may be.'

'More chance of finding a trace if we also have something of the wife and child,' Lance added, raising hopeful eyebrows.

'Their house was one of the many drowning.' Rafi Siti sadly gestured to the north-west, where the Jamuna had swamped low-lying lands.

'Oh,' Lance said, grimacing. Waterlogged items would not emanate sufficient traces of their owners to be useful to a limited finder like Fred.

'It will take a few days to—' Rafi Siti broke off when Lance raised his hand discouragingly. '*Accha!* That may be too many days?'

'No, the water. We have no strong finder available,' Kayankira said apologetically. 'We were lucky enough to muster the kinetics,' and she gestured at Lance Baden, who had never explained exactly *how* he and his men had managed to land safely at monsoon-swept Zia Airport. She felt the Bahadur's intense sorrow at his impotence, and inwardly grimaced because she could offer no real assistance. The monsoon had claimed so many lives.

Lance was equally distressed. Had Bárchenka not been so unreasonable in her demands on the Talents, the necessary teams would have been in place long before the flooding got out of hand. Lance clenched his fists. Well, he had to console himself that the telekinetics had got to Bangladesh at all – thanks to young Peter Reidinger, the 'skeleteam' that Rhyssa Owen was training at the Centre for Parapsychics in Jerhattan. 'Bring anything Bantam had handled a lot. We'll do what we can.'

The Bahadur brought his palms together and bowed his gratitude, slipping out of the Talents' temporary office with sorrow and dignity.

'We will do what we may,' Kayankira said. 'But first we need something to trace with.' She jotted a note down on her screen, adding to a list that was already many pages long.

'If we get hold of something traceable, Kayan,' Baden said, firmly resolving that he *would* do what he personally could, 'we can send it to Carmen Stein in Jerhattan. She's the best "finder" I know of. Or we could ask Rhyssa if we can borrow her.'

Kayankira gave a self-effacing grin. 'I have already asked, for I know her reputation. Rhyssa said she is desperately needed on some Linear problem. Maybe later.'

They both turned to more immediate problems, and all but forgot their resolve in the press of other emergencies.

The Bahadur had evidently delivered Tony Bantam's journal at a time when both Lance and Kayankira were out of the office. Lance found it six days later, when he could no longer delay the return of all his kinetics to Padrugoi Station. Cursing under his breath at failing to 'find' the missing couple, Lance was about to stuff the leather-bound book in his luggage when a picture fell out – one of the old flat type that had been largely replaced with tri-d's. All three Bantams had posed for this, their daughter sitting between

25

her parents, looking straight at the camera, her expression solemn, her hands crossed in her lap. Tony Bantam – Lance vaguely remembered seeing him at some of the South-east Asia conferences – and his exotic-looking wife were both looking down at their child with such proud and doting expressions that Lance felt a sudden stab of anguish. Surely they hadn't perished. They deserved to live long and happily together. He carefully slipped the photograph back into the journal, making sure it was secure before he closed the book and wrapped it in a hand towel so that the 'traces' of Tony Bantam would not be marred. He'd send the journal to Carmen Stein. She was good at finding lost people, especially families.

He must remember to mention getting the journal to Kayankira, who had already returned to Delhi where she was facing crises of her own. Meanwhile he had a shuttle to catch, and the newly promoted General John Greene might be casual about many things, but not about being on time for a launch. As Lance took his seat in the rattletrap ground vehicle that would take him to Zia, he thought that the heat in Bangladesh had one great advantage . . . Bantam's sweaty hands would have left very 'traceable' marks on the leather covers of his journal. Carmen Stein would find the Bantams. He was sure of it.

Weeks later, a report was forwarded from the Bahadur that the two Europeans, identified by their DNA as Tony and Nadezhda Bantam, had been found. Their bodies were trapped by debris in one of the little inlets along the Jamuna, several kilometres south of Chilmari. Their four-wheel-drive vehicle was discovered not far from their bodies. It survived its immersion. No trace of their daughter had been found. The theory was that such a small body had been flung free of the vehicle and the child had probably drowned.

That was when Lance Baden, so constantly plagued by Barchenka's demands, recalled that he had not sent the leather journal to Carmen. He found it, still wrapped in its clean towel, at the very back of his personal storage space.

He found the photo, and now he knew why he had felt unaccountable anguish at seeing it. The Bantams were already dead. He touched each face with a light finger of benediction for their deaths. Maybe . . . just maybe, the child had somehow survived. After all, her body had not been found.

He hesitated before rewrapping the journal: a clean towel was a treasure not lightly to be given away. Up on Padrugoi, clean clothes were a luxury, so he'd had all his clothes washed prior to leaving. With quick movements, he wrote a covering note to Carmen Stein, slipped it and the photograph back in the journal, relinquished the towel as a cover to protect whatever 'trace' the leather might bear, put it all in one of the special Talent-locked envelopes and sent it off with the next Talent shipment to go downside.

CHAPTER TWO

In her office in Beechwood, the old Henner estate over-looking the Hudson River, Rhyssa Owen Lehardt had just got through her morning's mail when three square white envelopes floated into the space she had just cleared.

Neatly done, Johnny, she said, able to identify a well-known mind behind the kinesis. She heard a soft, smug chuckle. She opened the one addressed to her, noting that her husband, David, and Peter Reidinger were to be the recipients of the other two.

Vellum envelope, no less, she said appreciatively to her unseen listener as she pulled out the formal, engraved invitation card.

    The Secretary of Space cordially invites you
    to the Inauguration of the Space Station
    Padrugoi on...

Really, Johnny, isn't he running a bit late with his invi-tations? I mean, the ceremony is January first – tomorrow?

Don't tell me you haven't a thing to wear? teased Johnny Greene, former etop pilot and currently the kinetic in charge of transport to the officially rechristened Padrugoi Space

28

Station. *My dear wife got a couturier special, but Senator Sally Greene was not among the Capitol Hill desirables so she has no place to wear it. I had to slot my guests into space available, considering anyone who could wangle an invitation has done so. Sheesh, you wouldn't believe the scheduling required!*

Even Rhyssa's mind boggled at the thought of transporting, or teleporting, the hundreds of very important personages to the Space Station.

Ah, a mere snap but it is time-consuming, and left me very little time to arrange our trip, Johnny continued. *Peter's got to be there even more than you.*

Rhyssa sat back in her chair, catching an undertone.

Johnny? She paused. *Are you expecting trouble?*

No, not exactly, came the reluctant reply, because telepaths did not, could not, lie to each other. *But I've reason to believe, well, sort of a hunch. Amalda doesn't confirm it so nothing may happen. Still, I don't trust Barchenka. She's been far too amenable.*

The completion bonus? Rhyssa suggested. They both knew how single-minded and arbitrary Space Station Construction Manager Ludmilla Barchenka had been in suborning all the material that would bring the project in online by its due date, including the forced employment of many Talents.

Ha! She'd her sights set on the early *completion bonus.* There was an even more satisfied edge to Johnny's voice because he had been instrumental in making sure that Barchenka had not finished before the contractual date.

So what's bothering you?

She's giving in too easily. She's been sooo cooperative, so helpful to Admiral Coetzer, that I smell a very large rat.

What does Madlyn say?

She's suspicious, too. So, I might add, are the grunts. They don't believe that they'll all be allowed to go downside. Though we've been transporting them down, as many as will fit in empty shuttles on their return leg. Which is another thing that worries me: she's letting them go.

She promised that, Rhyssa remarked, though a little frisson of tension shivered down her back. *With only repair teams needed now, it isn't economical to keep all those grunts on, using up air, food and space.*

Next thing you know, she'll be sending down the offies, and LEO will have to find another 'secure' facility to stash them in during their sentences.

Indeed. Rhyssa was not pleased to think that certain offenders might be returned to earth. But surely Padrugoi would need janitorial services, unless Admiral Coetzer was against such penal servitude. *Their quarters could be used for more storage space.* Rhyssa wondered why she was suddenly arguing on the side of Barchenka. *And Mallie says nothing?*

Nothing she can articulate, and his mental voice was definitely troubled. *You'll all come, won't you? Peter can 'port the three of you to Gate 134 at the Jerhattan Spaceport at GMT 0900 tomorrow. I'll be there.* Then his mental touch disappeared.

Rhyssa sat back in her chair, propping her elbow on the armrest and her chin on her hand. Peter had to be there, more than she? Hmmm. Well, Peter was the strongest kinetic. Even stronger than Johnny had become, once the former etop pilot got the hang of how Peter used generator gestalt to assist a launch. Peter would be thrilled to pieces to be at the inauguration. In fact, Rhyssa had had to talk sternly to herself when VIPs all over the world had received their invitations – and the Eastern Parapsychics hadn't received any. They were not, as a group or singly, despite the enormous help they had been to the difficult Barchenka, anywhere on her list of preferred guests.

Rhyssa examined the invitation, running the tip of her finger over the raised engraving, and felt the 'tingle' of an encoded line. Well, obviously one did not get into the inauguration without presenting *this* card.

'Hmmm. Taking no chances, huh, are you, Ludmilla?' So, there was a top-level security effort. As well there should be, she thought. And yet, Rhyssa frowned, why? Few could or would sabotage Padrugoi now it was built. The cost – in human lives as well as effort – had been staggering, including the on-completion bonus for Barchenka. The project had

had the enthusiastic support of every nation; it meant a way *off* overcrowded Earth, to the habitable planets already identified in this sector of the galaxy. The first-generation ship had been built in space over twenty years ago and launched to Procyon, eleven light years away, from the old, now defunct space station. Since then, in speedier space-ships, other journeys had been initiated.

Well, Rhyssa wanted badly to go to the inauguration. Now she would, and so would Peter. And Dave would, too, for their sakes. As she called up her non-psychic husband's office number, she heard a scratch at her door. Had she been 'broadcasting' the news that loudly?

'Come on in, Peter,' she called.

The door opened and Peter's invitation disappeared from her desktop and reappeared in his hand.

'I don't believe it, Rhyssa, I don't believe it,' he chortled, clutching it to his chest. 'What took 'em so long? And who else is coming with us?'

'Dave's coming.'

On cue, Dave answered her call. 'Yes, Rhyssa?'

'Take the day off tomorrow. We're going to the inaugur-ation. I've got the invitations.'

'We?'

'You, Peter and I,' she said, controlling the impatience she sometimes felt when he didn't pick up on what was so vivid in her own mind.

'Left it a bit late, haven't they?' Dave said in a dry tone of voice.

'Johnny Greene said it was the difficulty in arranging passenger space when so many have to get there on time,' Rhyssa replied, though that really didn't wash as a valid excuse.

'Gee, Rhyssa,' and Peter's facial expression was mixed confusion, annoyance and surprise. 'I could get us there.'

Yes, I know, dear, Rhyssa said, dealing with both her husband and her ward at the same time. 'However, we do have the formal invitations, complete with the integral security code.'

In front of her, Peter's eyes widened.

31

'That's good. I'd hate to be spaced because I had a bogus invite,' Dave said. 'See you tonight.'

'Security codes?' Peter tore open the envelope and put the invitation against his cheek to feel the embedded security. 'Wow!'

'Double wow! Not even my skeleteam,' Rhyssa rose from her desk, and came round to ruffle Peter's hair, 'would be able to enter Barchenka's lair without the proper code.'

'Oh,' and Peter lifted his eyebrows, running his finger over the code again. His expression altered to 'naughty boy'. 'I could!'

'We'll be legal tomorrow,' Rhyssa said, mildly chiding.

'Oh.' Peter's face changed – the naughty boy reminded of previous mischief. He looked down and subtly grounded his feet, which had been a centimetre above the carpet.

He had been paralysed since the day a wall had fallen on him and irreparably damaged his spine. A body brace that was supposed to give him some mobility had malfunctioned, and he had very little use of his arms as well. Until he had discovered an alternative method of moving himself – using kinesis. Mind, in this case, was very definitely over the mere matter of body. He had also learned how to imitate proper movement, using his remarkable gestalt, with any available source of electric power. Given sufficiently powerful generators, young Peter Reidinger had performed feats of telekinesis far beyond expectation, such as moving supply shuttles from Florida to Padrugoi Station. His youthfulness – Peter was just fifteen – had precluded his regular employment by the Eastern Parapsychic Centre: only his age had prevented him from being drafted onto the Space Station by Barchenka. Unknown to many, Rhyssa had had to make use of his particular abilities in several emergency situations, but she had been determined not to strain his blossoming Talent. Indeed, neither Lance Baden, the strongest of the other kinetic Talents, nor Sascha Roznine, who was the head of the Eastern Centre's training programme, had yet been able to assess Peter's full potential. Of course, now that Lance's conscription on Padrugoi was virtually over, he would be able to train and evaluate Peter Reidinger.

'Speaking of new clothes, though, Peter,' and Rhyssa eyed his casual attire, loose-fitting trousers, well worn and halfway up his calf. He was getting taller by the minute. 'You can't go like that. Give Tirla a shout. She'll grab any excuse to go shopping.' Rhyssa paused. 'She has excellent taste.'

Peter was quite willing to contact the former waif of Linear G, who was now living on Long Island with her foster parents, Lessud and Shria. Tirla waited, impatiently, until she reached her sixteenth birthday and was legally old enough to marry Sascha Roznine. She'd tagged him as 'hers' when he rescued her from subsistence-level living in the Linear.

The next morning, clad in an elegantly fashionable new tunic suit, Peter linked in with the Centre's generators and teleported Rhyssa and Dave Lehardt to the telepad that General John Greene had given as their destination.

'Neat placement, Pete,' he said, pushing himself upright from the vehicle he had been leaning against. He unfolded arms that had been crossed over the front of his dress uniform, the prestigious medals properly displayed. His face broke into a grin as he noticed Peter trying hard not to be self-conscious in the outfit that Tirla had bullied him into buying the day before. Then Johnny whistled at an elegantly garbed Rhyssa, dressed in a trouser suit of her favourite dark green. He nodded approval at Dave's dress tunic, trimmed in the same shade.

'Where're the generators?' Peter asked, noticing how far they were from the main buildings of the Jerhattan Spaceport.

'There!' and Johnny pointed to a seemingly innocent pile of vehicle shipping crates bunched together.

'Oh!' They could all hear his tentative 'lean' into the units as he tested their capacity. 'They'll do,' Peter said, and then glided to the vehicle, the small torpedo-shaped, windowless drone that Johnny had been leaning against. Its surface, while dull, was bare of the usual remnants of plastic shipping waybills that festooned such shippers.

33

'Tell us why we're here,' Dave asked, looking about at the drab edge of the huge landing field.

'Does this rendezvous have anything to do with the fact that each invitation was issued by a different VIP office?' Rhyssa put in. 'Are they really valid enough to get us admitted?'

'Oh, yes,' Johnny said, now urgently gesturing for them to enter the ship. They all had to crouch to do so. 'I made damned sure of that!'

Did you have *to steal them?* Rhyssa asked.

Not exactly steal. Johnny chided her for her suspicions. *Maybe purloin is the appropriate word because the last people Ludmilla wants on that Station today are Talents. And that's exactly why we have to be there.* He ducked to take his place where a jury-rigged control board had been sited. He gestured for Peter to take the seat beside him.

There were also just four places, seats obviously taken from AirForce units to judge by the style of the safety harness.

'I assume you have a very good reason for smuggling us in, Johnny,' Dave said.

'Oh, I do, but I don't know what it is, yet,' Johnny said. 'Not that I'm unnecessarily risking you three in a wild caper. Or my own neck. Madlyn's trying to get some information . . . she's still up there only because Ludmilla hasn't figured out yet that our Voice is Madlyn. And Maddie, bless her heart, volunteered to stay on during the switch-over to Admiral Coetzer as the duty kinetic. Madlyn does a good "scared-silly, mealy-mouthed" act around Ludmilla.'

The young telepath, Madlyn Luvaro, was gifted with a telepathic range that literally could be, and had been, heard from Padrugoi to Earth. Her kinetic ability, while minor compared to her telepathy, had been the ostensible reason she had been acceptable to Barchenka in the Talent Draft six months earlier. Sub rosa, she had done extraordinary service by keeping track of the hundreds of 'casual' workers, the grunts, who were unlucky enough to become disengaged from their safety tethers and drifted out into space.

One of the conditions that Rhyssa as head of the Eastern

Parapsychic Centre had made to make the Talent Draft palatable to kinetics was that all extravehicular workers, grunts as well as specialists, would have safety tethers. Barchenka hadn't cared how many grunts she lost to such accidents. She wouldn't spare the work hours, or vehicles to rescue them. Not only had she refused to allow teams to stand by to catch drifters, she had also limited the oxygen supplied to grunts so that, if they lost their grip, their oxygen supply lasted their shift, with little left over. Barchenka's indifference had been one of the many reasons why Talents had refused to work on the Station. Then Barchenka had invoked an archaic pre-glasnost statute, a Russian one that should have long ago been repealed, stating that it was *illegal* to be unemployed and that the state was the only employer, not the employer of last resort. This gave Barchenka the right, under Padrugoi's international charter, to draft any technicians, professionals or workers required for the construction of the Space Station. The parapsychics had accepted that with as good a grace as possible. But they had also, in the line of duty, done what they could to help their fellow workers.

Though Barchenka had callously used the Talents she conscripted, she had never bothered to learn exactly what their 'talents' were, above and beyond the specialists she needed to finish the Space Station on time. So she had no idea that kinetics, like Madlyn, were also telepaths.

'Not that I don't want to be on the Space Station for the celebration of such a splendid human achievement,' Dave said, 'but last night we all watched the tri-d of her showing Admiral Coetzer around as the new Commander.'

'What? That tri-d fooled a hardened PR man like you? She *had* to do that,' Johnny said deprecatingly. 'I was there . . .'

'As General Greene?' asked Dave.

'Well, not so as she'd've noticed,' Johnny replied. 'But there's something about her geniality,' and he grinned back at Rhyssa and Dave, 'that's very false. As well as totally out of character. Pete, don't help this "lift". I'll be using the push-pull method. I'd rather save you for later, if we should

35

just happen to need our "skeleteam".' He took a deep breath, closing his eyes.

There was no sense of movement – although lights ran in berserk patterns around Johnny's control panel. A metallic clank and a slight jar told the passengers that the drone had landed. Johnny swivelled, a finger across his lips for silence, sudden tension in every line of his body. A complicated rapping on the drone's hull made him relax.

'OK, kids, invitations front and centre. 'Scuse me,' he added as he squeezed around Rhyssa to get to the hatch to unlock it. The panel swung open to a very narrow aisle between towering storage vats and crates.

'Sir? The way's clear. The teams're in place and you've got ten minutes,' said an anonymous voice as Johnny stepped out. He had to sidestep to let the others disembark in the cramped space. He held out his hand to Rhyssa. Slim as she was, she had to tuck in her tummy, grateful that her pregnancy wasn't far enough along to impede her.

'Let's go then,' Johnny said.

What teams, Johnny?

Ssshhh.

The General led them a circuitous way through the high-piled stores to a lift door. Where a simple 'pass card' would ordinarily be inserted, a much bulkier unit was welded in place.

'Taking no chances,' Dave murmured.

'None,' Johnny said definitively, and carefully inserted his invitation card.

'Accepted,' said a mechanical voice and spewed the card back out. 'There are four persons to be carded.'

'It can count, too?' Rhyssa said, stepping up and inserting hers.

'Made it easier to keep track of bodies in and out,' Johnny said cryptically.

Only when all four invitations had been verified did the doors of the lift slide apart.

'Don't put 'em away,' Johnny advised as he punched the uppermost button. 'We've got to go through three more security checks before we get where we want to go.'

36

Johnny? The voice was a loud whisper that both Peter and Rhyssa recognized as Madlyn Luvaro's. *Is that you?*

Who else were you expecting?

I don't want to answer that. Madlyn's mental tone held a definite nervous edge.

Peter and Rhyssa, and Dave, are with me. Johnny grimaced in an apology to Dave for adding him as a seeming after-thought. *Who else did we manage to keep on board?*

Everyone you asked, Madlyn replied, the relief obvious in her voice.

Any ideas as to what's going down?

None, and her mental tone was as frantic as it was apologetic.

Don't worry. We're here, Johnny reassured her.

The lift stopped and its door opened. Johnny gestured for the others to get out as fast as possible. Even so, it nearly caught Dave's left foot it snapped shut so fast. Johnny gestured a turn down the next T-junction, urging speed. Rhyssa tried to estimate how long the lift ride had been but couldn't. What seemed most important was that the bleak halls were vacant of traffic. They were not, however, without a certain pervasive odour of air recycled with the unmistakable taints of overcrowded and under-washed humanity. She'd heard that eight men or women shared each inadequate cubicle. Rhyssa eyed the halls and functional doors that looked as if they led into dormitories.

'And none of the masses is permitted to join the festivities?' Rhyssa asked, as they reached the next lift column.

'You got it in one,' Johnny said, slipping his card in the slot and motioning the others to be quick. 'Of course, most of those are empty since Barchenka started shipping the grunts downside once she had no further use for their bods. The offies are on the lowest levels and kept there with double wristbands that allow no access elsewhere, unless they're working under guard. None of them'll be seen today.'

Again the lift doors didn't open until all four cards had been cleared.

John Greene checked his wristwatch, humming under his breath as he nodded his head to count the seconds.

'Time's going to be tight,' he said as he barrelled out of the lift, turning left.

This upper hall was wider, and the doors farther apart, indicating possibly better accommodations.

'Not really so,' Johnny remarked, picking up on Rhyssa's public thoughts. 'This is the level we moved the Talents out of.' He gestured upward with his thumb. 'At least they have the privacy shielding, and space, which Barchenka begrudged us.' He turned a corner abruptly, pointed to the lift at the end and started to jog. 'Third checkpoint.'

Peter glided past them and was already slotting in his card when they reached him.

'Air's better up here,' Dave remarked as they were taken upward again.

'Better be,' Johnny said, and the lift opened into another hall, painted an airforce blue. Only one door sported the security unit. Johnny held up his hand. 'We'll be emerging in the restroom area. Pretend you've just been and go if you need to.'

While his card was being processed, he straightened his tunic, brushed imaginary fluff from one sleeve, angled his soft hat more comfortably on his head and then strode diffidently out into the corridor, looking neither right nor left. Their destination lay in the large chamber where people were standing in groups, chatting brightly to each other as people do when passing time. No eyes seemed turned in their direction as they filed discreetly in. Rhyssa made a show of smoothing Peter's new tunic at the back, and then turned to put her arm through Dave's before they sauntered in.

I'll go hobnob with the service contingent, Rhyssa, Johnny told her. *Your seats are row H, 98, 99, 100. The hospitality suite is not far from them. Your seats should have reserved signs on them. Barchenka's more near-sighted than she'll admit, so I doubt she'll recognize you from the stage. Catch ya later.* And Johnny Greene moved obliquely left, slipping in among the uniforms.

Their timing had been excellent. Rhyssa barely had time to look around the foyer, which featured wall murals of various stages of Padrugoi's construction, taken from space, when she became aware of activity in the corridor they had just vacated. A squad of Station police in white dress tunics filed out of the rear door and began moving the invited guests towards the far end. There the huge folding doors were sliding open. A tiny audible click heralded an imminent broadcast, delivered in a slightly accented contralto voice.

'Distinguished guests, ladies and gentlemen, please display your invitations for inspection and proceed into the auditorium.'

A security check here too, huh? Johnny said from wherever he was. *And it looks like the official lighting-up will be exactly on* the *contractual hour,* he added with a snide chuckle.

Slowly the crowd entered what was designated on the Space Station plans as a mall for tourists and residents. Along the outer skin of the Station, transparent panels of one of the special alloys that had been developed for the purpose allowed a stunning view of the stars. Dark bulks were discernible, some of them in orbit around the Station. Peter's eyes widened, then he visibly relaxed as his other senses identified the dark objects to him.

Why can't we see them? he asked.

Barchenka has to turn on the lights officially. That's part of the ceremony, Rhyssa said.

They moved steadily forward to the wider space at the back of the arranged seating, where people were beginning to angle towards side aisles and their reserved places. There was no middle aisle.

Peter was looking all about him, gasping a little as he recognized the faces of well-known world leaders, all splendidly dressed for the occasion. While outwardly he was the epitome of patience, he kept up a running telepathic commentary of the notables.

I never thought I'd be so close to her. *D'ya see all those jewels, Rhyssa? And there's the triple world medallist in track. He did the 5,000 metres, the 10,000 and the 10,000 relay.* Peter especially envied runners.

They displayed their tickets to a hard-faced, white-coated

usher who was diligently checking every card. She directed them to the right-hand aisle, and down to row H. The first three seats bore 'reserved' cards. A large male usher hurried forward from the front to validate the tickets again, nodded and directed them to take their seats. In the next few minutes they had to get up several times to allow others to pass.

Careful, Pete. You're floating, Rhyssa said and casually pressed his arm to settle him more firmly in the seat.

All this upping and downing, Peter muttered, disgruntled, because those making their way to seats beyond him obscured his view out of the windows. *I can't wait until the lights come on and I can really* see.

At least we're far enough to one side so that the stage doesn't obscure your view, Rhyssa said in an encouraging voice.

Peter sat very straight, though she could hear the rumble of his discontent for what seemed like an intolerably long wait. Actually, the audience was in a hurry to be seated, and very shortly she felt the air of intense anticipation in the boy.

'Those ushers are military,' Dave murmured in her ear, smiling at her as if he had said something innocuous.

Rhyssa gave a look at the ones in front, facing the audience. The stance was unmistakable as a 'parade rest' – hands clasped behind their backs, legs slightly apart.

Johnny, where did she conscript her ushers? Rhyssa asked in a diffident tone.

Where d'you think? Moscow. She's got many connections downside and all over that part of old Russia. But I knew about them. *Sent many of 'em up myself so we had a chance to check 'em out unofficially,* Johnny replied. *They're not the ones we worry about.* They're *visible. Anyhow, all of my guests have got in safely. Lance Baden and Gordon Havers among 'em, though I thought someone might spot Lance and challenge him. And,* Rhyssa could hear his smug satisfaction, *the others are properly dispersed.*

She was about to quiz him on 'what others', when a wide door opened beyond her. She caught a glimpse of another large chamber, tables set along the outside and covered with trays of food. There seemed to be rather a lot of very big men and women, dressed in white waiters' jackets.

Are they indeed, said Johnny, catching her startled reaction. *Good to know. Knew I was wise to bring your sharp eyes along, Rhyssa. Oh, and incidentally, Pete, there's power on tap all over this level.*

Peter turned to look at Rhyssa, eyes puzzled.

What's going on, Johnny? Rhyssa asked crisply.

I honestly don't have a clue, yet.

'Hey, they're starting,' Dave said, pointing to other panels sliding open, where the wide steps to the stage were situated.

Space Station Construction Manager Ludmilla Barchenka led the procession, wearing a severe uniform of space blue with a chestful of decorations from her grateful motherland, a soft spacer's beret crammed on her large head. For once her expression was not sour: she had an air of triumph about her. Some facet of that emotion alerted Rhyssa.

I've never seen her this pleased before, Johnny. She is *up to something.*

Can you tell what?

Not as long as she wears that metal skullcap.

Yeah, and Johnny sounded disgusted.

Admiral Coetzer in the black uniform of his new responsibility followed her, leading others of his staff, each paired with Ludmilla's outgoing executives.

At least they're wearing different uniforms, Johnny added.

Can't they get on with it! Peter said impatiently as the seating on the stage filled with the honoured guests.

As the stage access door closed and the last person sat down, Peter emitted another gusty sigh.

Ludmilla Barchenka nodded abruptly to Admiral Coetzer, and they both went to the table placed to one side of the lectern. An aide rushed to pull off the velvet covering and exposed the gleaming metallic switch, atop a pedestal.

The Admiral smiled. Barchenka didn't.

'This is what you are here to see,' she said in her accented and guttural voice.

She grasped the control, held it up for all to see, and

then plunged the old-fashioned switch to the far side. Immediately, lights so brilliant that they momentarily dazzled the viewers came up outside, and Peter wasn't the only one to gasp in amazement. The great upper wheel of the Station, a connected polygon where moorings and airlocks were located, was agleam with lights. Massive arrays illuminated the hull of the spaceship that would be the first of many scheduled to leave the Station on colonial missions. The size of it dwarfed even the great wheel.

Peter Reidinger seemed to back away from the vision. Rhyssa saw tears in his eyes and a wishful expression on his mobile face. When his chest did not rise, she elbowed him and he took a deep breath.

Easy, love, she added, her mental touch gentling his emotional response to the sight. *You got here, to the Space Station, didn't you? You've come such a long way in a short period of time.*

Startled, Peter glanced quickly at her. *You don't mean I could go on her, do you?* He raised his hand in the direction of the spaceship.

Equally surprised, Rhyssa exchanged eye contact and drew her lips down in a regretful moue. *She'll be leaving on her first voyage this year. You won't be old enough, dear, even if a kinetic would be a wise addition to her crew. It's not as if you could push her to her destination, is it? We do have to know* where *we're 'porting something.*

We've got pretty good resolutions of the planetary systems they're going to . . . Peter couldn't actually wriggle his body, but that was the impression Rhyssa had of what he would have liked to do just then. *Time-resolved images, they call 'em,* he said, remembering some of his astronomy.

'Not clear enough to 'port to, Peter. Not yet,' she said sadly. Dave gave a sideways glance at the pair. 'Though God knows, that would reduce the voyage considerably.'

'You aiming to start shifting spaceships now, Peter?' Dave asked, referring to Peter's feat of the shuttle landing in Dhaka.

'Archimedes said, Give me where to stand and I can shift the earth,' Peter replied, grimacing up at Rhyssa.

'If you figure out where that is, Peter, you'll be assured of a place in history,' Dave said with a droll grin.

'I'm working on it,' the boy replied blithely.

On the podium now, the World President Martin Cimprich had replaced Admiral Coetzer. With many flowing and apparently sincere phrases, the President thanked Manager Barchenka for succeeding 'where so many others had been defeated by such a monumental task' in completing the Space Station on time. He added remarks about her devotion to the project, her immense personal achievement and how vital the Space Station would be to the peoples of Earth in their search for new worlds to inhabit. Barchenka, still standing, shifted from one foot to another, showing her usual impatience with speeches. As if Cimprich was aware of her restiveness, he cleared his throat and then, smiling at her, gestured for an aide to approach.

'It is my infinite and distinct pleasure, Manager Barchenka, to present you with this.' A splendid sculpture, a rectangle of glittering plastic showing Padrugoi Space Station hanging above the Russian quadrant of Earth, passed from the aide's hands to his. With a very courtly bow, Cimprich presented it to Barchenka.

With a very brief smile and an ungracious snatch, she took possession of the sculpture. Then, with a flick of her fingers, she dismissed President Cimprich to his seat. She turned to the lectern and settled the heavy sculpture on its top with a thud that echoed through the audio system.

'Why do they have to mess this all up with speeches?' Peter demanded and, once again, began to levitate until Rhyssa put a warning hand on his elbow. *Will we be able to get on board the spaceship while we're up here?*

I doubt it, Peter, so get your eyes full of her. We'll see about an official visit later. Admiral Coetzer knows of your part in the Bangladesh emergency.

'There is no way to keep the politicians and the orators away from such a fine opportunity to exercise their own voices,' Dave said quietly, in answer to Peter's spoken question. 'Especially during an election year.'

'Don't remind me,' Rhyssa said with a mock groan.

43

With no thanks to the President for his presentation, Barchenka began to enumerate the problems that she had had to overcome from day one of her assignment as Manager.

'*She* had to overcome?' Peter whispered, disgusted.

'Well, she did,' Rhyssa said, adding sourly, 'even us.'

Barchenka appeared determined to recite every one of the obstacles in the path of the successful completion of the first World Space Station. She phrased her words as an indictment of those who did not spring willingly to her aid when first approached.

' "Accosted" is more like it,' Dave said softly behind his hand. Rhyssa could not help a wry grin.

She says nothing about our *help,* Peter 'pathed sullenly to Rhyssa.

Did you expect her to? General John Greene asked from his seat among the military, on the far side of the auditorium.

If it weren't for us, Peter said angrily, *she wouldn't have finished on time, or ever.*

But she did, Johnny reminded him. *And I'm not sorry I helped.*

She should still give us credit.

Peter, Rhyssa replied firmly, *never will she give* us *any credit. No one does, and frankly, I'm all for anonymity. About ninety-nine per cent of the indigenous population of Earth is afraid of psionic abilities.*

Why? Peter frowned at his friend and mentor.

Because, lad, the parapsychic are different, said the distinctive voice of Australian Lance Baden, *and you, in particular, are much safer being anonymous.*

I don't want credit, Peter protested, turning his head to the left in Lance's direction. *But you* and the other Talents who got stuck up here deserve it.

We don't expect it, Johnny said in a blithe tone. *Nor do we want it from that source. Oops, well, she's taking credit for reducing loss of life on the Station too. Now to that I'll take exception.*

Peter was probably the only one who was aware that it was the General who 'reached out'. Even Peter didn't at first realize what John Greene had done with that slight kinetic 'pulse'. Suddenly Barchenka was scowling down at the prompter screen from which she had been reading her speech. She paused, scowled, lifted her hand to adjust dials, at first calmly, but when nothing seemed to improve, she thumped the screen in several places. Then, her expression registering fury, she slewed part-way round and imperiously beckoned to someone standing at the back, below the stage.

'Wait,' she said bluntly to the audience, clearing her throat and stepping aside as the technician hurried to assist her.

Peter hid the irreverent grin behind his hand. *Will she get it back?*

How would I know? Laughter rippled in Johnny's mental voice.

Peter watched as the technician made several adjustments, turning at last with a nervous smile for Barchenka and indicating that he had fixed the problem. When she again took her place and looked down at the screen, she called him back.

What did you do, Pete? Rhyssa asked without looking at her prize student.

Me? Peter's expression was so surprised that Rhyssa had to believe him as he lifted his hand towards his chest in an attitude of offended innocence.

The audience began to get restless, shifting feet, clearing throats and looking anywhere but at the glowering Barchenka. She was having words with the technician, and he was still trying to adjust the screen to solve the problem. Whatever it was.

A woman dressed in the Space Station's new black uniform rushed out carrying a replacement unit. Music flowed out of the audio system, to bridge the pause in the programme. The defective unit was removed quickly and with no fumbling and the replacement installed. Barchenka's speech disk was inserted and the two technicians stepped back, out of her way. The music faded.

'*Boze moi!*' were her first words. 'The disk has been corrupted.' She glared around at the technicians as if they were responsible. The woman, after a brief hesitation, stepped forward and murmured to the Manager. Barchenka flapped her hand about in an angry rejection. She turned back to the lectern long enough to eject her disk, and with a furious glare at the assembled, stormed off the platform and out of the auditorium. Somehow she left the impression that, if the door had not been automatic, it would have slammed shut.

The master of ceremonies launched himself at the lectern, tapping the tiny microphone to be sure he was audible.

'Sorry about that, but let's give Manager Barchenka the ovation she deserves.'

That she might not be able to hear through the thick panel did not register with him. His script required him to ask for an ovation. He did so. Very few dutifully stood, and the enthusiasm of a genuine ovation was noticeably lacking. The guests on the platform, as if they wished to provoke a more lively participation from the audience, were the last to cease bringing their hands together.

The master of ceremonies cocked his head, obviously listening to an engineer's report. He smiled, and, leaning tentatively over the lectern, said: 'I've been assured that we're back online, distinguished guests. I'm sure we're all sorry that some green gremlin,' and he paused to see if everyone responded to his little joke, 'has denied us the rest of Manager Barchenka's stirring speech but, as she so often did after the, ah, minor setbacks, let us proceed.' He turned slightly and spread his hand invitingly to Admiral Coetzer, who would now address the audience in his capacity as the newly appointed Station Manager.

Rhyssa was suddenly aware that what the assembled guests had heard of Barchenka's speech had not actually confirmed that transition of authority.

If the Admiral seemed to hesitate briefly as he inserted his speech disk into the prompter, his face mirrored a little pleased smile when the process appeared to be successful. He began to speak in a crisp voice. He immediately mentioned the many, many agencies whose workers had generously given their time, skill and thousands of work hours to see this worldwide dream come true. He made

46

special note of those whose work had been conscripted from the international Linear Labour Pool, and happily announced that thirty-two per cent of the 'casual workers' had elected to stay on the Station as maintenance crew.

No other speaker experienced any difficulty with the prompting screen, and kept their remarks laudably brief. The special music composed by a Russian for the occasion marked the end of the formal part of the programme and finally the master of ceremonies invited the audience to adjourn to the reception area.

Just what did you *do, Pete?* Johnny asked in a tight 'path as he homed in on Rhyssa, David and Peter, emerging from the crowd making for the refreshments. From another direction, Supreme Court Justice Gordon Havers joined his fellow psychics.

Peter eyed the General speculatively. *Banging her fist on the prompter wasn't a good idea. Possibly even scrambled her text.*

Good thinking.

Peter did grin at the wordplay.

'*Greene!*' and the harsh voice stopped both the General and Peter in their tracks. Barchenka, her face set with anger, pulled Johnny Greene round by the arm. Alarmed, Peter stepped backward, trying to disappear into the throng. But others were as quick to leave the Manager's presence, and Peter was halted, unable to move, unwilling to teleport. 'How did you get up here? How did you scramble my screen?' she shouted, thrusting her fist up under the General's nose. She was so intent in confronting him that she failed to notice Rhyssa fade behind Dave's tall figure, pulling Peter with her.

'I, Madam Barchenka? I did no such thing,' Johnny replied honestly, pushing her fist down and away, an action she tried unsuccessfully to resist.

'You have the capability,' she continued, saliva spattering Johnny's face. Then she imperiously clicked her fingers over her shoulder. 'Scan him, Grushkov,' she ordered her telempath, hovering indecisively behind her. 'Is he telling the truth? Let's hear you deny it now, Greene!' She folded her arms across her chest and glared up at the kinetic General, her complexion scarlet under her spacer's beret. 'Then you will tell me how you got invitations and who gave them to you.'

Peter wondered if he could unobtrusively teleport himself anywhere but where he was, half hidden behind Dave Lehardt's broad frame. How Rhyssa had prevailed against the Manager as long as she had showed the depth of Rhyssa's courage.

'I most certainly did not scramble the Manager's screen,' General John Greene said, looking steadily at Grushkov. 'My invitation came from the Secretary of Space himself in appreciation of my assistance in getting much-needed supplies to the Station, and on time.'

Grushkov was immediately disconcerted. 'Madam Barchenka, he is telling the truth. Furthermore, his public mind is completely open.'

If John Greene and Peter saw the telempath blink and give John a closer look, Barchenka did not notice the exchange, her bulging eyes fixed on Johnny's face.

'*Awrgh*,' she exclaimed hoarsely, clenching her fists and waving them about in frustration. Then she barrelled forward, shoving into Dave's shoulder and pushing Peter aside with a bruising sweep of her arm. Johnny exerted a kinetic prop as the boy was momentarily off balance. Barchenka stomped onward, swinging her arms from left to right to clear her way to the long bar set up on one side of the reception room.

Grushkov muttered apologies to everyone so rudely handled, as he and Barchenka's other white-coat aides followed in her wake.

I'm sorry now I helped her in any way, Peter said as Rhyssa, Dave and Johnny ringed him against any other contact.

She didn't bruise you, did she? Rhyssa asked, concerned. Peter was much sturdier now than he had been when he had joined the parapsychics, but he was still susceptible to contusions. Especially when he was not, as now, using any shields to prevent physical contact. *Uncouth woman!*

I've half a mind to spike her drink, Johnny murmured, glancing across at the catering unit.

With an emetic? Gordon Havers suggested.

Peter would have laughed if he hadn't been mulling over something in Barchenka's mind that upset him where her arm had made contact with his chest.

Her speech was very important, he gasped. *She wanted to impress the world leaders so much that they would relent and make her Station Manager in spite of appointing the Admiral. She's furious she couldn't finish it because . . .* Peter faltered, ducking his head, frowning, his expression puzzled.

'*What?*' Rhyssa said aloud, shocked by the very notion of Barchenka in control of the Space Station.

'Admiral Coetzer's already on his way up to the hub,' Johnny Greene said by way of reassurance.

You could read *her?* Rhyssa exclaimed. *How could you? She's wearing a metal skullcap.*

'If she is, it isn't very good,' Peter said in a low voice, glancing nervously in the direction Barchenka had gone. *She's going to take over the Station again. She's the only one she will allow to manage it. She's going to make us pay!* Peter added. *You most of all, Johnny.*

'What isn't very good?' asked Dave, noting the tension in Peter's slender body.

Rhyssa quietly explained the gist of the exchanges. Dave's eyes widened in alarm and he, too, looked around the crowd to spot Barchenka's current position.

'How could she do that?' Dave asked Johnny.

'She hasn't got enough clout left with those necessary to confirm such an assignment, even if the Space Authority was insane enough to let her,' Havers said, troubled.

What else did you sense, Peter? Johnny Greene asked, rocking back and forth on his heels, his jaw muscles tightening in dismay.

No one else has ever read her, Rhyssa repeated.

I think it was her whacking me like that. Peter lifted one arm to his ribs. He hadn't felt the blow, only reacted to the momentum of her thrust. *The physical connection, and she's so angry she isn't holding anything back. I think she's after*

Admiral Coetzer, too. That's what she's gone to do now.
He turned his upper body round, looking in the direction
Barchenka had gone.

Oh, there you are! All three telepaths winced as Madlyn
Luvaro's powerful 'voice' assaulted their minds. *Oops. Sorry.*

The telepaths glanced around, not immediately spotting
Madlyn. Then the pretty, dark brunette in an elegant red
dress suit stepped out of the throng. She was smiling
and nodding politely to those she passed, but there was a
definite, noticeable tension to her body and in the tightness
of her smile.

'Hello, there, Rhyssa, Peter, General Johnny. How great
to see you here,' she said aloud. *There's one godawful
rumour just starting the rounds in the workers' level; that
Barchenka's going to be made Manager again.* As she bowed
politely to everyone in the cluster, she continued. *The
rumour is that she'd end up her speech by telling you all that
she's taking over the Station.* Her smile was fixed. She had
modulated her extremely strong telepathic voice to a mere
whisper, a scared mental whisper. Now her eyes begged
Rhyssa to reassure her. *How* can *she? When she came
storming in here from the ceremony,* and Madlyn gestured
around the refreshment area, *she was jerking her hands
around at her white-coats and telling them that the plan would
proceed.* They *moved out on the double. With that skullcap of
hers, I couldn't read anything from her, and those muscle-
men can't think with the front of their brains, so she* has
been planning something all along. 'Can I bum a ride back
down with you, General?' she said aloud, tilting her head
coquettishly at Johnny, but her eyes were clouded with
anxiety.

Rhyssa said in a conversational tone. 'Are you all packed,
Madlyn?'

'Yessum,' and the telepath nodded, more like a teenager
than the confident executive she had become during her stint
on the Station.

'I think I'll just see how Grushkov is doing,' Johnny
Greene said with a wickedly raised eyebrow. *Stay here.*

He went his way into the crowd.

You don't think there's any chance she could get her way?
Madlyn asked warily, pretending to admire Peter's smartly
tailored outfit. 'I almost didn't recognize you, you're so
smart.'

'Tirla took me shopping.'

'She's got excellent taste.' *How does she think she can oust
Admiral Coetzer? The World Council officially appointed
him. He's such a nice guy. So calm. He impressed me when
he toured the grunt levels and talked to all of them. Even
descended to the offie levels. Never once wrinkled his nose
at the pong down there,* Madlyn said. *Neither did Igor
Koryakin, who's the new Maintenance Supervisor. How can
they possibly turn the Station back over to* her?

It just has to be wishful thinking on Barchenka's part,
Rhyssa said.

Peter was very uncertain now. Could he have imagined the
vivid sequences he'd seen in Barchenka's mind . . . like very
fast fast-forwarded scenes . . . almost as if she were going
over the plans in her mind. They couldn't have been precogs,
because Barchenka hadn't a vestige of psychic ability! He
looked warily around. There weren't that many of her white-
coat muscles in this area. He reviewed the brief glimpse of
the very satisfied expression on her face, echoing her mental
attitude. Then a sudden stir as the rank of doors beyond the
refreshment area burst open, like one of the glimpses he'd
had, and platoons of white-coated men and women strode
purposefully in, spreading out.

Peter carefully levitated himself enough to see over
nearby heads. *I don't like the feel of this.*

At the exact same moment, Johnny Greene broadcast. *The
Admiral's run into a bad snag. His telepathic aide, Shandin
Ross, is with him. They can't get the lift to work to the Central
Intelligence Control level.*

Ground yourself, Peter, Rhyssa said, pulling him back
down to the floor.

She's locked Coetzer out! Johnny said angrily. *Coetzer's
supposed to have the command codes. She's locked him
out.*

Johnny, can't we do *something?* Peter replied anxiously.

'What?' Madlyn Luvaro demanded, and put her hand to her lips.

The lifts aren't responding, even to his emergency codes, Johnny said, his mental tone both angry and anxious. *I'm reading Admiral Coetzer's mind. He's so furious right now he's dead easy to read. He's coming back here.*

I've got to get closer to Barchenka, Peter announced.

Before Rhyssa could protest or caution him, Peter was gone from her side.

'No one will notice,' Dave said, leaning down to whisper in her ear.

'You did.'

'I was watching him. Everyone else is watching Barchenka's guards,' Dave said. 'Can't we do something? Anything? Are there enough strong Talents just to inactivate her?'

Not with her metal skullcap, Johnny Greene replied telepathically as well as out loud. *Although, Peter? Peter, where's he got to?* he added, his tone agitated. *Madlyn, have you any idea how many goons she has? Where has she positioned them? Oh!* Johnny's voice was silent for three beats. *Really? Pete, how'd you do that?*

Johnny's astonishment was so intense that all the 'paths caught it.

My God, he's great. Madlyn Luvaro's voice was so strong, Rhyssa thought she had spoken out loud.

Yes, that's what I saw in her mind, Peter answered and shot Johnny, as well as the other psychics, the visuals he had seen passing through her public mind. *Her strategy.*

That'll certainly help, Havers remarked, his lanky body relaxing. *What now, Johnny?*

Just be ready to take control when we can, Johnny replied. *She's been too busy with her planning to watch her back.* And there was a note of distinct satisfaction in his tone.

Those mysterious teams of yours? Rhyssa asked.

What teams? Both Madlyn and Gordon Havers wanted to know.

'How could she lock the Admiral out of the command zone?' Dave murmured, not being privy to the lightning telepath exchanges. 'She formally handed over the pass-words and encryption codes when the watch changed at dawn. Coetzer's staff has been installed since six a.m. Station time. Why don't . . .' he continued, breaking off when there was a sudden rearrangement of the crowd as someone barged forward: Barchenka. She had a voice wand in her hand.

'HEAR THIS!' The volume on her wand was deafening, instantly producing the silence she wanted from the now agitated audience. 'I AM RESUMING THE MANAGE-MENT OF THIS STATION. THERE IS AN IN-SURRECTION ON THE LOWER LEVELS.'

That's a fat lie! Madlyn said.

'BE CALM! I WILL SAVE YOU. THE ADMIRAL YOU APPOINTED IS USELESS IN THIS EMER-GENCY. HE DOESN'T KNOW THE STATION AS I DO.'

'Because, madam,' and the Admiral appeared on cue through one open door, his aides spreading out on either side of him, hands on the holsters of their dart guns. He had an on-deck voice that could be heard without amplification, 'you have tampered with the main control systems. I am the officially appointed Station Manager.'

'I SHOULD BE. I WILL BE.' Barchenka's wild gestures had opened a path between her and the Admiral. He advanced to confront her. 'NO ONE KNOWS THIS STATION AS I DO, WHO HAVE PUT EVERY RIVET AND GIRDER IN IT. YOU SHALL NEVER RUN IT WITHOUT ME. I WAS GOING TO EXPLAIN HOW MUCH YOU NEEDED ME, BUT SOMEONE CORRUPTED MY SPEECH DISK.' Her eyes were bulging, her face suffused with blood, the cords in her neck visible with her tension.

The Admiral came to an abrupt halt, shaking his head in outrage at her ranting as Rhyssa, desperate to offer such help as her people had available, reached into his opened mind. She was startled to hear Peter's voice already there. *Mention password, Admiral. Ask her about the password.*

The Admiral gave his head one more shake, eyes sliding

quickly to Johnny Greene, whom he knew to be a Talent. He took another step forward, just as a thin arm in blue reached out of the crowd near Barchenka and touched her shoulder.

'You've changed the password, have you, Barchenka?' the Admiral said and, with an effort the Talents caught, gave her an amused smile. 'That's why the systems won't respond. You've overridden the codes you only just gave me.'

'I HAVE CHANGED ALL. SPECIAL PROGRAM ONLY I CAN OPERATE,' she cried dramatically, thumping her chest with her free hand. 'NO ONE ELSE WILL EVER RUN PADRUGOI SPACE STATION BUT ME!'

Shelkoonchik? What does that mean? Peter asked. *Sounds Russian with that 'chik' at the end of it. Madlyn, are there any Russian speakers on the Station?*

Hundreds down in the grunt and offie levels.

No, no, someone in a command position.

Johnny Greene's amused voice answered, *Yes, the Maintenance Supervisor, Koryakin. He's still trying to get the lift to work.*

Koryakin! All three 'pathed the name at once. Their effort was met with silence.

He only receives, guys, Madlyn added in a droll tone.

Koryakin, the password has been changed to 'shelkoonchik', Peter said, his mental tone so intense that even Madlyn winced.

Did he hear that? Rhyssa asked.

Every receiving telepath on the Station heard that, Johnny Greene said, imaging himself tenderly touching his earhole.

The Admiral had come within inches of Barchenka now, almost a stroll of an approach. Certainly he did not act either cowed or subservient as he stopped just short of the semi-circle of her white-coat guards.

'As the duly appointed Manager of Padrugoi, I must inform you that your deliberate attempt to undermine my authority can be considered an act of mutiny.'

'*Mutiny?*' She threw back her head and howled with laughter. 'When you can control nothing of this Station and all these are,' she swung her arm to indicate the prestigious and important government officials in the stunned assembly, 'hostages. Guests,' she amended, 'my guests until *my* appointment is irrevocably confirmed.'

That provoked angry denials and restlessness from an audience that included every world leader who had wished to attend the inauguration of the Space Station, which their own security guards had cleared as 'absolutely safe'. From several directions, angry men and women charged her position. And aborted their charge when her white-coats produced illegal heat-guns and let off bursts of energy, searing the attackers. Their cries of dismay ended abruptly as Barchenka's forces swung their weapons from one side of the crowd to the other. The wounded were eased back, out of sight.

Is anyone badly hurt? Rhyssa asked on a broad band that would reach anyone in the crowd with minimal Talent.

No, ma'am. The ones I can see just got a warning crease. But that means those white-coats know how to shoot. Rhyssa couldn't recognize the speaker's mental tone: whoever he was, he was 'shouting' to be heard at all. Anger had probably given him more range than normal.

'You want to get back to Earth?' Barchenka was saying now, her smile malicious. 'Obey me. Any further display of insurrection,' and her broad smile dared a response as her eyes swept the subdued crowd, 'and my troops will see how fire-resistant your fancy outfits really are. I'll space *any*one who defies me. I, Ludmilla Barchenka who *made* this Station, I am in complete control.'

In the stunned silence that now held the assembled, the little bleep was all the more audible.

'Are you?' asked the Admiral gently, his manner relaxed.

'What was that?' Ludmilla launched herself angrily at him and gestured for two of her guards to cover him. The Admiral didn't resist when she wrenched off his wristcom and, dropping it to the floor, stamped on it, kicking it away from her when she couldn't break the impact-resistant case.

'You will be first to breathe space, Coetzer,' she said, shaking her fist at him. Then she spoke into her own wrist unit. 'Yellow team to the reception area. You'll see, Coetzer.

You'll be Admiral,' and she snarled the rank in a contemptuous voice, 'of deep space. And that,' she waved her arm to include the audience, 'will be the fate of all who deny me.' Then she stopped, peering into the crowd, searching avidly.

Who's she looking for? Madlyn said, trying to shelter herself behind Dave's large frame.

Me, said Johnny Greene blithely, *but she won't find me. Watch out, Havers. She knows you by sight, too. Are you far enough back in the crowd, Rhyssa? She'll also come after you.*

'Yellow team, what's keeping you?' Barchenka demanded angrily into her wrist unit.

That's more than enough of this sort of entertainment, Johnny said cryptically. *Ready, set, GO!*

NOW! The clear mental command was not in General Greene's voice. Suddenly the grills on apertures halfway up the inner walls crashed down to the floor, and those whitecoats nearest reacted, blasting at the metal plates. To be shot down by the many standard tranquillizer rifles that appeared in the openings.

'What the—' Ludmilla began.

As she raised her hand to redirect her troops' weapons, a dart smacked into her throat. Even as she collapsed, tranquillizer darts rained down on her cohorts. A few, who had dropped to their knees and turned their weapons upward, were not hit. Abruptly, every one of those threw their weapons away as if too hot to handle. On the hands held up in surrender, Rhyssa saw the unmistakable red burn welts.

Which they are, Peter said smugly. *Tit for her tat!*

The Admiral stepped forward and removed the wristcom from Barchenka's limp arm and the weapon from her hand.

'Now hear this! Admiral Coetzer speaking. Ludmilla Barchenka has been taken prisoner. Surrender without further violence, and I guarantee safe return to the planetary surface. This mutiny is now over. Surrender to Station personnel immediately and in an orderly fashion. I repeat, Ludmilla Barchenka is under guard and her illegal force is disarmed. This is Admiral Coetzer speaking. This Station is now back under my command.

'Distinguished guests, ladies and gentlemen, please be calm,' and now he held his hands up, circling to be sure that he could be seen. 'Are there any medical personnel who can attend to our wounded?'

Johnny Greene suddenly levitated in front of the Admiral, appearing to hesitate in mid-air, reaching out with his right hand to deflect or catch something.

Got it! Johnny cried, dropping to his feet again as he showed the knife that had been thrown at the Admiral. In the same second, one of Barchenka's thugs who was kneeling on the floor doubled up, screaming in pain.

'I suggest that no one else attempt a similar breach of common sense,' Johnny said, slowly rotating on his heel to survey Barchenka's mutineers. *Pete, can you do a shield around the Admiral? We're not home clear yet.*

Sure! Peter Reidinger, looking frailer than ever against the tall, well-fleshed Admiral, stepped to his side and projected an invisible barrier.

'Secure that man,' the Admiral said, gesturing for two of his aides to deal with the writhing would-be assassin. Then he noticed Peter. 'Ah!'

'You need Pete right now, Admiral,' Johnny said quickly in an undertone. 'He's that skeleteam I'm sure you've been briefed on.'

The Admiral raised his eyebrows in surprise, gave Peter an abrupt nod and then continued to issue crisp orders.

'If some of my fellow guests would be so good as to collect the arms.' Both male and female guests leaped forward immediately. Some of them cautiously nudged the weapons out of reach, or gingerly touched the handles in case of residual heat. The arms were dumped in a pile that Johnny Greene then 'lifted' out of the reception area.

Rhyssa crouched down by Ludmilla Barchenka's limp body and pushed her beret back, exposing the shiny skullcap that had prevented any telepath from reading her mind.

'Oh, my word!' Rhyssa exclaimed. When she lifted off the close-fitting metal plate, a round patch of bare skin, reminiscent of an ancient monk's tonsure, was revealed: bare skin would further increase the protection offered by the cap.

'No wonder she felt dense,' Gordon Havers remarked.

'It figures,' Johnny Greene agreed after a quick glance. Then he grinned at Rhyssa. *Not that I'd like to peek into her twisted mind, but someone may have to, to make sure we've arrested everyone involved in this little, ah, mutiny.*

Rhyssa gave a little shudder of revulsion and stood up, hands clasped together under her chin in distress. Dave put a comforting arm about her shoulders.

'General Greene?' Admiral Coetzer asked, beckoning for Johnny to come closer. He looked meaningfully at Peter, who was in earshot in his protective position.

'I'll vouch for Pete, Admiral,' Johnny remarked in a low voice. Then he cocked his head, indicating he was all attention.

'How much of a force do you have, Greene? Enough to deal with this . . .' the Admiral hesitated over his choice of words.

'Mutiny, Coetzer?' And Johnny's ineffable humour provoked a slight twitch of the Admiral's lips. 'I don't have a "force", just some volunteers in strategic places.' He pointed up to the open grills. 'Another group reports that they tranked her yellow team in the hall, so you don't need to worry about her being reinforced.' Johnny ducked his head, scratching the nape of his neck and grimacing in embarrassment. 'Your own personnel should be yours to command again . . . once we find your wristcom. Ah, thanks, Pete,' he said, as a wrist unit was teleported against his medals. He grabbed it.

'Thank you, Pete,' Admiral Coetzer echoed, turning to the thin youth at his side before repossessing his communicator.

The Admiral cleared his throat before speaking, his eyes never leaving Peter's face. His scrutiny of his youthful guard was more interested than patronizing.

The military and naval guests had taken it upon themselves to secure Barchenka's former guards, conscious or tranquillized, assisted by Johnny's irregular troops. Leaving some on guard in the apertures, trank rifles trained below, others dropped from the hatches to secure the insurrectionists. Moments later, Admiral Coetzer's Station personnel arrived to take official charge of the captives.

Barchenka's limp body was soon draped over several chairs, strands of her sweaty blond hair lying across the shaved pate. Though the drug in the dart would keep her unconscious for several hours, her hands and feet had been yoked as a precaution.

Meanwhile, recovering from the confrontation, other dignitaries had decided that now was the appropriate time to circulate refreshments. Since the waiters and waitresses were unavailable, guests performed such duties as pouring glasses of the inaugural champagne, wines, sodas, juices and liquors set out on the tables. Some were passing trays of canapés and other finger foods, setting aside their official positions to help restore some semblance of 'occasion' to the reception area. Those who had been unduly distressed by the shocks of the last hour were being comforted. The noise soon reached a normal level for such a gathering.

'Greene,' the Admiral said, after answering another bleep on his wristcom. 'CIC reports shuttles leaving that were not cleared. Possibly some mutineers are trying to escape. I'd prefer not to christen the Station's defence system today, but the crews are not responding to orders to stop.'

'An exodus like that can best be handled from Station control, don't you agree?' Johnny said, gently guiding the Admiral towards the nearest exit. 'We'll need the services of our Voice,' he added, beckoning Madlyn to come forward. *We might need everyone in CIC.* 'I believe you've already met Ms Luvaro, Coetzer,' and when the Admiral acknowledged that with a little bow to her, Johnny went on. 'She's been our Station-to-Earth contact and she'll be very useful right now. I don't believe you've met Rhyssa and Dave Lehardt.'

'By reputation certainly, I know Ms Lehardt and her husband,' the Admiral said graciously, gesturing for the small knot of psychics to accompany him. 'And Justice Havers. Though I haven't formally met Mr Baden,' he said, turning to Lance with an extended hand. 'Your superb management of the Bangladesh Emergency was a fascinating advertisement for kinetics.'

'Not as much as today was,' Lance replied drolly.

On their way to the lift, they passed knots of white-coated men and women now guarded by personnel from Coetzer's command.

'Admiral, sir,' Madlyn began tentatively, 'you gotta re-assure the grunts.'

'I beg your pardon?' The Admiral leaned slightly towards the Voice, who was trotting to keep up with his long stride.

'The workers, down below, they're terrified of Barchenka and they think she's still in control. If you don't tell 'em *you* are, they might do just about anything.'

'That will be our second task, Ms Luvaro. You can't, by any chance, reassure them yourself?'

'Me? They wouldn't *hear* me, sir. None of 'em are re-ceivers. It's *your* voice they need to hear on the audio. They liked you, you know. You didn't sniff or cover your nose when you visited their quarters.'

Coetzer's lips twitched in an effort not to smile as he adapted his stride to her shorter one, taking her by the arm and guiding her into the lift.

'I'll see if we can't improve those conditions, Ms Luvaro.'

'They'll work their butts off for you if you do, Admiral,' Madlyn said feelingly. 'Oh, you know they will, Johnny,' she added forcefully as she caught the General's amused reaction to her candour. 'Only I still don't understand why Barchenka picked such a crazy password. She hated music, and wouldn't let anyone even whistle in her presence.'

The Admiral chuckled. 'What better one to choose than something totally unsuspected. Since *shelkoonchik* means nutcracker, and one figures in the Tchaikovsky ballet, it was relatively obscure given her habits. Koryakin told me the composer was a famous Russian.' He turned towards the psychics for their opinion.

'He is indeed,' said Gordon Havers. *Well done, Pete! Neat way to disarm opponents, too. You must tell me how you heated up their weapons.*

It seemed a good idea, Peter Reidinger replied modestly, but his visible smile was broad enough for two faces.

You did real good, Peter. Real good. Madlyn looked up at him so adoringly that Peter edged closer to Rhyssa as the lift doors parted on the Command level.

'Admiral on the bridge,' said the sentinel at the lift as Admiral Coetzer walked into the Central Intelligence Control, the CIC, of Padrugoi Space Station.

CHAPTER THREE

Once in command, Admiral Coetzer contacted the Commandant of the International AirForce to despatch Earth-to-Padrugoi (etop) fighters to prevent the three shuttles – which did indeed contain Barchenka's associates – from making good their escape. Scenes of an unconscious Ludmilla, white-coats packed into the Station's brig, others surrendering, patched through to the shuttles' screens, were sufficient proof of the mutiny's total failure. Coetzer repeated his guarantee of safety. Two vessels immediately hove to, awaiting an AirForce escort. The third changed trajectory and, throttles on full, tried to lose its pursuers. Coetzer did not hesitate, and authorized the etop pilots to use the missiles with which their fighters were armed. The resultant explosion was vivid enough to be visible from both the Station and the American East Coast, which was at that moment passing underneath the Station. A brief newscast reassured the public, promising a full report later that day. David Lehardt, in his role as the Eastern Parapsychic Centre PR chief, helped the Admiral's public relations staff to put together what the public needed to know. A full investigation of the circumstances was to be carried out, and the results made public at a later date.

In his initial report, General John Greene, on detached service to the Padrugoi Shuttle Squadron, crisply explained that he had possessed insufficient creditable data to present to his superiors: certainly nothing to suggest that a mutiny was being planned by Ludmilla Barchenka. He pointed out that the most sensitive of precognitive Talents, Amalda Vaden, had 'seen' nothing. He himself had no vestige of the precognitive aspect of psionic talent. On recent trips to and from Padrugoi, his interest had been caught by nebulous rumours from the grunts being returned to the surface. Nothing concrete, merely the vague and somewhat inarticulate mental anxiety of his passengers and the relief they felt when they had reached Earth again, as if they hadn't expected to survive. Enough, however, for him to become alert and to take such precautions as he could with a limited number of dedicated Talents. His personal doubts had been partially confirmed when Barchenka was so eager to clear the Station of all telekinetics; when she had 'neglected' to send invitations to prominent personages like Justice Gordon Havers and Rhyssa Owen Lehardt. He was, however, aware of the grievances Barchenka harboured against those people, that could certainly be the reasons why they had been excluded from the invitation list. When she began importing 'additional catering staff', one of the Talents, Madlyn Luvaro, asked him to find out how large a catering staff for the inauguration should be. He had privately instigated a check on the extra personnel that Barchenka was hiring to serve at the inauguration ceremony. Except that few of them had had any previous catering experience and they all came from Slavic nations, he couldn't contest their employment. Their numbers, however, were far in excess of what a reputable catering firm would employ for a similar occasion.

Though Amalda, the Washington precog, could not give any substance to Johnny's 'hunch', he decided to take certain precautions. If he was wrong, he could deal with that. Being right was unacceptable unless he prepared for that possibility. With the lowest grunt-level living quarters being closed down, it was relatively easy for Johnny to hide those who volunteered to remain on the Station – just in case. Nor was it difficult for these men and women to infiltrate the larger air-conditioning conduits and stand a discreet vigil during the ceremony.

When, after the fact of the mutiny, he taxed Mallie Vaden about her lack of 'foresight', she replied in her own defence, 'If the circumstances *hadn't* been altered by you, the mutiny would have succeeded and I would have "seen" it. Only you intervened, so it didn't happen for me to "see". Simple!'

Barchenka's mutiny had been stealthily plotted. For instance, her personnel manager, Per Duoml, had known nothing about it.

'As much because he was an honourable man – in his own way – and too upright to have condoned a takeover,' Rhyssa remarked.

'Not that so much,' Johnny Greene added in private to the other Talents after they had given their testimonies to the investigating committee, 'as the fact that he had finally become disenchanted with our dear Ludmilla and, in the last month or so, had begun to distance himself.'

'Did he do so because he suspected her mutiny?' Justice Havers asked. He would have loved to have sat on the tribunal appointed to hear Barchenka's case, but having been on the Station, he was considered prejudiced. Another prominent American jurist had been chosen for the panel of five.

'Couldn't say, Gordie,' Johnny replied with one of his shrugs. 'Duoml turned his office over to Coetzer's personnel manager the day before, and was out of there like he couldn't wait to get downside.' Johnny paused. 'Of course, you might conclude that he knew something was up, but he sure didn't want to be involved.'

Fortunately, the subsequent mental probe of Duoml by Jerhattan LEO Commissioner Boris Roznine, who had been assigned to the unsavoury duty by the international investigators, was able to exonerate the man of any complicity.

'Writhing with distaste and considerable animosity towards Barchenka,' Boris later told his twin brother, Sascha,

64

'but without personal involvement. I think, though he hid it well, he had his suspicions. There're enough involved as it is. Including, and you'll love this, old Flimflam, Ponsit Prosit.'

'*Who?*' Sascha gaped at Boris in astonishment. Sascha had deliberately put the scam artist out of his mind once the man had been assigned to Padrugoi as a janitor in the grunt level.

'Yup. Dirt loves dirt, and he'd've loved doing the dirty on any Talent.'

'Just don't,' Sascha paused significantly, 'even *think* of that scuzzball near Tirla.'

Boris gave his brother a you-think-I'm-crazy look. 'Nor in the vicinity of Rhyssa and Peter. They've all put that kidnapping behind them, and it'll stay there.'

'And Flimflam?' Sascha's voice and manner had hardened.

'Well,' Boris shrugged, 'I don't think Barchenka trusted him any more than we do. He was supposed to do one of his brainwashing Religious Interpretation gigs on offenders, to get them to support her. I get the impression he isn't the least bit rehabilitated. Bets a lot, but there's no law against that up there. He can work all the scams he wants on offies and grunts. I warned Commander Ottey in Padrugoi Security to watch out for any further problem from him and, well . . .' Boris left the rest of his sentence in the air. Sascha understood what wasn't said.

'And His Royal Highness Phanibal Shimaz is safely on First Base?' Sascha asked.

'The penal unit there is isolated from the main blocks,' Boris replied. 'Colonel Watari's tough. Goes by the book. Shimaz is out of the way for good. That child farm of his was too much even for his family.' Then Boris sighed deeply. 'And speaking of debasement, I hope I'm not required to probe Ludmilla again.' Despite his long service with Law Enforcement and Order, Boris gave a shudder of revulsion.

Sascha spared his brother a sympathetic look. 'Her trial's nearly over. I doubt you'll have to.'

'Appalling woman. *Hates* us.' Boris meant Talents.

'She has reason to,' Sascha remarked candidly. 'Of

course, if I were truly honest, I'd admit that I reciprocate her animosity with interest.'

'I won't tell.'

'You're all heart, bro,' replied Sascha.

'So, give me some good news to go on with. I've five more of Ludmilla's white-coats to scan for the hearings tomorrow,' Boris said with a heavy sigh. 'Is Lance going to start training your young genius?'

'He had to settle affairs in Adelaide but Rhyssa and Peter are expecting him any day now.'

The tribunal hearing the case of Padrugoi Independent Space Station versus Ludmilla Barchenka for mutiny proceeded inexorably but with impeccable impartiality to a conclusion. Even the attempted hostage-taking, grievous bodily harm done to several distinguished guests and her threats against their lives were sufficient in themselves to have heavy penalties imposed on her. She was found guilty of high treason by the unanimous agreement of the tribunal that had included a Ukrainian judge, and was duly sentenced to permanent house arrest in a small house outside Kiev. She wore the special double-banded wrist ID of a convicted criminal that restricted her to those premises. As an added precaution, she was surgically body-tagged with a detector that could not be removed short of her demise. The completion bonus for the Padrugoi Space Station was sequestered and placed in a special account that would defray her costs and was budgeted to last a reasonable projection of her life expectancy. Visitors to her quarters were severely limited, and those few who requested visits were scanned before and after. The pulverized remains of the plastic sculpture, which President Cimprich had presented to her, were found in the first week's refuse.

The trial itself formed a judicial precedent, being the first action of the independent entity, the Padrugoi Space Station, against an individual. Thus the entire world became aware of the legal independence of that entity.

*   *   *

'Her biggest single mistake was in refusing to let us attend,' Johnny said to Rhyssa and Peter two weeks later after Barchenka started serving her life sentence. They were seated in Rhyssa's second-floor office in the Henner mansion.

Johnny took a sip from his second cup of coffee and continued. 'When I found out that Gordie's name had been struck off the invite list, and bearing in mind my other information, I decided Lance and I needed to meet. In his shielded quarters on the Station, of course. He actually organized,' and he grinned wickedly, 'our volunteers. When the ever-lovin' Ludmilla formally ended his conscription – she kept calling it a "work contract" – she watched while he cleared his office and his computer system, not that he had left anything up on *that*. Then she had her white-coats personally conduct him to the shuttle.' Johnny chuckled. 'He walked on and then walked off through the service hatch. His was the bright idea of utilizing the ventilation ducts. Had to pick people who could fit in them, too. In fact, he'd been eavesdropping on white-coat barrack conversations, trying to figure out what was going to happen. I'll give her this – she picked the most close-mouthed bastards she could find as platoon leaders. And I suspect they didn't know the whole nine yards beforehand.'

Rhyssa slowly shook her head over Barchenka's tactics and how very close they had come to success.

Peter cleared his throat. 'You don't know when Admiral Coetzer will let me see the spaceship, do you?'

'It'll be a lot more interesting when it's nearer completion, Pete,' Johnny replied. 'Never fear, skeleteam! Dirk Coetzer is not one to forget his debts.'

A polite knock sounded on Rhyssa's door.

'Come in, Sascha, Lance,' she replied, adding a mental invitation, and the door opened for the visitors.

Sascha had a now-is-the-time smile on his face that he directed at Peter, as he stepped forward to allow the lanky Lance Baden to enter behind him. The Australian Centre chief gave a cheerful wave including all in the room, but he, too, was eyeing his new student.

Not that I don't think I'll be learning more from you, Pete, than you will from me.

Peter had risen to his feet, a courtesy that Lance appreciated, though he was in no way a formal person.

No need to be nervous, pal, Sascha said on a tight 'path to the boy.

Don't tease, Rhyssa added, imaging her face with a severe frown.

'Come in, sit down and let's *talk*, shall we?' she said aloud, setting the tone for the discussion of how to train a boy who was probably the most powerful telekinetic to be discovered anywhere on the planet.

Lance settled himself in one of the comfortable lounge chairs, crossing one long leg over the other and linking his fingers together, totally relaxed. Sascha took the other lounger and waved at Peter to seat himself.

'Now, I've a full month off from the Adelaide Centre,' Lance began, 'so what I'd like to do, Pete, is walk you through exactly what you *do* do and see if we can develop any theories on gestalt so that others can also boldly go.' He glanced over at John Greene, who shrugged from where he was stretched out in the leather chair.

'I won't be too much help, Lance,' the General said. 'I just learned to go with the flow, and I can't tell you how I managed to emulate Pete here, except that somehow I had to keep Dave from cracking his skull open on the edge of that swimming pool.'

'Using the electricity from the sunbeds for the gestalt?' Lance asked.

Johnny nodded. 'I wanted him to *move* over a metre away. He did.'

'And after that, you were floating drones and space shuttles to Padrugoi like so many pebbles skipping across the pond,' Lance remarked drily.

Again Johnny shrugged. 'That's all I thought I was doing.'

Lance looked questioningly at Peter.

'Sir, it *is* sort of like skipping pebbles across the water,' Peter said.

'Then how do you estimate just how much of a skip you have to take in gestalt from the generators?'

Peter opened both hands in a helpless gesture. He was trying to shrug his shoulders as John Greene did, but only his right shoulder twitched in response to his wish. 'Some things I touch with my mind just feel heavier than others. Like orange juice or plasteel. Just looking at some stuff even, I can tell it must weigh tons.'

'At the Base in Florida,' Rhyssa put in, 'the technician always had the gross weight figures of what Peter was to lift.'

'That still requires some sort of calculation, doesn't it?' Lance added when Peter opened his hands in a gesture of continued dismay.

'Pete started off using the four point five kph generator we installed for him at Dorotea's,' Rhyssa said. 'And half the time now he doesn't even need to access that.'

'Very interesting,' Lance said, nodding, with the expression of someone who hasn't heard anything significant. 'Did you use any auxiliary power during the mutiny? For instance, when you heated up the butts of the white-coats' weapons?'

Peter shook his head, looking more and more concerned. Then suddenly his face brightened. 'I did lean on the generators when I put a shield around the Admiral. I didn't want anything to get through.'

John Greene and Lance Baden made eye contact.

'I didn't feel any pulse,' Johnny said.

'I felt yours, Pete, when you shorted out that woman's prompt screen,' Lance said, grinning.

'He didn't, I did,' Johnny Greene said.

'That was you, Johnny?' Rhyssa was surprised.

The General raised one languid hand. 'Guilty. She was taking far too much credit.'

'And all along, I thought it was you, Pete.'

Now a very smug smile tugged at the boy's mouth and was echoed in his eyes. 'No, I corrupted her disk.'

'Ah, so that's why Grushkov thought you were totally innocent,' Lance said, pretending much relief at getting the culpability straight.

Johnny nodded. 'I wonder what would have happened if we *had* allowed her to finish that speech?'

'I'm as glad we didn't, frankly,' Lance said. 'So, Pete – you don't mind being Pete, do you?'

'No, sir.'

'When you were shielding the Admiral, how did you make the weapons too hot to handle?'

'I just "thought" them hot. But I didn't move them anywhere.'

'Oh, I see. So it wasn't telekinesis,' Lance remarked, one hand covering his mouth for a moment.

'Not really.' Peter paused.

Rhyssa cleared her throat, Sascha ducked his head and Johnny's eyes were brilliant with amusement.

'That's as well. Can you explain it to me?' asked Lance, leaning forward in his chair and resting his elbows on his knees, clasping his hands lightly together.

'Can you suggest something that doesn't have any mass, sir?'

'Pete,' and Lance waved his hands, 'enough of this "sir" stuff. I know Dorotea is very keen on social graces, but I'm just another Talent, like Johnny here.'

'Not at all like me, you wombat,' Johnny said with considerable force in his voice, despite his relaxed position.

'For which I am indeed grateful,' Lance shot in an aside to him before he turned back to a startled Peter Reidinger. 'You and me,' and he waggled his finger back and forth between them, 'are going to be working as close as mates, and you're to call me Lance, right?'

'Right, ssss— Lance.' Peter swallowed.

'Right! Now, I'm to suggest something that doesn't have – mass. Well, everything has mass, including orange juice. Do you employ gestalt to transfer grams?' Peter shook his head. 'Kilograms?' Peter began to nod. 'And definitely dead tons? Right?'

'Right.'

'Do you instinctively measure the volume of what you 'port?'

Peter considered this. 'Well, I did look at the mass of

drones and shuttles when I was doing them. I *know* that something's dense by the feel of it.'

'What has mass in this room that you'd need gestalt to move?'

Peter eyed the objects in Rhyssa's office and then, with a mischievous glint in his eye, pointed to Johnny Greene, and promptly, those in the office heard a distant generator hum and the General, chair and all, was lifted off the floor.

'Hey, just wait an effing minute,' Johnny said, his eyes round with surprise. He didn't move, but his body tensed a moment before he obviously forced himself to relax. 'Not even for you, Pete Reidinger,' and he shook his index finger at the grinning boy, 'will I be a display piece.'

He and his chair were put back in place with not so much as a jar to Johnny's extended legs, the heels of his shoes fitting exactly back into the marks on Rhyssa's thick carpet.

Sascha, Rhyssa and Lance were smirking at his indignant reaction.

'One of these days, my young friend . . .' and the threat went unspecified. 'Why didn't you pick on him?' Johnny continued, sitting upright and pointing to Baden. 'He outweighs me.'

'He's my trainer,' Peter replied with an impudent grin.

'That'll teach you, Johnny,' Rhyssa said, having thoroughly enjoyed his discomfiture.

'I don't know about *that*,' Johnny replied, losing all trace of petulance before indolently shooting the cuffs of his tunic and resettling himself in the lounge chair. Then he favoured Peter with a genuine smile. 'Just caught me unawares. I'll be very careful not to underestimate you again, young skeleteam.'

'Which reminds me, Lance,' Rhyssa said, putting her arms on her desk and leaning forward towards the Australian, 'to tell you that Peter was fifteen just six weeks ago.'

'I take due note, Rhyssa, that he is not a working Talent yet,' Lance replied. 'And with all kinetics and 'paths back on their jobs, I presume that you don't intend to use the skeleteam.'

'Emphatically not. Now don't argue, Peter,' she said to the

71

boy, who was levitating out of his chair in protest. 'Neither Sascha nor I would have condoned the use of your exceptional abilities under normal conditions. Now that we are definitely back online, we are morally obligated not to abuse your good nature and Talent in any way.'

'But you're letting Tirla work,' Peter began.

'Tirla is *in residence*,' Sascha broke in, scowling fiercely at the boy who recoiled from his expression, 'with Lessud, Shria and their family in a Long Island Residential Linear that is not remotely like Linear G in Jerhattan. She is definitely *not* working,' and Sascha strung out the last three syllables to emphasize the point.

'She took you and me shopping,' Peter murmured.

'Tirla has never considered *shopping* to be work,' Rhyssa said, 'pathing tightly to Sascha to *stay out of this*.

Sascha grinned broadly as if in response to her comment. 'She's putting in every other minute she's awake studying.'

'I'd say she'll need to do more shopping for you, skeleteam,' Johnny remarked, eyeing the bare leg below Peter's now too short everyday trousers.

'I could do with some duds myself,' Lance said. 'You blokes ought to get your thermostats fixed. This city's bloody cold.'

'It's spring,' Rhyssa said in surprise.

'Not to my goose bumps it ain't. C'mon, sprout,' Lance said, rising and nodding to Peter. 'Now we got the ground rules laid out, we can have a good chinwag on the way to getting me some warmer stuff. Or should we call on this Tirla you mentioned?'

'She's studying hard,' Sascha said firmly.

'With your permission, Rhyssa?'

'By all means, Lance. Begin as you mean to go on.' Rhyssa waved her hand towards the door.

Lance indicated that Peter should precede him to the door.

'Sascha and I have some schedules we must go over,' Rhyssa said, pulling some pencil files towards her. 'Johnny, don't you have someplace you have to be now?'

'Well, if you put it that way,' and, clipping his hand

towards his right eye in an airy salute, General John Greene disappeared, the generators humming slightly to indicate how he had effected his withdrawal.

Peter gave a little sniff of disdain as he exited. Behind him, Lance cocked an eyebrow at Rhyssa and Sascha and left.

'My private opinion,' Sascha remarked to his chief, 'is that Pete could probably 'port himself anywhere without gestalt.'

'You're probably right,' Rhyssa said with a sigh, and inserted the first file.

Halfway through the second week of his training time with Peter, Lance was interrupted by a telepathic touch.

Lance Baden? Carmen Stein. I have found her.

Found who? Lance was so intent on observing Peter doing a lift of half a ton of scrap metal from a yard to a steel foundry that he couldn't for the moment recall what 'her' Carmen Stein might have found.

The Bantam child.

I'm not usually this slow, Lance said, not willing to direct any attention away from the screen that was graphing Peter's use of power in gestalt. *Who?*

The daughter of Tony and Nadezhda Bantam. You sent me a leather-bound journal, with a photograph of the three of them. The parents are dead. I have located the daughter.

My God, you haven't! Are you sure?

There was a brief pause. *I am as sure as I can be.*

Where?

She's very far away. Still in Bangladesh. I can pinpoint her more accurately once I am there. I apologize for not getting back to this sooner, but I have been busy with LEO.

Of course you have, Carmen. We have both been occupied in other matters. If she is alive.

She is very much alive.

'Damn,' Lance said aloud, for the good news had cut his concentration on Peter's kinetic switch.

'Did I do something wrong?' Peter asked, picking up the monitor to find the mistake.

'No, boy, you didn't. But I just heard some very good

73

news that put me off what we're doing here. Sorry about that. Excuse me a sec.' *Carmen, are you free to travel right now?*

Yes, since you could not find the child on your own, and Lance caught amusement in her voice. *That picture is at least three years old. You might not recognize her.* Carmen subtly suggested that a male would not be able to make the leap of the child's alteration. *I definitely will.*

Lance was suddenly so full of what he needed to do now that he failed to recognize the note in her voice.

D'you know Kayankira of the Delhi Centre? he asked Carmen. *She'd arrange for local guides, unless you're fluent in Bangla, which I am not.*

Tirla is.

Ah, yes, the shopping Tirla. Good idea, and Lance grinned at the thought of finally meeting this young Talent whom Sascha was eager to protect and Rhyssa and Peter thought highly of. Peter usually saw his friend when he had an afternoon off, while Lance attended to Adelaide Centre business. *I'll ask Rhyssa if we can take Tirla with us.*

Better to ask Sascha, Carmen said.

Whoever! Lance brushed that remark aside. Fleetingly he remembered that Tirla, who had a phenomenal Talent in languages, was, like Peter, too young to be officially employed by the Centre. Why should Sascha be asked? Ah, he was head of training. Well, Lance would have to clear all travel plans for Peter, as well as Tirla, with Rhyssa, as Centre head. The trip to a totally different culture could be educational for both youngsters.

Speak to Rhyssa, Carmen said. *My time is clear for the next few days.*

Lance explained the circumstances to Rhyssa, and her sympathy for an orphaned child was immediate. She granted permission for an expedition involving Peter, Tirla and Carmen Stein.

I don't think Sascha will object, if Carmen is along.

Lance shook his head. *Why would Roznine object? I understand she's not in active training yet.*

Ah! Sascha has a special interest in Tirla. He rescued her from Linear G and *a kidnapping attempt. I'll tell you the full story another time. Although don't be surprised at anything Tirla says or does.*

I won't then, Lance promised, without at all knowing what that might entail.

Will Peter be doing the kinetics?

Johnny's been wanting a long-distance test of that new carrier he's had designed. Lightweight, just a shell really, but suitable for longer-distance teleporting. I'd like to see Peter using it. Kayankira is meeting us in Dhaka.

That's right. You're good friends. Have a nice trip, and Rhyssa's mental tone briefly bubbled with suppressed laughter.

'How would you like to take a short break from *our* studies?' Lance asked Peter, grinning. While he regretted an interruption to this session, he realized that, since he'd been released from Padrugoi, weeks ago now, he hadn't even thought to enquire of Carmen about her search for the Bantams' child.

'To do what?' Peter asked, surprised.

Lance was a single-minded instructor, a much stronger telekinetic than Rick Hobson was. Peter felt he already had far more control over his energy than ever before. He certainly didn't want to interrupt these lessons.

'Remember when you dropped me and the shuttle full of kinetics in Dhaka?'

Peter nodded.

'Well, I have some unfinished business over there. We can try Johnny's carrier and some of your push-pull techniques, which we really haven't been able to do here,' and Lance gestured around the old warehouse they were using as a schoolroom.

'I wouldn't mind,' Peter admitted. 'Though it's more Johnny's technique than mine.'

'Probably because Greene still doesn't have the power you've got in your big toe.'

Peter didn't like anyone criticizing his friend, and averted his face from Lance. He knew he had a long way to go before he could control his expression.

'Not that I'm criticizing the General in any way, Pete. It's just wise to recognize limitations, that's all. We're to be there at sunrise, their time.'

'Will we be using the new carrier he sent us? That's awesome,' the boy said, his eyes gleaming. He and Lance had 'ported about Jerhattan, but a long 'port would be a treat. 'Back to Dhaka, huh? Zia Airport again?' Peter asked. He swivelled around to the monitor, asking it for the global coordinates and sighing with impatience at the time it took to access them. He had a memory that was almost eidetic, so he hadn't had to call up a general map first. He'd practised memory techniques while still in the hospital, inert on an A-frame bed with little else to occupy a busy mind. 'It'd be nice to *be* there,' he remarked, placing his finger on the site.

'Call it education. You haven't been many places yet on this ol' Earth, and it's about time you did some travelling, to see how the other half lives.'

'Can we go to Australia, too, while we're nearly there? You promised me I'd get to see kangaroos and wallabies and wombats,' Peter said eagerly. 'And Ayers Rock and Alice Springs.'

'We can't just take off and go sightseeing whenever we want to.'

'But—'

'I've got an errand in Bangladesh.'

They spent some time looking at the towns and cities of Bangladesh. Peter was fascinated by the flat landscape, with not a single residential Linear or ziggurat on the flat, deltoid plains. Even Dhaka's architecture was mainly in the traditional Bengali patterns.

The next day at the very early hour of four on a bright, crisp morning in early March, Lance and Peter waited by the new passenger carrier shell that General John Greene had had constructed for the purpose of kinetic transportation. It had windows, which Lance thought a definite improvement. Carmen arrived with a slight, coffee-skinned, black-haired youngster, dressed modestly but with great style.

'Hi, Tirla, whatcha need that for?' Peter asked, lifting his arm to indicate her backpack. 'We'll only be gone a few hours.'

'Stuff and junk,' the girl responded in a clear, faintly accented voice. 'You're the Lance that makes Peter work so hard,' she added, tilting her head and giving the tall Australian a searching look.

'Perhaps not as hard as he works me, Tirla.' Then Lance handed a towel-wrapped parcel to her. 'Keep that safe for me, please?'

She considered his answer for a moment before giving a sharp nod of her head. 'Sure.' She took the parcel and stowed it carefully in her backpack with a see-why-I-need-it glare at Peter. Then she pointed to the carrier. 'We go in this? And Peter flies it?'

'I 'port it, Tir,' Peter corrected her. 'Let's go.' He glided forward.

The girl snorted and crossed his glide pattern so he'd have to halt. 'Ladies first!' She gestured for Carmen to precede her.

Carmen shot an are-you-ready-for-this, Lance? look before she ducked her head and took the right-hand rear seat. Tirla insinuated her slender body into the starboard-side front row.

'Hey . . .' Peter protested. 'Lance should be there.'

'Why?' Tirla said, regarding him for a long moment of condescension, and Lance ended a possible argument by taking the vacant place beside Carmen.

'I can watch from back here just as well,' he said.

'Oh, all right.' Peter was too eager to leave to delay over a minor detail. He placed an old-fashioned paper-filled notebook on the flat surface in front of him and opened it to the page he had drawn up the day before, under Lance's supervision. Peter had been studying air routes and co-ordinates of airports and, since he'd be travelling through some sort of space – just as he had kinetically flung shuttles to Padrugoi – he felt, and Lance agreed, that ordinary flight patterns could serve the purpose of orientation.

Tirla sat straight up, craning her neck to peruse his notations.

'Looks like gibberish to me.'

'You've never seen any flight plans, so you wouldn't know.'

Lance leaned forward. 'Commercial airlines do not allow passengers to talk to the pilot in take-off or landing modes.'

'I didn't think Peter was commercial yet,' Tirla replied, swivelling round to stare at Lance with confident and very beautiful pansy-brown eyes.

'We're working on it,' Lance replied.

Tirla continued to hold eye contact.

Be careful with this one, Carmen said, without looking at Lance.

She's not telepathic?

She can hear when she wants to. But so far, she only wants to hear Dorotea and Peter. And Sascha, of course.

I see.

I doubt it, Carmen replied.

'Peter, let's launch this. I've promised Greene a full report on its performance and comfort in long-distance hauling.'

'Peter's not supposed to *work*,' Tirla protested, casually giving Lance Baden another of her scrutinies.

'For Peter this is play, fun, and cream tea with scones,' Lance said, gesturing to Peter to proceed.

Abruptly they were not in the warehouse any more, but in very bright sunlight, planted on one leg of the telepad. Safely outside the circumference of the painted circle around the telepad, Kayankira was seated at the wheel of a battered four-wheel-drive ground vehicle.

She dismounted immediately, a slender woman with a thick braid of black hair down her back, dressed in traditional Bengali garb. She ran towards them, her face beaming with delight.

You have arrived. Scarcely have I stopped the engine and you are here. How many minutes, seconds does such a journey take? Then the Delhi Centre chief was shaking hands as the passengers emerged into dry and dehydrating heat. *I know you, Carmen Stein. Your mind is unmistakable. Lance, it is good to see your face, no longer contorted with the anxieties with which that appalling Barchenka burdened*

78

you. And has she not had her just deserts! And who is this? She took a short step backward, throwing her arms wide in a surprise welcome, as Tirla emerged, looking about her in total amazement at the sun-washed plain of Zia Airport.

She's frightened, Carmen said and smiled reassuringly, holding out her hand to Tirla. *She's never been anyplace this open or uninhabited.*

Ooh, but she looks like one of us. Kayankira touched her chest with both hands. She brought them together in the formal salute of her part of the world. Almost dazed, Tirla hesitated. In another second, she evidently recovered from culture shock. She folded her hands in front of her chest.

'*Namaskar ji,*' she said in flawless Hindi.

Kayankira's expressive face registered complete awe.

Did you tell her everything about me?

We told her nothing, Kayan, Lance replied with a broad grin.

She gets your language right from your head, ma'am, Peter explained quickly so that the Delhi Centre chief would not think badly of his good friend. *She doesn't know she does it but it's what she does best.*

*Ah, the little one I have heard about. '*Namaskar, kya hal he?*' Kayankira added aloud.

'Stick to English, please, Tirla,' Lance said. 'We all understand that.'

Tirla cocked an eyebrow in his direction. 'I am fine, thank you,' she said to Kayankira very, very politely.

Ah, when she is old enough to be employed, I have first dibs.

Get in line, Carmen said. 'Lord, but it's roasting out here.' She fanned herself with her hand. 'I need some shade where I can concentrate on locating. What *is* the child's name?'

'To the vehicle,' Kayankira said, pointing to it and gathering her passengers in the circle of her free arm to herd them towards it. Peter and Lance began shucking their jackets and rolling up their sleeves. Though Tirla was dressed for Jerhattan too, she strode as if mere climate was not affecting her.

79

She was glad enough to reach the shade, drink thick sweet coffee and munch her way through European-style breakfast breads in the Zia passenger terminal. She had eyes only for the fascinating promenade of passers-by and their sometimes exotic-looking burdens. Peter was trying to emulate Tirla's composed manner, but then she was more accustomed to Neesters, from her years in Linear G.

'So, what *is* the child's name, Lance?' Carmen repeated when she had had a restorative sip of the coffee.

'I don't know. Wasn't it mentioned in the journal?'

'I didn't read it. When I realized that the father was dead, I used the photograph of the child as a focus.'

Tirla paused long enough in her surveillance of the terminal to extract Lance's rectangle from her pack and hand it to the finder. Carmen passed it over to Lance who quickly riffled through the pages, trying to find personal references.

'Ah, Amariyah?' He stumbled over his pronunciation of the written word, putting the accent on the second syllable.

'Ama*ree*yah, I would say,' Kayankira replied. 'Though it is not a common Indian name, either Muslim or Hindu.'

'Nor does it sound Russian, which was the mother's nationality,' Lance said.

Peter groaned. *Not another* shelkoonchik?

'A nutcracker?' Tirla asked, frowning at Peter.

Kayankira's eyes threatened to pop out of their sockets. *Russian, too?*

Carmen gave a shrug. *She can do it with any language.*

How does *she do it?* the Delhi Centre chief asked.

As well ask how Peter heaves space shuttles about, Lance said with an equally diffident lift of his shoulders.

'What has a nutcracker to do with Amariyah?' and the name flowed prettily from Tirla's lips.

'Nothing, I believe. But Amariyah is the child we have come to find. Now, if you will all be quiet.' Carmen put a finger on the face of the child sitting so solemnly between her parents and closed her eyes.

Tirla closed her eyes too, so that she wouldn't inadvertently distract the 'finder'. That was one parapsychic courtesy she always observed. She was also fond of Carmen, now that she saw the great benefits that had come of Carmen's finding her in the first place.

'She's quite a ways from here,' Carmen finally said.

'I can*not* understand what you could have been thinking,' Sister Kathleen was saying, shaking with frustration and anger. She was holding a dusty Amariyah away from her, and the girl, usually so self-effacing and gentle, was trying to twist free, flailing her arms. To go right back to tearing more hair off the scalp of the hysterically weeping Lila, curled up in the wreckage of what everyone in the orphanage knew was Amariyah's garden. All the other girls were ringed about the little tableau, well out of range of either Amariyah's or Sister Kathleen's retribution, staring in round-eyed, open-mouthed fascination.

'I was thinking she has killed my garden,' Amariyah cried. 'She is still rolling in it. You are surely seeing that much!' Too tightly held in Sister Kathleen's capable, firm grip to pull more of Lila's luxuriant tresses from her head, the furious little girl now kicked dust at her victim with her bare feet.

From the corner of the main building, Sister Epiphania came rushing, to discover the cause of Lila's continuous shrieks. Epiphania paused a moment, taking in the incredible scene of the prostrate Lila and her colleague holding the struggling Amariyah.

'Oh, dear Lord, oh, dear Lord, save us,' Sister Epiphania chanted as she rushed forward to succour Lila, who screamed in terror when 'Phania touched her. She had her eyes tightly closed, as much against the dust Amariyah was kicking at her, as because she knew she had been caught doing something wicked. 'Lila, dear Lila, it is I.'

The voice reassuring her, Lila opened her eyes enough to see that she was safe. She clung to Sister Epiphania, shrieking out that she would never be married now, with all the hair pulled from her head.

'Nonsense,' Sister Kathleen said, coping with Amariyah's flailing. 'Do take that . . .' Kathleen firmly closed her lips on

81

the adjective she was going to apply to the malicious Lila, paused and rephrased her sentence, 'that child and bathe her scalp. She's by no means badly hurt. Certainly not enough to keep caterwauling.' Although, she thought candidly to herself, who they would marry such a mean-spirited creature to was moot.

Soothingly, Sister Epiphania managed to get Lila to her feet and lead her away through the circle of watching children.

'Now, Amariyah, let us deal with you,' Sister Kathleen said in her firmest no-nonsense voice. 'I cannot believe that *you*, of all the children here, would display a vicious streak!'

'She ruined my garden!' Amariyah suddenly collapsed, sinking into a pathetic bundle, tears streaming down her dusty face as she picked up first this clump of greenery and then that. She held them to her mouth, in the age-old gesture of grief, completely bereft. She did not scream, she did not sob, but the tears kept pouring out of her sorrowful blue eyes in a manner that totally unnerved Sister Kathleen.

'Oh, my dear child, do not take on so.' The nun pulled the little girl up, broken plants and all, stroking the tangled hair, rocking the slender body in her arms. 'You can replant the garden,' she said encouragingly.

'It is the dry season,' Amariyah wailed, though she surrendered to the motion of Sister Kathleen's body. 'Nothing will bud or bloom in the dry season. Surely you are knowing this.'

'Go about your tasks,' Sister Kathleen said, realizing that the entire orphanage was avid witness to the scene. She raised one arm to scatter the audience. 'Tula, Rabiah, take the washing down before the sun bleaches all the colour away. Soma, Lota, take the little ones to the banyan tree and finish telling them their story. Sakti, Reva, you were supposed to be drawing water. Be sure to put the jars in the shade to cool for our supper. Habibah, Risha, Uma . . . All of you big girls, you have not finished hoeing the potatoes.' She shooed them all about their sundry tasks, rocking Amariyah in time to her orders.

'Now, little one, what shall I do with you?' She held the child away from her, and was unutterably affected by the tears still rolling down the woebegone little face. 'Never, in all the time you have been with us, have you misbehaved!'

'My flowers (sob), my vege-(sob)-tables (sob) are all dead.' The murmured words were bitter. 'Nothing I can do will bring them back to life.' She opened her hands and displayed the limp and wilted remains of her once thriving plants. 'Why? Why did Lila kill them? They had done her no harm. She is an assassin!'

Sister Kathleen pressed her lips together, wondering why she wanted to cry, too. Crying was not an effective answer to any problem that she knew of. She was flummoxed by the fact that this was the first time Amariyah had wept tears. She was such a self-contained little body, diligent with her assigned tasks, willing to do anything required of her. She had been so good with the little ones when the fever struck, even deserting her garden during the emergency. Whatever had possessed Lila? Of course, the girl was older, starting her menses when, as every woman knew, females were more likely to be perverse. Especially the Bengali girls, who matured far too young, Sister Kathleen thought. Lila would soon be thirteen, and all her thoughts were on marriage. The girl refused even to consider the alternatives now available to the young women of Bangladesh. Well, Kathleen thought philosophically, you can lead a horse to water but you can't make it drink.

'Now, child, we will wash your face and hands and dry your tears.' She rose, trying to lift Amariyah to her feet, but the girl writhed out of her grasp.

Amariyah hunkered down and began tenderly gathering up the dead stalks and stems. 'You must be going into the compost. You will be going with my love because you were rewarding me with your beauty and your strength. After death there can be life in another form. It is written.'

Sister Kathleen stared in surprise, and watched as Amariyah finished collecting the remains and walked towards the efficient composting tank, the very welcome gift of some ladies' group in England. Kathleen did not remember where, but the gift was much appreciated.

'When you are done, Amariyah, I will wash your face and hands.'

She heard a murmured response, and rather thought it had to do with being able to wash her own self without help.

Sister Kathleen shook her head, wondering if, perhaps, she should have reminded the child of her manners. A reprimand right now was inappropriate. And besides, Amariyah was one of the few girls who could be counted on for scrupulous courtesy. Father Salih and the Bahadur had both commented on her deportment. She watched a moment longer as Amariyah returned for another load of damaged plants, her expression still woeful, but the amazing tears had stopped. Sister Kathleen turned towards the infirmary where little shrieks suggested that Sister Epiphania was anointing Lila's torn scalp. Sister Kathleen caught herself smiling. Lila deserved, at least in this small measure, physical and mental discomfort for such a random act of senseless destruction.

As the cool of evening settled in, Sister Kathleen had occasion to pass the spot where Amariyah's garden had flourished. She halted, staring at the place that had been raked clean of pebbles: not even so much as one of the twigs that had provided a little fence remained.

'Oh dear,' and Kathleen was truly and devastatingly appalled at the sight. 'Oh, poor dear Amariyah!' She looked about the little clumps of girls playing games. She couldn't spot Amariyah. Of course, Amariyah was *always* gardening at this hour. She looked again towards the wide-spreading limbs of the banyan tree where the girls were gathered. That is when she saw the dust-cloud rising in the distance. She thought little of it, since this was the hour when people did undertake journeys, when the fierce sun was setting.

She was astonished when, twenty minutes later, the sturdy ground vehicle came to a discreet halt at the orphanage gate. The driver descended and came to the gate, a Hindu to judge by her clothes, and indubitably high-caste. She scolded herself briefly for adding that to her first impression. The visitor saw her and folded her hands politely, smiling such a warm greeting that she smiled back.

'Is this the Orphanage of the Holy Innocents?' she asked.

'Yes, it is,' and she paused for her to identify herself.

'I am known as Kayankira,' she said, which surprised the Sister, 'and I am Chief of the Delhi Bureau.'

Kathleen noticed that she did not explain which bureau, but her manners and deference to her were so charming that she could not feel any harm in her.

'I am Sister Kathleen Rose. I am in charge here. My colleague is Sister Epiphania Gibson.'

'Ah, Sister Kathleen,' the Bureau Chief said with another polite bow, 'allow me to present my companions?' She turned to a woman of at least forty years, with the most serene face the Sister had ever seen on a layperson. 'This is Carmen Stein, an old friend of mine. Here is also her young friend, Tirla Tunnelle, who is travelling just now in Bangladesh. Also Peter Reidinger. And last but never least is my old friend, Lance Baden.'

Sister Kathleen acknowledged the introductions in a sort of daze. Then Sister Epiphania came rushing out to stand beside her, and the introductions were repeated. Sister Kathleen was aware that Carmen Stein was looking about from one knot of giggling girls to another – who had now realized the orphanage had received visitors of some importance. She did not notice the tension in both Ms Stein and Tirla.

Suddenly, interrupting Lance Baden just as he was about to explain their presence here, Tirla went rigid and pointed.

'She's there.'

'Yes, she is,' Carmen replied, a rush of relief and in-explicable joy flowing across her face. *Lord, but she's broadcasting enough frustration and outrage for even Tirla to hear it.* 'May we?'

'I don't understand,' Sister Kathleen began, automatically taking a step to impede any invasion of the orphanage space.

'It is all right,' Lance Baden said, stepping forward and taking her hands in his.

And suddenly Sister Kathleen knew it was, though she didn't know why or how. These people, even the gawky boy, radiated goodwill and confidence in the rightness of their presence here, this evening, in the little orphanage outside Bogra. Kathleen Rose stepped back, wondering how they had disarmed her so completely.

'Oh, I'm so happy for her,' Sister Epiphania said in a tremulous voice.

'Happy for who?' Kathleen asked, staring in amazement at her fellow nun.

'You know?' Lance Baden asked Epiphania, who smiled beatifically at him.

'For Amariyah, of course,' 'Phania said as if that were obvious.

'I don't understand,' Kathleen said, shaking her head.

The dark girl, who looked part Asian, was hurrying through the yard, past Amariyah's former garden, the boy following with a most unusual gliding step. Ms Stein followed more slowly, as if savouring the moment.

'Yes, we are come for Amariyah Bantam,' Kayankira said. 'It has taken a long while to go through all the records after the flood, Sister Kathleen.' She held out a sweat-stained journal, and opened it to the page containing a photograph. Kathleen was arrested by the picture of a much younger Amariyah, sitting straight and proud between two lovely people who obviously adored their child.

'Oh!' The odd distancing Kathleen experienced was obliterated by a sense of tremendous loss, the loss of Amariyah. 'Oh, dear Lord, I don't think the child ever did wash her hands and face, or comb her hair. It's all full of dead leaves.'

'Ah,' and Kayankira smiled understandingly, as if she knew all about the garden and Amariyah's most uncharacteristic attack on Lila. 'It is as nothing, for the essence of the child is known.'

The two Sisters now hurriedly followed the others towards the tree. How had this Tirla seen Amariyah? She was on the far side of the thick tree trunk, not at all visible from the gate. Yet as the visitors, the nuns in their wake, skirted the girls, Tirla had reached Amariyah. She hunkered down and began talking earnestly – in Bangla – to the blue-eyed orphan. The tall boy hovered behind Tirla as Ms Stein joined them, the most beautiful smile on her face as she leaned down, touching Amariyah gently on the forehead.

'We have come for you, Amariyah Bantam. You will have a garden all to yourself and no one will defile it.'

Those remarks stopped Sister Kathleen in her tracks, blinking in astonishment. Then it suddenly dawned on her that these people were psychics. They could read minds – and feelings. She hugged herself, even though she knew that the Church was tolerant of such phenomena, and worried about what her mind might have revealed to them.

Just then the squeal of brakes and the smell of petrol in the heavy air distracted her. Father Salih, too? Well, they had had the courtesy to inform *him*. That was correct. As if the photograph was not confirmation of her unusual waif's identity. But she must know more before she released the child to their care. Ms Stein was not a relative; although she was dark, she bore no resemblance to Amariyah. The birth mother had the same black hair as her daughter, with glints of red. Both parents had intelligent blue eyes.

'I have come as fast as it is possible to travel,' Father Salih was explaining as he joined those now observing Amariyah, Tirla and Carmen Stein. The boy, Peter, still hovered, not intruding but very interested. Lance Baden and the Bureau Chief had stopped a distance from the trio, and now turned to shake hands with Father Salih. 'Sister Kathleen, Sister Epiphania, it is all according to protocol. The Bishop of Dhaka himself is reassuring me. He is calling me on the system.' In excitement Father Salih often reverted to a purely Bangla cadence. 'He is giving his approval for these good people to take our Amariyah with them. They are being most respectable folk, to guard, guide and educate her. I am giving you reassurances on that head.'

Father Salih tended to be overly courteous, but Sister Kathleen thought he would bow himself off his hips any moment if he weren't careful. His eyes kept flicking to Amariyah, seated under the tree. She had ignored the approach of Tirla and Ms Stein but when the woman had so gently touched her, she had begun to shake off her apathy, regarding them with gradually widening, surprised eyes.

'Oh, dear Lord,' 'Phania murmured distractedly in Kathleen's ear, 'just look at the state of her. Her hair,' a little moan, 'and she didn't really wash her face before supper.'

'No one has noticed, nor is it important,' Kathleen replied, sighing for the hole she knew would be Amariyah's absence from her life. On the other hand, the mystery of the orphan from Sirajganj was solved. Her parents had been married: she had been loved and cared for as a child.

Lance Baden, whose accent she had now recognized as Australian, was addressing her. He was holding out official-looking documents, handing her his personal card. Blinking at it, she saw that he was from the Adelaide Centre, not Bureau, of the Parapsychic.

'Kayankira has been assisting us in finding young Amariyah. I knew her parents, Tony and Nadezhda Bantam. We met at area conferences, Sister Kathleen, so when he and his wife were listed as missing, I tried – unsuccessfully, I'm sorry to say – to locate them. We had assumed that Amariyah here had also perished. Carmen Stein,' and he gestured to the woman who was now kneeling in front of Amariyah and gently holding her by the hand, 'located her this morning.'

'You are psychics, aren't you?' Sister Kathleen heard herself asking.

Lance gave her an understandingly kind smile. 'We are.'

'She loves things that grow,' Kathleen said, and then pointed to the raked space by the outside fence. 'Her garden! She could make anything grow, even in the dry season.' Kathleen blinked, wondering why she should think that would interest this man. Absently she handed the documents to Father Salih, who had politely stretched out his hand for them.

'Really?' and the single word was imbued with keen interest, not bored enquiry. 'We shall encourage it.'

'She'll settle in better with you if she has a garden.' Then Kathleen gave herself a stern shake. 'Where are you taking her? Does she have family?'

'Yes. She will have family now.'

'Blood kin?' and Kathleen didn't know why she insisted.

'No, closer.'

Then Father Salih intruded on this quiet exchange, tapping the documents he was still holding. 'Ah, yes, now we know her surname. You must sign here, Sister Kathleen,' he said, handing her the papers and his pen. Then he turned round so she could use his back as a writing surface and she signed in her distinctive scrawl. Father Salih filled the space for the witness with his precise tight handwriting.

'I think she's glad to be going,' Sister Epiphania murmured to Kathleen, sounding upset.

'If she goes to where she will have a garden that will not be uprooted,' Kathleen began, 'she will not fret.' She paused, controlling her private regret at losing the girl. 'She is sure to be happy among those who are now her guardians.' Kathleen turned back again to Lance, and touched his arm. 'Is she psychic?'

'Possibly. That is why Carmen was able to locate her. She is young yet. Who knows where her Talent will lie?'

'In gardening, of course,' Sister 'Phania said, as close to being indignant as her gentle soul could get.

'Yes, gardening,' Lance replied. 'Exactly so.'

The other girls had turned silent, their wide brown eyes watching. Lila had thrown the end of her sari over her face and was visibly fuming that so much attention was being paid Amariyah. She glowered as Tirla, holding Amariyah's hand, walked with the boy Peter and Ms Stein to where the other visitors were standing.

'She *wants* to come with us,' Tirla announced to all, as if there had been any doubt. 'She's to have a garden.' Tirla stopped and uncannily turned to stare at Lila, who gave another shriek and buried her face in her hands. 'We will see that no one disturbs it.'

With that, Tirla led Amariyah, who did not so much as look in Lila's direction, towards the gate. As if in a daze,

Amariyah turned back and, folding her hands in front of her chest, gave the two Sisters a deep bow.

'I thank you for your help and kindness,' she said in a formal tone. 'I leave in sadness.'

Only Carmen and Tirla knew that there was no sadness at all in her mind as she proceeded to the ground vehicle.

'Go with God, child,' Kathleen said, making a quick sign of the cross at the departing orphan.

'Oh, dear, dear, dear,' Sister Epiphania said, wringing her hands until Kathleen patted them reassuringly.

'You will forgive our haste, Sister Kathleen, Sister Epiphania,' Kayankira was saying with much saluting and bowing. 'We have come far today, and we must return. We will send you a picture of Amariyah in her new home. She will be encouraged to write to you. You will be happy for her. We are happy to have found her.'

Father Salih was again folding himself near in half, agreeing with everything the Delhi Bureau Chief was saying, which Lance Baden reaffirmed as they reached the ground vehicle and began climbing into it, Tirla shoving Amariyah in front of her, then sitting protectively beside her. The boy, Peter, seemed to slide upward and took the jump seat, while Lance settled in the driver's seat with Kayankira beside him. Sisters Kathleen and Epiphania waved, Father Salih kept bowing, and then all the remaining girls – except Lila – rushed to the fence to wave and shriek farewell, good luck and be healthy. The nuns made the sign of the cross and bowed their heads in little prayers.

It took all Sister Kathleen's store of reserve to continue with the evening. First she had to reassure Father Salih, who was having second thoughts – even though the Bishop had authorized the transfer – about the sudden departure of the little one. And she had to comfort Sister Epiphania, and then see the girls into their dormitories and settle them for the night. Lila had been reduced to total silence by the inequity of Amariyah's leaving, when she was still in the orphanage and unmarried.

Her duties ended, Sister Kathleen climbed into the scant privacy offered by mosquito netting in the tiny room she shared with Epiphania. As she said her rosary, calmness seeped through her and her aching, empty heart. She fell asleep and dreamed of Amariyah in a garden of unusual blooms and plants, all thriving because of Amariyah's loving care.

Amariyah herself was asleep at this point, held on Carmen Stein's lap, as Peter Reidinger took them back to Jerhattan, their mission accomplished.

CHAPTER FOUR

'She's got a psionic mental signature,' Dorotea told Rhyssa, when they had put the sleeping child to bed in the room Tirla had once occupied in Dorotea's neat little house on the Henner estate. Despite her eighty-odd years, Dorotea sat bolt upright on the edge of her chair. Perhaps the glass of brandy was out of character for what she called her 'sweet harmless old lady' look, but she needed the drink. The pregnant Rhyssa was sipping cranberry juice.

'You can't guess what? Telepath, telekinetic, telempath?' Rhyssa asked. Dorotea was their pre-eminent assessor of psychic abilities.

Dorotea shook her head, sighed in a heavy gust and took another sip of her drink.

'Much too young to assess, but it *is* there. She's had quite a traumatic day.' Dorotea held up her hand as Rhyssa started to protest. *No, not the kinetic jump. She was fast asleep in Carmen's lap. Lance Baden knew better than to give her any more to deal with.* 'No, I got the awful distress of that little witch uprooting her plants just to be malicious. That garden meant more to Amariyah than anything else; food or drink or shelter. She doesn't like water.' Dorotea grinned. A bath had definitely been in order for the dusty, dishevelled

92

child before settling her between clean sheets. Tirla had solved the little contretemps over getting her into a bathtub by flinging off her own clothes and climbing in first. 'Except to use on plants, of course.'

'It'd be normal for her to have a trauma about water, nearly drowning in the flood,' Rhyssa said.

'Hmmm, yes,' Dorotea murmured through the glass at her lips. She took a good swig. 'However, she's unlikely to have *that* particular problem here in Jerhattan unless she falls in the fish pond. Since she also has no living relatives, and she *does* exhibit Talent, we'll just have her made a ward of the Centre. We've done that before to rescue children from far worse circumstances. Besides which, I can use help in the garden now it's springtime. Or supposed to be.'

'Are you willing to mind her?' Rhyssa was surprised. She had half planned to take the child into her home. Install her with two parental figures. That is, until Dorotea caught sight of the little waif.

'Well, you've moved Tirla out on me,' and Dorotea gave a disapproving sniff, 'though she enjoys the life with Lessud and Shria in their Linear.' Dorotea gave another sniff, for she certainly wouldn't have fancied such a lifestyle. 'You have enough on your plate with the Centre and being pregnant. And you certainly don't need another child in the house when your son arrives.'

Involuntarily Rhyssa's hand went to her abdomen. 'Well, I have no objections to accommodating her.'

'I do,' said Dorotea. 'I think I'm the right person for her. We can review this in a few weeks' time.' She shook a finger at Rhyssa. 'No one wants you overburdened, my dear. There! That's settled. You'd better get back to your house. Dave'll be in soon, and he'll want to hear all about this.'

He will? Rhyssa said with great amusement.

'I think he will,' Dorotea said firmly, and finished off her drink. 'Now,' and she settled in her chair, the control panel of her household unit appearing in front of her, 'I'll just order in some necessities.'

'What? And usurp Tirla's prerogative?' Rhyssa said with a laugh as she rose from the chair. 'I wouldn't dare.'

'Tirla said she'd come back in the morning to assist me. Meanwhile, the child must have something clean to wear tomorrow morning.' Dorotea gestured to the unit. 'As she's come from the sun-baked plains of Bangladesh, I'd say that shopping in a mall tomorrow might cause severe culture shock. We'll introduce her gradually to such pleasures.'

'Does Tirla have it all planned?'

Dorotea chuckled, glancing up at Rhyssa. 'You know, I think she might, and her instincts are invariably correct. She needs a break from wall-to-wall Teachering. Shopping for someone else will provide it. Amariyah! Such a lovely name. Tirla took instantly to the child, and you know how unusual that is. I think we'd be wrong to interfere with that budding friendship.'

Reflecting briefly on Tirla's complex personality, Rhyssa agreed. It was a wonder the way the girl had shaken off the trauma of the kidnapping and the physical abuse that wretched Flimflam did. Her feet showed no scars from the bastinado whipping that he had inflicted on her.

Tirla's a survivor, dear, Dorotea said reassuringly. Then she shooed Rhyssa away. 'You've still got all those files to deal with. I can still handle something simple like this. Peter'll be back from that warehouse of Lance's, and I'll need to fix him a snack.'

With Dorotea heading for the kitchen, Rhyssa knew it was time to leave. The walk across the lawn to the main house, and the wing she and Dave lived in, gave her a chance to organize her thoughts for the work that did indeed lie in wait on her desk.

The next morning Tirla was back at Dorotea's almost before the woman had arisen from her own bed. Certainly well before Peter was up.

She's still asleep, Dorotea said, a finger on her lips, as she met Tirla in the hallway.

'I thought she'd be up by now. It's well into day where she comes from,' Tirla said in a quiet voice. She could 'hear' Dorotea, as well as Peter, but she had never quite got into the habit of responding mentally. In her estimation, telepathy was something to be used in an emergency. 'Did you get her something to wear?'

The previous evening, Tirla had been indignant over the little sleeveless dress that Amariyah had arrived in.

'I did indeed. In the living room,' and she stepped aside to let Tirla through. *I'm getting breakfast. Did you wish for something?*

'What are you having?'

I'll just see what falls out of the fridge.

Tirla smelled the frying eggs and the toast as she finished inspecting the essential wardrobe that Dorotea had procured for Amariyah.

'I couldn't have done better,' Tirla said, beginning to set the round kitchen table for three, then adding a fourth setting.

'Is she awake?' Dorotea asked, one hand hovering over the egg bowl.

'Coming to.' Tirla slipped out of the kitchen.

'I'll let you handle it,' Dorotea said to the empty air, and wondered if eggs were part of a Bengali breakfast. Eggs were produced by hens no matter what country they inhabited.

She heard the murmur of girlish voices, one a little high-pitched at first, that settled into a less agitated tone halfway through the first sentence. She heard water in the hall bathroom, and then the two girls entered the kitchen. Amariyah stopped in the doorway, all eyes, but not alarmed as she surveyed the room.

'Good morning,' Amariyah said, giving a polite Bengali bow, folding her hands up to her chest.

'You don't need to do that any more,' Tirla said. 'It is not the custom here.'

'Sister Kathleen is saying that there is no country that is not having good manners,' she said mildly. Tirla stared at her in surprise. 'This one says I am to call you Dorotea. You are not a Sister?' The cadence in which she spoke was Bangla, her vocabulary unusual.

Dorotea thought her manners quaint and most acceptable, a change from Tirla's blunt, almost impudent ways.

'I am not a religious Sister,' Dorotea said.

'You may call her "dida",' Tirla suggested. *That means 'grandmother', Tirla explained, 'pathing on this occasion. It is very courteous for a much older woman.*

Thank you for that translation, Tirla, Dorotea replied at her drollest.

Tirla had the grace to flush.

Oblivious of the rapid flash of thoughts, Amariyah nodded. 'Thank you, dida. Thank you very much for the clothing, too.'

'You may sit, Amariyah. I will help the dida,' Tirla said.

From her I will accept the appellation, Tirla, but you will call me Dorotea or I will not serve you this good breakfast.

'I will help Dorotea,' Tirla repeated circumspectly. She put the plate of eggs and toast in front of Amariyah. 'Isn't Peter coming to breakfast? *Peter!*' she shouted down the hall, without waiting for an answer.

'I'm here, I'm here. Oh, good morning, Amariyah,' Peter said, surprised. He had obviously teleported himself into the kitchen, although the child had not seen him materialize. Now he 'walked' to the table. 'Ah, did you sleep OK?'

'I slept very soundly, thank you, Peter.'

The girl waited until the others were served, bowing her head over her hands clasped on the table edge. Dorotea hastily thought of a quick grace.

'Let us be thankful for the food we are about to enjoy,' she said. *She was raised in a Catholic orphanage. A little grace never hurt anyone,* she added to a surprised Peter.

If Amariyah hesitated another second, it was to observe how the others addressed their food. Tirla ate with gusto, thickly buttering and spreading jam on the toast, cutting up her egg into manageable portions, drinking milk almost noisily and chasing egg pieces around on her plate with her toast. Amariyah did not look up from her plate until nothing was left, then folded her hands in her lap.

'You wouldn't happen to have another egg, would you, Dorotea? Or more toast?' Peter asked plaintively. 'D'you want anything more, Amariyah?'

She gulped and shook her head. 'Oh, no thank you very much, Peter.'

I gather that seconds were never offered at the orphanage, Dorotea remarked repressively, resuming her position at the range.

Like Oliver Twist? asked Peter with a grin, as he physically took his plate to her rather than 'porting it.

Amariyah watched as Peter consumed two more eggs and three slices of well-buttered and jammed toast.

'I'm a growing boy,' Peter said in an almost apologetic tone to her.

She quickly ducked her head away, flushing with embarrassment to be caught staring at anyone.

'Dida, what are my duties now? Tirla has served the meal. I am careful with dishes. Where does one wash them here?'

'In the dishwasher,' Tirla said, pointing. 'We have better things to do with our time than wash dishes.'

Amariyah's eyes went round with surprise.

'That is so, dear,' Dorotea said gently as she rose. 'Come, we must select more clothing for you.'

'You have already given me these.' Amariyah touched the blue coverall.

'Jerhattan is much colder than Bogra,' Dorotea said, holding out her hand. 'Peter, you may fill the dishwasher.'

'Sure.' He paused, a devilish grin in his eye, and then meekly added, 'Dorotea.'

You'd better, young man. I want no didas out of you, either. Just thought I'd make Amariyah feel at home!

'You'd freeze outside wearing just that,' Tirla said, also holding out a hand to the child. 'Come. We will see what's to be had,' and the light of acquisition enlivened her face.

Oh, Lord, let's hope the treasury can stand it, Peter said. Tirla pretended she hadn't heard that.

For Amariyah the morning was sheer magic. Either Tirla or the dida kept her hand in theirs as they watched the selections slide across the screen. They encouraged her to choose the colours she liked, the styles that she seemed to prefer: she who had never had any choice or expected to be given any. The ordering seemed to be done by speaking into the big screen. A small window at one side then confirmed the purchase. It took Amariyah a little time to realize that there was no bargaining with the vendor. She found that odd, though the other two did not. Dida Dorotea was so kind, so generous, and Tirla was so much nicer than any of the other older girls at the orphanage, that Amariyah couldn't believe her change in circumstances. She had even been able, for a few moments in the rapture of owning more than one dress, to forget her dead garden.

'Now, we do have some tasks,' Dorotea said briskly. 'Off,' she added, and the screen went dark. 'If you will put this on, Amariyah,' she held out a warm fleece-lined jacket, 'we will go outside. Tirla will come, too.'

'I will?' Tirla was taken aback. 'But I thought I would access Teacher from here.'

'The fresh air will do you good, too. Dida commands, Tirla,' Dorotea said at her sweetest. She shrugged on an old jacket, shoved worn gloves in one pocket and a measuring tape in another. 'I believe you like gardens, Amariyah.' She was amazed by the vivacity flooding the child's solemn little face.

'Oh, I do, dida.'

Dorotea took her hand. 'Right now, of course, only the spring flowers are coming up, but there's a lot of maintenance to be done. This house faces south-east, so we have good sun on most of the beds all day. Things do not grow with quite the profusion that they do in Bangladesh, but I have reason to be proud of my green fingers.'

That unfamiliar idiom made Amariyah regard Dorotea's slender hands with surprise.

'It's an expression, my dear, meaning that one is good at gardening.'

'I have black fingers,' Tirla muttered, closing the front door behind them. 'Oh! Look at the tools, Amariyah! Just your size.'

Dorotea beamed with satisfaction as Amariyah gazed with rapture at the child-sized wheelbarrow, equipped with rake, fork, spade, trowel and watering can. She had to be encouraged to examine the tools and reassured that, yes, these were for her to use. Surely there'd been some toys in that orphanage. Or had her garden been her only 'toy'?

'Try them, Amariyah,' Tirla said, pushing the child towards the barrow. 'See, just the right size for your hands!' She had to close Amariyah's fingers about the rake handle. 'See? They were made for you!'

'Oh! Oh! Oh!' exclaimed Amariyah, hands clasping the rake in a grip that made her knuckles turn white, tears flowing down her cheeks.

'Now, now, it's no big thing, dear. I do need help, you see, and Tirla's best at shopping.' Dorotea reached into her coat pocket to find a tissue. 'Tirla, go get my trug and my stool from the shed. We'll need to rake some of last year's leaves away, Amariyah. Let's make a start, shall we? Just wheel your barrow over here, will you?' Dorotea gently ushered the dazed little girl towards the garden, where the green spires of daffodils poked through the mulch.

Tirla, returning with Dorotea's equipment, regarded Amariyah with consternation. *She's still crying.*

'Don't cry, Amariyah,' she said aloud, folding a sympathetic arm about the girl's slender shoulders. *She's not sobbing. She's just letting tears run down her face. How does she do that?* 'I told you you'd have a garden.'

'It's the dida's garden,' Amariyah murmured. Rake in hand, she took the final steps. 'But I will make it neater.'

'That's the girl. This dida needs help with her garden,' and Dorotea groaned artistically as she bent down. Amariyah was quick to help her to her knees. 'I can trust Tirla to find shopping bargains, but I wouldn't trust her to weed.' Dorotea could not resist flashing a sour look at Tirla.

'Why are you trusting me?' Amariyah asked.

'Because,' Dorotea said slowly for emphasis, 'I know that I can. Here, let's just clear the leaves from this patch. Do you have daffodils in Bangladesh?'

Setting the little rake carefully to the ground, Amariyah dropped to her knees beside Dorotea, oh so patiently coaxing the dead stuff away from the green shoots.

'I have never seen these before.'

99

For a moment, Tirla thought that Amariyah was sniffing the leaves, she had her face so close to them.

'Tirla, why don't you go and get my gardening book?'

'Why don't we access the screen?'

'That would mean we'd have to go inside,' Dorotea said, well aware of the ploys Tirla could come up with in order to get back to a screen. 'I think one of those printed books you find obsolete will do nicely.'

'Which one?' Tirla asked in a put-upon tone.

'Get the *Encyclopedia of North American Flora* first,' Dorotea said firmly. 'The title is printed on the spine, you know.' She turned back to her eager student. 'Now, there are five varieties of daffodils around the house, and eight of narcissi. They'll be coming up next.'

Tirla brought the book and, while Dorotea was turning the pages to the section on bulbs, she sneaked back to the house to turn on the Teacher. The avid gardeners stayed out for the entire morning. Tirla had a peek from the front window from time to time, seeing two rear ends waggling above the flowerbeds. Amariyah was evidently oblivious of everything but her hands in dirt and muck, and making certain that she'd cleared the last little bit of debris from the emerging plants.

When that bed had been cleared, Dorotea ushered her back into the house. 'Now wash your hands well, and be sure to brush your fingernails clean,' she said, nodding significantly to Tirla to oversee the process.

Dida Dorotea served warming soup, because the child was quite pale from cold under the tan the Bangladesh sun had given her. By then the new clothing had arrived, and Tirla insisted on a fashion show, making certain that everything fitted correctly, giving a long lecture on how Amariyah could mix and match the various items, and helping her put them away in the drawers.

Dorotea had had the notion of logging Amariyah on to Teacher in the afternoon so that they could see just where the child stood academically. That could wait until tomorrow. Today she would consolidate her position with the child by taking her on an afternoon stroll of the grounds so she could orient herself. Dorotea also hauled a protesting Tirla away from the monitor for more fresh air. The lawns were just beginning to green up, but the trees and shrubs were bare.

'There is a great deal of gardening to be done here, dida,' Amariyah said solemnly.

'This time of year is not the busiest for gardening here in North America,' Dorotea remarked. Because it was so obvious from Amariyah's manner that she looked forward to the challenge, she did not say that there were men who did nothing but take care of the gardens here on the old Henner estate.

'Where is the kitchen garden?' Amariyah asked.

Tirla managed to turn a laugh into a gurgle.

'I will show you where the vegetables are grown another day. You're cold. We shall go home and have a nice cup of tea.' Dorotea tightened her grip on the small hand.

'We forgot to buy gloves,' Tirla said. 'I'll get gardening gloves, too, if they make them in Maree's size.'

'I'm sure we'll find some,' Dorotea said.

How is our waif? Rhyssa asked as they made their way back to the house.

If Teacher was the key to our Tirla, a garden is Amariyah's. What worries me is that she hasn't smiled once, and I wonder if she knows how to laugh.

That's your department, dida.

Dorotea imagined herself as a giant cat, tracking down a mouse of a Rhyssa with malice intended.

I couldn't resist, dear. Then Rhyssa's mental tone altered. *We have got hold of Amariyah's birth certificate. She was born five years ago in Jakarta, August 17. Tony and Nadezhda were working on some ruins up-country. Just made it to the hospital, or so Kayankira discovered in her research. There are, as Kayankira said, no living relatives. Both parents were only children. Each had put the other down as 'next of kin'. We also accessed Tony's employment application, and security search lists no living relatives of any degree of kinship.*

So she's ours?

I'll file a formal request with the Children's Protection League and have her legally made our ward. Pause. *Kayan's very interested in our Tirla.*

Ha! was Dorotea's response to that.

And inordinately impressed by Peter.

As well she might be. Dorotea had a very soft spot for Peter Reidinger.

Are you comfortable with Amariyah?

I'll be more so when I can get her to laugh and smile.

So how does your garden grow? I saw you two out there. Did Tirla sneak in to the Teacher?

Dorotea indulged in a mental snort of disdain. *As soon as she could. Well, she was Linear-bred. I can't expect her to be horticulturally minded. Amariyah, on the other hand, is to the manner born.*

Those tools were sheer inspiration.

I thought so, too. But we must find her some patch somewhere on the estate, all hers. Mine is the dida's garden. She'd take on the entire grounds if we let her.

Maybe old Ted Comer will take her on as an apprentice.

Him? Dorotea and Ted were more frequently at odds over minor details of gardening than in charity with each other. *I have to get her on the Teacher program first. We'll see just how good her orphanage tuition was.*

The next morning, with Tirla assisting, Amariyah Bantam was found to understand the basics that any five-year-old should know. Her spelling was the English-English variety: her vocabulary and arithmetic adequate, her handwriting the cramped little script that 'saves paper', as Dorotea remarked. She was also fluent in Bangla. She knew nothing about technical Teacher aids, such as a computer, or even how to find her way around the tri-d. She informed them almost regally that only the older girls were given technical instruction. The orphanage had a communications system and a satellite connection, donated by the Presbyterian Women's Association. Occasionally they were all allowed to watch 'instructional' programmes and nature films.

Unexpectedly, her IQ testing ranged towards genius

level, but her schooling so far had not been in the least bit challenging. Concurring with Carmen Stein's assessment, Dorotea could also feel the spark that so often blossomed into a Talent.

It was Tirla, to whom such an item meant so much, who reminded Dorotea that Amariyah had no identification band.

'She'll hardly need it,' Dorotea began. 'She's not likely to go anywhere yet without an adult.'

'You haven't even stranded her!' Tirla cocked her arms at her waist and glared accusingly at Dorotea. 'We don't want another incident, do we?' she added, tilting her head, her eyes wise beyond her years as she obliquely referred for the first time to being kidnapped.

'Yes, you're quite right.' Dorotea was prompt to admit mistakes. Even those she herself made. 'If you'd just go up to the main house and get Sascha to give you some strands, you can weave them into her hair yourself.'

'Yes, Sascha would have strands, wouldn't he?' Tirla said and, flipping her own long black hair with its security strand over her shoulder, briskly strode out of the house on her errand. 'And I'll make him get an ID bracelet for Maree. Like an hour ago!'

'She's mute right now as far as telepathy is concerned,' Dorotea told Rhyssa when she dropped by after Amariyah had gone to bed, exhausted by an exciting day. Dorotea pursed her lips. 'We have, however, come to a compromise about how she will address me. Dida Tea is formal enough for her convent-trained sensibilities, and it at least sounds like my name.' Then Dorotea went on more thoughtfully. 'She *might* have some kinetic ability, although she didn't display any while we were weeding. She'd never seen daffodils. She's been inhaling garden encyclopedias like the print would fade.' She beamed over having another ardent plant lover as a companion. 'Never thought that old printed books would be more than a curiosity. I noticed today that the print *is* fading. Or at least some of the colour 'graphs in them. I've tried to explain to Amariyah about common and

103

Latin designations of flowers. My Latin's rusty, but Tirla and I did show her how to access Dictionary. She's been looking up all the big words as if her life depended on it. I think we'll plan a little trip to the Botanical Gardens once she's more acclimatized to this part of the world.'

'D'you think she's homesick for Bangladesh or the Sisters?'

Dorotea shook her head. 'She may be later on, when the novelty wears off. She asked to write to the Sisters. I must get the address from you. Oh, and she did smile at Peter tonight. Just a little smile, but enough to reassure me that she knows how.'

'Don't fret over that, Dorotea. She must be a little overwhelmed by her change in circumstances. Have you told her about her . . . lack of blood kin?'

'No, I didn't. She's far too involved with differentiating *asphodelus*, which is the Latin, from *narkissos*, which is the Greek, in case you didn't know.'

'I didn't,' Rhyssa said, rising and beating a strategic retreat.

When the earth warmed in the spring sunlight, Dorotea and her new ward had become fast friends, despite the age difference. Ted Comer was also taken with the solemn little girl, and was cajoled into giving her a garden plot all her own. He'd planned to put it into zinnias, which were not Dorotea's favourite flower, but Amariyah had endeared herself to him by naming every single shrub, tree and greening plant by their Latin names.

'I couldn't stop her learning. She's inhaling gardening terms,' Dorotea said in an aside to the surprised groundsman.

'I've some seeds I can give her.'

'Any vegetables?' Dorotea asked, eyeing him. 'She seems to feel that we are lacking in kitchen-garden space.'

Ted looked stunned.

'I do plan to take her to the greenhouses,' Dorotea went on. 'She wasn't that impressed with flowers and trees and shrubs being stuck indoors in the conservatory, but she took the point that some of them wouldn't flourish in the open.'

Ted nodded, with the vigour of someone who doesn't quite understand what he has just been told.

'We can let her have both, can't we? Vegetables and flowers?'

'If it makes the little girl happy, I ain't agin it,' Ted replied.

Only after she had planted it to her satisfaction did Amariyah show Tirla *her* garden. Tirla pretended a keen interest that took Dorotea by surprise.

'When did you start learning anything about gardening?' she asked Tirla when she had a chance.

The Linear-bred girl shrugged. 'I gotta keep in touch.'

Peter also feigned interest. He was able to make a brief escape from his horticulturally determined housemate because Rhyssa allowed him to accompany Lance Baden back to Adelaide, to continue their experiments in assessing his limits.

'If he has any,' Lance amended when he discussed the resettlement with Rhyssa and Sascha.

'Travelling is a good idea,' Sascha said, 'especially since we've got to keep him busy until he's old enough to be put on the roster.'

'I must get hold of Dirk Coetzer,' Lance said. 'Peter keeps harping on about that promise to tour the spaceship.'

'I'll check with Dirk,' Rhyssa said.

'And nudge Johnny Greene about it, too,' Sascha suggested.

'That's not a problem,' Rhyssa said. 'The outfitting of the *Andre Norton* is still on schedule.'

'So Barchenka's not the only one to make good,' Lance said slyly.

'And I'll make sure Peter's on the first tour available. There are promises that must be kept.'

' "And miles to go before I sleep," ' Lance quoted, surprising them all.

*   *   *

105

The Space Station Commander Admiral Dirk Coetzer did not forget his promise to young Peter Reidinger. Without any reminder from General John Greene, just before Peter's sixteenth birthday in September, the Admiral extended a special invitation to the young kinetic and to anyone else from the Eastern Parapsychic Centre who wished to come. Rhyssa was coping with her colicky son, Eoin, but insisted that Dave go along with Peter, Sascha, Lance and Boris Roznine. It turned out to be the first tour of the nearly completed spaceship, and the Talents were the only guests. Johnny Greene was present, too; he knew the great ship almost as well as her designers.

' "Every rivet and girder in it," ' and Johnny's grin was malicious as he quoted Ludmilla Barchenka.

'That's enough of that,' Dirk Coetzer said, and the others guessed that Johnny Greene was not above trying the Admiral's patience with occasional references. The former etop pilot remained the only other Talent who had sussed out and could effect Peter Reidinger's gestalt in telekinesis.

The colony spaceship was still moored in the construction quadrant, with access tunnels to the various hatches, and was surrounded by small rigs, with nets of supplies attached by tethers. For this visit, all but the engine and fuel-storage segments had been aired up and the artificial gravity turned on so the guests could move about more freely. The tour started in one of the levels in which cryogenically suspended astronauts would be stored in racks of specially engineered 'cradles'.

'We prefer "cradle" to "coffin" or "tank",' the Admiral said, patting the nearest empty container.

Peter eyed it speculatively. 'Like a single passenger carrier,' he said to Johnny Greene. Carefully, with well-rehearsed control, he was able to lay his hand, but not his fingers, flat against the container. John and Lance, knowing how difficult it was for Peter to make small motor gestures, exchanged glances over that little triumph.

'There are nine levels, so we can accommodate a suitable colonial gene pool,' Coetzer went on.

He showed them one of the storage holds, already half full

of supplies, and demonstrated how the locks would operate to prevent oxygen leakage from any hull penetration.

'No *Titanic* disasters in space,' Coetzer said with satisfaction. 'The *Andre Norton* has been built to survive. The ship is separated into units, each one self-sufficient. From the bridge, the captain can remotely initiate the revival of passengers, should that be necessary.'

'Let's hope it isn't,' murmured Dave.

The Admiral took his guests farther forward, into the living levels where the skeleton crew – Coetzer grinned at Peter – would be running the immense colony ship. Each crew member was to serve two years' duty on rotation for as long as the journey would last.

'Not that the *Andre Norton* will get to Altair any faster, but certainly eventually.' Of that the Admiral was certain.

'Some degree of privacy is essential to crew well-being,' he said, showing them one of the cabins where he demonstrated how cleverly furnishings had been built into the wall spaces. 'They also afford shielding,' and he nodded to Lance and Johnny. 'We learned that lesson, even if we aren't likely to ship any psychics in the crew.'

'Why not?' Peter asked, jerking his head round to the Admiral.

'None have volunteered, Pete.'

'I would,' Peter said firmly, almost belligerently.

'I know, son, I know,' the Admiral said, a reassuring hand on the boy's shoulder. Coetzer thought he'd fleshed up a bit, had lost the bony look he'd had at the inauguration. He was taller as well, and had an unmistakable but modest confidence about him now. Nothing succeeds like success, Coetzer thought, remembering the comments on young Reidinger's progress that Johnny Greene was always dropping. Which was why Coetzer had never forgotten his promise to the boy. 'But your future is linked with this planet. God knows, I'd give anything to sail this ship out of our system, on her way to Altair.'

'Why can't you?' Peter asked. Surely admirals could do what they wanted. Cut orders or something.

Coetzer chuckled. 'Doesn't work like that, Pete. Now,

come with me and I'll show you the nerve centre of this ship.'

'Admiral on the bridge,' was the ringing cry, causing officers and ratings to snap to attention.

'As you were. If you'll—' Coetzer began, and stopped as he saw the awed expression on Peter's face. He'd never quite got over the wonder of the scene that was visible on the forward screen of the *Andre Norton*, so he stood in respectful silence as Peter absorbed the panorama. The ship's prow, although parallel to the great wheel of Padrugoi, faced outer space. Sometimes the prospect terrified those with any degree of agoraphobia. Mostly the view reduced people to stark amazement and wonder, as it did Peter.

The hunger, the yearning for the unknown and the unreachable, was visible on the boy's face. For a long moment, the boy was stock-still, until Lance leaned forward and lightly touched his arm. Peter exhaled.

'Say again, Pete?' the Admiral asked, sure that he had heard words on that breath.

'I only need to know where to stand,' Peter murmured, eyes focused beyond the plasglass to the black space, pinpointed with stars.

'When you find out,' Johnny said gently, 'do let me know.'

Peter gave his head a shake, and grinned with sheepish apology at the Admiral.

'Well, then, let me show you how the *Andre Norton* operates.'

Peter was attentive, asked intelligent questions, but his eyes were constantly seeking the scene outside.

'He's mesmerized,' Lance remarked quietly to Johnny.

'Has that effect, all right,' Johnny replied, giving a short sharp sigh. 'Can't blame him. I ogle it every chance I get.'

Once the bridge tour was done, the Admiral offered his guests lunch in his quarters. It was obvious to the others that Peter would have gladly taken a sandwich to the bridge and stared at space until it was time to leave. But he had learned manners from Dorotea, and, though he kept looking at space

108

until the lift door closed it from sight, he recovered his poise on the way back to Padrugoi. He kept thanking the Admiral throughout the excellent lunch, asking now and then about details he wished to make clear in his own mind.

'Would it be against security if I asked if I could have some, well, sort of details, like how she masses? And, you know, some idea of her interior and her decks?' Peter asked, while the adults were having coffee. He didn't like any stimulants. He hadn't needed any medication since he'd left the hospital. Other than his paraplegia, he enjoyed very good health.

'We do have just the sort of documentation you'd like, Pete,' the Admiral said. 'Oh, nothing that breaches security or shows more than the general outlines, but the specs do include the dimensions as well as the mass, though that's estimated rather than actual. We know how much the components weigh in gravity. Of course, it isn't as if the *Andre Norton* was a seagoing ship and we'd know how much water she displaces.' The Admiral grinned. 'But yes, you may have what we've prepared as a press handout for her launch.' He leaned across the table to Peter, who was on his right. 'You will, of course, be on hand?'

'I'd be delighted, sir,' Peter replied, beaming with gratitude.

'Good, that's settled. You are high on the invitation list,' and the Admiral winked.

'Any time I can be of service, sir, you have only to think it.'

'Really?' and Dirk Coetzer rolled his eyes.

'Oh, not 'pathing you, sir, never,' Peter assured him hurriedly.

The Admiral grinned. 'Just teasing. I'm well aware of the high ethics of Talent.'

'Anyway,' and now Peter paused to smile impudently, 'you've got a natural shield that only lifts when you get very angry.'

'Oh? I do?' Coetzer was pleased.

Now you've done it, Johnny said with feigned disgust.

Done what?

I've had the Admiral believing I could read his mind so he'd tell me what I needed to know before I went in and found it.

Peter looked from Johnny to the Admiral who was still grinning with great satisfaction. Coetzer raised an eyebrow significantly at Johnny and sat back in his chair.

Looking without permission isn't ethical, Peter said, distressed that the man he admired most would do such a thing.

Who said I looked? Johnny replied. *He just thinks – thought, thanks to you – I could read him.*

Tsk, tsk, Lance Baden said, without glancing at their end of the table. He was chatting with unusual animation with the attractive engineering officer, Lieutenant Commander Pota Chatham.

A copy of the coveted plans, secured in a big envelope with *ISS ANDRE NORTON* blazoned on the front, was shortly delivered to the Admiral, who handed it over to Peter. Then the Talents rose from the table, thanked the Admiral and his officers for the tour and the lunch, and took the lift to the boat deck and the recently installed telepad. As they swung out of the lift, they nearly collided with a cleaning crew. Johnny felt a surge of menace, and looked around at the janitors running vacuum tubes over the deck and walls. The flicker of whatever-it-was was gone. Probably one of the grunts, annoyed by their appearance.

'Admiral Coetzer did say we were the first, didn't he?' Peter asked as he ducked into the personnel carrier, the envelope hugged to his chest. Lance was not the only one to notice that his fingers actually curled possessively on its edges.

'Yup,' Johnny said, climbing into the forward left-hand seat. 'Care to 'port us home, Peter?'

Peter hesitated and then, with careful hands and fingers, put the envelope on the forward shelf. He even managed an extra pat, as if telling the envelope to stay put.

'Sure,' he said.

Dave Lehardt was relatively accustomed now to tele-kinesis, but he was not accustomed to 'seeing' it happen: the view of the boat deck of Padrugoi was suddenly the sunny late afternoon of the Henner grounds, and not a hint of movement – just the abrupt alteration of physical position. Dave swallowed in awe at the ease with which Peter displayed his ability. The kid hadn't even taken a deep breath: just teleported them. Snap! Like that! Amazing.

'He was *holding* the envelope, Rhys,' he told his wife, imitating Peter's gestures. 'He cocked his fingers around the edges and he was holding it to his chest – like his most precious possession – with both hands flat, and definitely hugging it to him. He may not *know* he was doing it but Johnny, Lance and I saw him.'

Rhyssa smiled at her husband over the head of their son. 'He's been close to such small motor movements for some time now, but only when he isn't really trying to use them. Lance hasn't mentioned it to him, though he's told me. That's good news. Peter still has no feeling below the neck. Maybe he'll just forget trying and let his Talent take over. When he's not conscious of the need for movement, sometimes he just moves like an ordinary sixteen-year-old. He doesn't even hover just above the floor as much any more.'

Dave chuckled softly, sitting down to watch his wife feed Eoin. 'He would have liked to hover outside the *Andre Norton*. Seems to me that a kinetic would make a very good space traveller. He, or she, would function well in no gravity.'

'For goodness' sake, don't mention that to Peter. Or he'll be after permission to do space-walking next.'

'Why not? Johnny does. And Coetzer dropped a hint that they would like to contract Pete for assembly jobs.'

'I know that,' she said in a glum voice.

'You're going to have to let him, you know. You'd be wrong to fight it.'

Rhyssa gave him a long, hard stare that he returned, a little smile tugging at his lips.

'It's good public relations to plan ahead for every likely contingency, m' love. And look at it from Pete's perspective. Do you know anyone else who's so totally accustomed to no gravity?'

111

She gave a little laugh. 'I hadn't thought of his kinesis as no gravity.'

'It might be a little different, learning to cope with wearing a space suit. He does, after all, still have to breathe air. Or does he?' He gave Rhyssa a quirky glance.

'Of course he does,' she said. 'Only, why was it so important for him to get the plans?'

'Souvenir, of course. We were the first two civilians to see the finished product.'

'Yes, that makes sense.' Rhyssa paused, stroking her son's thin but waving hair. 'Does he know Coetzer wants to employ him when he's of age?'

'Nothing was specifically said in Peter's hearing. But the boy's not dumb. He'll figure it out. He'd have Johnny on his side.'

'That is, of course, a great consolation to me.' Rhyssa lifted her son to her shoulder to burp him.

'It is to me too,' Dave said, leaning back in the chair and stretching his legs out.

'Maree?' Peter called from his room. 'Can you give me a hand here?'

Amariyah appeared at the doorway, very much aware that her friend meant that literally. She knew that he did not use his body the way she could. She had even mentioned once, very tactfully, that he should remember to touch his heel to the floor first, then his toe. That's how people naturally walked. But she was quick to respond to any need he voiced.

'How?' she asked.

'I want to put this,' his index finger limply pointed to the unfolded sheet on his worktop. It depicted the *Andre Norton*, the sections colour-coded for the different functions: red for engineering, green for living, blue for life-support, orange for command, yellow for cryogenic and brown for storage, 'on the wall.' He swivelled his body, his finger now pointing to the display space. 'There.'

'You have the tacks?' she asked, coming forward. She was, as usual, dressed in gardening clothes, well washed

112

and well used. Dorotea had put extra pads on the knees.

Amariyah pushed a chair against the wall while the top drawer of his desk opened far enough to allow the box of pins to exit and float towards her. She got up on the chair.

'Here?' She tapped the wall, looking over her shoulder at him.

'That's right.' The thumbtack box hovered by her right hand. Then the sheet made its stately way across the room and flattened against the wall.

Amariyah straightened it slightly, took out the necessary tacks and neatly secured the corners, while Peter inhaled anxiously, wincing as each tack pierced the paper. She took the box out of the air, closed it and, descending from the chair, replaced it and closed the drawer. Then she regarded the neatly hung drawing.

'That's what you saw today?'

'Yesss,' and the awed tone Peter used made her regard him with polite surprise.

'You had a good look at it, then?' she asked, knowing how excited Peter had been to be invited for a tour of the spaceship.

'But you should have seen outside!'

She blinked. 'I thought it was inside that you wanted to see. What was outside that was worth seeing? You are telling me that space is all black.'

'Yes,' and Peter slowly shook his head from side to side, his eyes glowing, 'it is. But then there're stars and space.' The last word was reverently spoken.

'You and your space,' she murmured affectionately. She was well aware of Peter's intense interests. He had got into the habit of confiding in her. She listened intently and, unlike Tirla, his other confidante, she never interrupted or argued with him. Usually, of course, she was busy weeding. That gave them added privacy. Often he did what he could to help her because sometimes she tried to move things too heavy for her strength, like peat moss and fertilizer sacks, or heavy pots and tubs. He'd even thrust his insensitive fingers into the mud because it was her notion that somehow messing in mud and dirt would be good for him. He knew

Dorotea found gardening therapeutic, but not in quite the same way that Amariyah did. She had an almost religious fervour for *her* garden. He understood it better now – with the diagram of the *Andre Norton* on his wall.

'Thanks, Amariyah,' he said.

'You're hovering,' she replied, gently pressing on his shoulder until he was grounded.

'Thanks,' he said absently, his eyes going from stern to prow, up and down the decks, memorizing.

'Print won't fade, you know,' she said kindly, quoting Dorotea's oft-repeated maxim.

'It better not,' Peter said, but he smiled in her direction. 'She's beautiful, Amariyah. Just beautiful. Everything I imagined she'd be. Inside and out.'

'Do you want to go with her when she flies?'

Peter heaved a sigh, Amariyah slyly noting that his chest had actually lifted. When she had been in the Centre long enough to be able to ask personal questions, she had broached the subject of Peter to Dorotea – while they were companionably weeding the side bed – why did he move so oddly? Had he been born like that? Dorotea had explained about the wall falling on him, his paralysis, and then his unusual ability to use a 'connection', Dorotea had called it (though Amariyah learned later from Tirla that it was called a 'gestalt'), to use the power of his mind to move his damaged body. While she was on that subject, she said that Peter could also not use the toilet as others did, and wore a bag for waste disposal. Amariyah calmly accepted this explanation with a nod of her head.

Peter, Dorotea went on, couldn't feel anything, so they all had to watch out that he didn't inadvertently burn or injure himself. He was assiduous in doing the daily Reeve exercises to keep muscle tone, and in getting massage. Dorotea assured Amariyah that it was polite to remind Peter to keep his feet on the ground. When he got excited, he started to hover. Amariyah was to ignore any other unusual motions. Peter was still trying to control, by his mind, the smaller movements of hands and feet that everyone else took for granted.

114

'Are you going to move the spaceship when she's ready to go?' Amariyah asked. Several times now she had been in the personnel carrier, taken with Peter and Tirla on special educational trips.

'I wish.' Peter shook his head, altering mood. He grinned down at Amariyah. 'The *Andre Norton* has to get where she's going under her own power.'

'But you know where she's going. Why can't you just send her there? Is she too big for you?'

Amariyah was as aware as everyone at the Centre that Peter Reidinger had the most astounding telekinetic ability.

'I've got to know where to stand first,' Peter said, his eyes focusing on a distant goal.

She waited in case he had more to say. The shine in his eyes warned her that his thinking had turned very private. He'd said all he intended to right now. She slipped away, leaving him to thoughts that made his face both sad and glad. She was pleased that this Admiral person had kept his promise to Peter. It was good that important people kept promises. She was pleased, too, that Peter had confided in her as much as he did. She loved Peter.

She left his room, tiptoeing to the door which she closed quietly so as not to interrupt all his happy-sad thinking. She really did have to check on the seedlings. Ted was very pleased with the way hers came on. He said she had magic fingers, not just green ones, because her garden produced the most beautiful flowers and the tastiest vegetables. He had stopped trying to persuade her to concentrate on flowers; even stopped complaining that she bordered her garden with marigolds. She liked Ted: he was always smiling and cheerful. Just seeing his thin, weathered face made the day better. Dorotea liked him, too.

'Never a harsh word for anyone, bar insects and those dratted moles,' Dorotea said. 'A good man, our Ted. Knows his flora, too.'

'He mispronounces the Latin names.'

'But,' and Dorotea held up one hand in mild rebuke, 'he knows them.'

Amariyah was suitably chastened.

115

'Now, now, child. Remember, too, that he understands gardening in this climate. Which is quite different from Bangladesh.'

As Amariyah walked over to her garden, the other children at the Centre were also released from their Teaching sessions. There were fifteen children, six boys and nine girls, ranging from four to twelve. There were infants as well, but she didn't see much of them. Dorotea liked her to play with the older ones, and Amariyah endured activities such as hide and seek – as long as no one tried to injure the bushes they hid behind or stepped on *her* garden – and skipping. She had quick, clever feet and knew about rope-dancing from the orphanage. She learned the songs in English and added a few in Bangla. She did not, however, see any point in the endless tossing of the big ball up into the net circle. The ball was too heavy for her and the iron rim too high. Mostly the older boys and girls monopolized that outdoor activity. None of them were at all interested in gardening, but she was glad of that. They had no delicacy of touch, and might damage young plants. She never forgot the death of her garden at the orphanage, nor Lila. It was therefore odd that she had felt from the very moment of their meeting that Tirla was different, safe and trustworthy, though Tirla did somewhat resemble Lila in physical type. Tirla was as special to Amariyah as Peter was. Tirla was a sister to her, though sometimes the girl could be more motherly and demanding than Dorotea. Tirla considered Amariyah ineluctably *hers*. Tirla was also very smart about 'things' in Jerhattan and the Linears. When Tirla took her out and about, Dorotea always reminded Amariyah to listen to Tirla and do exactly as she said.

Amariyah reached her garden and stood where she could survey the bed. It had started out as a small rectangle, almost begrudged by Ted as a special concession to Dorotea. He had now enlarged it three times; one end had partial shade during the hottest part of the day, so she could grow those special flowers that did not do well with full sun. She was, as Dorotea called it, counting heads when the ball bounced

116

once, slamming into the display of narcissus, breaking heads off; bounced a second time and broke branches off the orange-coloured *Azalea indica.*

Amariyah let out a shriek that was heard throughout the grounds, both aurally and telepathically. The ball rolled from the *Azalea indica* down the slight slope and mashed down her marigold seedlings. Amariyah was not a violent child, but she kicked the ball so hard that she sent it high into one of the trees, where it stuck in a bole.

Peter got to her first because he could 'port himself. Dorotea was not far behind him, and Ted as well as two other groundsmen, Sascha and Sirikit from the control room and Rhyssa from her office, while apartment windows were flung open as people reacted to the loud scream.

Amariyah was on the ground in front of her flattened marigolds, keening and rocking back and forth, tears streaming down her cheeks. She ignored Peter, though he tried to put a consoling arm around her shoulders. She ignored Dorotea, and Sascha and Rhyssa and even Sirikit, whom she usually liked. Ted reached out to assess the damage and an invisible barrier blocked his hand. Startled, he looked to Dorotea, who shook her head, and he drew back, clucking his tongue at the damage.

'It isn't that much,' he muttered to Dorotea.

'*Any* damage is too much,' Dorotea said. 'Find out who was shooting baskets and shoot them.'

'They wouldn't have done it on purpose,' Ted said. 'Whyn't we just leave the ball up there?'

Dorotea followed the direction he pointed in and gave a sour grin.

'I could put anchor fencing round the court, help keep the ball inside,' he suggested. 'Like I have round the tennis courts.'

'Do so, Ted,' Rhyssa said, having heard their discussion. 'And no more basketball shooting until the fence is up.' *Did you get the same blast of fury and vengeance as I did?* she asked.

Is there anyone on the estate who didn't hear it? Dorotea countered wryly.

It's gone now, Sascha said, making eye contact with Rhyssa from the other end of Amariyah's garden bed. *Not a trace of telepathy from her now.* He ran a frustrated hand through his thick hair.

Did you have a chance to assess it, Dorotea? Rhyssa asked.

Dorotea shook her head. *Might only occur for protection.*

Peter said, *She sure tore hair out of a bigger and older girl's scalp at the orphanage. The nuns were amazed at her reaction. Is there anything we can do about the bush and the bulbs?* He reached out to pick up a narcissus bud and couldn't. He shoved his fingertips against the barrier and it dissolved. *She's got a barrier round it. So protective, yes, but I don't feel any 'pathing. And the barrier just went away.*

She trusts you, Peter, Dorotea said. *And I get no hint of Talent right now. She is a bit young.* She started to get down on her knees by the child.

'Don't,' Amariyah said sharply, but her voice was low and dispirited. 'I'll fix it.'

'Can you?' Peter asked, putting a world of sympathy and encouragement in his voice.

'I can, you can't. Go away!' Then Amariyah realized that she was speaking to the most important adults of the Centre. 'Please!'

'If you need any help, Maree,' Ted said, 'lemme know. I'll go and put up a fence so it can't happen again.'

'We'll find out who was playing,' Rhyssa began.

'No!' There was no 'please' to that sharp reply. 'Go away while there is still time.'

Time for what? Sascha asked.

Go away, she said, Peter added and, with an apology, 'ported everyone out of the immediate area, including himself.

Peter! Rhyssa, Dorotea and Sascha said in surprise, finding themselves back where they had been only a few minutes before.

He's right, Dorotea said to forestall rebuke. As well she was back in her kitchen. She rescued the cookies she'd been baking before they were crisped.

118

When Amariyah came in for her supper, she was unusually silent. To be expected under the circumstances, Dorotea thought, and didn't remark on it. Peter kept watching the child across the kitchen table. Her eyes were swollen from crying, despite the fact that she had washed her face. She hadn't quite got all the dirt from under her nails.

She's not unhappy, Peter remarked, *but she sure is tired.*

Amariyah finished her dinner, thanked Dorotea, rinsed her plate and utensils and put them in the dishwasher. Then she went to her room and was in bed, fast asleep, ten minutes later when Dorotea surreptitiously checked.

It was Ted who came knocking on Dorotea's door early the next morning, before anyone else was awake.

'You better see this, Ms Horvath,' he said, his eyes wide in their sockets and his whole body tense.

Dorotea flung a jacket over her dressing gown and followed him across the lawn to Amariyah's garden.

'What?' Dorotea stared, as amazed as Ted. The marigold seedlings that she had seen smashed were upright and whole. The *Azalea indica* had not a trace of broken boughs. The narcissus sported intact buds.

'She could have replaced the marigolds,' Dorotea told herself and Ted. 'She might also have changed bushes, though I can't imagine where she got another orange azalea at short notice.'

'It's the same one, missus. She didn't change it,' Ted said, slowly shaking his head from side to side. 'And bulbs don't transplant well when they're ready to bloom. They'd wilt.'

'You're right about that.'

Without a thought for grass or dirt stains on her elegant burgundy velvet housecoat, Dorotea knelt down and peered at the resurrected plants.

'And I sensed nothing at all. But then,' she murmured, fingers on her lips, 'I was busy with the cookies and then supper.' *Peter? Wake up. I want you to remember the state of Amariyah's garden in the orphanage when you saw it.*

HUH? What?

119

Dorotea repeated her question.

I didn't see it. Or rather, I saw where it had been; all neatly raked as if nothing had ever grown there.

Oh. That's a pity.

Why?

Well, and Dorotea accepted Ted's hand to help her to her feet, *I'll see if I can winkle it out of Amariyah.*

Why? Peter's tone was stronger, now he was wide awake.

I think she resurrected her garden.

So that's why she wanted everyone to go away. Before it was too late. But I didn't feel anything. Did you?

No. Did you know *that's what she was going to do?*

No, but it's what she did, isn't it? Plants would wilt real fast in Bangla weather. Here there'd be more of a lag. Wouldn't there?

Did you help her? Dorotea asked, trying to solve the puzzling resuscitation logically.

Me? No. I'm no help in a garden. Except for 'porting things. There was amusement in his voice. *Did she fix every-thing?*

As near as makes no never mind. 'Thank you, Ted,' she said out loud, patting the bemused man's arm placatingly. 'Just one more psychic mystery. Let's make no more of it, shall we?' She smiled brightly at the head gardener. 'And do put up that fence.' *Or maybe,* she added to herself in her innermost mind, almost ashamed of such a thought, *that's what we shouldn't do, so we'll find out what Amariyah does when her precious garden is threatened. Strange, I didn't 'feel' any output. I must be getting old or something.*

Dorotea told Rhyssa as soon as she sensed that her chief was in the office.

Well, I had one ear open for her, so to speak, Rhyssa said. *I perceived nothing. Though, come to think of it, later she was very tired, but not at all as miserable as she had been when she gave that shriek. And that was very definitely telepathed. In extremis!*

Then there's my mother, Dorotea said, her eyes thoughtful.

Your mother?

Yes, Ruth Horvath was a microTalent, you know, and never did know what she was doing because she did it on a subconscious level. When she tried *to manipulate on the microcellular level, she couldn't. It was spontaneous or it wasn't.*

What could Amariyah have done? To restore plants *to life?*

Probably just as elemental. Ah, well, I don't think we should interfere.

I agree completely, Rhyssa said firmly.

Ted's putting up the fencing today, Dorotea said.

Under the circumstances, is that right?

Morally right, Dorotea replied irritably. *I'm not sure I could live through another such incident. That'd be carrying research a shade too far.*

Right. How are we going to explain it, though?

You mean the garden? I'm not going to try, Dorotea said.

Good idea! Especially since we can't. Have a good day! Rhyssa advised in a bright, overly cheerful mental tone.

When the boys came to apologize, and they were sincere to their toenails, Amariyah was just finishing her breakfast. Dorotea 'heard' the boys approaching: two were promising empaths and Scott a possible kinetic, since he always made many more baskets than his peers. They had reached their decision to come independently. Drew Norton was the spokesperson, his eyes anguished as he led the trio into Dorotea's kitchen when she opened the door for them.

'Amariyah,' Drew began, swallowing hard and gulping, 'we're the ones you should beat up for smashing your garden.'

'Oh?' Her reply was non-committal as she turned in her chair to face them. Scott Gates and Moddy Hemphill shot quick glances at her and then ducked their heads.

'We were messing with the basketball,' Drew went on in a rush.

'And I kicked it, hard. I didn't *aim* at your garden, Amariyah. I really didn't,' Scott said.

She gave Scott a long look. 'I know you didn't. But my garden got messed up anyhow.'

121

'Can you *ever* forgive us?' Drew asked, his face contorted.

'*You* didn't mean it,' Amariyah said, accepting the apology and dismissing them with a nod of her head before she turned back to her hot toast.

Dorotea caught her thoughts; the flash of watching Lila deliberately uprooting her plants, stamping on them, kicking them, making sure even the little fence was destroyed. Then the arrogant girl's attempt to keep Amariyah from reaching her garden, from trying to save at least some of it. A very fleeting glimpse of Amariyah, head down, butting Lila to the ground, sitting on her chest and grabbing handfuls of hair to yank from the scalp. If Amariyah had any regrets, it was that taking vengeance on Lila delayed any possible chance of saving her plantings. But she'd been so enraged, she hadn't thought beyond giving Lila what punishment she could inflict, subconsciously knowing that the nuns might ignore the matter since 'only plants' had been involved.

There was a long pause while the boys tried to figure out if she had, or had not, forgiven them their trespasses. Dorotea cleared her throat.

'You are supposed to throw that ball, not kick it,' Amariyah said, realizing that some response from her was required.

'Ted's going to put up a fence to prevent, ah, any more wild shots,' Dorotea said.

Scott aimed her a quick look. 'We're not to shoot baskets for a week.'

Amariyah considered that, too. 'Just don't kick it any more,' she said, giving Scott a long hard look. 'You don't know your own strength.'

He hung his head. 'Guess so.'

'Thank you, boys, for coming forward. That takes a lot of moral courage,' Dorotea said, herding them to the door.

'Not when your parents're psychic, it doesn't,' Drew muttered.

'They're not here facing Amariyah,' Dorotea said. 'You appreciate that, don't you, Amariyah.'

'I am doing that,' the girl replied, and popped the last bite of toast into her mouth.

'I think that's all, boys. I thank you for coming,' Dorotea said.

'Only,' and now Scott, reprieved, touched Amariyah on the shoulder, 'how did you get the ball so far up the beech tree? Are you a kinetic?'

She shook her head, since she was chewing.

'She's far too young to know *what* sort of psychic ability she has,' Dorotea said, chuckling.

Oooh, that's a whopper of a lie, Peter told his mentor. He was hovering in the hall, waiting until the interview was over.

Not at all. We don't *know what sort of Talent she has.*

Yet, was Peter's capper.

She was busy herding the boys to the kitchen door. *Thanks for not appearing. It was hard enough for them to come and apologize no matter what parental pressure was put on them.*

Psychics must assume responsibility for the application of their talent, either conscious or inadvertent, Peter remarked loftily. *Hey, don't let Maree have all the toast.*

Dorotea popped four more slices in the appliance. *Come and get it!*

Did she repair the garden?

Were you eavesdropping? Dorotea demanded sternly.

No. I looked when the boys came in. What happens if they see that there's no damage now?

They went the other way round the house, Dorotea said with a mental chuckle. *So as not to view the scene of their crime.*

'Good morning,' Peter said cheerfully as he ambulated into the kitchen. 'Mistress Maree, how doth your garden grow this morning?'

Amariyah blinked and looked up at Peter's bland face.

PETER! Dorotea expressed indignation at such a gaffe.

'Quite well, thank you,' Amariyah said, speaking through her mouthful of toast, crumbs emerging in a spatter when she came to the 'th'.

'Really, Amariyah, how many times do I have to tell you not to speak with your mouth full?' Dorotea asked, pretending dismay.

'He asked. It's not polite to ignore a "good morning".'

'Gotcha,' said Peter, managing to cock his index finger at Dorotea, and winking.

'Polite response or not, do not speak with your mouth full, Amariyah, and use the napkin, please.'

The psychics who had responded to Amariyah's shriek followed the example of Rhyssa and Dorotea: they ignored it. Ted built the twelve-foot anchor mesh fence around the back of the basketball standard. Amariyah's garden prospered. If, in the next few years, she grew things that ought not to survive winters in Jerhattan, no one remarked on that. They enjoyed unseasonal blooms, fruits and vegetables. Even Tirla, who had no interest in gardening whatever, was complimentary.

Over the next two years, Amariyah studied the Basic Tuition courses and received high scores. On her own initiative, she studied elementary botany, biology and horticulture. She complained to Dorotea that the curriculum was much too basic, and asked for a more advanced course. She was also very good about keeping in touch with Sister Kathleen and Sister Epiphania on a regular basis. She received short notes in return. To prove that she had grown and was flourishing, she sent them a glossy of herself and Dida Tea in front of her flower garden. But she didn't say that it was her very own garden.

Peter, too, studied hard, and by the time he was eighteen, he had completed degree courses in engineering with an emphasis on astronautics, physics and astronomy. He read everything he could access on spaceship design, lunar habitats and ecology, and the constant flow of Martian reports, and he memorized the classified data that Johnny Greene slipped him from time to time about Mars's first manned station. Learning all he could helped Peter Reidinger pass the time until he was officially allowed to work for the Parapsychic Centres.

When Tirla married Sascha on her sixteenth birthday, her wedding bouquet contained *Stephanotis floribunda*, blossoming vigorously out of season. Amariyah, as an ecstatic bridesmaid for her dearest friend, wore a circlet made of the flower that was reputed to encourage happy marriages. Sascha was equipped with a sprig on his suit jacket, and so was his best man, his twin brother, Boris. Rhyssa also carried a generous matron of honour's spray of stephanotis. Dorotea and Shria, acting as 'mothers of the bride', wore corsages of traditional Greek wedding flowers. They sat proudly in the front row of the imposing lounge of the Henner mansion as Lessud escorted his foster daughter to Teresa Aiello, who, in her capacity as Mayor of Jerhattan, performed the marriage ceremony. The bride had said she would 'honour' her spouse, but emphatically refused to have the word 'obey' in the vows she took.

Mama Bobchik was the only representative of Linear G, and that was solely because she had been present at Tirla's illegal birth. And remembered the date. She was so awed by the company that she was rendered almost speechless, although the occasion did not inhibit her appetite. Nor did anyone 'notice' how much of the food disappeared from the buffet tables that Mama Bobchik continually browsed. Peter, serving as an usher at the intimate wedding, kept a check on her acquisitiveness in case small items of value from the reception rooms went astray. In this, Mama Bobchik was somewhat maligned, for she limited her temptation to food-stuffs.

Kayankira had appeared, still hopeful that she could contract for Tirla's services as soon as she turned eighteen, despite Rhyssa's constant assurances that the poly-linguist would definitely be stationed in Jerhattan to be near her husband. Carmen Stein was a guest, as were Cass Cutler and Suzanne Nbembi, the first psychics with whom Tirla had worked. Sirikit and Budworth in his mobility chair came down from the Incident control room.

After the traditional wedding cake was cut and distributed, the speeches made and toasts given, Peter 'ported the bride and groom to their secret honeymoon destination.

Dorotea and Shria wept, and so did Mama Bobchik. Boris heaved a sigh of relief that his brother was finally safely married to his most unusual bride. If anyone remarked on the disparity of ages between bride and groom, everyone who knew Tirla at all well recognized that she was sixteen going on sixty in real-life terms. She was more than a match for Sascha. It was devoutly hoped that *he* was a match for *her*.

CHAPTER FIVE

Starting the day after his eighteenth birthday, Peter Reidinger spent time in all the other Parapsychic Centres on Earth, getting to know the other registered kinetics, hoping that he could find one more who could employ the gestalt that had added such scope to his and Johnny Greene's abilities. He had already met other Centre chiefs when their travels brought them to Eastern on business with Rhyssa, but not all the other kinetics. Despite the ingenious tests that Lance Baden had set during his 'training period', Peter Reidinger had yet to learn the limits of his kinetic thrust. Even without using generator power to augment his kinesis, he could lift several tons: not very far, of course, but without visible strain. In gestalt, he apparently had no limit.

Lance reported to Rhyssa that he hesitated to try to explore the potential for fear of inadvertently pushing Peter too far, if there was a 'too far' for Peter's gestalt.

Rhyssa showed Johnny Greene Lance's report on his next visit to her office. It had become a frequent stop in his weekly schedule now that Jerhattan had officially opened a telepad and supplied generators capable of thrusting supply drones to Padrugoi. He let the hard copy drift down to her desk.

'Well, I'm satisfied with pumping stuff up to Padrugoi. That's pretty good for a banged-up, middle-aged ex-etop pilot,' Johnny said with a grin. 'Trouble is, it's not quite good enough any more.'

'What are you leading up to?' Rhyssa asked, cocking her head at him.

'Basically, how soon can I start using Pete?'

'What do you mean?'

'You know what I mean. Now that Padrugoi's looking ever outward, I'm useless.'

'Oh, go on!' Rhyssa said derisively.

'I'm serious. There's First Base expanding habitable blocks on the moon . . .'

'Lance is up there, handling construction tasks very well,' she said, trying to compose herself for what was really on J. Greene's mind.

'On the moon, yes, but not in space. Not when the Space Authority is looking to set up a permanent south-polar base on Mars.' He leaned sideways, his green-flecked amber eyes gleaming. 'We need Pete in space, Rhyssa, not stuck downside.' When she started to protest, he rapidly continued. 'Yeah, I know. He's trying to find you another gestalter.' Johnny's opinion of the prospect was low. 'If you haven't up till now, you're not likely to. Furthermore, Pete will feel that he's failed you if he doesn't.'

'Oh, come now, Johnny, that's a bit strong,' she replied, irritated.

'You know it isn't. The boy adores you. He's determined to make you proud of him.'

'I already am,' Rhyssa protested.

'Then let him perform where he's best suited. In space.'

'There are far too many things that can go wrong in space,' she said firmly.

'Like kidnappers?'

'Low blow, John Greene,' she snapped back. 'He's unique!'

'And we can't lose him,' he finished for her. 'But *you* will!' Johnny cocked his finger at her, his expression solemn. 'If you keep him down on Earth doing piddling little pushes, when what he really wants is space. He has since the moment he pushed that supply rocket up from Florida. Where you were quite happy to take him so you could show off his unique abilities!' He bracketed the last two words and gave her a challenging stare. 'Look, at least let him train on Padrugoi. Maybe you're right,' and Johnny took to pacing, throwing his hands in the air. 'Maybe he can't cut the mustard in space. Maybe he's agoraphobic, and the sight of so much "nothing" all around will freak him out.'

Johnny paused and gave Rhyssa a big grin. 'I sorta doubt it. He's been hanging in space, of a sort, since the first time he went out-of-body to find you. He needs to find out what his limitations are, because we sure as hell don't know them.'

'Did he put you up to this, Johnny?' Rhyssa managed to keep her voice level. Her thoughts were chaotic; she had sensed Peter's disappointment with his assignment to find more gestalting kinetics, though he had kept a tight shield on his thoughts, smiled and told her he'd do his best.

'Me? No.' He opened his mind so she'd know he was telling the truth. 'That's why I'm here now, making sure you make the right decision before he wonders where on earth you're going to stash him to "keep him safe". For Pete's sake,' and he gave her a droll grin for his use of the well-known exclamation, 'give him the permission before he asks you. You'll strengthen your position with him.'

She knew that was true.

'Contract him to Padrugoi,' Johnny went on. 'Dirk *likes* the boy. He *needs* him badly to finish off the *Arrakis*. They're behind schedule. He'll also make sure that he's thoroughly trained. If I'm wrong, and Pete can't hack space work, it'll be Dirk who tells him. Not you.'

Rhyssa dropped her eyes, sighing as she recognized the merits of that argument. From the moment Peter Reidinger had touched her sleeping mind, they had had a bond that she had done everything she could to strengthen. She also recalled Dave's warning about Peter's yearning to be involved with the spaceships, and space itself.

'And another thing, he can't really teach anyone what he does,' Johnny went on, pressing his advantage as he saw her waver. 'I'm as much a fluke as he is. I had advantages, true, being an etop pilot with an understanding of mechanics and flight. The only reason I lived through that crash is because I think I did something along the lines of a gestalt to keep from smashing myself irrevocably on the ground.' Johnny gave a self-deprecating chuckle.

'Would Padrugoi be enough for Peter?' she asked in a soft voice.

'Enough? I guarantee he'll be kept actively employed and well appreciated.' The mischief never far from Johnny Greene erupted. 'Think of the fee you can extract from the Space Authority for his services! The Centres will be rolling in credit.'

'Credit has never been a consideration,' Rhyssa said, pretending to be offended by monetary considerations.

'Ha! Who's kidding who? Sascha and Tirla could initiate that scanning programme of theirs, and you could fund that guy, Professor Gadriel, and his CERN project and the FermiLab physicists.' He started to tick off on his fingers the various projects that the Centres had in mind when the cash flow improved. 'The gene ID programme has only been held up since your grandfather's time. So has the research into therapeutic touch that Sister Justa Smith, Clive Bakster and Dolores Krieger pioneered in the nineteen-sixties.'

Rhyssa looked away from Johnny's uncharacteristically earnest expression, out of the window to the green lawns and flowering trees. And imagined the blackness of space from the gigantic spinning wheel of Padrugoi Station. She remembered Dave's description of Peter Reidinger's face when he had first looked out on the vastness and the far glow of the stars. She should stop being afraid for him: that was repressive. She knew he wanted to get out into space, somehow, in some capacity. Dave had reminded her of that. She would be wise to submit gracefully to the inevitable and let Peter go. Her grandfather had often said that, when you let someone go, they were more likely to return. Admiral Dirk Coetzer was not a Barchenka, trying to suborn unwilling workers. In this case the 'worker' was only too willing. And able.

'You'll be sure that he'll be drilled exhaustively?'

Johnny smiled, his mind exuding his relief at her surrender and his unreserved approval. 'I'll be as close to him as the skin of his extravehicular mobility unit. We'll have Madlyn on his case throughout, and you know she'll tell you *all*!'

Rhyssa gave a nervous little laugh. 'Even when I don't ask.'

'Know what you mean,' Johnny said, exuberant. 'Look, there's some groundwork I want to lay before you tell Pete. Sirikit says he's manning Lance's position as Adelaide Centre's kinetic right now. I'll just drop in.'

Rhyssa eyed the General suspiciously. 'What do you have in mind?'

'Nothing that puts our golden goose at risk. Just a sort . . .' and he grinned, 'a caper, if you will. I also have to give Dirk the good news.'

'*He*'s the one who put you up to this?'

'Of course. Ever since Pete screwed Barchenka's password out of her mind, he's had September the eighth red-circled on his notepad.'

'Really? I know Peter was very pleased to get a card from the Admiral.'

'He'd've had a contract if we'd thought you'd be the least bit willing. So, get it done now. Of course,' and Johnny scratched his head, 'we still have to convince the Space Authority to let an eighteen-year-old play with their precious cargoes.'

'Johnny Greene!' Rhyssa exploded with indignation at that admission. The man's gall was inexhaustible.

'Well, I didn't want to get their hopes up.'

She swooped up a fistful of pencil files, threatening to shower him with them, but he 'ported himself neatly out of her office, his laughter echoing in her mind.

On sober reflection and without his insidious presence, Rhyssa admitted to herself that, presuming the boy didn't have an unsuspected agoraphobia, his destiny – such a pompous word – was in space.

However, Rhyssa did check with Amalda Vaden to see if there was any hint of a disaster affecting Peter.

131

'Nope. Can't find one,' Mallie reported. 'You expecting any?'

'Just checking,' Rhyssa replied. 'But keep your precognitive eye on him over the next few weeks, will you?'

'Sure,' and there was a smile in her voice. 'Pete's a good kid. He'll do well on Padrugoi.'

'How did you know what he's going to do?'

'I'm the precog, you know,' was Mallie's parting shot.

Johnny Greene had set up his 'test' with Lance before the kinetic had gone on his latest construction contract with First Base. Johnny's telepathic range fell well short of Oceanus Procellarum, so the two men made advance plans . . . in case. They were both certain of two things: first, they needed incontrovertible proof for the Space Authority and second, Peter needed a real challenge. So Johnny 'flew' himself to Adelaide at the time Peter would be finishing his breakfast and before the rest of the Talents would arrive for work. Peter was surprised, and very pleased to see him stroll into the guest quarters of the Australian Parapsychic Centre just as Peter was 'porting his breakfast dishes into the kitchenette sink.

Nothing wrong, is there? Peter asked, gliding swiftly to the General's side as he stood looking about the foyer.

Johnny shook his head, shielding any wisp of thought the young man might catch. The General was still elated by his most satisfactory interview with Rhyssa.

'No one's here yet?' Johnny asked with innocent surprise as he walked on into the main Incident room. Peter followed him. Since Peter was in residence, and certainly able to handle any parapsychic emergencies, the other telepaths and kinetics went home after their duty hours.

'Not yet. Harry's usually first in. He bikes here, to keep fit,' and Peter sounded a bit wistful. He might be able to 'port himself anywhere on Earth, but a simple pastime like riding a bicycle was not an option. 'He swears he'll teach me how.'

'Harry might at that,' Johnny agreed affably as he swung the small bag he carried up onto the worktop. 'Start up the generators, will you, Pete? Got a small job for you. Lance needs this.'

'Lance? But he's on First Base,' Peter replied, startled.

'This isn't heavy,' Johnny said blithely, demonstrating by 'porting the bag from the surface without a gestalt and suspending it for a few moments. 'Three kilos.'

'But the moon?' Peter repeated, stunned.

'Look, Pete, you've managed to push forty tons four hundred and forty klicks without breaking into a sweat. Pushing three kilos four hundred thousand is not that much more effort, now is it?' Johnny gave a dismissive wave of his hand. 'I'll be ready to boost though, frankly, I think you can do it on your own. Either way, Lance says the engineers need these sensors like yesterday. Everything's held up waiting for them. I don't see why we can't *try* it. Window to the moon is open,' and he pointed out of the east-facing window where the lunar ghost was visible in the morning sky, 'and it's at perigee. Timing's right. If we're going to give it a go.' Johnny's tone was subtly challenging. 'Don't think it'll strain you, skeleteam.' A nice touch, that, reminding Pete of other triumphs. 'Lance wouldn't suggest it if he thought you and I couldn't cut the mustard.'

'Well . . .' Peter looked around the empty office. 'But I'd need to "see" where I . . . we were sending it.'

'Sure.' From the outside pocket of the small bag, Johnny whipped some glossies. He dropped the first one on the desk: the lunar coordinates of First Base, conveniently close to the equator in Oceanus Procellarum. 'Sort of in the back-yard of First Base, you see,' and he pointed to the shining dome in the background, moving his finger to a red and white striped bollard that was the selected target.

'What's that for?' Peter asked.

'Actually,' and Johnny frowned down at the bollard as if trying to remember, 'I believe it's a marker for the lunar-vehicle parking area. See that shadow?' This was barely visible, but Peter nodded as one will when one wishes to show that one has been closely observing details. 'It's one of the four-man articulated crawlers.' He deposited a second image from those in his hand and chuckled as he displayed it

133

to the kinetic. 'Even got a lunar licence plate: FB 3, no less. Detailed enough for you?'

Peter gave a dubious sniff, screwing his face up into a grimace.

'Ah, let's give it a try,' Johnny said nonchalantly. He had been intently listening for the generators to reach full power. Now he shot as strong a mental reassurance to his young colleague as he dared. He couldn't be too obvious about such a 'pathing, but he counted on having confused Peter with fast talk. 'Sit!' He pointed imperiously to the chair that was used for telekinetic sessions. 'I'll hook you up,' he said, putting a hand on Peter's chest to push him back into the padded seat. 'Have official readings on your performance.'

'Only three kilos?' Peter asked, eyeing the bag dubiously as Johnny bent to fit the sensitive pads of the recorder to his body.

'That's all, bag included. Ready?' Johnny didn't want to give Pete any time to think beyond the essential errand. He opened his mind, letting Peter feel his readiness. 'Set? *Go!*'

The generators whined at such a high pitch that, for a nanosecond, Johnny Greene wondered if the powerful drain might not overload them.

'Hey, I don't think you needed that much moxie on the 'port,' he exclaimed in feigned surprise. 'Ease up, will ya? It's not like you were trying for the moons of Jupiter.'

'Well, I wanted to be sure to reach the bollard.' Then Peter began to realize what he'd just done. 'I felt it connect. I have to have got it there. Don't I?'

'We'll know soon enough,' Johnny said easily.

'Say, you can't 'path as far as the moon. How'd you know about Lance needing the chips?'

'Madlyn,' Johnny replied enigmatically as he watched the printout on the recorder.

'Oh.' Pete frowned. 'Wait a minute. She can't 'path as far as the moon either. Or at least, she's never mentioned she could.'

'Sheeesh,' Johnny said, flicking his fingers dismissively. 'Com-contact, man. Which lesser mortals without your

134

advantage regularly use to communicate. Coetzer had Madlyn 'path me when the urgent request came through. I had to pull rank to get all the chips needed. Some were highly classified, you know.' He had glanced over the sensor report. 'Hope you didn't plough that bag. Be hard to replace those items.' He clicked his tongue in mild reproach as he showed Peter the readings. 'Bit of overkill on the power you used. You'll need to refine the long thrust, I think.'

Peter looked startled by Johnny's matter-of-fact appraisal, and Johnny grinned wryly as Peter gave a worried gulp.

'When will we know I did it right? If I did. And you weren't in on the thrust, either.' Peter glared accusingly at Johnny.

'I wasn't needed,' Johnny replied with injured innocence. 'Two of us might've blown the generators and really messed up that shipment.'

'So, when will we know?'

'Didn't think you could do it, did you?' Johnny said, grinning. He made a fist and gave Peter a mock blow to the jaw.

'But we don't know if I did.'

Johnny chuckled confidently. 'Lance should call through on the Centre's com,' and Johnny tilted his head at the com-unit. 'Lemme know when he does. I'm not worried. And I've got the figures to prove you did it, too.' He jerked his thumb at the read-out. 'Well, I'd better get back and reassure the wife. I forgot to tell Senator Sally I'd be missing early this morning. I'm sure she'd've sent you her love if she'd known I was going to see you.' He put a comradely arm about Peter's shoulders and guided him through the foyer to the door. ''Portation sure helps not having to deal with diurnal displacements. Give me a push, will ya?'

'Where?'

'Back home,' Johnny said, 'now I've got my own telepad. *Then* I've got shuttles to waft up to Dirk. Who sends you his regards.' He had landed his personal carrier neatly on the packed red dirt in front of the Centre. He had left the hatch up – for a quick getaway – and now slid back into the seat. 'Say "hi" to the gang here. Sorry to miss them.'

Then he closed the hatch. *Ready when you are, Pete.* He raised his hand in a farewell salute and touched the kinetic's mind.

Peter Reidinger accepted the contact and, still confused by Johnny's whirlwind visit, 'ported the carrier back to the Jerhattan telepad.

'G'day, Pete,' and Harry arrived on his pushbike. The mulga trees that obscured the Centre from the roadway half a mile away had also hidden Johnny's carrier. 'Up early, ain'tcha?'

'Nice day,' Peter said non-committally.

Later that morning, Lance contacted Adelaide, spoke at length to the duty officer and then asked to speak to Peter.

'Thanks for that package, Pete.'

'You got it? I didn't damage anything, did I?'

'Nope,' and Lance chuckled. 'Ploughed up a ridge of moon dust against the bollard, though. Some thrust!' His voice went offline for a moment. 'Hold it, guys, be right with you. We got those chips you've been looking for. Thanks again, Pete. See ya.'

A weary General was admitted to Admiral Dirk Coetzer's office on Padrugoi Station.

'Johnny, what brings you up here today?' The Admiral waved him into the nearest chair and gestured to the coffee pot on its warming plate that was a feature of most naval offices.

Greene shook his head as he sat heavily down.

'I did it,' he said.

'I don't think you mean the drones that arrived this afternoon.'

'Not them.' Johnny flapped his fingers in dismissal. 'I got Rhyssa Lehardt to see the wisdom of letting Peter Reidinger get into space, instead of farting around pushing junk from one continent to another.'

'How'd you do that?' That was the best news Coetzer had had all morning, what with the rumour that fuel prices were going up, and a very expensive component that had to be rescued from tumbling out of sight in space. 'I didn't think she'd put him at risk. I'd prefer that he had the gumption to speak up for himself.'

Johnny let go a sigh. 'I would, too, Dirk, but he's still in grateful mode for her rescuing him from the A frame, hospital and all that shit. I reminded her that he's less at risk up here than downside. Risk of boredom. He'd have real work to challenge him,' was Johnny Greene's reply. He cocked an eyebrow. 'Of course, you'll have to promise to give him the proper EVA training.'

'She'd permit him to work outside the Station? In space? That's where we could really use a powerful kinetic right now.'

'Sure. Why not? I reminded her, as I do you, that that young man's been manoeuvring himself in space ever since he learned how to gestalt. And he's much better at *that* than I am.'

'Could he manage a space suit to do the EVAs?'

'That's what you're to find out.'

'Ahhhh,' the Admiral drawled, comprehending. 'So if he isn't capable, it's me that gives him the no-go, not her? Right?'

Johnny chuckled. 'Well, he'd accept it from you. He wouldn't from Rhys. He'd always wonder if she prevented him from getting up here.'

'I noticed that he and Ms Lehardt have an unusual bond.'

'They do. She got him out of Jerhattan General Hospital and the prospect of a useless existence.'

'He's what – just eighteen?' Coetzer asked.

'By a couple of months. Kids join the Navy at that age all the time.'

'A point.'

'Hell, Dirk, he's much more powerful a kinetic than I am. You need him up here.'

'You don't have to convince me of that. But I'd hate to have to put an end to his aspirations if he can't make the grade in EVA.'

'If the grunts from the Linears can, he can.'

'*If* he doesn't freak out first time he goes extravehicular.' Dirk's expression mirrored a legitimate scepticism.

'Well, we'll just have to find out. And if, mind you, and it's a big if,' Johnny said, pointing his finger at the Admiral, 'he proves agoraphobic and useless in a space suit, he could probably do more kinesis from inside the Station than Baden did. He can also haul a lot more weight than I can.'

Dirk gave him a long sideways glance. 'Like all the way to First Base?' Johnny's reaction was not what Coetzer expected. He gave a diffident shrug.

'He might at that. At least he can stand on this Station to do his pushing. You've got all those powerful generators.' His smile was sly. 'Pete loves generators. The bigger the better.'

Dirk gave his head a twist, trying to conceal his elation at the prospect of having Reidinger on contract to him. 'Padrugoi is four-forty klicks from Earth. The moon's between four hundred and four hundred and fifty *thousand*.'

'I know. We can start when the moon's at perigee and work up to apogee,' was the blithe reply. 'Working him into the distance gradually, Dirk. Who knows what he'll be able to do when his Talent matures?'

Again the Admiral favoured the General with a long and speculative look.

'You're up to something, Greene.'

'Yeah, up on Padrugoi, and I want the guy who taught me all I know up here too. I owe Pete big.'

The Admiral couldn't suppress his suspicion that Greene had some hidden ulterior motive. Which, doubtless, would be confided in him at a time Greene thought appropriate. The former etop pilot and bodyguard of the Secretary of Space was Peter Reidinger's staunchest supporter. If he couched his admiration and respect for the young man in a slightly cynical manner, that was preferable to patronization or fawning. And Coetzer had plenty of proof that Greene was also his dedicated adherent in all matters that forwarded humanity's progress starward.

'All right, I'll make a formal application to the Eastern Parapsychic Centre for the services of the kinetic, Peter Reidinger. How much is she going to soak us for him?'

Johnny shrugged. 'That's between accountants. I just recruit.'

'Why doesn't Peter?' Coetzer asked sharply. 'Train more kinetics, I mean. God knows, we can use every one the Centres find.'

'There just ain't anyone else with his little knack, that's why. Not that Rhyssa and Baden haven't been looking under every psychic rock to find a likely student for him. I can do gestalt, but I don't know how I do it. Neither, in the final analysis, does Pete.' He rose stiffly. 'I'm for some sack time, Dirk. Catch ya later.' With a casual salute, he left the office.

Dirk Coetzer immediately put in a call to his Contracts Manager. He most certainly would grab the opportunity to employ Reidinger. He only hoped that Rhyssa Lehardt would not renege, beset by second thoughts. Greene had made Coetzer patently aware of how unusual and valuable Reidinger was considered by the parapsychics: a talent that they would not risk. How had Johnny Greene talked her into it against her better judgement? Coetzer dismissed the notion that he'd have trouble now that Johnny had told him the lad was available. Rhyssa was known for her integrity, and would honour her word to the General. Nor would he have misled Coetzer. The man was clever, an opportunist, devious, but he wouldn't misrepresent a matter as important as this. Of course, Greene knew how very much Coetzer wanted Reidinger's abilities up here on the Station. And, if the boy – young man – couldn't hack space after all, his kinetic talents used from the safety of the Station would still constitute an asset. Coetzer liked Peter Reidinger, admired a lad who had overcome such a massive physical disadvantage. The prospect that Peter might 'mature' into an even greater range and depth was even more tantalizing. What *would* the mature scope be? He gave a soft whistle.

Peter's juvenile use of kinesis had been spectacular. Johnny had seen to it that Coetzer received a file of Baden's training reports on Reidinger. Whether or not he was able to advance beyond his initial performances was moot. The prospect of teleporting freighters to First Base or – Coetzer inhaled sharply at the mere thought – or Mars, filled the Admiral with a sudden glorious ambition. Padrugoi had been humanity's first step on the path out of its star system. The installation at First Base was another. A permanent Mars colony replacing the present temporary exploration habitat would prove that humanity could adapt to an alien ecology. Earthlike worlds – M-5s – had been identified around many primaries in this galaxy. That new hush-hush telescope was able to find free oxygen in the ozone layers of several planets, meaning they could probably be inhabited without protective coverings or breathing apparatus. To make the most of such opportunities, humanity had better learn the lessons Earth's other satellites had to offer. First Base had already taught valuable techniques, a good preparation for the challenge of inhabiting Mars. In Coetzer's lifetime, Padrugoi had been conceived and constructed. The moon was inhabited. That he might live to see the day when Mars would be, too; that he might also be part of that triumph. What a prospect!

' "Or what's a heaven for?" ' Coetzer quoted to himself. He allowed himself a long moment to savour his new aspiration. His intercom buzzed and he dealt with the practical problems of contracting the means to the new goal he contemplated.

Assimilating Peter Reidinger into the Transport command of General Johnny Greene was the first step in his Padrugoi contract. He was hired as a 'civilian consultant' in Supply and Transport, nominally working under Greene. At the General's insistence, he was given the highest security clearance.

'He's going to handle sensitive stuff from the word go,' Johnny said when the Space Authority resisted. 'He wasn't a security risk when he started lobbing shuttles into space for you, and he hasn't developed any questionable habits since then. He also doesn't need some near-sighted spook snooping around him.'

In the first week of Peter's employment at Jerhattan Spaceport, he lifted more tonnage than Johnny did in a month, a fact that the General made sure everyone in the Space Authority knew. The only aspect of the job that Peter had objections to was the requirement to wear recording pads during gestalt.

'Look, Pete, it's necessary,' Johnny said, cutting through his demurral. 'You don't feel 'em anyhow, so what's your beef?'

'I have more than enough appliances glued to me,' Peter replied sourly.

Johnny gave him a quick look, but did not give in. 'They're a record, just like Incident reporting in the Centre, that *we* need. I wear 'em, too, OK? Now, let's just shift this last monster and call it a day.'

'I'm not tired, Johnny.'

'You aren't, but I am. I'm thirty years your senior, m' boy, and when I say it's quitting time, it's quitting time. Dorotea's got dinner waiting.'

After they had sent the freighter to Padrugoi on the first leg of its long journey to Oceanus Procellarum and First Base, Johnny gratefully shucked off his pads.

'C'mon, Pete. I've seen enough of these four walls today.'

When all parties involved had signed the contract with Padrugoi, Rhyssa suggested to Peter that perhaps he would prefer to have his own apartment in the Centre for those intervals when he was downside. The Space Authority had not queried the clause that required Peter to have one week in every four back on Earth. Despite his euphoria when Rhyssa explained the conditions of his contract, Peter 'knew' that she didn't want him living on his own. Nor did he. He liked Dorotea, and Amariyah made a much nicer sister than Katya ever had.

'I'd rather stay at Dorotea's,' Peter said quickly, and knew by the way Rhyssa relaxed that she'd hoped for this response. 'Dorotea says she doesn't mind me staying on. She's still trying to fatten me up, you know, even if I don't like to eat too often.' That was one of the few times Rhyssa heard him refer, even obliquely, to the appliance that collected his body wastes. 'It isn't as if the food isn't great on

141

Padrugoi.' He lifted his shoulders in a good imitation of Johnny Greene's characteristic gesture. He saw her lips twitch in recognition.

'It's your choice, Peter,' Rhyssa said, and tried not to broadcast her relief.

'Besides, Amariyah would miss me,' Peter added with an affectionate smile.

'That's true,' Rhyssa agreed. 'So would Eoin and Chester, young as he is.'

Peter grinned back. 'And impressionable. I don't want your kids to forget me.'

'I doubt they would,' she replied sincerely. Her son, Eoin, already showed an unusual empathy for a child, now just three and a quarter years old, and she hoped it would mature into a useful ability. Chester, at fifteen months, responded to her telepathic cues, turning from tears into smiles when she soothed him. Right now, they could be keenly aware of 'atmosphere' and respond to it, naughtily enough, at times, to try her patience severely. They seemed to sense that Peter was different, and curbed their horseplay. They never hung onto his hands the way they would their father's or Johnny Greene's. It was as if they knew they should respect his personal space.

Since Peter had been under the Centre's aegis, he had had less and less contact with his natural family. Until her death, his mother had religiously visited her son every month, but she had never been comfortable in his presence once he was mobile. He supported his father and his sharp-tongued jealous sister, Katya. They would have extorted more financial assistance from a guiltily generous Peter if their sporadic attempts to see him had got past Rhyssa's staff. After Peter was installed at the Centre, Katya appeared periodically at Beechwood, demanding that she be allowed to see her brother. Sirikit or Budworth would dutifully show her a duty roster and point out where in the world he was currently training with Lance Baden. Then she'd be escorted back to the transport tube. Shortly before his eighteenth birthday, she gave up. Half the time he had been at Dorotea's, a short walk from the Henner mansion.

142

So Dorotea, Amariyah and Rhyssa's children became 'family' for him.

Peter was assigned quarters in officer territory on the Station, and ate in the officers' mess. As pleasant as everyone was to him, he couldn't join in many of the off-duty activities, and he felt subtly out of place in the mixed service–civilian environment. Even the ensigns were several years older than he was, and, while he was too well mannered to read minds without express permission to do so, he was often aware of the strong emanations of uncertainty about him in the mess. Occasionally one of the older officers was patronizing, but he could ignore that. The only one of the Station's permanent staff he felt comfortable with was Madlyn Luvaro. She had such a crush on a certain Lieutenant Senior Grade Dash Sakai that generally her conversation orbited around the subject of the communications officer. The guy wasn't the least bit psychic, so he was blithely unaware of Madlyn's crush. Everyone else on the CIC recognized it. It wasn't as if Madlyn wasn't pretty, feminine and good company: it was just that Lieutenant Dash Sakai was career-motivated. Peter wondered if there was any way he could unobtrusively inform the com officer that having a psychic as a wife would enhance any officer's career.

In any case, he was glad to step back into the comfortable ambience of Dorotea's home every month. Amariyah got a trifle bored and short-tempered, like any younger sibling wanting to dominate a conversation, when he rattled on about space and the Station. Until the day he just happened to mention the Station's extensive hydroponics system that supplied both food and oxygen purification. Instantly her attitude altered, and she had to know all about the gardens.

'Then I shall be a space gardener,' she said in her resolute manner.

'First you have to learn hydroponics engineering,' Peter said repressively. That would be all he needed – a kid sister on Padrugoi.

'I shall learn all I need to know from Teacher. You just see

143

if I don't,' she added in such a quarrelsome mood that both Peter and Dorotea regarded her in surprise. 'Dida Tea, you will tell me what courses you took.'

Dorotea regarded her mildly. 'If you ask politely.'

Instantly, Amariyah looked penitent, her blue eyes filling with tears of shame for her outburst. 'Please, Dida Tea, will you help me?'

'It'll be hard work,' Peter said correctively.

'I already know a great deal about flowers and vegetables,' Amariyah reminded him, once again the argumentative sibling.

'You'll need to know a lot more,' Peter began.

'And so she shall,' Dorotea said, casting a warning look at Peter to subside. 'Come, Maree,' she said, holding out her hand to the girl, 'we'll just see what courses Teacher has online.'

'Yes, Dida Tea,' Amariyah said meekly. At the doorway, she flashed a glance back at Peter and stuck her tongue out.

While Peter's main task was 'porting supplies and personnel to the Station, he was also required to help 'port materials into the second colony ship, the *Arrakis*, being constructed at Padrugoi. He wanted very much to visit the hull and watch the various stages of its construction. But that would require a space suit. Peter wondered how he could broach the subject of getting trained. If Linear grunts could be taught to manage construction suits, he was sure he could.

He sensed tentative attitudes towards him from Madlyn's adored com officer, Dash Sakai, and Lieutenant Commander Pota Chatham, the chief engineering officer on whose watches he generally worked. He'd hinted as often as he could that he didn't need to be in the Station CIC to use the marvellously powerful generators. He could gestalt with them from anywhere within several miles, and certainly from the *Arrakis*, which was moored in the main construction and repair yard. When his allusions were ignored, he thought maybe he'd been premature. First the CIC officers would need to learn to trust him as much as Johnny Greene did, and, he was sure, Admiral Coetzer. They'd have to get accustomed to his work habits. He was always on time for his scheduled 'ports: he never took a break until Johnny called one, he maintained a strictly professional attitude at all times and he never left his post until the watch officer officially told him to 'stand down'. Not that he would have presumed, in any respect. He was not fragile. In fact, he was probably the safest, strongest person on the Station, especially since the first thing he'd been drilled in was emergency procedures if there was a Station alert. He knew where all the escape pods were and had amused himself in between 'ports by figuring out who he should rescue in order of importance. Admiral Coetzer was first, of course; Johnny Greene, if he was on-station at the time; then the executive officer, Linke Bevan. After them, his priorities altered, but he rather thought Madlyn, because she was the strongest 'path in all the Centres, and then Dash Sakai – because Madlyn would be inconsolable if Dash got wasted. He spent other idle moments figuring out how many he could 'port to safety in the first sixty seconds. He even tried putting air envelopes around groups, to give them oxygen and protection against bursting in vacuum.

Another favourite topic for speculation was how Rhyssa had been persuaded to let him take the Padrugoi contract in the first place. He knew how badly she wanted him to find and train kinetics in the gestalt. Considering how much he owed her and the Psychic Centres, he was willing to spend his whole life trying. But so far there'd been no kinetic for him to train . . . if he could. He suspected Johnny had had more of a hand in getting him on Padrugoi than the General was about to admit. Certainly Admiral Coetzer had given him a wholehearted welcome aboard the Station. He was a frequent guest at the Admiral's table when he was on board. (Maybe that's why some people avoided him.) Coetzer kept a paternal eye on him – at least that's what Peter heard Commander Temuri Bergkamp say when the engineering officer didn't realize Peter was in earshot. Peter did not 'listen' or 'peek', but sometimes people had 'loud' minds and he couldn't help but 'overhear', despite keeping up a light shield most of the time.

That was how he happened to learn that he could be a lot more use to the Admiral if he could 'hack the black', as the grunts phrased it.

'I got book on him,' one of them said as he and his mate swung into a service corridor ahead of Peter. As he didn't make any noise walking, they were unaware of his presence.

'For or agin?'

'Agin, a' course. Kid that young'll panic first time he has to hack the black. Ya know whaddi mean. Shit himself all over!' The first one gave a malicious chuckle of antici-pation.

'I doan think he will,' the other said defensively. 'General thinks he'd make it.'

'Then whyn't he being trained? Been here how many weeks now?'

'I dunno. Hear tell they doan wanna rush him, 'cos he's sorta fragile 'n' stuff. Sure is skinny.'

'Ha! We wasn't given no time. We hadda go out, an' that was that!'

'That's what we wuz hired for, dink. He's not just a grunt, ya know. Notice how he walks? Just like he was *in* a suit. Sort of smooth, like.' The man made a gliding gesture.

'Putcher money where yer mouth is.'

'Sure! An' we *book* the bet with Kibon. You ain't goin' slip me on this.'

'You're on. Slip me into a good downside binge, you will.' And the first man held out a hand to his buddy. Peter inserted himself in a doorway in case they caught a glimpse of him. They turned a corner at the next junction.

Peter digested that conversation and perked up consider-ably. Bets on him, were there? That he'd shit himself? Peter chuckled bitterly. They didn't know much about him, did they? He almost wished he *could* pee. Even if he couldn't 'hack the black', there wouldn't be that sort of evidence for anyone to see. But he knew he would hack it. He wanted to be out in space so badly. He wanted to prove to Johnny and the Admiral that he was more than just a transport mechanic. He could match construction units so smoothly no one would ever have to worry about them tumbling out of

146

control from reaction. He knew his physics: any action in no-gravity conditions caused a reaction. He had more control than any other kinetic, even Lance Baden. Why, he could speed up the construction of the *Arrakis* by months if they'd only let him help. He'd already 'ported many of its components into space. Placing them inside the hull would be child's play. He'd studied the *Andre Norton*'s designs – it was the sister ship of the *Arrakis* – so thoroughly he could close his eyes and still put anything in place. He'd wanted to be personally involved ever since his first glimpse of the *Andre Norton* at the inauguration ceremony. When the Admiral had invited him up to view the completed colony ship, he hoped he'd have a chance of working on the next one. All right, he couldn't *be* a colonist. He'd accepted that. But that didn't mean he couldn't have an integral part in the construction of the other two 'A-type' colony ships. He'd take a vital step towards that dream, if he could just talk them into letting him in space . . .

He'd do it now. He'd ask now. After all, the worst that could happen was to be told 'no'.

When Peter Reidinger suddenly appeared in the Admiral's outer office, Yeoman Nicola Nizukami was surprised. He'd never before just 'appeared' out of thin air, though she knew he could do such things. She didn't need to be psychic to see that the kinetic was nervous. He was very pale, and his Adam's apple kept jumping up and down in his throat. She wondered if he could sweat like other males.

'Are you all right, Mr Reidinger?' she asked, wondering what to do if he fainted or something. She knew some of his history, as did everyone on the Station, but, in this encounter, she seemed not to have all the information she should. She knew the Admiral wasn't expecting him.

'If the Admiral's available. I mean, I don't want to interrupt or anything,' he managed to say.

She gave him an encouraging smile. He was much too skinny, she thought. Why doesn't someone put some weight on his bones!

He blinked and she caught her breath, hoping he

hadn't read what she'd been thinking. She'd been briefed, as everyone had on the Station, that he would be too well mannered to do that. The psychics considered uninvited mental intrusion to be against professional scruples.

'I'll just see if he's free,' she said hastily, lifting her wrist-com to her lips. 'Admiral Coetzer, Mr Reidinger would like a moment of your time.'

'Send him in,' was the immediate response.

She turned to operate the door control and she thought again that the kid would faint, he had turned so white.

'He won't bite you, Mr Reidinger,' she whispered and stood aside, giving him an encouraging wave.

Slowly he glided forward, like an ensign knowing he was in for a tongue-lashing, she thought. Not that Admiral Coetzer was a martinet. And Mr Reidinger was definitely in the Admiral's good books. The door slid shut. Yeoman Nizukami resumed processing the many end-of-month reports to the Space Authority headquarters downside.

She was interrupted by an incredible wave of exultation and looked round her, trying to figure out the source and reason. She was alone. The door to the Admiral's office slid open and Peter Reidinger soared out. She blinked because he was a good foot off the floor.

'Ahem, Pete,' said the Admiral, who had followed him to the threshold. 'You're levitating. Nicola won't mind, but you might turn a few heads in the corridor.' There was a big smile on Coetzer's broad, pleasant face and an expression of paternal affection for his visitor.

'Oh! Thanks, sir,' and Mr Reidinger descended. He beamed at Nicola, shaking his head ever so slightly as the outer door opened and he glided out into the corridor, feet on the ground and knees lifting in his usual approximation of an ordinary gait.

Nicola was used to all kinds of people coming and going from the Admiral's office, and just about every sort of response to interviews, but to see someone *sailing* past her was most unusual.

'Sir?' she said, in the hopes of an explanation.

Dirk Coetzer laughed, rubbing his hands together with

immense satisfaction. 'Just made that young man very happy, by giving him permission to do exactly what I want him to do.'

'Sir?' Nicola was no wiser.

'Get me CPO Ryk Silversmith on the com,' and the Admiral turned back into his office, chuckling and continuing to scrub his hands.

Whose exultation, then, had she thought she felt? She had a useful amount of empathy that made her a good secretary. As she obediently got Chief Petty Officer Silversmith on the com, she realized that he was in charge of training personnel in EVA.

'So Pete couldn't wait any longer, huh?' Johnny said, when Coetzer contacted him about the interview.

'He was the shade of a sheet,' Dirk said, delighted to be able to discuss this remarkable development with the man who'd most appreciate it. He chuckled. 'He'd've been shaking like a leaf, if he could. Took all my self-control not to whoop out loud.'

'So he got up the gumption to ask.' Johnny grinned smugly. 'I wonder what prompted him? Not that I'm not delighted. I've seen him staring at every team of grunts, broadcasting envy. But I like him making his own move. Oh, well, EVA's not my favourite pastime, but I'll get my suit checked out.'

'You're not involved,' Dirk Coetzer said.

'I'm not?' The General sounded indignant. 'I promised Rhyssa I wouldn't—'

'Silversmith'll train him. Same way he trained you, I understand.'

'Silversmith?' There was a brief pause on the other end of the comline. That was the second time in a day the Admiral had trouble suppressing laughter. 'None better.'

'Thought you'd see it like that. You and I, however, can discreetly follow his progress. You can accompany him on his first official EVA, I'll grant you that much.'

'You mean you won't go along too, Dirk?' Johnny's tone was sly.

149

'I get a few perks, you know.' He allowed himself to chuckle then. 'That is, of course, if he can hack the black.'

'Care to make a bet?'

'No, I don't think I do,' the Admiral said in a slow drawl. 'But you'll get pretty good odds if you check with Kibon, the Station bookie.'

'They're making book on it?'

Dirk Coetzer gave a deprecating snort. 'Scuttlebutt about Reidinger has been . . . quite informative.'

'I'll check out the odds first.'

'Don't tell me you're sceptical?'

'Dirk, I want to be sure whose money I'd be taking on a sure thing. I don't want one of those offies you have up here looking to waste me.'

CPO Ryk Silversmith was a compact man, one of the few who took advantage of the naval tradition of wearing a beard, grizzled and neatly trimmed against his jawline. Scuttlebutt suggested he waxed it at night. He had not previously encountered his latest student, but he was well aware of the bets laid for and against Reidinger's ability to hack the black. He'd heard that one of the offies, a janitor, had placed an enormous sum 'against' the lad. His reputation as a trainer did not permit him to bet on a student. So far, there'd been no casualties among *his* graduates. He did wonder, when he saw the skinny kid sitting as bolt upright as a cadet, if maybe this one would ruin his record. He'd also been adroitly informed that this Reidinger was special, so he'd better pass.

A half-hour into the first session of classroom basics, and Silversmith was of two minds: whether or not to like the kid. Reidinger knew his physics better than any newly commissioned ensign. The naval manual on EMU maintenance and repair was up on his notepad. Though he listened intently to Silversmith's spiel on space suits, it was as if the kid was checking a mental list to be sure the chief didn't miss a point. Kid didn't act know-it-all either: wasn't the least bit smart-ass, respectful, but not an ass-licker. Whatever. Silversmith proceeded inexorably with the standard introductory session. When, as was his habit, he required Reidinger to repeat from time to time what he had just said, the answer was spot-on. At the end of the hour, he hauled out the demonstration model.

'This,' he said, flipping the sleeves, tapping the helmet and the belt, 'is an extravehicular mobility suit. Also known as a space suit, Mr Reidinger. You will refer to it from now on as an EMU. Do you read me?'

His student was staring at the EMU with such shining eyes and eagerness that Silversmith had to clamp down hard on the usual sarcastic retorts he had coined over the years, to depress the stupid ideas some dinks – and he included Reidinger in that number – had about extravehicular activities and/or space suits.

'You will need one. You will never exit this Station without the one that has been assigned you, and without checking your EMU before and after every use. Do you read me?'

'Yes, sir.'

'Reidinger?' the chief barked.

'Sir?'

'I'm not a "sir". I'm Chief. Chief Silversmith, to be explicit. Get me?'

'Yes! Chief Silversmith.'

'Strip off that coverall,' and the Chief, not to spare Reidinger's feelings but because he didn't care to waste any unnecessary time on modesty, turned slightly to one side, looking at his clipboard.

To his surprise, the kid immediately peeled off his one-piece coverall and stood in his briefs. Looking at the long, skinny frame, with very little muscle on it, Silversmith knew there wouldn't be anything on board the Padrugoi that could be made to fit. Seemed a shame to waste money on a custom job when who knew if the kid could cut the mustard. Bets were heavy against him. The Chief had seen worse physical specimens make out, but he had his doubts about Reidinger. Orders were orders, and Silversmith deftly took the necessary measurements, slightly puzzled by the odd

151

bulge down the kid's left side. Funny place to wear a security pouch. He gestured for Reidinger to dress.

'Take a while to make your suit up, Reidinger,' and he tapped the clipboard with his light-pen. 'Next lesson's oh-nine-hundred tomorrow.'

'Yes, Chief. Thank you, Chief Silversmith.' And the kid sort of flowed out of the room.

Silversmith was surprised when Reidinger's EMU came up from downside two days later. He inspected it, to be certain the dimensions matched his exact measurements. The helmet was fitted out with unusual toggles and pressure switches, and the two halves of the EMU had far more sensor pads than regulation ones. Even those for officers. He called downside for an explanation, ready to chew out the manufacturer if needed.

'Additional specs came in with your figures, Chief. Tongue-switches and special pressure points so the wearer can use the jetpack. Sensor pads to register heartbeat, respiration, BP, that sort of medical stuff. Everything's according to the special instructions I got from the Admiral's office. Initialled by him, too. Know his fist.'

Chief kept his opinion of 'special instructions' he didn't know about to himself, though he examined the additions carefully. There were some odd things about that kid. Was it wishful thinking on the Admiral's part that Reidinger would pass without a hitch? Did the Admiral know something about the kid that he didn't already know from scuttlebutt?

Instruction nearly came to a halt on the day when the Chief considered that Reidinger was ready to put on his space suit for the first time. He had already drilled the kid on the special tongue-switches and pressure points in the head-piece. 'Minute your helmet's locked in place, you gotta have air, and it's smart to have your com-unit operating, too. You got that?'

'I got it, Chief.'

'Now, Reidinger, you start with the pants of a space suit, like this,' and Silversmith stepped into his pants, one leg at a time, and demonstrated the private connections. The kid looked squeamish. Well, if he wanted to get into space, he'd better get used to it. When Silversmith had the pants on, he sat down. Activating the automatics, he held his arms above his head as the upper part of his suit lowered slowly, enclosed his arms, and enveloped his torso until it settled on his shoulders, leaving his head free. There had been many changes in space-suit manufacture since the Russian Yuri Gagarin was launched above the Earth. If they were now less cumbersome, they were still awkward to put on. Even if a man could get suited up by himself these days.

Reidinger gave the most imperceptible shake of his head.

'What's the matter, Reidinger? It's simple enough. Step in, plug yourself up to the sanitary stuff, sit, then activate this button,' and the Chief touched the control again.

'I can't do it that way, Chief.'

'Whaddya mean, you can't do it this way? Only way you can . . .' The Chief stared, shook his head, because the kid was somehow in the pants with the top coming down over him and the Chief *knew* no one could get into a space suit *that* fast.

'You gotta attach the evacuation tubes,' he said.

'I did.' The kid's face fired up.

'I didn't see you,' the Chief said bluntly.

'I did. I just have to do it differently.'

'I'll just check you out on that,' the Chief said, separating his words angrily. Giving a practised heave to his feet, he strode over to Reidinger who got to his feet, oddly more graceful than most, their first time in a suit. The Chief lifted the kid's right arm to see the read-out on the belt. 'How'd you do that?'

'But I did, didn't I?'

'*How*'d you do that?' the Chief repeated.

'I'm a kinetic.' Reidinger offered that as a complete explanation. That did nothing to mollify the Chief's growing annoyance. 'I don't move the way you do.' With that, the helmet lifted from its rack and settled over the kid's head. Without assistance, it locked into place. 'Like this.' His voice was muffled.

The Chief stared at his suited pupil. Automatically he grabbed the kid's shoulder and twisted him to inspect the

153

suit lights. If the kid suffocated himself, who'd they blame? Air was flowing and the com-unit light was green. The Chief snapped his mouth shut on a desire to snarl at the kid. He got control of his temper.

'All right then, let's run through the purpose of all those fancy switches; so I know you know why you're pressing what.'

The Chief's tone bordered on the sarcastic. He swallowed his disappointment when Reidinger ran through the additions, naming each one correctly. Of course, neither wore jetpacks for this session. If, and the Chief paused lovingly after the conjunction, if the kid got any further in his EVA training and ever needed to use a suit's jetpack.

'All right, Mr Reidinger!' The Chief placed his helmet on his head and locked it into the safety position with a jerk that almost put him off-balance. He backed up to Reidinger. 'You check my EMU lights now.'

'All green, Chief.'

'Right, Reidinger.' The Chief moved with accustomed ease from the ready room to the airlock. He almost wished that the safety net was not in place outside. That the kid would freak out when he saw nothing between him and anything else beyond the airlock. He hadn't placed a bet, since that went against his scruples. Now he wished he'd had Chief Turnbull place an anonymous one with Kibon. Winning would do much to absorb his growing irritation. Then there was his suspicion that the kid had somehow faked the sanitary connections. It'd be his own fault if he messed himself.

The Chief punched his glove at the wide pad that closed the inner hatch. He waited until it had cycled from green to red. He walked to the outer one, and his peevishness increased when he saw how smoothly Reidinger moved in the EMU, like he was still gliding. The Chief tried to damp down his reaction, but this skinny kid in a custom-made suit that must have cost the Station critical credits was getting on his wick.

'Right! I'm going to open the airlock,' and he slammed his fist on the red-coloured pad. The green light went off and the warning blink of 'airlock activated' came up. The 'open door' hooter began. The hatch moved slowly into the hull. 'Reidinger, what's the first thing you do now?'

'Clip on my safety tether,' Reidinger said.

'Do so!'

With a grand gesture, the Chief waved him forward, keenly anticipating that the kid would draw back in horror as he caught sight of wide-open, black space. Of course the net was there and the area floodlit so the full impact was reduced. But he'd seen so many freak out. Most needed a little push, and he was lifting his arm to give one. Before he could make contact with the kid's back, he'd stepped off the edge like a willing sacrifice to this challenge of his courage.

Silversmith listened hard to hear panic breathing, a cry, anything. What he heard was one quick inhalation of breath and a small, soft sigh. No freaking out, no scream of terror; Reidinger floated gently outward, without flailing his arms or legs, his initial step into space taking him slowly to the end of his tether. Then he made an expert turn and faced up, looking out beyond the lights of the Station wheel to black space.

The Chief gave a surprised grunt and, clipping his tether onto the bar over the hatch, he pushed off to the upwardly dangling Reidinger. The kid was oblivious of his approach and, before Silversmith reached him, he began hauling himself down the net, turning his head in every direction as if he couldn't get enough.

From the moment the Chief gestured him out of the airlock, Peter was unaware of anything else. He paused only a moment and let himself fall into space. Oh, he was peripherally aware that there was a spacenet but it did not obscure his view of the black. And he could hack it! Gratefully! Yes, he thought to himself, remembering to breathe after what was an almost overwhelming spiritual awakening, yes, I am in space. I can hack the black! I *love* the black!

Then he let himself float outward, completely in control of his body. He had taken good heed of the maxim that 'action causes reaction in space'. He had never felt such utter freedom, even the moment he had learned to move his body

155

kinetically. That was a poor second to his elation now. He felt the little tug of his space tether and, making exactly the appropriate move, turned to face up, the lights of the Station wheel glittering in his face plate, a benediction from Padrugoi herself. Smiling to himself, Peter began to explore the limits of the net, looking constantly around him, taking it all in. At last! This was where he belonged. In space!

'So young Reidinger can hack the black. Well done, Chief,' said the Admiral's voice on Silversmith's helmet com, startling him into a violent action of dismay. 'Well done, Chief.'

Catching himself with a deft twitch of his safety line, the Chief closed his eyes and mentally reviewed the last half-hour. How long had the Admiral been watching, listening? Had he said anything to the kid that he'd be called on to explain? Who'd patched his com-unit into the Admiral's private channel?

'General Greene said he'd be a natural. He was right,' the Admiral added, to the Chief's utter chagrin.

'Aye, sir, he certainly is,' Silversmith hastily agreed. 'Like he'd been in space all his life.'

'Well, certainly the past four years or so,' the Admiral remarked enigmatically. 'Tomorrow you can belay that net and use a longer tether. Drill him on manoeuvring. I want you to put him through every emergency routine we've got in the manual.'

'Aye, sir. Of course, sir.' With a sense of reprieve, Silversmith heard the faint click that meant the Admiral was off-line. 'All right, now, Reidinger. See if you can get your ass back to the airlock.'

Increasing the Chief's vexation, Reidinger gave just enough of a twitch to the safety tether to drift slowly back to the lock.

'Now,' the Chief said in a steely voice, 'see if you can make a smooth passage to the downside of the net.'

If the Admiral wanted this kid to be competent in space, there was no time like the present to begin the drill. Silversmith kept him at it until he heard the click again.

'Are you still out there with him, Chief?' asked the Admiral.

'Aye, sir. He's a natural, sir.'

'That's enough for his first space walk, Chief.'

'Aye, aye, sir.'

Silversmith had to haul on Reidinger's tether to get him back to the airlock. When the Chief removed the kid's helmet in the ready room, there was a rapt look on his face that worried Silversmith more than any other reaction could. Reidinger was space-mad. He was going to have to watch this one.

Silversmith was also present in the mess when he heard that the heavy offie bettor had to pay up, damn near roughing up Kibon. The winners in the CPO's mess were loud with celebrations of 'an easy win'. Silversmith made a note of the man's name – Bert Ponce – so he could check the records on what the guy had done to get him sent up to the Station. The Chief was a little surprised not to be able to access those records, but he did find out that Ponce was stuck up here as a menial worker until his natural death. Whatever he'd done, it had to have been worse than awful. One thing was sure: after losing every credit in his account (and Silversmith did discover that Ponce had a *lot* of credits), the guy wanted the kid's guts. The Chief hated a sore loser.

So, for two good reasons, Silversmith never took his eyes off the kid as he put him through every space acrobatic he knew of, ready to lasso the kid in if he started drifting into outer space. Grudgingly the Chief had to admit that the kid never disobeyed him, never lost control, never resorted to any of the antics some space-happy yeomen did. But he was always alert. You never knew with that type. The Chief made sure Reidinger could cope with a damaged oxygen connection, with drifting, with tumbling, with suit pressure dropping (and a 'technical' leak in his EMU). Since the Admiral said the kid's main job would be matching construction units without causing any action that would, in turn, cause displacement, Silversmith made him 'join' empty tanks over and over. Reidinger acted as if this was the

157

greatest treat in occupied space. Silversmith got more and more nervous. Something would happen, he was sure of it. The training could not go on without some sort of glitch. Somehow that sonofabitch Ponce would take revenge on the kid for losing him so much credit. The situation wasn't normal.

After Silversmith had to agree that Reidinger could hack the black, he welcomed the addition of General Greene to the team working on the *Arrakis*'s hull. Not that that put a stop to Reidinger's fascination with space. The General, Silversmith noticed, was keeping as close an eye on the kid as he was. As if the brass didn't think the Chief was making a thorough job of training the kid.

Admiral Coetzer made matters worse by joining the three of them to watch Reidinger's first assignment – taking a heavy drive component from the 'net' and manipulating it across the fifty yards of space to the hole in the hull left open for convenient insertion.

'Nice work, Reidinger,' the Admiral said with, to Silversmith's mind, just the right degree of approval. 'I think we would certify him as space-safe now, wouldn't you, Chief?'

Silversmith hoped that Admiral Coetzer, or the General, who was hovering even closer to the Chief, did not accurately interpret his gargle of surprise.

'Aye, sir, I do believe you could, sir,' he responded hastily and with appropriate sincerity.

'Good. Continue, Reidinger. We've got a deadline to meet, and you're going to make all the difference. Carry on, Chief,' the Admiral added to Silversmith. Then, with due care, the Admiral activated his jetpack and returned to the Station.

Silversmith was acutely aware that the General remained for the duration of the EVA, observing Reidinger and limiting his remarks. He kept himself tethered to the net rim, which suggested to the Chief that the General was not as happy in space as the kid was. He wondered, should he mention Bert Ponce to the General? Of course, he had nothing but a gut feeling that the offie wanted to get back at the kid. And how could he get to Reidinger when he was wearing an offie's double wristband?

Silversmith had to spend a full six days space-dogging Reidinger as he worked in and outside the *Arrakis*'s hull. On the second day of this purgatory, Silversmith noticed that the construction crews must have been detailed to keep their eyes open, too. There were always at least five nearby, just in case the kid tumbled himself or some of the expensive units he was handling. It aggravated the Chief no end that the kid moved expertly among the components moored by tethers around the hull. It was like watching a quarterhorse – the Chief had spent the first eighteen years of his life on a cattle ranch outside Austin – work a calf out of the herd. Reidinger would home in on the required item, give it just the right spin or push to send it out of the net and to the exact place it would spend the rest of its working life in the hull.

Reidinger seemed to know an awful lot about the internal design features of the *Arrakis*, too. He didn't argue, but at times, even the on-site naval architect and the construction boss, even the General, deferred to him. That galled Silversmith even more. To cap it all, the Admiral gave Silversmith a commendation for his 'expert training and guidance of one Peter Reidinger, to the level of space safety required by the Authority.' Silversmith was torn between hoping the kid never did tumble off into space, thus keeping the Chief's record untarnished, and hoping the kid disappeared without trace, a victim of the black. Perversely, the Chief put one of his own secret security locks on the rack where the kid's suit hung. No grunt, blackmailed by that Ponce scuzz, was going to sabotage it. The Chief had a reputation to maintain. When Silversmith was given another assignment, he removed his security lock, never realizing that several attempts had been made to open that rack; none, of course, successful.

Then he heard that Reidinger had conned one of the limo pilots into training him on the Station's simulators. He supposed that the Admiral would check the kid out on them, too, and decided that the Navy had gone to hell in a handcart if it would certify the space-mad on a self-destruction course.

On the few subsequent times when the Chief happened to pass Reidinger in the corridors, he didn't look quite so much like a 'kid' any more.

CHAPTER SIX

Rhyssa invited Peter, Dorotea and Amariyah to dinner with her family on his second night downside. Dorotea discreetly informed her that the first thing Peter had done was to ask Amariyah to help him pin up a digital print of the *Arrakis* over his treasured diagram of the *Andre Norton*. The second thing was to take a stroll through the grounds with Amariyah hanging onto his hand, so that she could show him what she'd been doing while he'd been away, and question him about anything new in the Station hydroponics unit.

When he walked into Rhyssa's house the next night, she was instantly conscious of his air of competence and assurance. She embraced him gladly, allowing him to feel her delight in seeing him and her pride in his latest accomplishment.

I'm not at risk in space any more, Rhys.

As Johnny would have it, you've been 'in space' since I sprang you from that awful hospital bed, she responded. 'Oops, the thundering herd knows you're back!'

She stepped aside as her rumbustious son Eoin stampeded into the living room, yelling, 'Petey, Petey, Petey.' Instantly Peter folded himself down to the child's level, smiling warmly, holding out one hand.

'Hey there, Eoin, how's the man!'

In his brother's wake, Chester toddled as fast as he could pump his legs to clasp the other hand, squealing with delight.

They ignored Dorotea and Amariyah, dancing about until their mother settled their good friend on the couch where they could climb up on him.

'I guess I know who counts,' Dorotea said with a disdainful sniff. 'Evening, Dave,' she added when Lehardt arrived with a tray of drinks and handed her the dry sherry she preferred.

'They don't see Peter every day like they do us,' Amariyah remarked imperturbably, sitting on the velvet footstool beside Dorotea's chair and smoothing the dress she and Tirla had bought for the occasion. It was the one Peter had liked best when they were shopping that afternoon. Going shopping – and to the Old-fashioned Parlour of Gastronomical Delights – was almost a ritual for the three of them. 'Thank you, Dave,' she said, accepting the fruit juice Dave served her.

'Didn't know what you'd be drinking now that you're a certified space walker, Pete.'

'Same thing I drank when I wasn't,' Peter replied, draping his arm about each of the two limpet-like boys as they snuggled into him.

Rhyssa sat close enough to remove either or both of her sons if they squirmed too much. Peter did slip free of one clinging paw so he could 'hold' the glass of ice water Dave offered. The boys, who were close to their bedtime, were being very good so they could stay up longer. Rhyssa was grateful that Peter hadn't lost his calming effect on them. Rachelle would shortly come to take them for their bath.

'How d'you get on in space, Pete?' Dave asked as he gave his wife her cocktail and settled himself with his in the leather conformable chair.

'Well, book was made on whether or not I could hack the black.'

'No kidding. They had a wager going?' Dave was amused. Rhyssa was not.

'Standard operating procedures, Rhys,' Peter said, sensing

162

her annoyance. 'They're always betting up there. On anything, from who'll be the next one to take a tumble, or how big the fine'll be for losing man hours.'

'And I'll bet,' Dorotea said proudly, 'you were far too deft to incur a fine.'

'I had to prove to Chief Silversmith that I wouldn't, you know.'

'Oh?' asked Rhyssa, catching a flash of suppressed hubris. 'The Chief didn't like you?'

'Well,' and Peter demurred, 'I think I irritated him . . .' He shot a quick look at Rhyssa over Chester's head. *Honest, I didn't peek. The guy radiated such waves of hostility I'd have to have been mute not to be aware.* Aloud he said, 'I don't quite know why I annoyed him so much. I did everything he told me to.'

Dorotea gave a polite chortle, tapping her lips with her knuckles, her eyes dancing.

'That might have had something to do with it,' Rhyssa remarked.

'Probably he's never met anyone quite like you before,' Dave said in a dry voice.

'There isn't anyone else like Peter,' Amariyah said primly, eyeing Dave in dignified reproof.

Dave was accustomed to her blunt remarks and grinned. 'You're quite right, of course, Amariyah, but petty officers in the Navy are often a law unto themselves.'

'Chief Silversmith had to keep his reputation as an instructor,' Peter told Amariyah. 'I certainly didn't want him to fail with me.' He made eye contact with Rhyssa. 'He didn't have a bet on me, either way. I had the sense he didn't know which he wanted most – for me to fail or succeed.'

'You had a choice?' Dave asked lightly.

'What do you think, Dave?' Rhyssa replied, wishing not for the first time that her husband had some empathy. He winked at her, and she knew she'd taken his bait. She made a face at him. 'Of course you had to succeed. Johnny was sure you would.'

'Is that why he personally bird-dogged me, and had extra grunts assigned to wherever I was working? I *know* for a fact

163

he's not keen on EVA. And don't think I didn't feel Madlyn's touch every minute I was outside.'

Rhyssa had the grace to look abashed. *You know I had to.*

'How do you know Johnny doesn't like working in space?' Dave asked, surprised.

'I just do,' Peter said, and he lifted his shoulders in the General's characteristic shrug. 'You get to know who likes EVA and who's the least bit nervous.' *A genuine case of mind over matter, Rhyssa.*

'Why do they work in space then, if they're nervous?' Amariyah wanted to know.

'It's a good job and pays well,' Peter said.

'And safe enough, once Barchenka was no longer in charge,' Dave remarked.

'Why? Wasn't it always safe?' Amariyah tilted her head enquiringly at Peter, wanting his opinion.

'No, it wasn't, Maree, but no one needs to worry about getting lost in space any more.'

'Why? Do you rescue them?' she asked, although she indicated there could be but one answer.

Peter dropped his eyes to his drink.

'Well, do you?' she insisted, leaning towards him. 'You can do anything you want.'

'I suspect that if Peter needed to rescue anyone, they wouldn't be aware of it. Would they, Peter?' Rhyssa asked.

He grinned at her. 'More or less. Didn't happen often, anyway. All they needed was a bit of a halt to stop their spin.'

'Did you have eyes in the back of your helmet?' asked Dave, amused.

'No, I had Madlyn looking out for me and she knew the signs. So,' and his grin was self-deprecating, 'it was more her than me, Maree, preventing the need for rescue.'

'When I've learned hydroponics and work on the Space Station, will I get to go out into space? Will you rescue me if I need it, Peter?' Amariyah asked.

'Of course I will,' he said stoutly.

Rachelle appeared in the doorway. Eoin and Chester saw her and clung to Peter's arms.

'You've had an extra fifteen minutes, boys,' their father said, gesturing for them to go to Rachelle. They grumbled and shifted about, hoping for a reprieve.

'C'mon, boys. The bubbles are all ready for your swim,' Rachelle said, holding out both hands.

'Which bubbles?' Eoin wanted to know, reluctant to leave Peter.

'I'll be back tomorrow morning, Eoin. You can tell me which ones then,' Peter said, and gave the little boy a subtle push off the couch. Rachelle saw the obstinate look on Chester's round face and went to scoop him off the couch. 'I'll see you tomorrow morning too, Chester. It's great to be back!'

'I think dinner's ready,' Rhyssa said, rising to her feet and gesturing for Dave to escort Dorotea to the dining room.

During dinner, Rhyssa brought Peter up to date on all the Centre news. Lance Baden was back in Adelaide, flown directly into the Woomera Space Station, his contract for the moon expansion completed. He would probably sign up for another. Dorotea had Peter repeat some of the tales he had recounted the previous evening of his experiences on Padrugoi. Rhyssa was not unaware of some of the pressures he had experienced. That was why the subtle Dorotea had prompted him to repeat them. Rhyssa had plenty of food for thought while Peter, with great relish, ate the meal she had prepared for him.

'Not that I can't get anything I want up at Padrugoi,' he hastily amended.

'Food eaten in the company of good friends always has more savour,' Dorotea said pontifically.

'Why? We're eating the same things you cooked last night,' Amariyah said.

Dorotea cleared her throat and rolled her eyes heavenward at such tactlessness. Dave guffawed.

A bit like Tirla, isn't she? Peter said, reassuring Rhyssa with a wide grin. 'I'd like seconds of the garlic potatoes, please. That's one thing they don't use on the Station.'

'Why not? Garlic has many healthful properties,' Amariyah said.

165

'It also has one effect that may not be appreciated in a recycled-air environment,' Dave said.

'What?' Amariyah asked.

'Bad breath,' Dave replied, ignoring flatulence.

'Elephant garlic has no odour,' the girl said.

'We take the point, Maree,' Peter said, grinning with mischief.

'He's growing up,' Rhyssa said wistfully to her husband when they were getting ready for bed that night.

''Bout time. And he's enjoying life. *All* of it, I hope,' and Dave rolled his eyes.

'David!' she said in protest, because his expression was slightly salacious. 'He's only eighteen!'

'Honey, I'd had my first sex by the time I was sixteen.'

'You did?'

'We won't go into that. It was youthful exuberance, love!'

'Peter's not sterile,' she added. 'The medics say that paraplegics can, you know.'

'I know. I asked,' Dave said.

'Then kindly don't encourage him.'

'It's not for a *guy* to encourage him,' Dave said with a second suggestive leer.

'David!'

'And he's closer to nineteen, you know.' He tried to change the subject. 'So he has a week home, and then another three being a stevedore?'

'Stevedore?' Rhyssa gave him another hard look for his word choice.

'All right, transport and construction kinetic!'

'That's better. I wonder who else we could send up to Padrugoi from the Centre?'

'I thought you didn't want him to experience "life" yet?' Dave asked, stacking the pillows behind him so he could watch Rhyssa at her nightly beauty ritual. Privately he didn't think she needed to fuss with creams and lotions, but he liked watching her.

'Another *male* his age. He's very lonely. I caught that.'

166

'He is? I thought he was having the time of his life, doing what he's wanted most! Building a colony ship.'

Rhyssa swung round from her dressing-table mirror. 'I couldn't let him go on a colony ship.'

'Did I say he wanted to go on one? But sometimes, my telepathic darling, you don't notice the obvious.'

Rhyssa blinked her eyes, then had to blot the cream out of them.

'He feels out of place,' Dave explained. 'He hasn't formed any friendships with the Station personnel.'

'Even now he's doing EVA?'

'Dorotea noticed it. Amariyah didn't.'

'How would you know that?' she asked.

'She'd've been on it like a shark. She doesn't miss much about Pete, you know.'

'Oh, dear,' and Rhyssa paused in wiping off her cleansing cream. 'We don't have another Tirla–Sascha item, do we?'

Dave shrugged. 'That wouldn't be all bad, would it? What does Dorotea say?'

'It's true that Maree adores him. Almost,' and Rhyssa paused to chuckle, 'as much as she does gardening.'

'There're gardens on Padrugoi and at First Base. And I suspect they'll be even more important on that proposed Mars Base.'

'If,' and again Rhyssa paused a beat, 'the Space Authority ever makes its mind up on the project.'

'They have Pete now.'

Rhyssa finished removing the cleanser. 'Yes, they do, but do they know what they have in him?'

'I doubt it. Hey, come to bed, love.'

On his nineteenth birthday, Peter opted to take his special friends to dinner in a well-recommended uptown ziggurat restaurant. Rhyssa, Dave, Johnny Greene, Lance Baden, Tirla, Sascha, Dorotea and Amariyah were his guests. It was Amariyah's first 'adult' outing, and Tirla had taken her shopping. Amariyah Bantam had inherited her parents' estate, including their insurances, and they had been prudent managers, so she had 'independent' means. (Although the interest from the total – which was carefully invested by the Centre's Financial Office – was more often spent in acquiring horticultural rarities, she could afford to dress herself stylishly.) Peter had reserved a first-balcony table, which had not only the hanging baskets of exotic flowers that fascinated Amariyah, but an impressive, downtown view of Jerhattan. Theirs was a more sedate party than the one on the balcony above, which got louder and louder as the evening progressed.

Rhyssa, watch out! Amalda Vaden's telepathed warning distracted her from accepting her slice of birthday cake. It took Rhyssa a moment to wonder what Mallie was warning her against, and then it was almost too late. She had little time to react, because events had already been set in motion. The party above them had erupted into angry shouts and curses. She had time to *try* to get a shield out over Peter's guests. The next moment, two bodies hurtled over the balcony railing and dropped, striking Peter flat against the table, knocking both Rhyssa and Amariyah, seated next to him, off their chairs.

Johnny and Lance 'lifted' the pair off, dumping them unceremoniously to the floor to continue flailing at each other. Dave helped Rhyssa to her feet; Sascha went to Amariyah, who had been dazed by a blow to her head. Dorotea was bending over the unconscious Peter, feeling for a neck pulse. Amariyah surged to her feet, covered with cake, and lunged for Peter with an inarticulate cry. Tirla, being nearest, caught her. The child struggled, moaning with anguish.

He didn't have his shields up! Dorotea cried in consternation.

Why would he? At his birthday party, and in a respectable restaurant, Rhyssa replied, caustic with fear and anger as Dave steadied her. *I tried to help. Is Peter all right?* She pulled Dave with her as she joined Dorotea in examining him. *How is Amariyah?*

She's got cake all over her, Tirla said in disgust, and reached for napkins and a water glass.

Secure those two, Rhyssa said needlessly, because Johnny

and Lance had already exerted force on the drunken pair and they were locked motionless, face to face on the floor, arms outstretched as each was aiming blows at the other. Gargling sounds came from their throats, but they couldn't move. *I want a medical team here instantly, Sirikit,* she 'pathed to the Duty Office at the Centre. *Johnny and Lance can 'port them. Just tell me who!*

All conversation had ceased in the restaurant at the sound of the crash. Now curious guests were trying to see what had happened. Those on the upper floor were leaning over, their queries slurred by the drink they had taken. Two waiters came forward, one of them beckoning urgently to the maître d', who hurried up the short flight of steps, undoubtedly forming apologies and stopping short as he took in the damage and the inert body.

The lights of the restaurant dimmed as Johnny and Lance used that source of power to effect the arrival of the medicopter. Instantly the emergency trio homed in on Peter.

He's got broken bones, Dorotea said, anxiously wringing her hands. Peter had not yet developed osteoporosis, but brittle bones were associated with long-term paralysis. His exercises on the Reeve board and frequent massage were supposed to slow the onset.

Dave had an arm about Rhyssa's shoulders, trying to console her. Sascha gave them a short nod, indicating that he had reported the incident to LEO headquarters.

Boris is coming. Johnny, Lance, bring him in, Sascha added, and suddenly there was a LEO 'copter hovering sideways outside the windows. Boris Roznine peered into the restaurant and then gave crisp orders. The 'copter swept away to the helipad on the next level. In moments, uniformed officers were rounding up those in the disruptive party. Boris arrived on the first balcony with two more officers. He halted when he saw Peter.

Is he all right? he asked Sascha.

We're checking. Those are the ones responsible. Bury them deep in the LEO cells, will you, bro?

As deep as the law allows me, was Boris's response and he signalled for assistance.

'Fractures to the right arm, leg and ribcage,' the emergency medic was reporting to Rhyssa. 'I don't think his neck, or his back, are injured. His pelvis might be. A portable scanner's on its way in.'

Rhyssa came as near to fainting as she ever had, leaning into Dave's supporting body. Dorotea started to weep. Lance, who was nearest, assisted her to a chair and ordered a brandy. Cursing dire threats in a variety of languages, Tirla was attempting to clean cake off Amariyah's pretty dress. Amariyah, tears streaming down her face, kept her eyes on Peter. Then Tirla grabbed the arm of one of the medics and pointed to Amariyah.

'She's in shock,' she said, and the woman swung round to check the dazed child.

I'm terribly, terribly sorry, Rhyssa, Mallie said. *It all blew up so suddenly. One moment it was all right, and then I felt the precog. How badly is Peter hurt?*

We don't know yet. I saw the falling bodies and tried to shield him. The portable scanner just got here. He's alive. Tell me something good will come of this, Mallie. There's got to be something good out of it.

A long pause. He isn't going to die. He can't hurt, you know. He'll heal. I see nothing else.

Thanks.

Wish I'd been just that little bit faster. Mallie's repentant voice dwindled into silence.

'He will be all right, Rhyssa,' Dave said. 'He survived the wall. He'll survive this. He *is* a survivor!'

The portable MRI scanner was in place, clicking as it was slowly passed over the unconscious victim. Rhyssa leaned close enough to see the monitor that Bob Gerace, the emergency medic, was intently watching.

'Yup, buckle fracture of the humerus, three, no four, broken ribs, a hairline fracture of the right pelvic bone, a break in the femur, fortunately just past the joint so he'll,' Gerace hesitated on 'walk again', and then continued briskly, 'Well, nothing that won't mend. No internal injuries that are visible on the portable. It could have been worse, Rhyssa.'

'It's quite bad enough as it is, Bob,' she said tartly, and felt Dave's hands on her elbows, calming her. 'No further damage to his spine?' she asked, because she had to know.

'He had enough to begin with, Rhyssa,' Gerace said with a grimace. 'It was obviously a glancing blow; all the injuries are on the right side. OK, people, let's immobilize him.' He visibly winced at his choice of words, apologizing for his gaffe even as he placed a protective shell over Peter's upper arm.

With skill and speed, the breaks were given first aid. Johnny and Lance kinetically turned him over and laid him very, very carefully on the litter.

'D'you know Henry Hudson Hospital?' Gerace asked of no one in particular. 'It's nearest.'

'I do,' Rhyssa said, turning to Johnny and Lance. *Take the placement from my mind.* She let them 'see' the Accident and Emergency facility at the uptown hospital.

Again the lights dimmed as the 'port was made.

On the level above, indignant guests were complaining about being detained by LEO officers. Conversations were muted in the main dining room, and most of the curious diners had gone back to their tables.

'C'mon,' Boris said, with a jerk of his head in the direction of the stairs. 'I'll fly the rest of you there.'

'I think, if you don't mind, I'd like to take Amariyah home,' Dorotea said.

'We'll come with you,' Tirla said, gesturing for Sascha to accompany them.

'I'll get transport,' said Boris, giving a crisp order on his wristcom.

The maître d' was hovering on the fringe. 'Ah, there's the matter of the bill . . .' he began, and then backed off, scissoring his hands to indicate he hadn't meant that at all as Boris and Sascha both glared fiercely at him.

Boris motioned for the others to follow him to the helipad. They reached the accident ward just as Peter was being taken to surgery. He had not regained consciousness, but Bob Gerace and the resident orthopaedics man had conferred over the results of the MRI and decided how

171

to proceed. Gerace was trying to argue the doctor out of anaesthesia since Peter already had no feeling in his body.

'What if he wakes up in the middle of the procedure?' the man demanded.

'I am Rhyssa Owen Lehardt,' she said, marching up to him. 'I will be present, just in case he decides to 'port himself out of reach. Which is, I assure you, the more likely danger than that he would have any sensation. He also reacts badly to anaesthesia.'

'Oh.' The doctor acquiesced without a single word about hospital protocol.

'We'll be right outside,' Johnny said in his best military voice.

Peter did not regain consciousness until he was in the bed of a private suite of rooms in the Henry Hudson Hospital.

You're all right, Peter, Rhyssa said in the softest possible 'path when his eyes slowly opened. *I'm right here.*

He blinked, swallowing. He couldn't feel a thing, but he could smell 'hospital' around him. He turned his head towards her.

'What happened? One minute I'm cutting the cake.'

She explained tersely.

'I can't feel a thing, you know.'

'Fortunately,' she replied in a light tone. 'They've glued you back together. You're in one piece again.'

'That's good,' he said, matching her levity. 'Maybe I should have taken you all up to Padrugoi. The view there is terrific too, you know.'

'You'd've at least had your shield protecting you up there,' she retorted, letting some of her anxiety show.

He made a face. 'I should've kept a shield up. I'm sorry, Rhyssa, but I didn't think I'd need it at my birthday party. And in such a respectable restaurant.' Scaring her, he shot upright in the bed. 'Did anyone remember to pay the bill?'

Rhyssa was on her feet beside him, trying to get him to lie back as the monitor caught the rise in his vital signs and set off the alarm. Nurses and a doctor rushed in, gawking at the multiple-fracture patient able to sit upright in the bed.

'He's all right. He's a kinetic. He can do this,' Rhyssa explained.

'I don't care what he is, madam,' the doctor said, attempting to push Peter down on the mattress. 'He's on complete bedrest.'

'Peter!' Rhyssa said, urging him with voice and gesture to a supine position.

'How'd he do that?' asked the nurse, who was examining the monitor screen.

'Trade secret,' Peter said, suddenly hoarse. 'I'm thirsty and hungry and I missed my birthday cake.'

The intern was not amused, but, after he had assured himself that the 'antics' had not interfered with the newly set bones, he left.

Rhyssa didn't know whether to cry with relief or give Peter a piece of her mind.

No need to do either, Peter said. 'But I am hungry and I am thirsty, and I don't know where the kitchens are in this place.'

'We have one handy,' Rhyssa said, and went to the serving facility of the suite to see what was on hand. 'Just about anything you want. A piece of birthday cake will take a little longer.'

I'll make one immediately, Dorotea said in her mind, immeasurably relieved.

How long have you been listening? Rhyssa wanted to know.

I didn't stop listening, Dorotea replied in a tart mental tone. *What kind of cake do you want?*

I'd like double chocolate with boiled icing, Peter promptly replied.

I'll just turn the oven on and get Amariyah to help me. And if she isn't allowed to see Peter at the first available moment, I won't be responsible for her mental state.

Could she hear me, Dorotea? Peter asked, his expression anxious.

173

Try. She might just be receptive. She's been so worried about you! Good Lord, I think she did hear you. She's just stopped that silent weeping of hers. She's got the funniest expression on her face. Yes, Amariyah, Rhyssa's with him and we're to bake a chocolate cake with boiled icing to make up for the one he didn't get to eat. All right, now just get out the big bowls.

'Is Dorotea 'pathing to her?' Peter asked, astonished.

'No, she's vocalizing to Amariyah. Juice? There's anything you can name.'

'Apple if there is some.'

'Apple it is,' and Rhyssa returned quickly with a large glass. 'Don't you dare sit up again, Peter Reidinger. You're to use a straw or that monitor will have them all in here again.'

While he dutifully sipped, she sent word to those waiting anxiously to hear from her. Dave, Lance and Johnny were in the cafeteria, drinking coffee. They came up to reassure themselves with the vision of Peter 'porting the glass and dutifully sipping from a straw. Then Dave insisted on taking Rhyssa home. Johnny said he'd take the first shift, and Lance made himself comfortable in the small guest room of the suite.

'Can't I have pretty nurses?' Peter asked with mock petulance.

'I know it's breakfast time,' Dorotea said when she and an anxious Amariyah arrived in Peter's room the next morning, bearing a covered cake dish and a bouquet of choice blooms from their gardens.

Amariyah instantly put the flowers down and laid her hands delicately on Peter's right arm.

'Do you hurt?' she asked, gently touching each of the break sites as if to reassure herself.

'I can't hurt, honey. My body has no feeling, you know.'

'That doesn't mean you can't hurt,' she replied, her fingers lingering. Then she reached into her pocket and pulled out a carefully folded square. 'Where shall I put it?' she asked, unfolding the paper.

174

Peter identified the drawing as a copy of his talisman, the diagram of the *Andre Norton.*

'Good thinking, Maree. Over there, right across from the bed. Stick it over that stupid print. Did you bring tape?'

She nodded, bringing the roll out of the other pocket. 'I knew you'd need this to help you get well,' she told Peter.

Alerted by their voices, Lance entered the patient's room and helped her stick it up.

'You're here early, Dorotea,' he said, finishing that task.

'You didn't think I had much choice, did you?' Dorotea said drily, indicating Amariyah.

The girl settled herself on the chair at the foot of Peter's bed and said not another word, except 'thank you' when she was offered her slice of cake.

The staff of Henry Hudson Hospital began to remark on the various notable people who came to visit the young multiple-fracture case on the thirty-sixth floor of the medical ziggurat. Rhyssa, who came daily, was identified by one of the empaths in the hospital as the head of the Eastern Para-psychic Centre. The fact that there were LEO guards posted in the waiting room on Peter's hall was soon common gossip. The floor nurses mentioned that he was a nice young man, not at all demanding, unfailingly polite, cute in a 'young' way and very personable. One oddity, though, was that he had not been prescribed pain medication, despite having six fractures and severe contusions. Everyone loved a mystery, which spiced up dull and repetitive duties no end. And he had such visitors! LEO Commissioner Boris Roznine was recognized. He arrived with his twin brother, Sascha, and Sascha's exotic-looking young wife, Tirla. She and her husband were in every day. Jerhattan Mayor Teresa Aiello paid several short visits. But when General John Greene, on whom one of the radiologists had had a crush since he had survived his crash as a famous etop pilot, arrived with his wife, the Senator, in the company of Admiral Dirk Coetzer, Peter Reidinger was established as a 'celebrity'. Their colleagues tried to find out why a nineteen-year-old boy attracted such distinguished guests, and quizzed the

175

floor nurses. Naturally, every ambulatory patient who could found some business on the thirty-sixth floor, welcoming the diversion.

A spry older silver-haired woman and a pretty black-haired girl visited every day with flowers and home-made cakes and cookies, but they weren't relatives nor were they recognizable personages. His grandmother and perhaps his sister, though the patient bore no resemblance to either.

Of course, the circumstances of the disgraceful accident were public knowledge. An entire chapter of a fraternal organization was charged with drunk and disorderly conduct, as well as causing grievous bodily harm during a fracas in one of the uptown restaurants. The LEO guard made certain that no known member of the media dallied on the floor to pester the victim. Nevertheless, Peter's amiability was sorely stretched by casual visits from fellow patients and staff.

'I don't mind, really,' Peter told Rhyssa on the morning of his sixth day in hospital, 'but I can't even change my damned bag unless I lock the door. And then they pound on it, asking if I'm all right.'

'At least I was able to get the vid-cam turned off so you *can* be private.' She pointed to the wall brackets, where a security camera had been located.

'Look, Rhys, can't you get it through their heads that I'm OK? That I can leave here?'

'Not until those breaks begin to mend, Peter,' Rhyssa said firmly to end that argument.

'Do I have to stay in this damned bed all the time?'

'It really is wiser, Peter. You may not feel anything, but the least little jar might displace those bones. You've seen the scan report. You know how many fractures you have. Give them a chance. I'll spring you from here,' and she smiled winningly, 'as soon as possible. There's no reason why you can't stay at Dorotea's, you know.'

'So this is my vacation for the year?' He 'ported his right arm up, cast and all, gesturing around the room.

'Don't do that to me, Peter,' Rhyssa said, hand on her chest in alarm at his movement. 'And no, this is sick leave.

Which I don't think you've claimed ever since you came to the Centre. Where would you like to go to convalesce? Down to Florida . . . lie in the sun, swim in the sea?'

'I just want to get out of here,' he repeated, as near to sulky as Peter ever got, shaking his head from side to side on the pillows. 'And I'd rather be on Padrugoi than Florida,' he added.

Johnny! Johnny! Please wake up, Johnny. Peter's urgent voice roused the General.

'Huh? What?'

Johnny, it's Peter. Wake up!

Johnny tried to focus his eyes on the digital clock on the bedside table. *For God's sake, d'you know the time?*

She's giving me a bath.

Who's giving you a bath? Johnny gave the clock a second look. Yes, it was three-thirty in the morning.

The nurse.

Which one? Johnny said, suddenly quite alert and grinning.

Does it matter which one? Peter's voice sounded desperate. *I had a bath this morning!*

If you don't want a bath, or anything else, dump her in the corridor with the bathwater, lock the door and let me get back to sleep.

He settled the covers over his shoulders and snuggled up to his wife's warm body. He wondered if it was the red-headed nurse who was trying to seduce the kid.

As far as Johnny knew, Peter followed his advice, but he certainly never referred to Peter's three-thirty a.m. call for advice. During his morning visit the next day, he avoided eye contact. He did notice that Peter's face was flushed when he entered. So Johnny became all business. He'd brought with him some of the elements that were waiting to be transported, one way or another, to the Moon Base.

'I know this accident has put us all off schedule, Pete,' Johnny said, pulling a chair closer to the bed. 'And it's going to affect their perception of you.'

'Why? I didn't *have* an accident, it happened *to* me.'

'I know, I know, Pete. But you're going to have to convalesce and pass their physical before you'll be allowed back up to the Station.'

At the flow of indignant curses Peter let out, Johnny realized that one facet of his education had been remarkably enhanced during his Station employment.

'Where'd you learn all that?' asked the General.

'Oh, the grunts are colourful.'

'Just don't let Rhyssa or Dorotea hear that kind of language, or my name'll be mud.'

'I'm not stupid,' Peter said sharply.

'Never thought you were, Pete. Well, to the matter at hand. Dirk's on our side,' Johnny said, passing sheets over that Peter 'held' in front of him. 'Especially after I showed him the bollard thrust. I've been saving that one for a propitious moment. But we've now got to overcome the reaction to your broken bones.'

'It's not my bones that teleport,' Peter said in an angry, sullen tone. He *hated* hospitals. He *hated* nurses – especially after last night's incident. He *had* dumped the bathwater on her after he had kinetically ejected her from his room. Bet she hadn't known he could do *that*! But the incident had upset him a great deal. She'd thought he was helpless. Everyone thought he was helpless: built like one of those beanpoles in Amariyah's vegetable garden. No one knew what he could *really* do if he set his mind to it. Even himself! Then he caught Johnny's blink of surprise, and he tried to suppress his anger and deep frustration.

On his part, Johnny had never heard that tone from him. Peter was invariably good-humoured and willing. He wondered if he should have responded differently to that early-morning conversation. He shot a sideways glance at his profile. Pete wasn't bad-looking, in a young sort of way. He had the sort of features that would age well. And right now, he'd have an especial appeal that could easily rouse feminine lust. Or was it the 'mothering' instinct that Pete awakened?

'We always bill you as the mind-over-matter kid,

178

skeleteam,' Johnny said in a careless drawl. 'So let's use that strength to our advantage. Now the design of these babies,' and he indicated the glossies of the grossly clumsy freighters that Peter was examining. 'Originally, we were shoving projectiles, especially devised to break free of gravity and penetrate an atmosphere. These,' and he flicked one with his finger that was a collection of diversely shaped objects secured to a framework, 'wouldn't last in gravity, but should be easy to manoeuvre in space.'

Peter moved that one out of the hovering pack and examined it closely. He gave a little snort and glanced down at the manifest, noting its dimensions and mass.

'We shifted heavier stuff than this from Earth to Padrugoi,' Peter responded, slightly indignant. 'If nothing's fallen off it before now, it won't in a 'portation.'

'I figured that out myself,' Johnny said caustically. 'I know, you know, Lance knows, Dirk knows. No one – except Rhyssa – thought you could land a shuttle in a monsoon at Dhaka. You did. Only a few folks thought you could shift heavy drones from surface to Station, too. We'll just have to shift something like these – the pick-up-sticks' and he added the picture of a massive bundle of plasteel girders to those orbiting Peter's face, '– to convince their plodding earth-bound minds.'

Peter made a face. 'They're not that massive.'

'Neither were the chips you sent to Lance,' Johnny said.

Peter shot him a glance. 'These are not that light,' and quickly he broke eye contact, flushing again.

'It's still a matter of mathematics, Pete,' Johnny reminded him. 'And you don't have to cope with gravity. Just a slow easy thrust . . . sending the load on its way.'

Peter's expression altered from outright denial to thoughtful consideration.

'Look, Pete, you keep telling me that all you need is a place to stand. Right?' And when Peter hesitated, Johnny went on. 'So you stand on Padrugoi and 'port to First Base. You'd have all that power available, and that's megawatts more than you had for the monsoon caper. Even more than in Florida, until I made them upgrade the power system.'

179

Johnny's lips twitched, remembering just how quickly he'd been able to get funding for additional power once Barchenka started seeing the supply shuttles homing in. The bitch had been good for something.

'But that's still a lot of mass to shift!'

'OK, so we shift mass.'

'We?' Peter caught him up on the use of that pronoun with an ironic grin.

'Yeah, yeah, this time I'd be in the 'port, I promise you,' and Johnny crossed his heart. 'But I proved to you that you could shift something all the way to the moon, didn't I? So, we build on that. We use windows when the moon's at perigee, in respect to the Station.'

'That only cuts it down about fifty thousand klicks.' Peter was still sceptical.

'Every bit helps,' Johnny blithely reminded him. 'Or,' and he pretended to submit a second option, 'we could send lighter components. Reassembly's an option, you know. First Base has the technicians.'

'Is Lance back up there?'

'No, but he could be,' Johnny reassured him. 'We could push and Lance could catch. No matter how little or how much we send on its way, First Base is that much farther ahead. Look, it's put-up or shut-up time, Pete. Fuel's just gone up in cost, and you know how much those guzzling freighters take to break loose from the Padrugoi orbit. Dirk's counting on you, too. If we don't show the Space Authority a cheaper way to continue with our expansion into this system,' and Johnny paused a beat to emphasize his next words, 'they might abandon it entirely.'

'*No!*' Peter jerked upright at that, staring in alarm at the General, his face paling at the thought.

'Well, I wouldn't like that any more than you would, Pete. We'd both be out of the jobs we love. So, look this stuff over. Get familiar with the shape and mass of them. Think hard about just easing them,' and Johnny linked his hands, emulating wings gliding through the air, 'where they need to go.' He dumped the pile of pictures onto Peter's lap. 'Hell, for that matter,' and this was an honest inspiration, 'we could get them to set up a midway station. All I'm asking you to do now is think about it.'

Peter looked over at the door and Johnny heard the click as he locked it. 'People barge in here all the time.' He activated the electrical unit that altered the bed into a sitting position. He rearranged the pictures into a semicircle in the air around him.

'Whatever suits you, Pete.' Johnny settled back down on the chair by the bed and, crossing his legs, idly swung one foot as his partner looked keenly at each picture.

There was a tentative knock on the door. 'Who is it?' Johnny called.

'Nurse Roche,' was the reply.

Peter's eyes rounded and he shook his head vigorously. *Don't let her in!*

'Come back in a few minutes, nurse,' Johnny called, without interrupting the motion of his swinging foot. He kept his expression bland.

'D'you think those girders will give us a problem?'

'Uh? Oh, no, I don't think so.' Peter glanced back at the specs, glad to concentrate on them. 'Those plasglass panels might. Odd shapes.'

He hadn't looked at more than three sheets before there was another knock on the door.

'Who is it?' Johnny called.

'Dorotea and Amariyah,' was the muffled response.

'Oh, in that case, advance and be recognized,' Johnny quipped, unlocking the door and standing up. He swept a low bow to the visitors, who were laden with flowers and Peter's favourite cookies.

Johnny didn't stay long after that, but took the sheets with him. 'Top secret, you know. Bye, now,' and he waggled his fingers at Dorotea and Amariyah.

Peter was safe enough with them. However, the nurse he passed on his way down the hall was a very attractive redhead. She had a determined look on her face as she stopped outside the room he had just left. He wondered if she were Nurse Roche.

*   *   *

Peter was released from hospital three days later, the orthopaedic specialist astounded by the rapidity with which the fractures had knitted. The ribs and the humerus fracture were almost healed.

'Most unusual, most unusual,' he said, frowning at the evidence on the scan monitor. 'Especially with the presence of some osteopenia and muscle atrophy.'

'He's good about his board exercises, swims almost daily and has been conscientious in taking supplements. He's never been sick,' Rhyssa said. 'Since he joined the Centre, that is,' she added hastily when the doctor's eyebrows rose in surprise. She was equally surprised, but wondered if such a rapid recovery was some facet of Peter's maturing talent. He was bound and determined to leave the hospital at the earliest opportunity. Not that she blamed him, knowing his antipathy to a hospital environment. With all the visitors, he wasn't getting enough rest either, but she couldn't exactly hint to the Admiral or the Mayor to suspend their kindly meant visits. 'Since there is bone knitting, can he leave now? We'll take very good care of him, I assure you. We're just as anxious that he heals completely as you are. He spent so long in the hospital after the other accident, I know he'll progress much more rapidly at home.'

'Highly irregular, Ms Lehardt. Ordinarily I would insist that he went to a convalescent home, where proper nursing care is available twenty-four hours.'

'He isn't ordinary, Doctor,' Rhyssa said gently, and the doctor flushed. 'He'll do much better with Ms Horvath, I assure you. She's an excellent nurse and very strict. She won't let him lift a finger.' She smiled at her most radiant and charmingly insistent, and with firm mental assurances.

'Medically I have no reason to keep him here,' he said, tapping the scan's evidence. 'It isn't as if he's on a course of medication.'

Rhyssa was able to 'sense' the reason the doctor wanted him to remain – he'd never had a chance to examine a parapsychic before. There had to be *something* that would show up on a Somatosensory Evoke Potential. But he doubted he could get permission to do one. This kid was too well connected to be used as a guinea pig. Reluctantly he agreed, and signed the release.

Peter was nearly bouncing off the firm hospital mattress before the doctor was out of the door.

'Hang on, will you, Peter? I've got the Centre ground vehicle in the parking lot. The hospital'll insist you go down on a grav-pad but don't . . . for Pete's sake,' and she grinned at him, 'fall out of your multiple-fracture role. OK?'

He 'ported the clothes she had brought, and she discreetly retired to the guest room while he put them on. Then she called for the transport and waited, Peter almost vibrating with anticipation. It seemed to take a long time. Then both of them became aware of voices in the hall, growing louder and louder. She opened the door to see four nurses arguing, with some heat, as to who was to escort Mr Reidinger. If Peter pulled his head back in dismay, he also came as close to levitating his body onto the grav-pad as made no difference. The other nurses followed them to the elevator, pleasantly chatting about how glad they were he was well enough to go home, how he was to take it easy and not overdo it, and how pleased they were to have been of assistance to him.

Only when the ground vehicle swung away from the exit did he seem to relax into his seat with an exaggerated sigh of relief.

'That glad to go home, Peter?' Rhyssa asked.

'You've no idea,' he said fervently.

CHAPTER SEVEN

Rhyssa was especially grateful that Peter would be at Dorotea's during his convalescence. If Dorotea didn't have an eye on him, Amariyah would. Neither would let him do anything that might jeopardize the knitting of his broken bones.

Both Rhyssa and Dorotea thought that Admiral Coetzer's brief visit, three days later, prompted Peter's demand that he be allowed to work a 'light schedule'.

'I listened,' Dorotea said belligerently. She had been conspicuously in the garden when the Admiral arrived. 'He has Peter's best interests at heart, and it's obvious Dirk Coetzer misses the boy.' Peter would always be a 'boy' to Dorotea.

'What did he say?' Rhyssa asked anxiously. It was cold standing outside, with an unseasonably brisk September wind. 'It's the Space Authority who want medical updates on Peter, not the Admiral.'

Dorotea gave a dismissive sniff, settling back to her gardening stool while they were chatting. 'Them! Coetzer didn't even mention work to Peter, or ask for a time when he'd be able to work again. He remarked on seeing the old *Andre Norton* diagrams superseded by the *Arrakis*, recommended some books. Said that his downside leave was over.

184

Never a mention that he applied for it the moment he heard from Madlyn that Peter'd been injured. Of course, I suppose he can administer the Station from wherever he is, and possibly had meetings with the Space Authority down here. I got the feeling,' Dorotea remarked thoughtfully, 'that he's having trouble with them.'

'Bureaucracy in its usual obstructive role,' Rhyssa said drolly. 'Anything else?'

'Dirk Coetzer admires our Peter very much indeed. He was very nice to Amariyah, too.'

'I'd expect that. Was she on her best behaviour?'

Dorotea chuckled. 'She quizzed the Admiral rather closely about Station hydroponics. He was startled, but he recovered well and answered her quite fully.'

'Did she mention her current ambition?'

'Of course, and Coetzer recommended the Controlled Environment Support System course at Columbia. There's one in Alaska, too.'

Rhyssa grinned. 'No matter what her rating is from Teacher, she still has to wait until she's eighteen.'

'Then the Admiral took a polite leave and departed to that fancy ground machine with the Space Authority emblem plastered all over it. The sort that glows in the dark.' She paused. 'Will you allow Peter some 'ports? He isn't sufficiently occupied right now, despite everything Maree and I can invent. Even Tirla's running out of amusing incidents of the trouble those year-old twins of hers get into.'

'I know,' Rhyssa said in a dire tone, since Mischa and Miriam had been in her house with Rachelle while Tirla visited Peter. They made Eoin and Chester look like saints in comparison.

'I'll bet you do. However did that girl survive childhood in a Linear!' And Dorotea plunged her trowel back into the dirt, digging a small cavity for the hardy pansies she was planting. 'I'd let Peter do something, Rhyssa.'

'I will. Maybe he won't ask right away.'

Peter did, the same afternoon.

'I don't *do* anything with my body.' Peter argued with Rhyssa to give him some sort of work, no matter how limited. 'I lie totally still when I 'port. You know I do. I'm sick and tired of being a convalescent.' He emphasized the word with contempt. 'I'm bored with reading and watching the news. The current daytime programmes are abysmal, and I've memorized most of those old films and replays of the good classics.'

'You should keep in touch with what else goes on in the world, Peter,' Rhyssa said. She ignored the pile of visuals that he seemed to spend a lot of time reviewing.

'I watch the newscasts. But I *need* to work!' He put a lot of feeling into that statement. 'I was safer on Padrugoi!' he added sullenly.

She accepted that remark with equanimity and yielded to the inevitable, getting Rick Hobson to replace the old generator outside Peter's room with a much heavier new one. Though Peter hadn't said it, she knew he was keen to get back to Padrugoi and further EVAs, or whatever that pile of visuals he kept examining represented. If doing some work delayed his return until his bones were fully healed, she must be grateful.

When the members of the fraternity that had disrupted his birthday celebration were brought to trial, his name – and that of the Eastern Parapsychic Centre – was not mentioned. The Space Authority's bureaucracy had so decreed it. The restaurant actually filed the complaint and appeared as plaintiff. The severe fine, awarded to the restaurant, depleted the group's treasury and effectively disbanded them. Those whom LEO had charged with drunk and disorderly conduct were sentenced to three months' community service. Not all at the dinner had over-indulged, although, as the judge remarked in delivering his verdict, they should have restrained their offending colleagues. The two who had crashed into Peter had heavier fines and were given a six-months sentence for the grievous bodily harm of an unidentified diner. One of them, a man in his middle years who had held the position of deputy chief in the fraternity, made certain allegations about what he'd do when he was free again. His threats, for that's what the listeners took

186

them to be, were duly noted down by Cass Cutler, who had attended the court hearings in her capacity as crowd-control empath.

In his third visit to Peter at Dorotea's, Johnny Greene brought Admiral Coetzer's representations to Rhyssa that Peter could actually return to Padrugoi: his welfare would be their constant concern.

'I know I'm being protective,' Rhyssa told Johnny Greene and, seeing his expression, added, 'possibly *over*protective, but the medical opinion is that we'd be smarter to let him heal both from the breaks and the trauma of the affair.'

'Trauma?' Johnny asked, eyebrows rising on his forehead. Then his expression of surprised dismay altered. 'Well, I suppose it was. I certainly "felt" how he hates hospitals. It's just that Coetzer needs him badly.' He came to an abrupt halt.

Rhyssa caught something in his voice that sounded false. *What are you up to now, Greene?*

He gave her a wide-eyed innocent stare.

And don't try that *on me. Let me guess. You and Coetzer need all that stuff Peter keeps looking at on the moon, don't you?* Rhyssa said.

'Yeah, to be honest.'

Rhyssa gave him a long, hard look. 'And you want that boy . . .'

'He's not a kid any longer, Rhyssa,' Johnny interrupted. 'And we both know I don't have Peter's heft.'

'You think he could 'port as far as the moon?' Privately Rhyssa thought Peter was capable of such a feat, but that was loyalty speaking, unsupported by proof. They still hadn't reached the limit of his thrust.

'Lance thinks so,' Johnny replied. 'I do, too.' It was not yet the time to tell her about Peter's bollard-bag special lunar delivery.

'He isn't well enough,' Rhyssa said, almost too quickly. And flushed as Johnny cocked an eyebrow at her for her vehemence.

'We'll be glad to have him back, when and as soon as he's well enough. Got any guesstimate I can placate Dirk with?'

'He's only been home two weeks. Give him another couple of months. At least.'

Johnny snorted in disgust, caught her determination not to let Peter be rushed, and nodded. 'Six weeks, maybe?' His expression beseeched her.

'Only if the scan shows those bones are completely knitted.'

'I thought they were! OK, I'll just pop in and see how he's doing.'

Peter was doing fine. When Johnny arrived, Amariyah was giving him his daily massage. Since Peter wasn't yet allowed to continue his Reeve board exercises, massage with healing oils was at least an alternative passive muscle toning. Amariyah had watched the therapist until she knew each of the movements, and then insisted that she be allowed to help. The therapist had remarked on how strong her hands were.

'All that gardening,' Peter said teasingly.

Despite his lack of physical sensation, Peter always felt better after massage. Oddly enough, Dorotea noticed that he wasn't as nervous with Amariyah as he was with the therapist, an attractive girl as well as an empath. Dorotea was also keen to have Amariyah take on a change of duty from Teacher and her garden. If she tended towards caring, that would be a good career for her and might nourish whatever Talent Amariyah had. Gardening was, in its own way, a form of nurturing.

'Well, hi there, skeleteam,' Johnny said, peering into Peter's room.

'Heard you coming,' Peter said, prone on the massage plinth, not bothering to turn his head towards the visitor. 'Any luck on getting me back up to Padrugoi?'

'Nope.' Johnny sat himself down in the specially built chair in front of Peter's worktop. Idly he swung it about on its gimbals. 'She's giving you another three weeks lounging around down here. Can't say as I blame her.' He eyed Pete's long, bony frame, shiny from the oils, a towel draped over his hips. 'If you were up there, you'd be working your butt off. Sorry, Amariyah.'

188

The girl had given him a sharp frown.

Peter chuckled. 'She doesn't want to lose her patient. Nags me all the time, she does.'

'I don't,' said Amariyah, her dark blue eyes protesting. 'Dorotea's the one who nags at you. "Eat this, have more of that. You're too skinny." ' Her mimicry of Dorotea's tone was perfect. Then she demonstrated the point, trying to pinch Peter's thin waist above the towel to show how little flesh there was. She then soothed the reddened spot.

'Are those ribs healed, Maree?' Johnny asked, noticing where she had nipped him.

'Of course,' she said. Then she stroked the other fractured places with comforting pats of her hand. 'He was scanned two days ago. He is showing progress.' With a deft flick of her arms, she flipped a long towel over Peter's prone body. 'There. That is enough for today. You have Johnny to talk to. Would you care for some refreshments?' she asked, turning solicitously to the General.

'As long as it's home-baked,' and Johnny licked his lips in anticipation. 'Don't get much of that up on Padrugoi.'

'That is not what Peter tells us,' she said as she left.

What is *the situation on Padrugoi, Johnny?*

The General grimaced with dissatisfaction. *I've gone as far as I can go, Pete. The cargo corrals are bursting the edges of their nets. For the next exciting instalment, we need you. In the new contract with SpaceShifters International, shipping costs went up eight per cent. Not only do freighters require full crews – talk about feather-bedding – the thrust to get them under way guzzles fuel. Once a freighter's up to speed, it can drift down to the moon, make a braking orbit, and use a brief burn to assume orbit. More to start back to Padrugoi. Hell, we could send down twice as much payload if we didn't have to use up so much cargo space for fuel and all that extra crew.*

An expense that you hope I'll be able to reduce?

You got it in one, Pete. That was when Johnny noticed Peter's treasured picture of the *Andre Norton* was partially obscured by the *Arrakis*, and high-resolution shots of First Base and the moonscape surrounding it. *Simulating limo flights, huh?* He swung the chair about and ran a finger down one of the glide-pattern lines, ending at the First Base field and three lonely cargo containers, their hatches open to their emptiness.

Well, it beats watching the tri-d.

Johnny grinned at Peter's sudden flush and decided that the kid was embarrassed to be caught at it. No harm really in his studying shuttle piloting, when he had little else to do while healing.

You know, Johnny added casually, adding another bone for Peter to worry while he was convalescing, *I've been doing some energy-use study on myself, like how many calories I burn when I'm lifting. Rather interesting.* He took a pencil file from his blouse pocket and set it on the worktop. *Here are Lance's study records of you, lifting this, that and everything here, there and everywhere. I think you'll notice that you're much more economical, calorifically speaking.*

Having spoken his piece, he was properly appreciative of the tea, sandwiches and little pastries which Dorotea and Amariyah brought in. They had an enjoyable conversation. When Johnny took his leave, he paused briefly.

'Oh, Station scuttlebutt has Madlyn dating Dash Sakai.'

'She is?' Peter grinned with delight. 'He noticed?'

'You might say her interest was brought to his attention,' and Johnny Greene gave them all a farewell salute.

Two months later, the Centre's chief medical consultant, Martin McNulty, and Dr Coulson, an orthopaedics specialist sent in by the Space Authority for an impartial opinion, pronounced Peter medically fit.

'In fact, if we didn't have the accident scans to compare with,' the orthopaedics man said, 'I'd wonder if they ever had been broken. There is, as I'm sure you're aware, McNulty, some osteopenia.'

'Peter takes dietary supplements against loss of bone mineralization.'

'Not as much muscle atrophy as I'd expect.'

Peter did not like the way Coulson regarded him: as an object rather than a person. He hated being discussed as if he wasn't there, as if he were nothing more than a pronoun.

'Of course, Peter regularly uses his Reeve board in exercising, has frequent deep-tissue massage, swims, and he doesn't put any strain on his skeleton,' the Centre's medic remarked, eyeing his patient. Martin McNulty was empathic with some contact telepathy to augment that ability. 'Being kinetic has some advantages, doesn't it, Pete?'

Peter nodded, his eyes darting to Coulson's incredulous expression as he looked from the accident MRI image to the one on the monitor. His professional manner did not conceal doubt from his very perceptive patient.

'Of course, there'd be less weight on those bones in space,' Martin went on.

'Padrugoi Station has gravity!'

'Yes, but still only point seven-five of Earth normal, now that the Station is in full operation. Visitors find that more comfortable, you know,' Martin replied.

'Whichever,' and Coulson flicked his fingers in dismissal of the difference. 'I have to concede that those bones are clinically whole.' He touched Peter on the shoulder, unaware that Talents, especially Peter, disliked casual physical contact. 'You can go back to work as soon as they'll have you,' he said, with a patronizing smile.

Pete, Martin said warningly when the patient shifted his body away from the orthopaedics man's touch. *He doesn't know better.*

'Thank you, Dr Coulson,' Peter said, gliding away from tactile range.

Martin deftly manoeuvred the specialist out of the treatment room. 'If you'll just sign the certificate that Pete'll have to produce for his employers, Sidney,' he said, a subtle empathy reinforcing his suggestion, 'we won't need to take up any more of your time.' He closed the door behind him, which was as well, because Peter 'ported himself back to his room, where he let out a burst of exultation.

You've been cleared? Dorotea asked from the kitchen.

Now don't worry, Tea. Dr Coulson doubted I'd ever broken anything, despite all the scans.

Really? You've healed that well?

Peter was far too elated to hear the odd tone of her voice.

191

He only knew that he could go back up to Padrugoi as soon as he could organize his departure.

Do wait until after dinner, dear, Dorotea said placidly. *I've got your favourite casserole in the oven, and Amariyah's done you an apricot pie for dessert. Besides which, you'd better speak to Rhyssa.*

Rhyssa already knows, Rhyssa and Peter replied in unison. Peter's triumphant laugh echoed down the hall to the kitchen and telepathically up to Rhyssa in her office.

Rhyssa? Peter added. *Can you tell Johnny Greene? Madlyn should be on watch, and can pass the good news along.*

Of course, Rhyssa replied with no hint of her mixed feelings. She was, of course, delighted that Peter had passed the physical, but she was also depressed that he was so eager to return to Padrugoi.

You can understand his urgency, though, can't you? Dorotea said on a tight message.

Yes, I can.

Don't sound so defeated. Why don't you and Dave come down for pie? Amariyah's crust is always flakier than mine. When are you going to be able to ship up that empath and the hydroponics specialist? Peter needs some empathic company up there.

I've held Ceara Scott back to go up with him, and Ping Yung is already on Station.

Then you'll have done your best for him once again.

Oh, I do hope so.

Of course you have, and Dorotea's tone was testily reassuring. *Though perhaps he should be doing more for himself.*

I beg your pardon?

Now don't get huffy with me, Rhyssa Owen Lehardt! Dorotea replied tartly. *One of these days he's going to get into a situation he'll have to get himself out of, you know!*

Yes, and Rhyssa's mental tone was abruptly contrite.

You can't be worried any more about those stupid threats Cass overheard in court? Dorotea went on. *As if that drunk would ever be hired onto the Station in any capacity. He*

192

wouldn't pass the age limit, much less the physical. Peter is safer on Padrugoi, doing what he's good at and loves.

Ceara Scott was a space-medicine physician, joining Padrugoi Station for several jobs: one, to do her grant experimentation on the effect of weightlessness on the bone mass of the 'casual workers' – the polite term for grunts. Another was to monitor Peter's physical condition, and the last was to discern any possible antagonism towards him, either personally or in his capacity as a teleport/telepath.

When Rhyssa announced that she had to be ready to take up her assignment on Padrugoi by ten p.m. that day, she was instantly flustered.

'I haven't got anything packed, Ms Lehardt. I mean, I knew I'd be going *soon*, but that's awful soon.'

'Ten o'clock tomorrow morning?'

'Oh, no, I mean, yes, I could probably make that, but . . .' The young woman was clearly rattled.

'Just pack what you'd need for the first few days, Ceara, and we'll see that the rest follows. Would that help?'

'Noon?' was the tremulous option suggested.

'That will be fine. Shall I send Sirikit over to give you a hand?'

'Oh, would you? Please. I'm sorry to be a nuisance.'

'Not at all, Ceara. The delay suits me fine,' Rhyssa said, and with a cheerful smile, broke the com connection.

'Putting off the inevitable?'

'You heard Ceara,' Rhyssa said, trying not to sound defensive. 'She's the delay.'

Dave grinned at her. 'When are we invited for apricot pie?'

'About seven-thirty.'

'Just us?'

'I suspect so.'

'Then why are you wringing your hands, Rhys?' Dave asked, cocking his right eyebrow at her.

'I am?' Rhyssa hastily rubbed her hands on her pant legs. She stood up. 'I think I will actually be relieved to have him back on Padrugoi.'

193

'Look, Rhys,' and he put his arms about her waist, drawing her to him, 'the drunk and disorderly guys haven't finished their term of community service and, double-banded as they are by LEO, there's no way they could get into the Centre here. And there's even less chance of one getting onto Padrugoi.'

'You saw the latest of their online threats.'

'And,' he said, hugging her, 'I saw Boris's report of how quickly the pair were arrested. The Faithful Brotherhood of the whatever they called their little coven are now all tagged, and their associations identified as well. You *know* that.'

She sighed. 'I know it. Do they?'

'Pete'll be safe for the next four weeks. You can always suggest he take his free week at Johnny's.' When he felt her stiffen slightly: 'OK, so that's the most obvious alternative. At Lance's, then, or Kayankira's; at your parents' place in Montana.'

'Dorotea and Amariyah would never forgive me.'

'At Tirla's then. *No one* could ask for better security than that. It wouldn't arouse Peter's suspicions, unless you broadcast them. Dorotea and Amariyah can go there. You know Maree is great with Tirla's hypertwins.'

Rhyssa gave her husband a reproachful look.

'Well, they're a handful,' Dave said.

'Our kids aren't?'

'We had them one at a time and got used to 'em.'

'Which reminds me, I promised to read Eoin a story. Did I tell you I actually got reproductions of the *Dr Seuss* books?'

'Several times.' He kissed her and let her go. He didn't have an ounce of psychic ability, but he'd been reading her body language – with great appreciation – for six years. He might not know exactly *what* was worrying his wife, but he knew when she was upset and could comfort her.

Peter Reidinger had been all set to dislike Dr Ceara Scott on sight, when he found out from Rhyssa that the space-medicine specialist had been unable to leave the moment he had clearance. She arrived at the Jerhattan telepad in a ground vehicle filled with family and three carrying cases. She'd taken another twelve hours to pack that *little*?

Some people organize their packing, Rhyssa reminded him. She had said her goodbye the previous evening; Dorotea, affectionately but not fussily ten minutes ago. It had been Amariyah who had clung to him, her fingers patting each one of the old fractures as if reassuring herself of his health. Peter hated it when Amariyah cried, the silent tears streaming down her face.

'No dear,' Dorotea had said firmly. 'Give Peter a happy face.'

An obedient grimace sent the tears to one side of the nine-year-old face.

'See? I'm smiling,' Amariyah said, spoiling it with a gulping sob.

'I promise, Maree,' Peter said, leaning down to rest his cheek against her wet face, 'I'll see if you can come up on a visitor's pass. You and Dorotea.'

'Don't include me,' Dorotea said, urgently waving away the offer.

'Well, you and Ted, too, so you can both see the hydroponic gardens.'

'The gardens? I could see them?' The child brightened.

'Didn't I promise?'

Go now, Peter, Dorotea said, lightly putting her hands on Amariyah's shoulders and drawing her away from Peter.

Peter 'ported himself to the Jerhattan telepad and waited. He hoped that Amariyah would stop crying.

She's accessed this morning's Teacher, Peter. Don't worry about her, Dorotea said.

I'm not worrying about her.

Hmmm. Yes, of course not. Bye.

Peter settled his one duffel bag behind the passenger seats and waited. He checked the personnel carrier. He glided over to the generators and inspected them. He waited. Shading his eyes, he saw a ground car on the perimeter road. He flicked out his mind. He had had no contact with this Ceara Scott, so he doubted that he could 'path to see if she was in it. He did, to his surprise, feel anxiety, nervousness,

195

fear and keen anticipation. Rhyssa had told him Ceara Scott was a latent empath, her talent revealed when she was interning. Dr Scott had been advised that Peter could answer any additional questions she might have on her empathy while she did her year's tour on Padrugoi. He waited more patiently.

When he identified her as the second person to emerge from the crowded vehicle, he was agreeably surprised. She had the most glorious red hair, curling vigorously around her head. She also had the almost translucent skin that often went with such colouring, and her eyes, anxiously seeking his, were an amazing shade of blue. He stared.

Manners, Peter, manners! Dorotea rebuked him.

'Dr Scott?' he began, making sure he looked as if he were walking. During his convalescence he had also tried to improve his 'walking'. Sometimes he could almost feel the surface beneath his feet. 'Tell me what you're bringing with you, and I'll store it for you,' he said, extending his hand. He even managed to curl his fingers about her knuckles. He savoured her essence, though the contact was very short since she was full of repentant haste.

'Mr Reidinger, thanks, but Stu will put my packs in,' she said, indicating the young man, also a redhead, but bearing no facial resemblance to her.

The dark-haired woman who had emerged first was now directing Stu, with a maternal air, to hurry and be sure to get them all in.

'My mother,' Ceara Scott said. 'I was told this wasn't a secured base, so they insisted on coming. My father, my sister Terry, my sister Fiona and her husband, Dr Richard Jude,' she went on, introducing all the passengers.

'No, it's not exactly a secured base,' Peter said. No other hands were offered him, so Ceara must have warned them.

Her brother stowed the three bags, of which only one was very large. Ceara stood looking around.

'Isn't the pilot here?' she asked.

'I'm the pilot,' Peter said, lifting one hand to his chest and smiling confidently.

'Oh, how silly of me,' Ceara said, flushing. 'Mr Reidinger's the telekinetic I was telling you about, Dad.'

The elder Scott nodded. 'Then kiss me a hug, girl, and let's not delay him any longer.'

Kissing and hugging included every one of her party, but as soon as the farewells were done, she walked briskly to the carrier. Peter gestured for her to take a front seat and she settled herself.

'If you'll all stand back,' and Peter pointed to the side of the telepad that was farthest from the generators. 'Nice to meet you,' he added as he watched them scatter hurriedly out of the way.

'I didn't delay you too much, did I, Mr Reidinger?'

'It's just gone noon,' Peter said, 'and I'm Peter, not "Mr" anything, Ceara.'

'Thank you,' she said. 'How long does it take to get to Padrugoi?'

Peter leaned lightly into the generators. 'Not very long,' he replied, unable to resist grinning. The field vanished and they were on the telepad in Padrugoi's transit bay, a cleaning gang just beyond the telepad circle, goggling at the suddenly materializing personnel shell.

'Ohhhhh,' her gasp was a startled, indrawn breath. For a long moment, eyes wide, mouth slightly ajar, she stared out of the forward window at the abruptly altered view. 'Ohhh,' she said again. Closing her mouth, her very blue eyes still wide, she turned to him. ' "Not very long", huh? More like instantaneous, wasn't it, Peter?'

'That's kinetics for you,' he said, opening the hatch and lifting himself out. He hadn't quite got the hang of doing that as a normal person would. She didn't seem to notice as she emerged.

'Oh!' she said, immediately aware of the lower station gravity.

'You'll get used to it quickly,' Peter said.

Just then the Station alarm went off.

Pete? said Johnny, his tone urgent. *Get up here! Fast! Some goddamn dink of a freighter captain just sliced through a very full cargo net, and containers are popping out of it like pus out of a wound. Some are headed towards the wheel. We need your ass up here.*

The ensign who had been awaiting Peter and Dr Scott didn't know what to do with the alarm wailing.

'Escort Dr Scott to the sick bay, Mr Ahh—' Peter picked the man's name out of his head, 'Patterson, and then proceed to your duty station. Nothing to be alarmed about, Ceara. Safety drill sort of thing,' he added mendaciously. 'Excuse me.'

And he 'ported himself to the CIC, where everyone was scrambling to their stations. The main screen had been divided into multiple windows: the freighter with its empty cargo rack tangled with the cargo net; the stream of containers let loose from the corral; the gigs and tugs speeding to head off those in a trajectory towards the wheel of the Station; and the space-suited workers jetting to converge on the loose objects.

'Neatly timed, Pete,' Admiral Coetzer said, arriving from his ready room. 'Linke, have we identified the freighter? Who's the Captain? And I want him in here as soon as he gets his damned vessel out of the net and moored properly! Find out who his employer is, and about getting his contract and his licence revoked. Portmaster Honeybald is apoplectic. Who's EV watch officer? Who do we have out there that can assume command and bring order to that chaos? Pete,' and Coetzer motioned to the upper left-hand screen, 'can you stop that one from tumbling? It looks to be on a collision course.'

'Yes, sir,' Peter said. He immediately repositioned himself at the engineer's station manned by Lieutenant Junior Grade Spencer Ci. Peter hadn't worked with him before. Not that he needed gestalt to tip the upper facet of the cube the Admiral had pointed to. He pressed against it, perceptibly slowing its end-over-end motion and bringing it to a halt in space, relative to the wheel.

Good catch, Johnny Greene said, striding into the CIC. 'Where do you want me, Admiral?'

'Screen three, Johnny. See what you can do with *that* mess.' The Station generators picked up revolutions as the General tapped their power.

'Sir, Bergkamp here, I've got a full unit suited up and cycling through the lock.'

'Good. Proceed to the wheel and deflect any incoming. Peter, do us a mean favour and detach that fragging freighter from the net and put it where it belongs. The dolt who's driving it doesn't know his ass from his elbow.' While the Admiral's suggestion was facetiously delivered, it was no less the appropriate measure to take. To judge by the erratic use of his manoeuvring thrusters, the Captain was only making matters worse by pushing the rest of the captives hard against the far side of the net that bulged ominously. Without conscious thought, Peter leaned into the Station's power and turned off the vessel's thruster rockets, picked it out of the net and deposited it at the nearest empty gate in the commercial mooring section. Pieces of the cables it had severed or tangled with floated in reaction in space. The CPO in charge of the nearest crew sent men to secure those before they constituted an additional hazard. Almost as an afterthought, Peter secured the freighter to the wharf and connected the accordion airlock to its main hatch.

Well done, Pete! Johnny exclaimed.

'Thank you very much, Mr Reidinger,' the Admiral said with great aplomb, slapping his armrest in one-handed applause. Cheers from the other officers echoed Coetzer's sentiment. 'Now, let's round up those strays, patch that net.'

Lift that barge, tote that bale, the irrepressible General Greene sang inaccurately.

'And restore chaos to confusion.' Oblivious of the 'path, the Admiral finished his command. Peter choked on suppressed laughter.

Don't do that to me, Johnny, he said.

Relief, lad, sheer relief, Greene replied. *Now help me get that inward-bound quartet of dome arcs. Their shape makes their trajectory erratic.*

Where shall we put them?

Just stop 'em. Here comes the cavalry, and Johnny pointed to the lower left-hand screen where EMU-clad figures were jetting into view.

'Bergkamp, get your men on those dome arcs. General, are you available?'

'On the mark, Admiral,' Johnny replied.

'Mr Sakai, I want a secure link to Mr Honeybald at the Portmaster's office,' the Admiral went on, handling other aspects of the emergency.

Peter, and the unmistakable voice of Madlyn Luvaro nearly deafened him, *I have three tumblers outward-bound from the net, sou'-sou'-east at five thousand kps relative to the Station.*

I'll get 'em. Where do you want them?

The 822 looks to be the nearest gig. It's not all that far from where they spun off. They're panicking. Maybe Dash hasn't heard them, with so much confusion on the bands.

Peter found the grunts easily enough by opening his mind, augmenting his telepathic range with gestalt from the generators, just as the communications officer reported their predicament.

'I have them, Lieutenant Sakai,' Peter said into the com-unit.

'You do?' Dash Sakai swung his chair round towards the engineering station in surprise.

'Madlyn,' Peter said in explanation.

'Oh. Very good. Thank you, Reidinger. They didn't think we'd see them with so much else going on.'

A simple case of 'quis custodiet', Madlyn said smugly.

To himself, Peter thought her quote inappropriate, but her watchfulness was not.

The pilot of the gig to which Peter shifted the three grunts acknowledged their proximity and gave them a tow back to the Station.

'Admiral Coetzer, I have the Captain of the CCD online demanding to know who turned off his manoeuvring engines and who . . .' and Sakai paused.

'Let me have it, Lieutenant,' the Admiral said with a malicious smile.

'The hell endangered his crew with that – I'd rather not repeat that, sir – precipitous mooring?'

'Inform the Captain of the CCD that he is to be in my

office with his log file at sixteen-hundred hours. Inform Mr Honeybald that the crew is not allowed shore leave, and that the Captain is not to be admitted back on board without direct orders from me.'

The emergency lasted two hours, of which only the first three-quarters were critical: the rest were spent mending the broken net cables and herding the captured cargo back into confinement.

Peter did not admit to anyone how tired he was from that spate of concentrated activity. He was unexpectedly relieved when the Admiral stood the watch down from the scramble. Coetzer gave a 'well done' and a special nod of thanks to Peter and Johnny before he left the CIC for his office. Peter was surprised to see others reacting to the all-clear. Temuri Bergkamp sat back from the engineering panels, dramatically mopping his sweaty forehead.

'Never appreciated what you guys can really do,' he said. 'I know you shift cargo up here, but bouncing a freighter with its thrusters on is something else again.'

'I turned the thrusters off first, and I thought the Admiral meant what he said,' Peter replied.

'He did,' Temuri replied feelingly. 'I just don't think he thought you could do it that fast.'

'No problem with the generators the Station has,' Peter said, feeling his face flush at the praise.

'Pete loves generators, Bergkamp,' Johnny said with a wide smile. 'The bigger the better. He can do anything with the right amount of power . . . and a place to stand.'

There are moments, General, when you're a pain in the ass, Peter remarked.

If anything, the General's smile got wider.

Sorry, Pete. Let's blow this joint. 'Thanks for your help, Bergkamp. C'mon, Pete, I know you didn't get a chance to settle in.' *And I won't mention the beautiful redhead you brought up with you.*

You just did.

Rank has some privileges. I'm grabbing some lunch. What about you?

I need to unpack.

Catch ya later. Johnny Greene turned in the other direction and Peter gratefully went to his quarters. He'd left his bag in the personnel carrier, and now 'ported it up to his cabin. He would have to apologize to Dr Scott for leaving her in the abrupt way he had. Maybe they would have explained it all to her when she reached the sick bay. Thinking of apologies reminded him that his remarks to the General had been uncalled for, even if Johnny had not apparently taken offence. But Peter was annoyed with himself for snapping like that.

Peter changed his waste bag and showered, closing his eyes as he levered shampoo to his head. He stood under the fine air-driven hard spray until he no longer felt the sting of soap on his sweaty face. The warm air circulated through the shower enclosure and died away as the cubicle's sensors ceased registering moisture to be recycled.

Peter lay down on the bunk, lifting the light cover over his bare body.

'I'll just close my eyes,' he murmured. He did, and was startled by the strident buzz of the intercom.

'The Admiral's compliments, Mr Reidinger,' said a voice he recognized as Yeoman Nicola Nizukami, 'and would you kindly join him for dinner at twenty-one-thirty hours?'

Peter saw that he had an hour to get dressed.

'Yes, certainly, Ms Nizukami. Delighted.'

He must have slept nearly three hours. He'd have to get fit. There was a Reeve board up here for him to use, and he could rig the hydrotherapy bath for swimming against a current. He'd start tomorrow morning. That is, if his schedule allowed.

CHAPTER EIGHT

'Asked their permission?' Incredulity and outrage coloured Johnny Greene's voice as Peter Reidinger arrived at the Admiral's lounge, promptly at 2130 hours. 'Asked their permission to *move* the freighter?'

'Or so the company spokesman informed me,' the Admiral said, his tone amused.

'Then that Captain should have asked our permission for tangling in our net,' Johnny said.

'The net was not where it was supposed to be,' Dirk replied in the manner of someone reporting conversation. 'Good evening, Pete. Barney, see what Mr Reidinger wants to drink.'

'Lit up like a Christmas tree,' Johnny went on, 'dense enough to be clearly visible on the antiquated screens those tubs use, and three klicks from where he should have been to reach the mooring Honeybald assigned him. That Captain is suffering from a serious visual malfunction.' Then as an afterthought, 'Or he wasn't even on the bridge.'

'How did you know?' Dirk said, grinning. 'And he's Captain no longer.'

'Good!' Johnny took a swig of his drink like a toast to

that dismissal. 'We've got enough problems up here without someone inventing more. Freighting's a boring job. I wouldn't want it. But that,' and he pointed his finger at the Admiral, 'doesn't mean I would be a damned fool.'

'Ah, Dr Scott,' the Admiral said, leaving Johnny to greet another guest. 'Hope that little flap on your arrival didn't give you a false impression of our hospitality.'

'Of course not. I was impressed by the way you all handled the emergency. Good evening, Peter,' she added, nodding to him.

Ceara Scott was certainly not flustered this evening. She wore a burgundy silk suit that was a stunning contrast to her upswept red hair, and fitted her extremely well. She certainly didn't look like any medical person he'd ever encountered.

'Admiral?' Johnny's tone chided Coetzer to introduce him and, grinning, Dirk did so.

'A pleasure to meet you, Dr Scott,' the General said, with a wide grin and appreciative glances.

'So you are the famous John Greene,' she said. 'I was warned about you.'

'You were?' Johnny pretended surprised dismay. 'Who would cast aspersions on my innocent head?'

'My uncle, Jerry Scott, was in your etop squadron.'

'Rosie Scott?' Johnny's surprise was no longer pretend. 'You're Rosie's niece?'

She nodded and sighed. 'Rosie!' she added, with a grimace. 'He hated that nickname.'

'Then he shouldn't have been saddled with that shade of red hair,' Johnny replied. 'Damned good etop, though,' he said in an aside to Dirk.

Dash Sakai and Madlyn Luvaro, who looked elegant in a rich emerald green, Pota Chatham and Shandin Ross arrived in a group, and that completed the Admiral's table.

Peter sat across from Ceara Scott and tried not to stare at her or worry if she was noticing him. He felt unaccountably awkward with knife and fork. He also felt awkward in answering her questions, especially when the Admiral, Johnny, Madlyn and Dash informed her of his particular part in coping with the emergency. She had watched the space drama from the sick bay.

'Didn't put you off a space walk, did it?' Shandin Ross asked.

'If anything, I was reassured,' she replied, her glance flicking from Peter to Johnny.

'Just let us kinetics know when you're ready to try, and we'll stand by,' Johnny said.

'A space walk is not obligatory, you know,' Madlyn said. 'I'm one of those who can't "hack the black", as they say up here.' She gave a little shudder.

'I'd like to try, but only after I've got my experiments started,' Ceara Scott replied.

Johnny asked her what area of space medicine she specialized in.

'It's esoteric, and I'd bore you all stiff with the process, but I'd be happy to show you my lab work, if you're interested.' She smiled at Johnny's startled reaction to her invitation and turned to the Admiral. 'You must be very proud of the facilities you have up here. So much has already been done. Even under Ludmilla Barchenka.'

'Yes, so I understand,' the Admiral replied at his blandest. Ceara blushed.

Peter caught her embarrassed thought that possibly the name of the previous Station Commander revived unpleasant memories.

Madlyn Luvaro reassured her, and then the entrée was served and everyone's attention was turned to the excellent roast. It was, all told, a very pleasant evening and, towards the end of it, Peter relaxed sufficiently to enjoy it as much as the others did.

Three days later, he awoke to see a message flashing on the monitor. It was from the Admiral's office, and indicated that a personnel carrier had to be 'ported to Padrugoi at 0845. He must have been sleeping very soundly to miss the bleep of incoming mail.

Johnny?

Join me for breakfast. His mental tone indicated he did not wish to engage in further discussion at that moment. Like many people, he was more sociable after several cups of coffee. *We got time.*

Not much, Peter thought, seeing the screen clock registering 0815.

Why didn't you wake me?

I had enough trouble waking me. *I'd've thought the bleep would have rise-and-shined you.*

When Peter reached the officers' mess, Johnny was already seated at a corner table in an almost empty room. The steward bustled over to settle the new arrival, promptly serving the herbal tea that Peter preferred. The General went on getting coffee inside him and nodded a welcome.

I needed that, Johnny said, with a sigh of repletion as he finished the cup and beckoned the steward for a refill.

What's the matter? Peter asked.

You're not prescient?

You're procrastinating.

Well, I'll give you time to have some of that swill of yours before I totally ruin your breakfast, Johnny replied with a wry grin.

It's that bad?

Ah. Depends on how you look at it, Johnny said with the sort of shrug that Peter had learned to associate with bad news.

Who's after our hides for saving the Station three days ago?

Johnny rolled his eyes and, thanking the attentive steward with a wave, blew on the surface of the hot beverage.

The Space Authority is alarmed by the rate at which we acquit our duties.

They're the ones coming up? Why? Monday was no fault of the Station's.

Johnny leaned back, crooking one arm over the back of the chair. *In an odd way, it is. We're too damned quick and efficient. There are also too many 'dangerously' full cargo nets, what they hold not yet delivered to their ultimate destination. Also the Mercantile Union demands a full investigation of ex-Captain Maggert's unfortunate encounter with the net.* Johnny planted one thumb on his chest and reversed it towards Peter. *And/or us.*

Was someone on the CCD hurt after all?

Bruises. They should have been strapped in anyhow, since they were technically still in flight.

But it was Maggert's fault. The log proves it.

Of course it does, Johnny said with a snort. *The Union's just posturing because the freight captains want a rise in fees. Union claims that Padrugoi does not employ enough of their members because the surface-to-station run is unavailable.*

It hasn't been available for five years.

True, and the Union was more than happy to stop having to deal with Barchenka. Admiral Coetzer is a different kettle of fish. On the other hand, the Space Authority says the Station is not making expeditious use of available shipping to supply First Base and its construction timetable.

But the SA is the one complaining about fuel costs. The turnover would be faster if the freighters could use longer burns. Peter stopped because they both knew the answer to that. Longer burns took more fuel.

Johnny nodded, his eyes twinkling. 'You got it, Pete. We're caught either side of that barrel. Unless, of course . . .'

You want us to heave stuff to First Base.

Now did I say that? Johnny demanded, sipping his coffee and raising his curved eyebrows up his forehead.

No, but it's the only way to clear that much of a backlog, and you know it. Peter tried not to sound either alarmed, which he was, or angry, which was another way of being alarmed. He should have known where all this was leading. He should have known not to fall into Johnny's little trap in Adelaide with the chips Lance 'had so urgently needed'. He'd wondered when Johnny was going to bring the bollard-bag special-delivery 'port out in the open.

The Union will be seriously annoyed, Peter said with a sigh.

There will still be plenty of things for SpaceShifters; junk I sure as hell don't want to bust my gut sending, with or without your help. We gotta lay down some rules, you know, Johnny said.

'You ever tell anyone about Adelaide?' he asked softly, aloud. *Not even Dirk Coetzer?*

'No, kid, I haven't. Wasn't the right time.'

'It is now.'

Johnny had the grace to nod, grimacing at the necessity.

Well, Dirk may suspect something. Our pet Admiral has ambitions. We're both essential to them. Then Johnny leaned forward across the table, speaking softly, although there was no one else in the mess, bar the steward who was working in the serving alcove. 'Anyway, it's much too soon after those fractures for you to be shoving stuff, Pete, but if we could just get one light unit to First Base, it would solve a lot of problems.'

'I like the "we".'

'Now, kid, at Adelaide I wanted most to prove your range to *you*,' he said, cocking his finger at Peter.

Peter caught the note in the General's voice. 'And now to them. Right?'

'You got it in one.'

While Peter doubted himself, it irked him immensely that the Space Authority, which already owed a great deal to his and Johnny's telekinetic abilities, had hesitations.

'Have they asked if I – we – could?'

'That's one of the reasons they're here today, unless I miss my guess.' He paused. 'But I know that crowd. What with fuel prices going sky-high,' and he made a face at using that phrase, 'the SA is not at all pleased at the hike in expenses. You and me are their best bet for completing the additions at First Base. And quite likely the Mars project.'

'The moon today and Mars tomorrow?' Peter gawked. 'They don't want much, do they?'

'You might get a reprieve on Mars until after First Base is fully operational.'

Peter stared at Johnny, because the General's tone suggested that this was within the realms of possibility.

'You're not kidding, are you?'

Johnny shook his head solemnly and then started to grin. 'Pete, I have every confidence in you.'

'What if?'

208

'What if be damned, Reidinger. You'll never know until you reach the limits of your envelope,' Johnny said in a flat, serious tone. 'They once said that we'd never break the sound barrier, that we'd never land on the moon, that we'd never find other habitable worlds in this galaxy. For that matter, the abilities we have were discredited and scorned until Henry Darrow presented "scientific proof".'

'Now wait a minute, General Greene.' Peter lifted his hand, holding out his fingers in an urgent 'stop' motion.

'Jesus, look at the time.' Gulping down the last of his coffee, Johnny Greene rose to his feet. 'We'd better get to CIC and 'port 'em up or they'll be late for this meeting they want. Let's 'port to the corridor outside. We haven't the excuse of an emergency today.'

Johnny glanced over his shoulder to check if the steward was still out of sight, and then nodded 'go'.

They went, and then strode purposefully into the CIC facility. The XO gave them a cheerful greeting. 'Admiral's got a side party waiting to welcome our guests, gentlemen.'

'Who-all's due up?' Johnny asked, pausing by Linke Bevan.

'Secretary of Space Abubakar himself, his chief financial officer, Alicia Taddesse, Mai Leitao.'

'Oh, the bottom-liners,' Johnny said with a displeased twitch of his lips. 'Bean counters.'

'A senior officer, Georg Fraga. That's all.'

'That's enough. C'mon, Pete. Let's haul their asses up here.'

Are those people difficult?

I forget that you haven't had to deal with the Space Authority Administration before. 'Pota Chatham's scheduled, isn't she?'

'As you requested, General.'

'Morning, Bergkamp,' the General said aloud as they reached the engineering station. 'Are the generators online for our use?'

'Aye, sir, they are,' Temuri Bergkamp replied formally, and gestured for the two kinetics to help themselves.

209

'General Greene,' said Dash Sakai from his com work-station, 'I have a request from Jerhattan to lift the personnel carrier whenever you're ready.'

Johnny shot a glance at the time icon that read 0843 and slipped into 0844 as they watched. Johnny nodded his head and Peter joined him to make the lift. Eyes twinkling, Johnny made a gesture at Dash Sakai, asking him to open the monitor at the landing bay. As the scene lit up, they all heard the bosun's whistle announcing the arrival on board of distinguished guests.

'Thanks, Bergkamp. C'mon, Pete. I need more coffee,' Johnny said, acknowledging the others on the watch as the two kinetics made their way out of CIC.

'Coffee, pu-lease, Barney,' Johnny said as he opened the door into the conference room where the meeting would take place.

'Aye, sir. Mr Reidinger, tea for you?'

'Please.'

Johnny paused by the conference table, looking around it. 'We got stalls today.' He pointed to the nameplates distributed in a semicircle facing the wide rectangular pro-grammable screen taking up the far wall. 'Ah, and whaddaya wanna bet we'll be in direct contact with Colonel Hiroga Watari at First Base?'

'You didn't mention him,' Peter said. He had already been introduced to the AirForce commander of the Moon Base on one of his infrequent downside trips. The Colonel had given Peter a searching scrutiny and dismissed him. Though Peter was somewhat accustomed to such a reaction to his skinny, unprepossessing teenage appearance, the Colonel's scathing regard had rankled, the encounter leaving behind it an offensive taint. Whether the Colonel was aware of it or not, he exuded negative empathy. Or maybe it was just to nonentities like Peter Reidinger.

Yeoman Nicola Nizukami stepped forward from the other end of the room.

'Colonel Watari is on the schedule, General.'

Peter was surprised at her tone; maybe she didn't like the Colonel either. Of course, he had come to realize that she adored the Admiral and guarded his privacy, and reputation, with the tenacity of a pit bull. Barney came forward and offered them their beverages.

'Ah-ha, Hiroga's struck again, has he?' Johnny said, teasing her. He took a quick sip of his coffee as she flushed, needlessly straightening the hard copy at the first two places. He liked to have hard copy for important meetings. He could doodle on it.

Peter regarded her intently, and then realized with dismay that he had come close to scanning her.

'You're his superior in rank, General,' she remarked in what might be a total non sequitur.

'That I am,' Johnny said cheerfully.

'Your seat's there; Mr Reidinger is on the Admiral's left.' Again she coloured unaccountably. 'Secretary Abubakar on the right.'

Johnny leaned round to see who bracketed him at the table. 'I certainly don't mind Commander Chatham, but do I have to have the CFO on the other side?'

'You've met Ms Taddesse?'

'I've heard about her,' Johnny grimaced.

'Come now, General, a woman you can't get on the good side of?' Nicola said, teasing in her own turn.

'There are some it isn't worth trying with.'

'Even for the good of the Station?' Nicola tilted her head enquiringly.

They heard voices in the corridor, and Nicola stepped back to the chair by the workstation.

A yeoman opened the door and then stood back to allow the guests to enter. The first woman who entered, her hair skinned back from her strong-featured face, was Alicia Taddesse, according to the large print of her Station visitor's badge. She glanced at Nicola, who politely indicated her nametag on the table. Ms Taddesse shot the General a sharp look, swinging her hard-sided briefcase onto the table. The second woman, with a slightly Asian cast to her features, very dark eyes and well-cut short black hair, entered nervously. She was so loudly broadcasting her dislike of the mode of transportation she had just had to endure that mentally, Peter reared back. The yeoman indicated her position at the table and she immediately sat down, as if a chair provided security. Then came Secretary of Space Abubakar, a scrawny-looking man with heavy jowls, a small but noticeable paunch under the loose black tunic he wore and a luxuriant head of white hair, brushed back from a high forehead. He smiled, his eyes moving from Johnny Greene to Peter, Nicola, and Barney, who stood attentively in the serving alcove. Behind him, as physically opposite to the Secretary as possible, slouched a tall man who unconsciously ducked his head to enter the room, though the portal was certainly high enough to allow clearance to the tallest man on the Station. Georg Fraga nodded pleasantly to Johnny Greene, gave Peter a searching look, and then stood by his chair. Lieutenant Commander Pota Chatham preceded Admiral Dirk Coetzer.

'Pota, when will First Base be online?' he asked as he entered.

'They should be on,' said Commander Chatham, looking at her com-unit, 'on my mark in five minutes, sir. Mark!'

'Thank you. Secretary Abubakar, ladies, General, Peter, if you'll all take your seats?' the Admiral said. 'If you'll be good enough to give Barney here your choice of beverage, we can get that detail attended to before we start the hard work.'

The newcomers, with the exception of Mai Leitao, who asked for water, preferred coffee. Peter used that brief diversion to seat himself next to Mai Leitao, who made herself very busy, precisely setting out her notepad and light-pen, fussing with the hard copy in front of her.

'Good Navy coffee,' said the Secretary with a pleasant smile at Barney. His glance fell briefly on Peter.

'Might as well leave a carafe on the table for us before you leave, Barney,' the Admiral said. 'Secretary, have you been officially introduced to Peter Reidinger, the General's colleague in Supply and Transport?'

Peter heard Mai Leitao's surprised intake of breath. He didn't need to look round to know that she immediately leaned as far away from him as her armchair permitted.

212

Bitch! Johnny Greene said. *Ignore her, Pete. She's along for the prestige.*

And didn't like the ride, Peter said.

Don't take that to heart. She feels agoraphobic to me.

'Ms Leitao,' Georg Fraga said, rising to his feet. 'You're going to need more space. Why don't you change with me? If the Admiral doesn't mind?' He looked enquiringly to Coetzer at the centre of the table.

As Coetzer spread his hands to indicate permission, he pointedly did not look at either the woman or Peter.

Peter, with as much nonchalance as he could muster, took a sip of his herbal tea and glanced down the table while the exchange was made. Commander Chatham's rigid attention stance relaxed as her com-unit chimed.

'Contact, Admiral Coetzer,' she said in her cool alto voice.

The monitor that had been positioned to face the crescent of viewers now flickered as the contact was established. Three men stood, two at attention, in front of a table in the conference room at First Base.

'Admiral Coetzer,' said the swarthy-complexioned man in the middle with a bow of his head that Peter decided might have accompanied an unseen click of his heels. 'Hiroga Watari here.'

Lance Baden grinned and said an Australian 'G'day', nodding to all.

'Sirs,' and the third man did salute, 'ladies.' He was as tall as the lanky Baden, but broader in the shoulders. He had curly blond hair and eyes that were vividly blue in a wide face. 'Major Cyberal at your command.'

'Thank you, gentlemen. Please be seated,' said the Admiral, and when they had, he banged his fist on the table. 'This meeting is called to order. Yeoman, prepare to record.'

'Aye, sir,' said Nicola's voice from Peter's left.

'Get it off your chest, Secretary,' the Admiral advised.

'My office is adamant that we achieve a flow of materials to First Base with no further delays,' Abubakar said with no preamble, rising to the challenge.

'Without, of course, increasing costs,' said Johnny Greene.

'General, you're out of order,' Alicia Taddesse said, giving him a stern look.

'Well, that's the size of it, isn't it?' Johnny said blandly, and took a sip of his coffee.

'The budget will not allow it,' Mai Leitao said, shaking her head as she passed her light-pen over the pad and brought up figures. 'There is no room for additional expenditure.'

'Our operation is daily dropping behind schedule due to lack of essential supplies,' Colonel Watari said, scowling, an expression that intensified his Japanese features. 'We have immediate needs that have not been met, despite frequent urgent requests.'

'The price of fuel is rising,' Leitao said.

Peter winced. Her voice had a whining edge to it, like a mosquito.

'We must reduce, not increase, the number of flights, Colonel,' she added.

'Then how, might I enquire,' and the Colonel's scowl deepened, 'are we to keep our schedule?'

'Cut back on the development, of course,' Alicia Taddesse said sharply.

Instantly the Secretary raised his hand in denial of that remark.

'Use the Discretionary Fund to meet fuel costs,' Johnny suggested, looking up from the doodles he was making on the hard copy. Mai Leitao stared at him, her mouth dropping. Georg Fraga had a funny expression on his face. 'Or, better still, use the kitty from Weapons Research and Development, which is obsolete anyway, except for appearing on the International Budget.'

'Now, now, General,' the Secretary said soothingly, his eyes on Johnny.

'Well, if you're using that for something else, Secretary, why not the—'

Abubakar cut into his sentence with a set smile. 'And you think we haven't culled those sources already, General?'

Alicia Taddesse glared at Greene.

'I was trying to be helpful. How's that "alternative fuel source" research going? Haven't heard a peep from that

214

bunch in months. They sounded as if they were onto something with the recombinant.'

Admiral Coetzer cleared his throat.

'Oh, yeah. I'm not supposed to know about that, am I?' Johnny asked rhetorically.

'I would ask how you do, General,' Georg Fraga remarked mildly, his hands clasped idly on the table in front of him, 'except I know your security clearance permits you to keep abreast of all new developments.'

'A recombinant?' Colonel Watari asked, his eyes widening with interest.

'Need-to-know, Colonel,' Johnny said with a wave of his hand and a slight emphasis on the rank.

'Yes, sir.' Watari's scowl returned.

'Whereas,' and now the Secretary turned back to Johnny Greene, 'you are supposed to be sitting on the answer to our prayers?' He looked pointedly at Peter.

'The kid?' Watari said dismissively, glaring at him. 'I don't understand, Admiral, why a civilian,' and the sneer was thinly veiled, 'is in on a high-level, high-security conference.'

'Are you referring to Mr Reidinger?' the Admiral asked in a very gentle voice. 'General Greene's colleague?'

'*My* instructor,' Lance put in, his tone unusually harsh. 'Same sort of "civilian" I am, Colonel.'

The Colonel leaned back in his chair, looking away from the screen, attempting to modify his thoughts appropriately to the clues given by his superior officers.

'Tell me, Mr Secretary, is the Space Authority in any way obligated to the fuel suppliers?' Johnny asked.

'What do you mean by that?' asked Georg Fraga, washing his hands in what looked like an idle gesture.

Peter wondered, and discovered that Georg Fraga had a tight mental shield. Alicia Taddesse did not, and her tension was visible to him despite her controlled expression of polite surprise. Her public mind was swirling with frank replies, and how she was to phrase them more discreetly. Mai Leitao's eyes were getting wider and she was broadcasting a tight swirl of anxiety.

'No, we are not,' the Secretary said. 'We advertise publicly for tenders from suppliers of liquid hydrogen and oxygen.'

'Who use recycled tanks?' Johnny asked.

'Yes, of course,' Abubakar said in a doesn't-everyone-know tone.

'What agency checks those tanks to be sure they haven't sprung leaks?'

'Leaks?' Georg Fraga gave a laugh. 'Is your point that the SA might be paying for more fuel than the freighters get to use?'

'Got it in one,' Johnny said with a curt nod of his head.

'Have you any proof?'

'Indeed I have. Yeoman, be good enough to screen the file marked CCD Number One – Fuel Consumption. It's the one I just put on your desk.'

Admiral Coetzer nodded for Nicola to do so. Peter sensed that this was no surprise to Dirk. Colonel Watari was clearing his throat and beetling his eyebrows. Peter got the distinct impression that this was not how the Base Commander had thought the meeting would proceed. As the file was being beamed to First Base at the same time, all saw the report simultaneously. Colonel Watari's frown deepened, Major Cyberal looked shocked and Lance gave a long sigh, shifting position so that he could rest his chin on his raised hand.

'According to all specifications for a freighter of the CCD's size and bulk cargo capability,' Johnny said, 'she should have had enough fuel left on her return to Padrugoi to navigate without problems to her assigned mooring.' Figures scrolled down the screen. 'Because she was lighter on fuel than the Captain realized when he made his first burn, he couldn't make a long enough one to put her on her assigned trajectory. She was off course coming into Padrugoi. What little fuel was left in the thrusters was not enough for her to correct her entry. That was not the first time this has happened to a freighter. Yet the tanks were supposed to be full when the CCD left Padrugoi outward bound. Captain Maggert knew, and did not report the discrepancy. His first mate did. Is that correct, Commander Chatham?'

'It is, sir,' Pota Chatham said, standing up and angling her wristcom so she could read from her notes. 'The Station has noted similar late arrivals over the past few months. In fact, it's becoming the norm instead of unusual. We have had complaints from the Portmaster, too.' She turned to the Admiral. 'You may remember Commander Bernabe's report three months ago on leakage traces discovered during fuel loading. Of course, those tanks were returned as faulty. We've had no report from the suppliers about how such leakages occurred. Nor what is being done to ensure that Padrugoi receives certified full tanks.'

'You may recall, Admiral,' Johnny said, 'that I have mentioned the mass differentiation.'

'Mass differentiation?' Georg Fraga asked, surprised.

'Yes, didn't you know? A telekinetic is very much aware of how much mass he or she shifts.'

'How?' Fraga asked.

On the First Base screen, Lance sat up again, grinning.

'We keep records of how much thrust is needed for each item logged in for transport,' Johnny said with a casual wave of his hand. 'And how many calories the telekinetic burns in each lift. That's how we figure the cost, you know.'

'No, I didn't,' said Alicia Taddesse, her expression grim.

Johnny gave a negligent shrug of his shoulder. 'I'd be happy to show you our costing equation.'

Taddesse looked from Johnny to Fraga, and her eyes slid over Peter.

Are they cheating the Station, Johnny? Peter asked.

Someone is. Or at least trying to charge Padrugoi a full dollar for sixty cents' worth of fuel. We don't know who. Sometimes only fifty cents gets to us. Welcome to big business and politics, Pete. Easy, lad, don't let them know how this upsets you, and Johnny sent soothing thoughts. *This has to be sorted out, now. Especially since we can prove our allegations. Ignore the negative vibes.*

'I'd be very interested in how you arrive at your figures, General.'

Johnny extracted a pencil file from his breast pocket and

217

kinetically wafted it to the table in front of Taddesse. 'No charge for special delivery.'

Show-off, Peter said, imaging himself grinning, though he was careful not to let the smile show on his face.

Coetzer and Abubakar had no such reservations.

Just then, a wave of increased mental stress reached Peter. One of the most constant fears of the non-psychic was that telepaths could read their minds all the time. Why a telepath would want to was rarely considered. Mai Leitao was broadcasting her fear that the General and that awful boy knew 'all' about her. Peter promptly turned her 'off' in his head.

Taddesse inserted the file in her notepad and studied it.

'Even *after*,' and the Secretary emphasized the word, 'we have put a stop to such shortages, there will not be a significant saving in fuel costs. My office is committed to enlarging First Base as the jump point for the Mars project. We can't have one without the other.' Abubakar leaned back in his chair, politely inclining his head to the Admiral.

'Padrugoi Station is also committed to both projects. That's why General Greene and Mr Reidinger are here.'

'General Greene is known for his assistance,' Abubakar said, and lifted his eyebrows enquiringly.

'Mr Reidinger taught me all I know,' Johnny said.

'The—' 'Kid' was what Alicia Taddesse did not say out loud, but it hung in the pause that followed. 'I find that hard to believe, General.'

'Don't,' said the Admiral. 'We have never made public the role Peter Reidinger played in foiling Ludmilla Barchenka's White-Coat Mutiny. Without his timely assistance, you might have had to deal with *her* on this subject.'

Abubakar cleared his throat noisily. 'I didn't know.'

Alicia Taddesse was surprised, Georg Fraga was dumbfounded, Colonel Watari incredulous, Cyberal curious, and Lance Baden's smile was broad. Peter did not look in Mai Leitao's direction. Some part of him was very pleased with the reactions. But that was not professional, and he was going to need all his professionalism to cope with whatever came next.

You're right there, lad, Johnny said.

218

But he's a kid! Alicia's public mind shouted in denial.

'Mr Secretary, the security was "need-to-know". You need to know that Peter Reidinger was the most important factor in quelling the Mutiny. He was not of an age to be added to the roster of the Parapsychic Centre then, but he has been with us now for several years.'

'He's the one who, ah . . .' and Georg Fraga paused.

'The one who untangled the freighter and put it where it belonged, yes,' the Admiral said. He gave Peter a grateful nod.

'The General and I worked together,' Peter said firmly, deepening his voice to make him sound older. He noticed that Johnny raised one eyebrow as everyone regarded him.

'Actually, to be truthful, Peter shifted the freighter. I was too busy rounding up containers before they got too far away.'

Why did you say that? Peter demanded, trying to keep his face from registering his dismay.

You'll see.

That's what I'm afraid of.

You'll let these mundanes misjudge you?

'He's the strongest telekinetic on earth,' Johnny went on, oblivious of Peter's serious attempt to shut him up. 'Right, Lance?'

'Right, General.'

'And *he's* your solution to the fuel-cost rise?' Alicia Taddesse demanded simultaneously with the Secretary's excited, 'He can kinetically reach the moon from Padrugoi?'

'He already has,' Lance put in. 'If the Colonel will oblige?'

'Oblige? Oblige in what way?' and Watari was suspicious.

'You will remember that we were in urgent need of certain chips, Colonel, on the tenth of May last year?'

'Yes, I do. How did you manage—' The Colonel broke off, goggling first at Lance and then in Peter's direction.

'Would you access that proof of delivery, Cyberal?' Lance asked the Major, who bent to an unseen notepad.

'Yes,' and the blond officer frowned as the record came up. 'Sergeant Gendro collected a bag from the vehicle parking field.'

'The third bollard from the right?' asked Johnny.

Peter seethed, and felt Johnny raise his shield against him for the first time in their long association.

'Yes, you're correct. How did you know that detail, General?' Cyberal asked.

'That's where I told Peter Reidinger to put it.' Johnny waited a moment to allow that information to be absorbed. 'You have a time registered for the delivery?'

Cyberal nodded, spoke a few commands and a window opened up on the conference screen and showed a replica of the May 10 date and early-morning hour.

'Very interesting,' and Secretary Abubakar gave Peter an approving smile.

That the Admiral had not known was obvious to Peter, but Coetzer concealed that behind his broad smile.

'The bag only weighed three kilos,' Peter said, hoping to forestall what must be inevitable.

'Well,' Alicia said with a condescending little smile and a twist of her elegantly clad shoulders, 'three kilos is scarcely something to brag about.'

Peter felt a surge of anger for such belittling.

Hold that thought, Pete, Johnny said so sharply that Peter blinked. While the General's public manner was relaxed and slightly amused, Peter sensed that Johnny Greene felt the same way about Taddesse's dismissal as he did.

'Three kilos?' Colonel Watari asked eagerly.

'In point of fact,' Lance said in a languid drawl, 'we very badly need that shipment from Chipsink.' He consulted his wristpad: 'Waybill number 51161708, that cleared Jerhattan terminal at eight-forty-five today. Brought up to Padrugoi with the Secretary's party, I believe.'

Commander Chatham was already tapping in the designation. 'Yes, we have it on board.'

'It weighs five kilos, Peter.'

Every eye was on him, and he felt trapped.

Not trapped, Pete. It's just show time for the doubters.

Five kilos today, five hundred tomorrow, five thousand the next day. Peter felt perversely rebellious as well as anxious. He sternly reminded himself that this was what he had dreamed of doing when he was lying in hospital, what he and Johnny had talked about doing. He thought of how he'd just *jumped* into the accident with the CCD and did what had to be done, including shifting the freighter out of the way. Everyone was turned towards him, faces friendly and faces decidedly sceptical. He caught the ironic gleam in Johnny's eyes, subtly reminding him of that early morning at the Adelaide Centre. Damn General Greene for springing it on him without warning! Then he saw Alicia Taddesse's haughty and dubious expression, the stunned incredulity on Georg Fraga's face, the bland query on the Secretary's and the hint of anxiety in Admiral Coetzer's eyes. OK, Peter, he said to himself. It *is* show time. Five kilos! Only a question of mathematics.

'May I see the shipment?' His voice sounded unusually calm for someone about to make history – officially – with the longest-distance teleport.

'Certainly, sir,' said Chatham, and a window opened to the transit bay, showing an innocuous white plastic shipping carton, 51161708 clearly stencilled in black on the side.

What he could 'see' he could 'port. He 'felt' it to heft its mass. He tapped into the ship's generators. Had Johnny warned Engineering to be ready? He didn't much care. He wanted to alter the expressions on the faces of Alicia Taddesse and Georg Fraga. Scare the living daylights, once and for all, out of the stupid, intolerant Mai Leitao, and prove himself to the Admiral. And especially to Johnny Greene, who was waiting, all but breathless, to see what Peter would decide.

Peter leaned lightly into the generators; no sense ploughing the package into the surface of the moon. It was only five kilos. He 'saw' the bollard as he had 'seen' it that morning in Adelaide; he didn't need the shadow of the moon crawler. Been there before. Can do it again. He 'ported the carton.

The tension in the room was palpable. Peter let it sit there for a long moment. First Johnny, then Lance began to smile.

'Lance,' Peter said, 'since Sergeant Gendro's already collected one delivery at that bollard, perhaps you could rely on him again.'

221

Johnny let out a cowboy roar, clapping his hands over his head and swinging himself around in his chair in an excess of jubilation. The Admiral grinned broadly and settled back, relieved. Commander Chatham and, in the corner, Nicola Nizukami were also smiling. The Secretary alone appeared to keep his cool, but the expression on Alicia Taddesse's face was one of shocked and dismayed surprise.

So she'd thought he couldn't do it? Peter thought, not letting any sign of triumph leak into his expression. He'd shown her! And himself!

At the end of the table, Georg Fraga looked unexpectedly worried, and Mai Leitao collapsed across the table, knocking over her glass of water.

'Medic on the double, Admiral's conference room,' Commander Chatham said into her wristcom. 'Yeoman, bring me more water.'

Peter rescued Leitao's notepad and light-pen and 'lifted' Barney's serving towel to soak up the spill.

'What did you do to her?' Alicia Taddesse demanded of Peter, glaring at him. She had jumped to her feet, but made no move to assist her colleague.

'Peter did nothing to Mai Leitao,' Johnny replied sharply to the CFO. 'She did it to herself.'

'How could she?' Taddesse began and, seeing the fury on the General's face, broke off.

How could she think I'd do anything to another human being? Peter said, close to panic.

Stupidity, Pete, pure stupidity. Calm down. You have done absolutely nothing wrong today. Nothing!

'Ms Leitao seemed a little unnerved by,' the Secretary began, paused, and started again, 'by reaching the Station so quickly.'

Fraga had his fingers around her limp wrist. 'She's got a pulse,' he said reassuringly. Commander Chatham touched Leitao's throat and confirmed that with a brief nod. Helpfully, Nicola held out a glass of water.

A discreet tap on the door heralded the arrival of the medical team. Peter was overwhelmingly relieved to see Ceara Scott leading them. She gave him the briefest but most emphatic encouraging nod as she made a quick examination of Mai Leitao.

'She fainted?' she asked in a non-judgemental tone, looking around the table.

'It would appear so, Dr Scott,' the Admiral said. 'We have no idea why.'

'I'll want to know exactly what caused a perfectly healthy woman to collapse, Doctor,' Taddesse said in a gritty voice.

'Of course,' Ceara said with a nod of her head, and gestured for the stretcher team to approach. Deftly, she and the ratings transferred the slight, limp body to the litter, blanketed it and left the conference room. Peter didn't know why, but Ceara's presence had unaccountably relieved him. 'We'll do a full scan as soon as we get the patient to the sick bay.'

'Thank you,' Alicia Taddesse said. She sat down again and moved her notepad into precise alignment with the edge of the table. 'Colonel Watari, have you recovered the five kilos?'

'Not yet.' The Colonel was startled.

'It takes time to suit up, Ms Taddesse,' Lance said. 'So where were we?'

'We are nowhere, Mr Baden, until that sergeant returns with proof of delivery,' Taddesse said, closing her lips in a firm line.

'I don't see how you can entertain doubts, Ms Taddesse,' Lance said. 'Peter sent it. Ask the CIC engineer what readings he had on the generators.'

'What good does that do?' she demanded of Lance.

'I think you failed to assimilate the significance of General Greene's file, Ms Taddesse,' said the Admiral in the gentlest of tones that should have warned the CFO.

'The significance is, if I may, Admiral,' the Secretary interrupted, also in a mild tone, 'that every telekinetic thrust can be recorded.'

'And is, especially here on Padrugoi,' Johnny said, a malicious smile on his lips, 'so there is scientific proof that kinetic energy has been expended in a gestalt with the Station generators.' He waved his hand towards Nicola, back at her workstation. 'Please ask Lieutenant Bergkamp to forward the last five minutes of generator usage to our screen.'

'Aye, sir,' she said with alacrity.

With equal speed, another small window opened on the bottom of the monitor. It displayed readings in three categories, which were described as elapsed time, generators at rest and usage. The slight surge as Peter made the brief gestalt was duly recorded.

'I don't believe those figures,' Taddesse said belligerently.

'And tell me why we should wish to deceive you, Ms Taddesse?' the Admiral asked.

She pointed her finger at Peter, her eyes flashing with anger, incredulity and fear.

'I cannot, absolutely cannot, believe a boy that young could send even three grams all the way to the moon. It's over four hundred thousand kilometres from here!'

'Mathematics, Ms Taddesse,' Johnny said, 'which you as a CFO should certainly appreciate. Ten tons of equipment four hundred and forty kilometres from Earth's surface to Padrugoi, or five kilos four hundred thousand to the moon. Peter has the range.'

'Does boggle the mind,' the Secretary remarked tactfully. 'But then, the mind, ah, minds,' and he nodded apologetically to Johnny Greene, 'that could transport some five hundred kilos of personnel carrier from the Earth's surface to Padrugoi this morning do not have to prove themselves to me. It is greatly to the benefit of our entire programme, CFO, that the ability is at this moment in time available to us. Otherwise,' and his voice softened, 'we might have to look for new jobs.'

Unconvinced, Alicia Taddesse folded her arms in front of her, her eyes flashing and darting about the conference room, her lips thin with denial.

A com-unit blip startled everyone.

'Admiral? Commander de Aruya. Dr Scott said you wished to be told as soon as we had examined Ms Leitao. She is conscious, and I'm treating her for shock. The MRI scan shows no cerebral damage or cardiac failure. Ms Leitao is anaemic, and requires other essential minerals as dietary supplements and stands in need of a holiday. I would hazard the guess that she's been working much too hard, or has been under severe pressure lately. She should be well enough – I beg your pardon.' Those listening heard a thin background noise and the doctor had evidently turned away from the com-unit, his voice fading. 'When you have a private moment, Admiral, I'd like a few words with you.'

'Thank you, Commander de Aruya.'

'No doubt Ms Leitao would prefer a different mode of return,' said Johnny, his eyes glinting maliciously as he looked up from his doodling.

'Hmmm. You may be right, General,' the Admiral agreed.

Secretary Abubakar clicked his tongue in annoyance; Taddesse tightened her crossed arms.

'All this excitement,' Georg Fraga began. 'Leitao's rarely out of the office, you know. She may not even be aware of—' With a helpless gesture of one hand, he broke off in chagrin.

'The strides made in the parapsychic sciences?' asked the General.

'How long does it take a man to suit up and retrieve a parcel?' asked Taddesse irritably, drumming her fingers on her upper arm. 'That is, of course, if there is one.'

'Actually, Pete holds the record for getting into his EMU,' Johnny said in a pleasant, conversational voice. 'I find it takes me five minutes to be properly suited up and go through the checks. And I'm supposed to be fast.'

Johnny, are you doing us any good by needling her so? Peter asked, getting more and more peeved.

She may be the CFO, but plain mathematics will require her to employ your kinetic ability, as opposed to the fuel bill they'd have to pay if they don't. She'll have no possible argument now that Abubakar is on our side.

Is he?

Yes.

What have we proved today? That I can fling five kilos to the moon?

Yes, but also that you did it, Peter. And with no strain at all.

225

How can you determine that? Peter demanded, since he wasn't hooked up to the usual sensors.

We know exactly what use you made of the generator gestalt, Pete, that's how.

Peter had no further argument. So Johnny had trapped him into this display, at this time, and before such sceptics. He could have, but Peter didn't think the Admiral had. Certainly the people from the Space Authority hadn't been party to this, not with the way that CFO felt about him. Fraga looked sick with worry. As for Ms Leitao, what had made her faint like that? He'd been careful not to so much as think in her direction.

'Admiral Coetzer?' Colonel Watari's deep voice roused Peter from his unhappy deliberation. 'Sergeant Gendro has found a package at the bollard. The waybill number reads 51161708 from Chipsink, shipping date's today and time of shipment is marked as eight-forty-five. Show 'em the tag, Sergeant.'

The First Base window altered to display the details.

'I think that proves delivery,' Lance said, looking slightly smug.

'Bring the package in on the double, Sergeant,' the Colonel said in sharp command.

'We can sure use those chips right away,' Major Cyberal said, very pleased.

'Chips are the least of our worries,' Watari muttered.

The Secretary turned to Peter, approval and relief apparent in his expression. 'The question now is, how much mass can you send at a time, Mr Reidinger?'

'I don't know, Mr Secretary,' Peter said honestly, and heard the derisive noise that came from the direction of Alicia Taddesse. 'I'd be willing to try to increase mass.'

'Increasing slowly over a period,' Johnny put in, 'with me assisting.'

'Frankly, we have never been able to ascertain what Pete's limit is, Mr Secretary,' Lance added, sitting forward.

'You said it was all mathematical,' Taddesse said, almost snarling at Johnny.

'So it is,' Johnny replied, unruffled. 'And, with Pete's

permission, we'll keep pushing. By the same token, it's inadvisable to overload or overuse his telekinetic ability.'

You said you'd be helping me.

So I will, but we both know that I have a limit. It's you we're selling to save the projects.

'Until, or if, we discover a finite limit,' Johnny continued, 'we should be able to come to a useful working schedule. We already have some guidelines,' and Peter knew that Johnny was attempting to convince him more than anyone else in the room, 'in terms of generator power used and calories burned.'

'The General and I have finite limits to the mass *we* can teleport and how far,' Lance put in. 'I, too, advise that we proceed slowly. John gets as much as one thousand tons from surface to station at a go. What're you up to, Johnny? Eight loads a day?'

'One an hour,' Johnny said. 'Of course, we can do two or more small to medium lots within the half-hour, but I watch my calorie burn carefully and don't exceed what I know my daily limit is.'

'I can thrust small masses – a hundred pound limit – but not as far as the General can,' Lance went on. 'Anything under ten kilos, or a hundred K telekinetic pressure, say, as I had to during the Bangladesh flood conditions. I can handle that sort of work for upwards of several hours. But then I have to rest for a similar period.'

'And Mr Reidinger?' asked the Secretary, clearly impressed by the details from the two older men.

Grinning, Lance spread his hands wide, a gesture that Johnny Greene repeated.

'We found out something new today, ladies and gentlemen,' Johnny said. 'Let's proceed cautiously with this valuable natural resource.'

'Using what as the primary guideline, the use of the generators, or the calorific expenditure?' asked the Secretary.

'Calories mean energy expended. That's the most important criterion.'

'What are your favourite foods, Mr Reidinger?' the Secretary asked with a mischievous smile.

As Peter blinked in surprise at such an unexpected question, Johnny roared with laughter, Lance guffawed and the Admiral grinned broadly, leaning back in his chair in relief. Fraga's smile was polite, but Alicia Taddesse did not seem to appreciate their levity at all.

'Once we establish a safe calorific expenditure for you, Mr Reidinger,' Georg Fraga said, taking out his notepad, 'can we present you with a delivery schedule for the material most urgently needed at First Base?'

I think you should handle this, Pete, Johnny said, stretching his legs out under the table.

Peter hid his annoyance at Johnny Greene's manipulation of the meeting, even if it was to his advantage and that of parapsychics in general. He did feel great satisfaction at proving his ability to doubters like Alicia Taddesse. The Secretary appeared to be open-minded. What position did Georg Fraga hold in the Space Authority? Senior what?

Pete turned his mind from that to how to set fair parameters. Johnny had made him test his own abilities. And, to be truthful, it had been relatively easy. Especially knowing that he had already managed to reach First Base from Adelaide. How much mass could he shift if he *really* tried? Obviously, he should set parameters now. What sort? Johnny was always trying to get him to reach out a little further. How far would please him? Peter wondered. For that matter, 'how far' would please Peter Reidinger? Today had opened up possibilities he had only tentatively dreamed about. And possibilities that he oughtn't to dream about – yet. The qualifier startled him.

He brought his attention back to the matter under discussion.

'I need to have comparison figures on what,' Alicia Taddesse began, glaring briefly at Fraga as she pulled her notepad towards her, 'Mr Reidinger's services will cost the SA as opposed to traditional fuel.'

'Ms Taddesse, I am already under contract to the SA,' Peter replied gently.

Ha, she forgot that, Johnny said.

'My salary on a per diem basis is a quarter of the cost of a pair of *full* . . .' and Peter could not resist lightly emphasizing that adjective, 'fuel tanks, and most freighters require ten for a round trip.'

She spoke figures into her notepad. A hint of a smile played on her lips.

'Less urgent supplies would still have to be freighted,' Peter said, steepling his fingers in an attitude he thought would make him appear more assured than he was.

You're doing fine, Pete, Johnny said, a grin in his voice, though he kept his expression politely attentive.

'I would like to visit the moon physically, if that's all right with you, Colonel Watari,' Peter said, and smiled at Lance Baden. 'I would need good telepad sites.'

'Telepad?' the Colonel repeated.

'Like the X in a circle that designates a helicopter landing site. I doubt if you would want me to place shipments at the third bollard from the right in the parking lot.'

'I see no problem with establishing formal delivery locations,' the Secretary said, smiling as he looked over at Johnny Greene. 'If you'd care to accompany Mr Reidinger, General? I know you haven't made it to First Base yet.' When Johnny nodded, Abubakar went on. 'I think we can provide you both with a personal inspection of the facilities, don't you, Colonel?'

'Yes, yes, of course, Secretary,' Watari replied. 'We've a Rest and Re-enlistment flight going out tomorrow, in fact. It's returning with some urgently needed personnel, but there's certainly room for Mr Reidinger and General Greene.'

'I appreciate that, Secretary.'

'That would take over a week,' Alicia Taddesse said, not quite protesting, 'even if they only stayed a day to site these, ah, telepads.'

'A necessary condition,' Peter said. 'I must also remind you that my current contractual schedule is three weeks on Station, one week on the surface.'

Taddesse shot upright in her chair, startled. 'But—'

Peter managed an indolent Greenesque shrug. 'That schedule is in my current contract,' Peter said in a tone that brooked no argument. She stared at him, all hint of the smile wiped from her expression. 'The Eastern Parapsychic Centre would strenuously resist any amendment at this point in time.'

'I find that unacceptable,' she began.

'I do not,' said the Admiral firmly. 'We are lucky to have Mr Reidinger at any time, Ms Taddesse. His presence on the Station was the reason Monday's fiasco did not turn into a major disaster.'

'My contract does include emergency assistance, Ms Taddesse,' Peter added politely.

Taddesse turned to the Admiral. 'Aren't there emergency crews on standby at all times?'

'Of course there are, Ms Taddesse,' the Admiral replied. 'Rescue gigs are on patrol in every quadrant, and they moved quickly into position, as you can see on the visuals when you review the tapes. Mr Reidinger and General Greene expedited rescue and containment, reducing damage to personnel, freighter and cargo.'

'Excuse me, sir,' Colonel Watari said. 'Engineering would be very grateful if Mr Reidinger could send us waybill number AF22BH47503.'

'What's the mass?' Peter asked, wanting to show Taddesse that he was cooperative.

Watari looked off-screen. 'One hundred and five kilos.'

Ask if that figure includes its packaging, Pete, Johnny said.

'That includes packaging, Pete,' Lance said from First Base.

Great minds, Johnny said with a chuckle.

'How *much* of that mass is packaging?' asked Peter aloud.

'You'd need the packaging,' Watari protested.

'Packaging's forty kilos,' Lance said, and Watari gave him a sharp look for his response. 'The volume is one hundred by forty by sixty. Centimetres.'

'Those seleno-seismic sensors can't be bounced about,' the Colonel objected.

'They won't be,' Lance said, with a sideways, almost condescending glance at the Base Commander. 'I can receive, Pete, if you think I'm needed.'

He doesn't think he is, Johnny said so emphatically that Peter ignored the growing doubt in Taddesse's attitude. He trusted Lance implicitly. He trusted Johnny, too, but not the General's propensity to get him into situations before he realized he was involved.

'We'll have to locate the item first,' Peter said, trying to sound very businesslike.

'Of course,' the Admiral said, and turned to give orders to his yeoman and Commander Chatham, who had anticipated the request and were busy at their notepads.

'I'm not so sure about removing the packaging,' Taddesse said, regarding Peter with narrowed eyes.

'I don't drop things,' Peter said, irritated by her continued scepticism. 'If I am to be effective as a courier, the less unessential mass I have to teleport the better, and the more I can shift per working hour.'

That's right, Pete, don't let her bully you. She needs you far more than we need her. Johnny imagined himself as a rooster, crowing on a rooftop at sunrise.

'A good point,' the Secretary said, tactfully overriding that concern.

'I've located the shipment, sir,' Commander Chatham said.

'If you'll put up the coordinates, Pota,' Johnny said, losing his pose of indolence. 'Naturally it's one in that temporary net.' He gave a long-suffering sigh. 'But at least it's in the priority section.'

'That poses a problem, General?' Taddesse said, and it was obvious that she hoped there was one.

'Do you want it in here?' Johnny asked.

'You wouldn't want it in here, General,' Commander Chatham said. 'Not with all that packing.'

'Oh, I stripped off the unessentials,' said Johnny, and leaned back in his chair.

Of everyone in the room, only Peter was aware that the General had employed a light gestalt. He couldn't resist grinning.

The three sensors, in lightweight, transparent bubble pack, appeared on the end of the conference table where Mai

231

Leitao had been seated. Taddesse gasped, one hand going to her throat. Colonel Watari jerked out of his chair on First Base.

'Careful with those!' Colonel Watari cried, one hand extended in an unconscious protective gesture.

'I didn't hear so much as a bump, Colonel,' Secretary Abubakar said soothingly.

'More like a swoosh as it slid into place,' Fraga added encouragingly.

'Do you enjoy playing hopscotch, General?' Taddesse said in an acid tone of voice.

'Only with those who can't see the numbers on the paving, Ms Taddesse,' Johnny said, showing his teeth at her.

Whatever the CFO might have said, and her anger was palpable in her flushed cheeks and rapid breath, the Secretary held up his hand to forestall it. With a visible shake of her head, she subsided, staring at the montage of Padrugoi on the opposite wall.

During that brief exchange, Peter had 'felt' the substance of the sensors, mentally examining the volume, as someone would take a cautious taste of unfamiliar food. Most times he didn't need to do any psychic 'handling', since the manifests always told him what he was about to 'port.

'I think it would be wisest for me to deliver them directly to your office, Colonel,' Peter said. 'Lance, may I have the exact coordinates?'

'Of course, Pete,' and yet another window opened at the base of the conference-room screen with the lunar location. First Base in Oceanus Procellarum was situated near the moon's equator at 3°11'40'' south latitude, and 23°23'8'' longitude.

Take your time, Pete, Johnny said. Aloud he added, 'Commander Chatham, you might have one of the standby gigs collect the packaging before someone in the marshalling yard sounds an alarm. It's in the priority section of the corral.'

'Very good, sir.'

You can get a direct contact with Bergkamp, Pete.

'Admiral, may I have a direct contact with Engineering?'

Peter said, hoping he sounded calm. Was it his imagination, or did his voice shake a little?

No! was Johnny Greene's firm reassurance.

'Of course,' and Dirk Coetzer, his blue eyes decidedly twinkling, 'and I think, so that we can watch you in action, let's have the engineering station board up on our screen, Pota.'

'Very good, sir.'

Another window crowded against the others on the bottom of the screen.

'I'm ready,' Peter said, wondering if all those on his side were in league to give him more time. 'Lance? I'll put the sensors on the worktop behind you.' Peter leaned into the gestalt; the surge on the generators' gauges flickered at the highest point and fell back as he eased off to what he now sensed was just the right amount of power required. He tried very hard not to think of the immense distance involved. Only that these sensors, their specific volume, had to be placed elsewhere, on the worktop behind Lance. For a nanosecond he felt Lance's mind, reacting in exultation over this second display of pure, boundless telekinetic power.

'Wait!' That was all the time Colonel Watari had to utter a protest before the teleportation was completed.

'Neatly done,' Lance said, grinning from ear to ear as he swung round in his chair to face the delivered package.

With a cry of alarm, Colonel Watari leaped across the room, anxious hands examining it, gesturing for Cyberal to help him remove the one outer plastic sheet so he could assure himself that the sensors had not taken any harm during their unique journey through space.

'I heard only a slither,' Lance was saying, and turned back to the screen to those in the Station conference room. 'Neat, Pete.'

'Would you be in need of a mid-morning snack, Mr Reidinger?' Secretary Abubakar asked with attentive courtesy. 'To replace the calories you just burned up?'

'That's very kind of you, sir,' Peter replied, inclining his head graciously to the Secretary. 'Yes, thank you.'

233

'I think we are all in need of sustenance,' the Admiral said, and raised his voice, 'Barney?'

OK there, Pete? Johnny asked. 'A marvellous idea,' he added aloud.

'Could we have a reading on the . . .' Fraga began, looking at Peter beside him, his fingers still steepled together. Alicia Taddesse was apparently deprived of speech; she sat staring at the space where the three sensors had been. '. . . the gestalt. Is that what you call it, Mr Reidinger?'

'I use a gestalt, Mr Fraga,' Peter said. 'What Engineering's records tell us is how much generator power was involved in the teleport.'

'I see.'

I wonder if he really does appreciate the distinction, Johnny remarked. *You're tired, Pete. No more showing off today. Got me?*

Showing off? Me? Peter imaged himself with a huge mouth, lower lip drooping to the floor. Johnny gave a smug mental chuckle.

Admiral Coetzer suggested that perhaps they should end the conference on this good note. Peter could see that the Colonel was tight strung with the desire to get the sensors into place. Lunar 'quakes were a constant hazard to new construction. Watari was certainly more than polite when he went efficiently offline. The Admiral and the Secretary exchanged grins.

Teleportations or schedules were not even discussed during the break. Before the proceedings at Padrugoi ended, the Secretary had dropped the formal Mr Reidinger and was calling him Peter. Georg Fraga seemed anxious. One of those, Peter thought, who did not realize that parapsychics were still people, with minds that worked differently. Alicia Taddesse confined her remarks to agreeing with her superior or with the Admiral. She did request a report on Mai Leitao. The senior medical officer responded that Ms Leitao was in a deep and restful sleep.

'I can 'port her,' Johnny offered, 'to whatever destination you suggest. The infirmary at your headquarters, perhaps.'

Taddesse reared back in her chair, scowling. 'Not when we know that she's terrified of teleportation.'

'She needn't know,' replied the General with a shrug. 'You can tell her she was brought down from the Station on a regular transport. Which is no lie, since I regularly 'port personnel downside.'

'Commander de Aruya recommended that she have immediate treatment for her, ah, malnutrition,' the Secretary said, 'and a holiday.'

'There's not another regular, self-powered shuttle going down for a week,' the Admiral put in, his expression solicitous. 'She need never know.'

'I think that's wisest, Alicia,' Fraga said earnestly.

'We can ask the medic at the headquarters infirmary to keep her sedated overnight. She obviously needs the rest. I hadn't realized I was working her so hard,' Abubakar said, his expression anxious.

'She's meticulous in the performance of her duties,' Taddesse said in a low voice.

'I'm sure,' the Secretary murmured. He rose, offering his hand to the Admiral, who got to his feet. Then he approached Peter.

'Mr Reidinger,' and he grinned over the formal title, 'Peter, I am deeply grateful for your willingness to extend yourself. You must tell me quite frankly if we overwork you at any point.'

'I will, sir.'

If you don't, I will, Pete, Johnny said, also rising. *There is no way I'm going to allow anyone to risk the skeleteam.*

Except you! Peter tried to keep his tone jesting.

Johnny gave him a very long, thoughtful look. *Especially me.* Then he broke mental contact to stride around the table, helping Fraga collect Leitao's possessions.

CHAPTER NINE

When Peter got to the officers' mess, he wasn't sure that he
was hungry. He wasn't sure what he felt. By rights, he should
have been elated at having 'ported two packages all the way
to the moon. He kept seeing the expression on Mai Leitao's
face, her scrambling move away from him. As if he was
unclean, or his talent was a disease that could infect her. She
reminded him of his mother and her altered perception of
him. He also realized that he had been shielded from such
mundane attitudes and reactions. Carefully shielded. Maybe
he should opt for his own apartment, and not live in the
Talents' special enclave, where he would gain no realistic
knowledge of how his sort were perceived by the other 99.97
per cent of Earth's inhabitants.

'Peter?' said a cheerful voice behind him. He spun about.
'It's just Ceara Scott,' she added, reassuring him before he
had completed the turn to face the redhead. 'I didn't mean
to startle you. I just saw you there, and . . .' she gestured to
the empty mess, 'thought it would be nice to have someone
to eat with. If you're eating? I'm taking a break before this
place gets too crowded, and all the best entrées are gone.
There's fried chicken today.' She sniffed deeply. 'Doesn't it
smell divine?'

236

Despite her red hair, she wasn't at all like Nurse Roche. The colour was different too: not the same shade of red, Peter thought.

Her smile began to waver.

'I didn't mean to intrude.'

'No, no, not at all, Ceara. I'd like company, too. The fried chicken does smell good.' He raised his arm to gesture for her to lead the way. She chose a table at one side of the mess.

They were served deftly by the rating, who suggested the corn bread and okra as suitable companions to the chicken.

'Good eatin', ma'am, suh,' he said, grinning broadly. 'Smart of you to get in here 'fore the rush starts.'

'And keep away from it, too,' Ceara said in a low voice, when he had gone off with their order.

'Are you settling in here all right, Ceara?' Peter asked, thinking he heard an uncertain note in her voice.

'Oh, yes,' she said quickly. 'They're all *very* helpful. It's so different from university labs, where the competition can be fierce.' She paused, searching his face: Peter saw anxiety. 'Sometimes it's difficult being an empath. You can't avoid sensing what other people are thinking.'

'You're an empath?'

'Yes,' she seemed surprised. 'Didn't you know? A latent, I admit,' and she smiled shyly. 'I just didn't know *how* I knew some of the things I did – like how other students felt about me. It was almost a relief to know it was a perfectly normal empathetic response.'

'I see.'

'Do you?' She gave him a sad little smile. 'They said at the Centre that I'm not obliged to inform people I'm an empath, since I'm not all that strong and I'm not really working as one. I thought I'd better tell you.' She made eye contact as she lightly touched his right hand where he had placed it on the table.

The physical contact was meant to allow him to 'feel' that she was telling the truth. Hadn't anyone mentioned he didn't like to be touched? Well, no, why should they? Empaths and telepaths preferred to make tactile contact; that was how

237

they were able to reach a mind the next time. She must have been briefed about him, that a wall had paralysed his legs and then the damned body brace had shorted the nerves in his arms. That is, if she hadn't guessed by the odd way he moved about. Her public mind was earnest, anxious and orderly. He would have expected that in someone trained in medicine. She was certainly speaking the truth, though he also perceived that she was anxious about his acceptance of her.

'Thank you, Ceara,' Peter said. 'It's sort of a relief,' and he gave her a reassuring grin, 'to have another Centre person up here.'

'Yeah,' she said with a little smile. 'I'm glad you're here, too. I don't know many other psychics. It's all new to me. Just like this grant.' She still had her hand on his, and he could feel her 'sparkling' with excitement, pride and anticipation.

'How come you were sent up to the conference room?' he heard himself asking.

She shrugged both shoulders. 'Coincidence. I am a licensed medical practitioner as well as a medical researcher. I want to keep my hand in, and so I said yes when they asked me if I would assist in medical emergencies. They put me up on the duty roster so fast I couldn't renege. So I was next up when the call came in. I don't think I ever want to be *that* dedicated to my work.' She wrinkled her nose in distaste. 'Agoraphobic as well as psychophobic. What a combination! Ah, here comes lunch.'

The meal did look especially appetizing, and Peter felt his mouth salivating. He never felt his stomach rumble, of course. He was grateful that he could smell and taste what he ate. The officers' mess on Padrugoi served excellent food, not that Dorotea wasn't the best cook in the world, but it was nice to taste other cuisines. There was quite a selection of international dishes available here.

'Your family sure didn't want you to leave,' he said. 'Neither did my sister. Dorotea wouldn't let her come to the telepad.'

'Dorotea?'

Peter could sense her curiosity, even though she maintained a polite expression.

'Dorotea's my adopted grandmother. I've been staying with her at the Henner estate, you see, since I emerged as a kinetic. I'm a ward of the Parapsychic Centre.'

'The scuttlebutt is that you're stronger than General Greene.'

'Well,' Peter demurred, 'that's still debatable. But I've been living at the Centre and so has Amariyah. She's an orphan. Her parents died in the floods in Bangladesh, oh, five or so years ago now. We're sort of brother and sister. She's crazy about flowers. We'd have plants all over the house if Dorotea let her. Maree wants to be a hydroponic specialist when she grows up. She's not quite ten now. Sorry, I'm babbling,' Peter said.

'That's all right. I'm the one who usually does that,' Ceara said, smiling until her eyes crinkled.

The steward came by their table, offering seconds before the chicken was wolfed down, or dessert. Ceara ordered pecan pie, and talked Peter into it, and a herbal tea.

'I prefer them,' she admitted shyly. 'Too much caffeine and my eyesight blurs when I'm doing slides.'

'Funny, I can drink tea with no bad effects but coffee's no good for me. Johnny – General Greene, that is – can't function without constant cups of coffee.'

'Probably because he's been a pilot so long,' she said with a disarming crinkle of her nose.

The topic of likes and dislikes was being discussed when the steward returned with their orders. It wasn't until Ceara's wristcom bleeped a reminder that they parted, with some reluctance on Peter's part. He briefly wondered if he had felt so comfortable with her because she was empathic. But he didn't care. He *had* felt comfortable with her, and had unconsciously relaxed from the stress of the morning.

Peter went back to his quarters. He planned to go to the gym and work out on the Reeve board; he fancied he felt a tingling in his chest and upper arms. Or was it a reaction to

239

the pleasant time he'd had with Ceara? When he got in, the message light on his com-unit was blinking.

'Pete? Greene here. We got transport at oh-three-hundred tomorrow, Limo 34. First Base's in conjunction for another five days, so we'd better get cracking if you want to do a walkabout at Oceanus Procellarum. Not that there's much to see, since they planted the Base on the most uninteresting real estate the Apollos could find. Please check in with me.'

The formal request, not the usual flip 'catch me, will ya?' that was Johnny Greene's usual style, was as troubling as it was, in another fashion, satisfying. The General was worried that he had overstepped the parameters of their long associ-ation in this morning's meeting. Ordinarily, Johnny just made telepathic contact when they were both on Station. And they were going in a limo, huh? Peter grinned. Maybe he was just in the way of giving General J. Greene a surprise on this lunar insertion moon orbit shuttle.

When he did make mental contact, Johnny sounded a bit tentative.

Just sent the SA party down. Leitao was totally out of it. Fraga was closer to her than a blister. Wonder if there's something between them? I'm checking out the crate I'll be flying.

I thought the Admiral said there wouldn't be transport until late tomorrow?

I'm speeding things up. Silversmith is checking out our EMUs. I used rank to get the galley stuffed with decent chow instead of standard grub. I bumped one other passenger so we could stow as much of Watari's wish list as the shuttle'll take. Since he now knows who to ask, he sent us another list of urgent items. We take 'em with us, he's got no gripe that you're joyriding to the moon. On a totally different tack, the General added: *Did you have that fried chicken they were serving in the officers' mess?*

Peter hesitated briefly. Had some of Leitao's paranoia rubbed off on him that morning? Was Johnny serving notice that Peter had been seen with Ceara Scott? Or just being friendly?

Yeah, with the corn bread and pecan pie.

240

I missed a good meal, and everyone informed me that I had, and there was genuine regret in his voice.

Does Rhyssa know we're going to First Base?

Yeah. I had Madlyn tell her that.

And about the meeting? Peter really didn't want Rhyssa to be upset about the responsibilities he had just undertaken.

Nooo, not exactly, Johnny said, hedging, sounding more like himself. *Madlyn didn't know either, so scuttlebutt's been contained. For a while,* he added cynically. *We'll make our getaway before that goes public. See ya down at boat bay twenty-nine, kit and caboodle, no later than oh-two-thirty. Get an early night. OK?*

OK!

Curious about which pilot would be flying the Limo 34 with them, Peter put in a call to Nicola Nizukami, who was certainly quite willing to tell him that Lieutenant Xiang Liu would co-pilot the flight with General Greene. Peter thanked her, smiling to himself. Couldn't be better. A limo had a crew of four and accommodated a dozen passengers, including service personnel, who could be counted on to stand a watch. He began to pack, knowing he was limited to one kilo since a limo's facilities were spartan. First in was his EMU skin. So he was really going to get to the moon. Almost absently, he slipped in the papers he'd need.

That done, he decided that he'd better put some time in now on the Reeve board. He needed a workout, if only to get rid of the tissue salts built up by the morning's tensions. Maybe it would take care of the tingling he'd been getting. He didn't have time to be sick or anything. Not when he could get to First Base.

Johnny made his way to the limo's cockpit as the rest of the passengers and crew settled themselves and strapped in. He noted the three seismic engineers from the Japanese Army, the three servicemen in First Base slate-grey fatigues on their way back after R and R, the two replacement cooks, both women, and the four men who must be the solar heating engineers. Johnny nodded greetings to the young lieutenant in the co-pilot's seat.

241

'Well, Mr Liu, I can see that the Admiral is sparing none but the best for our jaunt,' Johnny said with a grin. He looked around, noticed that Peter had taken the engineer's chair and absently waved him out of it. 'Peter, that's the chair for the third officer. We stand three watches on a limo.' He turned back to Xiang Liu. 'Who have we got for third watch – Carnegie?'

Lieutenant Liu glanced at Peter before replying blandly. 'Sir, we're at full complement now.'

'What?' Johnny groaned. 'We're going to fly this tub watch and watch?'

Peter cleared his throat. 'The Admiral thought I could stand in.'

'You?' Johnny's green-flecked amber eyes widened. 'Peter, flying a limo is serious work, it's—'

'Ninety-eight per cent boredom and two per cent sheer terror,' Peter said, finishing Johnny's famous quote. He pulled some flimsies from his pocket. 'Here's my flight certificate, simulator log book and rating.'

Behind him, Liu nodded and smiled encouragingly.

Johnny spluttered. 'But those ratings have to be signed—'

'By Admiral Coetzer himself, sir,' the lieutenant said. 'He's taken a great interest in Mr Reidinger's progress.'

Johnny narrowed his eyes at the young lieutenant. 'And what do you have to do with this?'

'Xiang was one of my three flight instructors,' Peter replied. 'Don't you remember encouraging me to learn more while I was busy healing?'

'Coming up on our launch window in two minutes, sir,' Lieutenant Liu reported in a circumspect tone of voice, forcing the General to make a decision.

Johnny frowned. *Peter, you don't have to do this, you know.*

But I do!

General John Greene pursed his lips tightly. After some moments he nodded abruptly. 'Very well, Mr Reidinger, is the ship secure?'

Peter suppressed an exhilarated grin, forcing himself to check the engineering gauges. 'Cargo locks secured, portside passenger lock closing – now!' he said, adding formally, 'Sir, the ship is secure.'

'CIC's hailing us, sir,' Lieutenant Liu said, tapping his headset.

Johnny tensed to respond and then sat back, waiting. Peter didn't need the hint to know that as a junior he was responsible for all radio traffic. He adjusted his headset and responded, 'CIC, this is Limo Thirty-four.'

Admiral Coetzer himself responded. 'Roger, Limo Thirty-four, what's your status?'

Peter turned to Johnny. 'CIC asks what's our status, sir.'

'And what is our status, Mr Reidinger?' Johnny replied, continuing his own test of Peter's knowledge.

Peter glanced over the control panels. Environmental: green, electrical: green, nav and com: green, RCS: green, main engines: green, computer—

'Sir, there's a fault on Main Processing Unit Two,' Peter said.

Lieutenant Liu glanced up from his pre-flight check, toggled a switch and went back to work.

'Taking MPU Two offline,' Liu announced. He muttered, 'We've got five more.'

'Sir, our status is green,' Peter said. 'Will you check me?'

Johnny smiled. 'Yes, Mr Reidinger, I check you. Our status is green.'

'CIC, Limo Thirty-four reports status green.'

'Roger Thirty-four, you are cleared for departure. Once clear, contact Padrugoi Departure on one two zero point four,' the Admiral replied.

'One two zero point four for Limo Thirty-four,' Peter repeated, punching in Padrugoi Departure's frequency on the second radio. To Johnny he said, 'Clear for departure, sir.'

'Roger,' Johnny said. To Liu, 'Unlock clamps two forward, three aft, four aft and one forward.'

Liu ran quick fingers over the control panels. 'All clamps unlocked.'

Johnny pursed his lips for a moment, then said, 'Mr Reidinger, take us out.'

Again Peter had to suppress a surge of excitement as he punched in the codes to power his thruster control panel. 'Mr Liu, are we scheduled for a standard departure?'

'Yes,' was the prompt reply.

Peter nodded and put in the standard codes he had memorized under Xiang Liu's guidance and radioed CIC. 'Limo Thirty-four is free and thrusting negative-y at five point zero metres per second on standard departure vector.'

Peter half expected Johnny to quiz him for saying 'negative-y' instead of 'down' – a question he'd been asked many times in training, and he had his answer ready. 'Down' is too vague in space; saying that you're thrusting on the negative-y axis states exactly what you're doing relative to Padrugoi – which is the largest craft.

And all spacecraft manoeuvres use the largest craft's frame of reference – a very good explanation! Johnny agreed with a chuckle.

Peter was chagrined to discover that his sub-vocalization had been so 'loud' that Johnny had heard it.

'Roger, Thirty-four,' a new voice, not the Admiral's, responded. 'Radar has a clean separation. You are go for de-rendezvous manoeuvres.'

Peter knew from his long hours in the simulators that the motions of the two spacecraft in close orbit were not at all intuitive. In fact, in order to slip behind Padrugoi, Limo 34 would have to speed *up* – and it would take a wild ride around the front of Padrugoi before the shuttle got behind the Space Station. But first the limo would have to crawl to a safe distance from the Space Station before it could fire its thrusters. Moving at a metre a second, it would take over three minutes – Peter checked the countdown clock – before the shuttle could begin that de-rendezvous manoeuvre which would put Padrugoi safely out of harm's way.

There was an age-old tradition in the military and para-military services of hazing any new trainee or officer. Because of his duties and peculiar condition, Peter had escaped that. John Greene felt that most of the hazing he had ever seen had been cruel and a waste of effort all round. With one exception.

'Mr Reidinger, outline our flight profile,' Johnny ordered.

'Yes, sir,' Peter replied. 'Our de-rendezvous manoeuvre will move us from a circular orbit identical to Padrugoi's, to an elliptical orbit with an apogee five thousand kilometres above Padrugoi's orbit – and change the time it takes to orbit the Earth from eighty-eight minutes to one hundred and forty-two minutes.'

Johnny motioned for Peter to continue.

'That burn is designated OAM-1,' Peter continued. 'The next burn occurs at the top of that orbit, seventy-one minutes later. The purpose of the burn is to change the inclination of our orbit from Padrugoi's twenty-eight-point-five-degree inclination to the Earth, to the moon's five-degree inclination – so that we are in line with the moon.

'That burn is designated OIM-2, orbital inclination manoeuvre 2,' Peter went on. He could feel Xiang's approval. He didn't dare reach for Johnny's yet. 'Seventy-one minutes after that we will be back at our closest point to the Earth—'

'Where will Padrugoi be then?' Johnny asked quickly.

Peter had his answer ready. He'd done his homework. 'Padrugoi will be at the same altitude, but two hundred and twenty degrees away from us.'

'Why?'

'Because our elliptical orbit takes longer to complete than Padrugoi's circular orbit. Padrugoi will have made a full orbit, and nearly two-thirds of its next one, before we're back down to the same altitude,' Peter answered smoothly. He took a deep breath and continued. 'At that point – if all systems are go – we will initiate our translunar orbit insertion and head out to the moon. That burn will be TLI-3. Just short of five days from now – by thirty-six point five minutes – we will be on the far side of the moon and initiate our lunar landing insertion burn, designated LLI-4. At that point, barring some short manoeuvring burns to handle the effects of lunar mass concentrations, we'll be locked in for a landing at First Base fifty-nine minutes later.'

'And how much fuel will be required?' Johnny asked, continuing the interrogation.

Peter refused to be rattled. The Admiral had lectured him on fuel requirements often enough.

'Our propellant to payload ratio is two point zero zero,' Peter said, 'but because we also want to take the limo with us, we have to provide fuel for it, too. So the total propellant ratio is two point two zero.'

'And how much fuel should we have on board?'

Peter sensed a trick question. 'Our fuel is liquid hydrogen, which we burn with liquid oxygen. We burn twice the volume of hydrogen as we do oxygen. Limo Thirty-four in its current configuration masses two thousand two hundred and three point five kilograms, and our payload including crew and passengers masses eleven thousand and four kilograms. Total final mass at First Base will be thirteen thousand two hundred and seven point five kilograms. Or thirteen point two metric tonnes. That will require three thousand two hundred and forty-six kilograms of liquid hydrogen and twenty-five thousand nine hundred and sixty-eight kilograms of liquid oxygen.'

He glanced at his display. 'But we are carrying a ten per cent fuel reserve, which changes the fuel loading to fifty point one metric tonnes.'

'What's limo stand for?'

Peter grinned. 'Lunar insertion moon orbit, sir.'

Johnny allowed the silence that followed to stretch out uncomfortably, but Peter knew he'd answered fully and correctly. 'Sir, we are in position for OAM-1.'

'Roger,' Johnny said, 'initiate OAM-1.'

'Aye, sir,' Peter said, aware that he had passed the test. 'Departure, this is Limo Thirty-four, we are go for OAM-1.'

'Limo Thirty-four, OAM-1 at your discretion,' Padrugoi Departure responded.

Peter let Limo 34's remaining five computers start OAM-1. When the shuttle's three main rocket engines fired off with a gentle kick, Peter added, 'OAM-1.'

'Roger, OAM-1 for Limo Thirty-four,' Padrugoi Departure confirmed. As soon as the engines shut down, Departure radioed back. 'Our computers have you in the green on that burn, Limo Thirty-four.'

Peter checked the shuttle's computers. He frowned, ran diagnostics on MPU Five and said, 'Computer Five is voting against the solution, sir.'

Johnny had followed Peter's diagnostics on his control panels. 'I see.'

Xiang Liu snorted. 'That's why we carry six computers on board. They're always going down.'

'Sir,' Peter said, remembering his drills, 'flight rules state that we report when we fall below five voting computers.'

'If we tell them, Peter, we won't be going anywhere,' Johnny replied at his drollest.

'Let me see if I can jog it back online,' Lieutenant Liu offered. 'And I'll look at MPU Two while I'm at it.' He got out of his seat, graceful in free fall as he pulled himself over to the MPU control rack and started pulling off access panels.

'Good idea, Mr Liu,' Johnny agreed.

Peter was still uncomfortable. 'Sir, I was told that there were no old, bold pilots.'

Johnny snorted at Peter's re-rendering of the old saw: there are old pilots and there are bold pilots, but there are no old bold pilots.

'Mr Reidinger,' Johnny said, 'we have seventy-one minutes until OIM-2. If we can't get one of the computers back by then, we'll abort the mission. In the meantime, I want you to stand watch while Mr Liu and I troubleshoot these wonders of electronics provided to the Space Station by the lowest bidder.'

'Probably Russia,' the co-pilot murmured, but only Peter heard him.

Xiang Liu managed to get MPU Five back online after jiggering with it for some minutes.

'OK, now we'll be go for OIM-2,' Johnny told Peter. 'I'm going to head aft and suss out the rest of the crew and the passengers.'

Before he gave permission to unclip safety harnesses, Johnny gave the usual reminders about the hazards of free fall, the procedures to take in the event of nausea and the action-reaction phenomenon. He advised the newbies to

247

keep one hand on something. Anything a luminous pale blue was safe to grab. Peter quickly recognized who had travelled in space before. The non-coms floated gracefully up and away from the safety seats; two of the Japanese Army officers moved with equal facility and were encouraging their tentative and nervous comrade. The solar heating engineers, all civilians, were very cautious about moving at all: obviously the matter of action-reaction had been emphasized in their briefing for this journey.

Johnny checked read-outs with the co-pilot and then assigned watches. Sergeant Bat Singh and Corporal Gopal Ahn were getting crew pay on this leg of the journey, and Peter was to get experience. Then Johnny called a coffee break.

'This your first time in space, Reidinger?' one of the non-coms asked, watching Peter glide easily towards the galley while evading the clumsier movements of the engineers.

'I've done some EVA,' Peter replied, grinning modestly. 'Great feeling, being weightless.'

'Not that you carry much,' the sergeant remarked, eyeing Peter's light frame. Bat Singh had massive shoulders, a heavy torso and arms disproportionately long for his height.

'Wrestler?' Peter asked.

Bat Singh shrugged and nodded, pleased by the guess.

Just then one of the engineers vomited. Liu hurriedly slapped the access panel back over the control rack to prevent any further accidents occurring with the ship's computers.

'There's always one,' Singh remarked in an undertone that only Peter was near enough to hear, as the sergeant pushed off the side of the cabin to get a spew-bag.

The sicker was strapped into his bunk in the sleeping area, where he was assured he would recover.

'What if I don't?' he asked anxiously as he was assisted aft.

'I haven't heard of anyone who hasn't,' Bat Singh replied genially. 'Not if you passed phobics.'

Peter was relieved of his watch by Xiang Liu, who told him with a certain amount of disgust, 'Those computers are always going down and I'm sick of babying 'em. Why don't you take a break? You did real good, *Mister* Reidinger.' He grinned as he gave the thumbs-up of approval. 'You can come back up for OIM-2.'

'Yes, sir,' Peter said, happily floating towards the rear of the cabin.

The passengers were all grouped around the ports, looking at Earth. Peter found himself following the Earth's geography and referencing the list of gestalt-capable generators at the same time. Let's see, he said to himself, Dhaka had the Ehrain Station, then Hong Kong, Brisbane, Melbourne, Auckland, Midway, Honolulu, Seattle, Portland, San Francisco, Los Angeles and San Diego all at once, followed by Denver, Dallas, Jerhattan, Miami and Buenos Aires. Then there were no big stations until Europe. Peter hadn't worked with many, but he'd seen pictures of the huge installation built by the CERN people in Geneva.

He did know that the nice people at the Conseil Européen pour la Recherche Nucléaire had been the first to put together gestalt circuitry. *They* were trying to understand how psychic powers worked in the physical world, so the gestalt was more of a scientific curiosity than a practicality for them. Peter remembered hearing Rhyssa comment once about how the CERN and FermiLab physicists were vying for the very small amount of research time the Eastern Parapsychic Centre allotted for telekinetics. If it hadn't been that Professor Gadriel had had some minor telekinetic ability, that vital research might never have been as enthusiastically pursued. And Gadriel was always trying to get complete energy-use readings for his investigations – like those that Peter and Johnny had been generating for their Padrugoi contract. Peter made a note to contact the Professor, and see about giving him copies of the data.

It seemed like five minutes, not the sixty-five that had really passed, when Johnny hailed Peter back to the cockpit.

'I think you've had enough excitement for your first flight,' Johnny said. 'I just want you to observe the next couple of burns.'

Peter grinned. 'That's fine with me, sir.' He strapped

himself back into the engineer's seat and walked through the OIM-2 pre-burn checklist.

In his mind, Peter called up the carefully memorized schematics of the limo's construction. Limo 34, part of the 30 series, was the fourth of its class completely assembled at Padrugoi. The Limo 10 series had been mostly assembled on Earth, with only the bolt-together occurring in orbit. The Limo 20 series crafts were about seventy per cent complete when brought up from Earth.

Because they had never had to be lifted from Earth as nearly-completed craft, the Limo 30s looked the least like a traditional spacecraft than anything since the lunar module of ancient Apollo days. For all of that, the Limo 30 still bore a striking resemblance of plan to the US Space Shuttle – but stretched.

The long cargo compartment was almost exactly twice the length of the old Space Shuttle's cargo compartment, because it was constructed from the original Space Shuttle tool-and-die set. There were no wings because they were not needed; the limo was never intended to re-enter the Earth's atmosphere. At the rear of the lengthened cargo bays, where the wings might have been mounted, there were instead the spacecraft's fuel tanks. Stubby landing pads were located under the fuel tanks – with the forward pair sticking out from the front of the crew compartment. Instead of the black heat tiles and white heat-resistant felt covering, the limo gleamed all over with protective gold Mylar covering. The forward compartment was a modified version of the Space Shuttle shirtsleeve crew section – nearly half the length again – and there were three EVA airlocks.

The limo didn't require the three huge Space Shuttle main engines which, right there, saved a lot of mass. For its engines, Limo 34 had two OMS kits – Orbital Manoeuvring Systems – at the rear, and a series of manoeuvring thrusters on the ship's nose. The OMS kits were another Space Shuttle hand-me-down, and included both the large 26.7 kilo Newton thrusters and a series of smaller manoeuvring ones. And the limo did not need a tail – instead, the designers had mounted an antenna array in the same spot. As a safety precaution, the limo designers had made the entire rear section of the limo – tanks, antennae, OMS and all – to be ejectable.

'Of course,' Lieutenant Liu had remarked to Peter when he had explained this feature months ago during his training, 'all you'd have left then was enough life support to keep you alive until you could get to the life pods, and enough manoeuvring thrusters to stop the ship from tumbling. If you were lucky.'

Peter didn't need Xiang Liu to tell him that any crew which had to jettison their propulsion system was quite obviously *not* lucky.

While the first burn, OAM-1, had required only 76 per cent of full power for just a little over a second – and a thrust of a little more than a tenth of standard gravity, OIM-2 would require the limo's two main engines to use 95 per cent of full power for nearly two seconds – but again at the same thrust.

The burn went perfectly. Except that MPUs Five and One both went out.

'What is it with these things?' Liu muttered angrily under his breath, as he pulled the two failed units offline and opened the access panel to reach them. It took him the better part of half an hour before he got MPU One back online. He spent the next thirty minutes working with Bat Singh as they tried to troubleshoot MPU Five.

'Computers report high oxygen readings,' Peter told Johnny.

'Accept their change,' Johnny said. 'They reported the same problem about half an hour ago, and I took their advice. We're feeling no pain, are we?'

Peter had to agree. He yawned. Maybe the stress of the mission was beginning to get to him.

'Liu, Singh, cover up that access panel and get into position. We're coming up on TLI-3,' Johnny ordered. 'After that, we'll coast on up to good ol' Luna for five days and drop ourselves in on Colonel Watari.' He switched on the limo's intercom and called the passengers. 'Everyone strapped in back there?'

251

When he got no response, Johnny sent Sergeant Singh back to check up. The sergeant came back in a few minutes with a big grin on his face. He yawned hugely for a moment, then excused himself. 'Sorry, sir. Everyone back there is all netted into their bunks and asleep.'

'Can't blame them,' Johnny said. 'Passengers usually crash about now – although they tend to gawk down at Earth until TLI.'

'Three minutes until TLI-3,' Lieutenant Liu reported.

Peter checked his engineering panel again. 'Computers are reporting that the oxygen levels have crept back up.'

Johnny yawned and nodded. 'I see it. I'm correcting it.'

Oxygen levels were very special in space. The limo's environmental control system regulated oxygen by partial pressure. On Earth, while total air pressure was one standard atmosphere, oxygen made up only 21 per cent of the air, and so the partial pressure was 21 per cent of one standard atmosphere. In space, rather than building spacecraft capable of handling Earth's standard atmosphere, a lower pressure was used with a correspondingly higher percentage of oxygen, so that astronauts could have the same amount of oxygen.

Fires consumed oxygen when they burned, and a fire in pure oxygen could burn much hotter and faster than the same fire in a standard atmosphere. Until the Apollo 1 disaster – when one such pure oxygen fire in the Apollo capsule had claimed the lives of three astronauts – the United States had used a pure oxygen system. Afterwards, the US switched to a mix of oxygen with just enough nitrogen to prevent explosive fires.

If the oxygen pressure got too high, it could cause euphoria and loss of concentration as well as damage to nerves, especially in the eyes. If the oxygen pressure got too low, the astronauts could be asphyxiated.

Space flight was still a tricky and expensive venture. Because of that, any spacecraft on any flight was subject to intense scrutiny. Since the days of the US Space Shuttle, there had been ways to keep in contact with ground stations, regardless

252

of the shuttle's position above Earth, and in modern times, those methods had been considerably improved. Tracking Data Relay Satellites, or TDRSs, ringed Earth and provided continuous telemetry and communication between spacecraft, Padrugoi and Earth.

Limo 34, by virtue of its crew and mission, was subject to more scrutiny than most.

Commander Sakai had made special arrangements to get a data feed to his console, and had monitored all the problems the limo had experienced.

While he had followed many limos in their flights to the moon, there was something about this one that bothered him. He couldn't put his finger on it, at least not enough to call it to General Greene's attention, or suggest to Admiral Coetzer that the mission be scrubbed, but – there was something. He scratched his head, trying to make sense of it.

'You know, we're being watched,' Johnny said with a laugh. 'Watched like a hawk.'

Lieutenant Liu nodded. 'All the time. Coming up on TLI in thirty seconds.'

'Committing TLI parameters to the computer,' Johnny said. 'Now all we have to do is sit back and relax.' He turned to Peter. 'Pretty soon you'll be able to walk around the old Apollo 12 site. It's just a hop, skip and a jump from First Base, you know.'

Peter spent a moment recalling pictures of the Apollo 12 memorial park. He had enlargements up on the board in his room. He'd watched the tour videos, too. He felt a thrill run down his spine as he imagined *being* there himself: the kid who'd never once thought he'd get out of that damned hospital bed. You never knew, did you?

'You know,' Bat Singh said to no one in particular, startling Peter with almost his exact words, 'either I could use some sleep myself, or I could use a beer.'

RHYSSA! Amalda Vaden's sharp cry jolted Rhyssa out of a deep sleep. *Something's wrong. With Peter.*

In the Eastern Parapsychic Centre alarms blared suddenly, alerting everyone on duty.

What is it? Rhyssa demanded of both Mallie Vaden and Budworth, the watch officer.

The precogs! They've got something, Budworth replied. *I've got five corroborations, all strong.*

What? Rhyssa shot back, willing Mallie, the strongest precog she had set on watch for anything involving Peter, to answer.

Fire in the sky. They all see a huge fire in the sky, said Budworth.

So did I, and there was a profound sorrow in Mallie's mental tone.

Fire in the sky? Peter? *Oh, my God! Peter! Fire in the sky!*

Confounded by Limo 34's telemetry, Commander Sakai leaned back in his chair, stretched and indulged in a good yawn. He forced his mouth shut halfway through and arched out of the chair, punching up Limo 34's frequency.

'Limo Thirty-four, Limo Thirty-four, declare an emergency,' he yelled into his headset.

'Oxygen levels are going back up again.' Johnny swore as he did a final scan of the control panels just before the computers commenced the TLI-3 burn. 'That can't be right.'

'Well, the computers all agree,' the co-pilot replied, 'the levels are too low.'

'They don't feel low,' Johnny said, narrowing his eyes in suspicion.

Peter yawned again, his cheeks tingling.

'Limo Thirty-four, Limo Thirty-four, declare an emergency,' the voice of Commander Sakai blared over their headsets.

Oh, my God! Peter! Rhyssa's voice shrieked in Peter's head. *Fire in the sky!*

'The computers have initiated TLI-3,' Lieutenant Liu reported.

The computers! Peter shouted to Johnny. Johnny responded with a moment of sheer terror that he rapidly brought under control, but it was too much for Peter.

254

*　　*　　*

Later, no one could quite remember what happened. Rhyssa felt a sudden wrench in her contact with Peter, and collapsed against Dave. At the site of the newly commissioned CERN gestalt generators, Professor Gadriel swore as his latest set of circuits burned out, while in the background the generators keened in agony.

Commander Sakai dropped back to his seat in horror as the TDRS relayed the growing fireball in the sky, as Limo 34's fuel tanks exploded.

With the image still burning in his mind, Commander Sakai punched up the Admiral's office.

'Sir, this is Commander Sakai,' he said, trying to keep his voice even. 'There's been a terrible accident.'

CHAPTER TEN

Lance was updating the flight manifests when Colonel Watari found him. The Colonel looked more solemn than usual.

'What's up?' Lance asked with no preamble.

The Colonel's eyes sparked with anger for a moment, and then faded. 'Word just in from Padrugoi. Limo Thirty-four's fuel tanks exploded when they started TLI-3. No survivors. They didn't even have time to make it to the escape pods.'

Lance opened his mouth, tried to speak, and shook his head wordlessly, denying what he had just been told.

'Not that it helps,' Colonel Watari offered, 'but it was probably instantaneous. They never felt a thing.'

From behind him a voice drawled, 'Oh, I wouldn't quite say that. I've one helluva hangover.'

'Johnny?' Lance shouted, instantly on his feet, his face lit with a huge grin at the welcome sight of a rumpled General, looking very much alive if slightly grey in the face. He started to rush towards the General but stopped himself, adding phlegmatically, 'I shoulda known they couldn't kill you.'

'They nearly did,' Johnny replied with a sour grin, rubbing the back of his neck. 'And the way this headache feels.'

It had been Rhyssa's terrified shout that had warned them. And Peter's frantic reaction that had saved them. In the instant Peter and Johnny realized that the computers had been sabotaged, Peter recognized that his fatigue and tingling cheeks were signs of oxygen starvation. He had slapped the emergency shutdown on the ship's computers, jettisoned the engines and fuel tanks and – Johnny still didn't quite know how – 'ported Limo 34 to the safest place he could visualize in that horrible moment: two hundred metres away from Apollo 12. And four hundred million metres from the fireball.

Then Peter had collapsed, leaving Johnny to power up MPU Two – the one computer that hadn't been sabotaged and so had been consistently overridden by the faulty ones – and to teleport himself into First Base.

Johnny shook off the pain of his oxygen-starved headache and pointed to Watari. 'You've got to get rescue vehicles over to the Apollo 12 site, like ten minutes ago.'

'What?' Colonel Watari had recovered from his shock, but his dislike for anyone ordering him about in his own office showed in the frown on his face. 'What's there? How'd you get here? What's going on?'

'In the order of your questions, Colonel, the Limo Thirty-four or what's left of it. Minus the aft end. I 'ported me here. We were sabotaged.'

'How? Who? What?' Lance babbled with delayed relief.

Johnny waved him off. 'Later. There's not much oxygen left, and what's there is mostly stale. If you please, Colonel Watari?' He flicked his hand at the control panels.

Even at the breakneck speed with which the First Base Commander organized the rescue party, it was still over twenty minutes before the cumbersome airlock bus was on its way and those in the cab on the lower deck of the facility could see the wreck. On the ground below it, a figure in an EMU waved urgently for more speed.

Is that Peter? Lance asked Johnny who was clenching and unclenching his hands on the oh-my-God bar in the bus. This part of Oceanus Procellarum was relatively smooth as *mares* go on the moon, so Johnny's grasp was more nerves than need. They were all in EMUs, for Johnny wanted to investigate the limo almost as much as Watari did.

Should be, Johnny replied. *Peter had his EMU with him, checked and sealed by Silversmith. I didn't say he could go for a moonwalk, but I won't fault him. The ambience in the crew compartment would be pretty dense for his innate sensitivity. Thank God for it. The EMU has its own oxygen, and God knows, one less inside leaves more for the others to breathe. Can't this thing go faster?*

My GOD! And you landed that!

They were close enough to see details now, as the disturbed moon dust was finally settling to the surface around the crash site. Watari and the driver in the cab of the airbus echoed Lance's exclamation of disbelief. The nose of the broken shuttle perched drunkenly on its forward landing skid, the rear cargo section resting on the lunar soil. The gold Mylar skin had peeled back several metres, lifted from the metal hull by the heat of the exploding fuel tanks.

'A good landing is one you walk away from, believe me,' Johnny said out loud, in a sardonic tone. 'Peter's being outside suggests that there weren't any more booby traps. You see, someone had epoxied the escape-pod clamps, so even if there'd been time to get to them, we wouldn't've escaped.' His expression turned grimmer.

'My God! Who'd perpetrate such a crime?' Watari asked. To him, space travel and everything associated with it was sacrosanct. 'Admiral Coetzer will be overjoyed to learn that you're safe. I should have reported immediately.'

'No, you shouldn't,' Johnny said with such vigour that Watari stared at him. 'Because we're not going to tell him just yet.'

'Not even how you miraculously got here?'

That really puzzled Watari, but Johnny wasn't about to enlighten him. He shook his head vigorously.

Watari spluttered in outrage. 'For God's sake, why not?'

'Because, as I said, Colonel, someone tried to sabotage us,' Johnny replied. 'And the sooner they find out they've failed, the sooner they'll try again.'

'Sabotage?'

'Yes, Colonel, sabotage.' Johnny's tone was almost kindly as he repeated his verdict.

The airlock bus was almost to the airlock, Peter moving cautiously in the moon's gravity out of its way.

He could be the one, Peter said, alarmed by Johnny's candour.

Naw. Lives by the book, this one, Johnny replied.

Too right, Lance said supportively.

Watching anxiously as the bus airlock closed very gently on the limo's single undamaged hatch, Peter could hear the amusement in the Australian's tone. He had previously mentioned to Peter that Watari's pernickety notions were irritating, but he ran a tight Base.

Watari's narrowed eyes were examining the crumpled space shuttle, noticing the heat-peeled Mylar skin at the end of the cargo compartment and the buckled condition of the other portside airlock.

'Sabotage. No doubt about it. Very well. Irregularities,' and now he winced at the proximity of the limo to the hallowed ground of the Apollo 12 site on one side, and the Surveyor landing monument on the other. 'Irregularities to save lives are another matter entirely. I will expect a full report when we return to First Base.' He tapped his headset. 'First Base, I want a security squad out here on the double.'

'On the double, Colonel,' was the instant reply. Peter recognized Major Cyberal's baritone voice.

Watari was completing the checks on his EMU suit so that he could exit the cab and examine the wreck first-hand.

'Limo's passengers and crew are to be accorded all privileges but are to be housed separately until this investigation is concluded. No contact with any Base personnel.'

'Quarters are available in DiMaggio Block, sir. Security as ordered, sir.'

'Oversee the transfer from the bus at that entry yourself, Major.'

'Yes, sir, over and out.'

'What about the personnel driving the airlock bus, Colonel?' Johnny asked.

259

The Colonel turned himself so that his helmeted face was visible to the General. Lance could see Watari's profile, his lips parted to show his teeth, demonstrating dislike of the General's implied criticism.

'The airlock is, of necessity, separated from the transport vehicle, General,' Watari said, his body stiff with resentment.

'Just making sure there is no contact,' Johnny replied blandly.

'Lieutenant Marr is in charge of the operation, and has been party to all orders. Have you not, Lieutenant?'

'Yes, sir, I have, sir,' was the crisp reply in a female voice. 'The airlock is now positioned and cycling through to the limo, sir. We will have secure transport in forty seconds!'

'Lieutenant Liu,' Johnny said, leaning over the bus's com-unit and pausing while Xiang came online, 'inform the passengers that they can now debark into the airlock. They are to bring all personal effects with them. You will secure the ship and await the arrival of a security team.'

'Yes, sir.'

'Do you require an EMU, Lieutenant?' Colonel Watari asked.

'No, sir. I'm currently wearing mine.'

'Peter, have you heard all that?' Johnny asked, turning his attention to the EMU-suited figure standing to the port of the bus.

'Loud and clear,' Peter said, watching with interest as he saw the slight movement of the bus airlock connection, indicating that people were disembarking from the wreck. From where he stood on the ground, he could see heads on the upper level of the bus, and guessed the relief of those breathing fresher air.

Xiang Liu had more or less ordered him to get into his EMU, saying that it would save air for someone else. With Sergeant Bat Singh and Corporal Ahn, they had examined the one remaining airlock with great attention to the possibility of additional sabotage. But they'd found none, so Peter, almost overwhelmed by the thick emotions of those so recently delivered from death, had gratefully disembarked.

His first steps on the moon were therefore not as ecstatic as he had anticipated. Sheer relief flooded his mind. And fatigue. He had kept linked to Johnny, and had been amused by Watari's reactions. The Colonel's efficient organization of the rescue had given Peter a boost but it seemed to him as if the lumbering airbus had taken for ever to bring fresh air and rescue to the limo. Briefly, he wondered if he shouldn't really have stayed behind with the others. He'd caught no resentment in anyone's mind, but then no one had wasted any effort not involved in breathing. A wisp of relief did reach him, that there'd be one less in the cabin using what oxygen was left. In fact, they were relieved that he'd been able to get out of the airlock. Then, too, no one else could fit into his EMU, so it was silly of him not to use it.

Watching the airbus loading up, Peter now roused himself to wonder where he should 'port his baggage, still on board the limo. Maybe to that table in the Colonel's office, so his things could be inspected, too, he thought wryly. He felt very queer all over. Probably the bad air, or just plain funk at the relief of arriving safely – or at all.

'Ready to disengage, Lieutenant.' Peter heard a crisp female voice on his helmet com. 'Colonel, all passengers aboard or accounted for.'

'Very well. Proceed to the Base and disembark the passengers at DiMaggio Block. No communication with anyone at this point in time,' Watari ordered.

'Yes, sir.'

D'you want to go in the bus, Pete? Johnny asked.

And be incommunicado in DiMaggio? Peter was amused that baseball idols were being immortalized on First Base. But then, the moon facility had been built jointly by American and Japanese engineers, both countries being baseball enthusiasts.

You're only the engineer. Johnny was teasing, Peter knew, to keep his flagging energy going.

Hang on a mo, Pete, Lance added. *I'm in my EMU. I can take you back. You're quartered in Clemens Block, next to me, anyhow. I'll just requisition one of those lunar rovers coming in. I doubt Watari'll want me to help investigate that wreck.*

Too right, mate, Johnny said, imitating Lance. *Certainly Watari likes to run his own look-sees. I think you should get a message back to Padrugoi. Very discreet.*

Watari has all messages recorded, Lance said. *At least, the official ones.*

Peter listened, wondering if this was the time to suggest that maybe they wouldn't *need* official channels back to Padrugoi. Only how, exactly, were they to explain what had happened? When Peter himself wasn't sure? And they were much earlier now, than the normal five days to First Base. But getting a quiet word back to Madlyn, who could then privately reassure Rhyssa, was an option. He hated to think of Rhyssa, Dorotea and Amariyah believing him burned to a crisp. If he could get Madlyn's attention. Most of the brunette's mental ruminations dwelt on Commander Dash Sakai. He could visualize Madlyn, chin on her hand, a dreamy smile on her face. Was visualization the key to 'send' or 'touch'?

Not now, he told himself wearily. You can barely 'port to Lance and Johnny. I'm tired, he admitted, recognizing the difference between the adrenalin high of being safely *on the moon* as opposed to being strong with physical vigour. He might not have limits to his telepathy and teleportation, but he did have a finite measure of energy. All the odd sensations that he was experiencing were fatigue, that's all.

Suddenly, a space-suited figure bounced up to him. 'I've borrowed that rover,' Lance said, and pointed in the appropriate direction.

That was when Peter noticed that the airbus was backing away from the limo and that there were men – the security squad probably – swarming about the wreck. The hatch opened again and Lieutenant Liu stood there, saluting to the two men waiting to get aboard.

'This way, Pete,' Lance said, touching his arm. With relief, Peter drifted beside Lance, and didn't object when Lance gave him a little kinetic push on the way. *So what did you tap into to get here so precipitously? Watari's dying to know.*

262

So am I, Peter said ruefully.

Did you really 'port all the way from your TLI-3 burn?
Lance was impressed.

Peter nodded his helmet. *With the boost we got from –
somewhere.* He wasn't sure if he should confide in Lance,
though it went against his grain to prevaricate to someone he
knew so well. But he was so security conscious right now
after such a near thing. Lance would surely understand the
reticence.

Peter stumbled, aware that there was little to stumble over
on this smooth *mare.* Lance put his hand under Peter's arm,
reducing the effort Peter had to make.

I think my last meal just ran out, Peter said.

We're nearly there, Lance encouraged him, and half shoved
him into the lunar rover. Once Peter was strapped in, he let
fatigue wash over him.

Thing is, you made it. Well done. Now to find out who.

And why, Peter added.

'Hold on now, Reidinger,' Lance said out loud, aware that
there'd be someone monitoring them.

Peter let himself relax, feeling safe and secure in Lance's
company. Peter barely took in Lance's explanation of the
geography of First Base as he was driven to the nearest
airlock. Then they were being cycled through it, Lance helping him from the rover, encountering the three-quarters
Earth gravity that First Base maintained within the dome;
unsuiting in the ready room, Lance getting the sergeant to
take charge of their EMUs; getting Peter's Base ID, room
assignment, and ration card – all the necessary bureaucratic
details required by security.

Not much longer, Pete, Lance said. 'If you're hungry,
Reidinger, I can show you where the mess is.'

'If it's all the same, Lance, I'd rather get to my quarters.'

'Right y'are,' Lance replied amiably, and indicated that
they should hang a right as they came to a five-way junction
of corridors, the widest one being the main route to the
Central Intelligence Control offices in Akahiro Block. Babe
Ruth Block was in that direction as well. Despite his fatigue,
Peter noticed the steel doors that would seal off sections in

each corridor. He saw the alcoves containing glass-fronted cabinets of emergency oxygen masks. He thought in passing that this was just the place for someone who liked to follow the book.

They turned up one of the narrower hallways down to a Y-junction, where Lance took a right again.

'Clemens Block – where us transient specialists are housed. But the tucker's good. Did you bring in the new cooks?'

'We did.'

'Good! One needs a change in the hand that stirs the chowder.'

The hallway was lined with doors, and Lance stopped at the fourth one on the left.

'We got you a single, Pete. I'm next door. Call addie is five-seven-seven-five. Or you can *call me.*

Politely, Lance took the plastic room card from Peter's limp grasp and slid it into the slot; a soft snick and the door opened. He gave Peter a gentle shove inside and then led him to the bunk, wider by a good metre than the limo's accommodation.

Lie down. I'll get your boots off and tuck you in, m' friend. You're one weary chook.

Peter made no complaint, and willingly laid his body down, faintly aware of the blanket covering him. He was asleep before Lance dropped the first boot to the floor.

Pete? Pete? Pe-ter! The voice was soft but insistent. Peter woke. *Pete? You're awake? Ah, yes, you are. Rhyssa's having knicker fits until she has an eyes-on report from Madlyn that you* are *here.*

Johnny?

That's who. C'mon, get up. I'll give you time to shower and clothe the bod.

Did you find out anything?

About the sabotage? Not much, except that we're not dealing with stupids. Someone rigged the MPUs raw-ther, and Johnny drawled the words, *deftly. And it had to be someone* on *Padrugoi. No time to import anything, or anyone, 'cos I*

264

was the chief importer. I sent folks downside. I didn't bring anything up-station that hadn't gone through security. On Earth, or again on Padrugoi.

I'm awake, Peter reassured the General, aware that he had to drain the waste-bag like, right now! He levitated up, found the toilet and emptied the appliance as Johnny continued his instructions.

I'll send a guide. You'll need one.

A guide? Or a bodyguard?

A little of both. And check it out. I can 'feel' a menacing presence from time to time, Johnny added grimly. *Lance warned me. I'm warning you.*

Peter exhaled at that intelligence. He looked around, realizing that he hadn't even noticed his accommodation when Lance had brought him here. Was it last night? Well, whenever it was. His small bag was on the desk and he 'pulled' out a fresh coverall and shorts. He returned to the bathroom. A notice on the shower enclosure warned him that water usage was limited: he was advised to soap before turning the taps on.

He did and felt refreshed despite the brevity of the wash. He was closing his coverall when he heard a brief tap on his door.

'Corporal Hinojosa, sir,' a female voice announced.

'Be right with you, Corporal,' he said and slid his fleece-lined shoes over his feet.

'Good morning, Mr Reidinger,' she said when he opened the door. She must be just within the height limit for the service, and he felt he towered above her. She had a lot of black curls, dark eyes and a ready smile. 'This way, sir.' She gestured gracefully towards the intersection. 'You're expected in Akahiro Block, that's the original facility, if you haven't had time to study a map of First Base.'

He deliberately matched his steps to hers; she had a long stride for a person her size. First Base's slate-grey uniform looked fashionable on her.

'I know who Babe Ruth and DiMaggio were, but who was Akahiro?'

She flashed him a smile. 'He was the most outstanding

first baseman of the international Japanese Nippon Nicks baseball team this century, sir. Popped more home runs than the legendary Mark McGwire. The North Americans didn't happen to have a baseball celebrity whose name began with an A, so the Japanese got first crack. They didn't have a C either, so Clemens got his innings, as it were.'

Peter responded to her wit with a genuine laugh. He enjoyed the walk – at least until they went through the major lock to Babe Ruth Block. There he caught malevolence so palpable that he staggered. Johnny had done well to warn him. But where did it come from? Men and women, clad in the slate-grey uniforms, seemed to be moving briskly on errands. A group of four wearing gym suits ambled more casually along the main corridor. Then the hate disappeared as if an impenetrable door had closed it off. Peter looked quickly up and down the long main access corridor, and then the corporal was gesturing for him to enter Akahiro Block.

I felt it in the Babe Ruth block, Johnny.

Same here. And that'd take a lot of sifting, since that block holds the main living quarters, mess halls and leisure amenities for both service personnel and consultants, and ends up at the prison wing that has its own airlock. Hurry along there, will ya?

I'm following my leader, Peter said, not at all averse to doing so.

'We're nearly there, Mr Reidinger,' the corporal said, pausing at an elevator shaft and slipping an ID into the slot at one side. The leaves parted and they entered.

Peter felt the upward motion through his feet, and then they reached their destination: the CIC of First Base. As he stepped out, a staggering panorama of moonscape was spread out, hazed slightly by the material of the enclosing dome, but nonetheless magnificent. So was the landing field the limo should have used. The pathetic-looking wreck was on the left-hand side, near smaller, separate domes that must be repair and maintenance facilities. A gantry surrounded the limo and technicians were busy. Three other spaceships, a little four-man courier rocket and two limos, both smaller than the 34, were parked to the right near the landing

266

terminal that was the official debarkation area. Beyond them on the widest part of the terminal apron, two freight lighters were parked, waiting to bring down cargo from the next orbiting freighter. So, in spite of all the problems, freighters were still transporting supplies to First Base.

'Colonel Watari's office is just here, Mr Reidinger,' Corporal Hinojosa said, having given him a few moments to appreciate the view before she stepped to the door and pressed the 'open' plate.

'Thank you, Corporal.'

'My pleasure, Mr Reidinger.'

'Pete!' Johnny waved expansively for him to hurry in. The General looked remarkably refreshed in a dark blue coverall that was a contrast to the slate-grey fatigues of Colonel Watari and Major Cyberal. Lance Baden in his preferred sand-coloured shorts, shirt and boots grinned a welcome.

'Come in, come in. Watari, we can place that call now. Pete, sit here.' He slapped the back of a chair he'd pulled out from the conference table where the First Base officers were sitting.

As Peter moved to obey, he caught a glimpse on his left of the worktop where he'd put the precious seismic sensors only days before. Watari scowled, but the Major nodded a more amiable greeting.

'Have you got the Admiral yet?' Watari asked, leaning towards the com-unit set into the panel of the table.

'On screen, sir. Now!'

There was the Admiral, seated in the centre of his conference table. On one side of him Madlyn wiggled her fingers as the image cleared, Commander Chatham beyond her. On the other side of Coetzer was Dr Scott, who seemed unbelievably glad to set eyes on those at the Base, and two security officers that Peter recognized from seeing them in the mess.

'Pete, you're a vision for sore eyes,' the Admiral said. 'Madlyn's relaying to Rhyssa that she's eyeballing you. I don't think she'd take *my* word unconfirmed,' and Coetzer's one-sided grin suggested to Peter that Rhyssa had been difficult. 'Bindra and Ottey here are going over the security tapes of the boat bay, all recent visitors, and we hope to figure out who tampered with the limo.'

'Madlyn,' Johnny said, with a polite nod to the Admiral for interrupting, 'you need empaths up there. I've got more than the usual emanations of dislike for psychics recently. And Lance, Pete, and I sensed a virulent presence here.'

'On First Base?' Watari exclaimed, as if denying the possibility.

'You do have quite a few lifetime prisoners on First Base, Watari,' Johnny said, his face inscrutable.

'We've offenders here, too,' the Admiral said, shaking his head slowly. 'The double wristbands prevent them from entering any sensitive area. Bindra, check the entire roster of offies. Could you "hear" anything from them, Madlyn?'

'Sir, I'm not an empath,' she replied, almost apologetically. 'But you can have the best at your disposal the moment you ask.'

'Please be so good as to make that request right now, Madlyn,' Dirk said, and then spoke over his shoulder to his yeoman. 'Send an official signal to Ms Lehardt at the Eastern Centre, Yeoman Nizukami, asking for empathic assistance as soon as possible.' Then Coetzer looked back to the screen.

'You may be sure we'll check our resident offenders,' Watari said stiffly.

'You may be sure I'll help him,' Johnny Greene added.

'I can't see how anyone here could have had any part in the sabotage of the limo,' Watari said.

'Possibly not,' Johnny agreed amiably. 'But right now I'd rather not have an unknown quantity that can project such malice in my vicinity. Much less Pete's.'

'His security is in our hands,' Watari said. And, when Johnny raised his eyebrows in query, he added, 'Corporal Hinojosa is a martial arts specialist, and far more dangerous than she appears.'

'Really?'

'Really!' Watari said in a flat voice.

'I'd like additional surveillance for Pete. I'll take Sergeant Singh for mine.' Johnny glared at Watari. 'Lance?'

The Australian shrugged. 'I don't work outside alone, Johnny. I'm in full view of the construction team. I've never felt any threat in Clemens Block.'

'Gentlemen,' and the Admiral entered firmly into the conversation, 'we shall continue our investigations with vigour. As soon as Mr Reidinger has seen all that he requires of First Base, and you can assure us that Limo Thirty-four is operational *and* secure, please contact us again. I will, of course, let you know of any developments at Padrugoi. Pete, Baden, General, Colonel, Major, good evening.'

The screen went blank. Johnny heaved himself to his feet. 'Pete, you need to eat. So do I. Lance, are you joining us?'

'If there is nothing pending, Colonel?' and Lance rose, looking politely to Watari for his answer.

'You are scheduled to accompany Mr Reidinger to be sure he and General Greene see all that they need to.' Almost as if he resented the courtesy it represented, Watari got to his feet and gave a stiff bow in Peter's direction. 'I hope you will not hesitate to ask for anything you need.'

'Did we bring you the most urgent items, Colonel?' Peter asked politely.

'Yes. Thank you.' Watari hesitated, then went on quickly, 'But they would not have been worth your life, Mr Reidinger.'

Well, get that! Johnny said, turning towards the door.

He meant it, too, Lance added, gesturing for Peter to precede him out of the door. The corporal snapped to attention as she saw them emerging. Peter locked his eyes on the fabulous western aspect of First Base of Oceanus Procellarum, one of the few *mares* that was not bounded by mountains or fault scarps.

'The nearest mess hall, please, Corporal,' Johnny said, strolling towards the lift. 'I'm hungry enough to eat a horse, and Pete here's been burning far too many calories.'

Peter did wonder what was 'burning' in him right now, but dismissed it. It was time to be hungry.

'Sir?' the corporal asked, concern in her voice.

'Don't mind him, Nina,' Lance said with easy cordiality. 'He'd never harm a horse.'

Rhyssa was overwhelmingly relieved to receive Madlyn's shout from Padrugoi.

I'm looking at him right now, Rhyssa, and he seems a bit sleepy, his hair is still wet from a shower, but otherwise he's fine. Oh, and the Admiral's about to request empaths from you. They think one of the offenders up here might be responsible for the sabotage.

An offie? Rhyssa was aghast. What station-held offender could possibly . . . ? *I'll check with Boris immediately and see who's been sentenced up-station recently. Someone with technical skills. Thanks, Maddie. I'll reassure Dorotea.*

She did that – news that was received with fervent thanks from Dorotea – before she put in a call to Boris Roznine for him to contact her telepathically as soon as possible. She barely had time to disseminate the good news about Peter through the main office, before she felt Boris's unmistakable touch.

Technically trained offies, Rhyssa? he repeated. *Far too many,* was the LEO Commissioner's immediate response. *I'll send you a full roster, but . . .* He broke off. *I'll check.*

Who, Boris? I caught that! Oh!

Yes, oh. 'Fraid you might, Rhyssa. Justice sentenced Albert Ponce, aka Flimflam, aka Ponsit Prosit, over five years ago to life incarceration on Padrugoi Station. He's still there. He was also peripherally involved in the White-Coat Mutiny. He lost all the benefits he'd earned by previous good behaviour, supporting her. Not that he was perceived to have taken a major role in the Mutiny. Even Barchenka didn't trust him. But he has more than ample reason to hate Peter. Though I don't believe the two ever met. Did they?

Not really. Peter was unconscious while Flimflam was beating Tirla. She had been his primary target at the time. Peter was caught up in the grab for her.

Parole officer notes Flimflam does a lot of betting, but that's not a crime up-station.

Does he win?

Boris's mental tone turned wry. *I can find out. I'd hate to owe Flimflam.*

270

I do. And I'm going to pay that debt, Rhyssa said with such vehemence that Boris protested.

As LEO Commissioner, Rhyssa, I can't turn a blind eye to everything the Centre does.

Rhyssa, said another mental voice on a very tight focus, *you won't need to if that man has harmed Peter.*

Dorotea! Rhyssa exclaimed, as shocked by the implacable tone in the older woman's voice as Boris had probably been by hers.

I think it's about time LEO paid an unofficial but immediate visit to Padrugoi Station, Boris said. *I'm sure Secretary Abubakar will authorize such an inspection. It is to the Station's benefit.*

You, too? To see I play fair, Boris?

Let's say to ascertain if offenders resident on the Station have set up an illegal network.

Oh. Rhyssa had to admit that that excuse was legitimate. She paused. *Only we'll have to make our own way up-station. Our kinetics are all on the moon.*

Leave that detail to me, Rhyssa, Boris replied. *Only don't tell Madlyn we're coming.*

She's not indiscreet, Boris, Rhyssa reminded him. *Especially about parapsychic business.*

She's in love, was Boris's unequivocal reply.

Clearance to Padrugoi Station was not a problem with the documentation Rhyssa, Dorotea and Amariyah were able to produce, especially with Admiral Coetzer's official sanction. They went as a family group, grandmother, mother and daughter. Amariyah was bubbling with excitement at going to see the Padrugoi hydroponic facilities. Rhyssa had arranged for Ping Yung, the empathic specialist already on Padrugoi, to show her the extensive gardens. The girl chattered away on the trip up with Rhyssa and Dorotea. Dorotea held Rhyssa's hand, physically and mentally, during the rocket flight.

I never thought I'd be doing this, Dorotea said several times. *I'm too old to travel perpendicular to Earth. I'm too old to go this fast anywhere.*

I feel much the same way, Rhyssa agreed, though she rather enjoyed the tremendous power in the shuttle's rockets as they took off. Boris Roznine, seated three rows down and frowning at whatever files he was reading, had paid them no attention. Neither did Cass Cutler, travelling as his aide, nor Lieutenant Ranjit Youssef, who successfully looked the part of a menial worker bound for six months' work up-station. He was at the very back of the thirty-passenger vehicle. Both Cutler and Youssef had encountered Albert Ponce aka Flimflam before, although he was unlikely to recognize them.

Dorotea managed a little smile when she felt both Cutler and Youssef trying to soothe her fears and apprehensions.

I'm not afraid, people, nor am I apprehensive. I just don't like this mode of travel. I like solid earth beneath my feet, she told them. *I am also not a crowd person.*

She felt Cass's amusement while Ranjit discreetly withdrew his encouraging thoughts. Cass's unique parapsychic ability was crowd control, generally used to prevent a large mass of people from turning into a riot by subtly broadcasting neutralizing reassurances. Cass was subtle enough so that even Dorotea could not tell if she had stopped emanating.

The initial ten minutes of the flight featured a tri-d about Padrugoi Station, including the history of its internationally sponsored construction. (The White-Coat Mutiny was not part of the spiel.) More importantly, the programme explained what visitors could and could not do, should and should not expect, and how to react to an emergency. By then, Padrugoi was visible on the forward screens, and grew rapidly to dominate the view as the shuttle seemed to inch closer.

Since her trip to Padrugoi for the inauguration had been by Johnny's teleport, Rhyssa hadn't seen Padrugoi in all its complexity. She was as astounded by the view as those seeing it for the first time. She tried to take it all in, especially the cargo nets, flashing with buoy lights where Peter and Johnny had reduced disaster to calamity, the corner she could glimpse at this angle of the construction

272

yard, and the dry dock surrounding the *Arrakis*. Amariyah wanted to know what all the little lights were.

'People working in space suits. The lights are their jet-packs, moving them about in weightless space,' Rhyssa told her.

'Like Peter does.'

'Like Peter does.' Did the girl really understand what Peter did?

'Will I be able to go out in a space suit with a jetpack when I come up to Padrugoi to work?' Amariyah asked.

'You won't need to go out into space. The hydroponic gardens are inside the Station,' Dorotea replied with a sigh of relief.

'When will I get to see them? Are we nearly there?'

'Almost,' Rhyssa said placidly. She'd forgotten how convenient it was to have telekinetic transportation. Instantaneously. Going by shuttle, she was able to appreciate the distance separating Earth and Padrugoi.

Amariyah had to have everything explained to her: the nets, the gigs towing construction units or cargo containers, where the larger freighters were unloading cargo. Rhyssa wondered if the Station was ever quiet. 'Day' had no meaning on Padrugoi, and it probably took all twenty-four hours and its vast crew to keep it running.

CHAPTER ELEVEN

Finally they were docked and permitted to disembark. The security officer didn't seem to take any notice once their retinal check matched their trip IDs.

Rhyssa? And she felt the touch of Shandin Ross, Coetzer's aide and telepath. *I'm officially here as escort for Commissioner Roznine, but the Admiral would very much like you to have lunch with him. Yeoman Nizukami will collect you after your tour of the hydroponics. It's nice to see you again, Dorotea. Ping Yung is looking forward eagerly to showing off his gardens.*

The aide stepped aside, making room in the cramped entryway for the short, compact Ping Yung, who eagerly surveyed the crowd until his eyes rested on her.

'It is an honour to have you here, Ms Horvath, Ms Lehardt and Miss Bantam. If you would be so good as to follow me, Ms Horvath, Ms Lehardt and Miss Bantam,' he said, bowing to each in turn in the fashion of his culture.

'You are of Chinese origin?' Amariyah asked very politely.

'Yes, Miss Bantam, from Hong Kong,' and he bowed to indicate that being Hong Kong Chinese was special. 'I have looked forward to this hour, when I have the pleasure of showing you how we garden in space. This way, please.' He led them off.

Rhyssa, telepathically aware of the LEO Commissioner, heard Shandin's greeting as Boris and Cass now disembarked. She was also aware that Ranjit was being hurried off in another direction by his contact. He, too, would immediately start work, investigating Flimflam's activities on-station. As it happened, only Cass Cutler of the parapsychics had had any sustained mental contact with the suspect, during Flimflam's appearance in Linear G as head of a Religious Interpretation Group. Ranjit could do the background investigating, hopefully discovering as much as he could about Flimflam, and any possible confederates, before an active move was attempted. One man, no matter how professionally adept, could not have undertaken the sabotage of the limo in the time available. Boris was required to deal with provable facts rather than the intuitive or psychic realities.

According to the work roster, Albert Ponce, aka Flimflam, was supposed to be on a rest shift in the quarters he shared with seven other criminals detained on Padrugoi. He was not in his quarters, and when Ranjit subtly pressed the minds of the four present in the room, his whereabouts were unknown. This was generally the case. Bert, as his cellmates called him, only slept there. They had long since learned not to 'know' how he spent his waking hours. Technically, so long as he reported for his work shift, his off-duty activities were not monitored. The double wristband would not permit a detainee access to 'sensitive' areas on Padrugoi. Ranjit then found out where he could find the main Station bookie, also an offender.

Kibon had established an 'office' in a supplies closet, cleared of its authorized equipment. The furnishings, such as they were, provided the bookie with a 'desk', that was more like a nineteenth-century clerk's stand (to fit in the cramped space), a stool and pencil files neatly arranged in cubbyholes on the walls. With the use of a long-armed gripper tool, Kibon could reach any file without moving from his stool. An old-style thin screen was mounted on the wall, and there was an equally obsolete pressure keyplate on the desk.

'Who, what, date and wager,' Kibon said in a flat, rasping tone without looking up, when Ranjit entered. He was a squat man of indeterminate age, his round face scarred with acne. His hands, the first joint on both little fingers missing, were poised over the keys to make the entry. He wore a janitor's tabs on a well-worn, dingy red one-piece coverall that had been Barchenkan issue, patched and frayed at cuffs and collar and almost threadbare at the closings.

Ranjit had had dealings with illegal bookmaking operators before, and was primed.

'The kid,' he said, using the on-station title awarded Peter Reidinger, 'return, within two weeks, ten credits. What're the odds?'

Kibon glanced up only long enough to read Ranjit's ID number. He grunted. 'New here, arncha? Ten to one against.'

'I'll take it.'

Ranjit also 'took' Kibon's public thoughts about 'the kid', and the wager, as the disguised LEO lieutenant carefully counted the credits, in small denominations, into the meaty, thick-fingered hand Kibon held out. Kibon had no opinions one way or another about 'the kid'. He was aware that Peter was one of them psi-kicks. He'd made money on the wager that 'the kid' wouldn't hack the black. He was willing to enjoy profit on this bet, too.

'Bert said it's a winner,' the lieutenant said, imbuing his tone with a wistful hope. Kibon grunted; his thoughts about 'Bert' were uncomplimentary and very wary. Especially since Bert had suddenly taken out of Kibon's keeping a great deal of credit. Certain other persons – Ranjit caught flashes of their faces – also frequent customers, had suddenly been flush enough to put substantial bets against 'the kid' making it to First Base. Kibon was glad to see the credits returned so quickly to his keeping.

Scrupulously counting the quarters and halves piece by piece, Kibon slipped Ranjit's credits into a slot to one side of the keypad. Ranjit could hear them hitting others, and realized that the entire body of the desk was Kibon's safe deposit box. The bookie, also listening intently to the sound, thought that he'd better empty it tonight and deposit it. He also inadvertently thought of where the deposit was to be made. Ranjit filed away that information for future reference.

Kibon gave Ranjit a cold stare. 'That all?'

Ranjit nodded, bowed humbly and retreated quickly from the office, bumping into the skinny man who was waiting to enter. Again quick with his apologies, Ranjit bowed himself away, down the narrow hall and into a broader corridor. He went to the first toilet area that reeked mainly of antiseptic and into a stall, where he could make his report unobserved. Allah granted to every man some small space of privacy at least once a day.

Commissioner?

Yes, Ranjit?

And the lieutenant flashed Boris Roznine the faces he had caught from Kibon's mind and reported that Bert, although off duty, was not in his quarters, nor did his cellmates know where he was. Boris thanked him and relayed that report to Ottey and Bindra, the Padrugoi security officers who were with him.

Go on a walkabout, Ranjit, just in case you might come across Flimflam.

Very good, sir.

'Do you want me to do some lurking too, Commissioner?' Cass asked, since she, too, could identify Bert.

'That might not be a bad idea, Cass.'

'An offender can't get above Ten Deck, or in the Malls without guards,' Ottey said.

Cass smiled and slipped out of the office.

'Could he?' Bindra asked Ottey.

'He's not *supposed* to have access,' Ottey replied, scowling.

'With someone like Flimflam, one can never be sure,' Boris said mildly, and then asked to view the ID images of all offenders currently on the station. 'The janitor staff as well. Flimflam can work a crowd a treat.'

                    *   *   *

'This,' and Ping Yung proudly pressed the entrance plate to
his plant kingdom, 'is the major Controlled Environment
Life Support System, CELSS, on Padrugoi. There are other,
smaller units elsewhere throughout the Station.'

His guests followed him onto the balcony that overlooked
the many-levelled hydroponic unit that was a deep well
in the main stem of the Station. Amariyah gasped, hands
crossed over her chest, blue eyes enormous as she saw
what was, to her, a horticulturist's heaven. The air was
slightly humid and redolent of hints of fertilizing substances.
Dorotea was impressed by its compactness, and the amazing
variety of recognizable plants in the tanks on the levels
below. She had not given much thought to how air was
purified on Padrugoi, nor how it managed to feed its population on a daily basis. She'd heard enough about the problem
of fuel and supply; but not much about feeding folks, though
Peter had told her the food 'wasn't that bad'.

Rhyssa watched the reactions of her two gardening
enthusiasts and smiled. It was worth the trip just to see their
faces.

They were not the only ones in the unit. Figures moved
about this and the lower levels, checking the flow of
nutrients into the hundreds, perhaps thousands, of tanks.
Rhyssa knew enough about growing things to recognize
certain foliage and identify the edibles produced. Carrots
and radishes were very obvious, but their inclusion surprised
her and she was about to comment when Amariyah pointed
to the tank beside her.

'You're growing *Lycopersicum esculentum* in space?'

'Yes, indeed,' Ping said, beaming at her. 'Tomatoes are, of
course, very nutritious, containing vitamin C and being the
basis for many recipes. How do you know the Latin name for
them?'

'It is important to know such things if I wish to become a hydroponic gardener and work on the Station, too,'
Amariyah replied with as serious an expression as her tone
of voice. 'What varietals do you have? What does best on the
Station in the tanks? Bush or cordon?'

Rhyssa had no trouble in 'hearing' Ping Yung's amazement at such questions from a youngster, but he was also delighted to have someone so knowledgeable to speak to, whatever her age. A nice man, in many ways as eagerly innocent as her ward.

'Amariyah is intensely interested in gardening,' she said.

'That is easy to see,' Ping replied with a little bow, and held out his hand to Amariyah. 'We have both bush and cordon. For the most part, we cultivate Plumito and Tigarella in the bush; Mirabelle and Dombito in the cordon. But we vary them with cultigens.'

'Apples?' Rhyssa asked, spotting that unmistakable fruit, trained to grow against the curving wall.

'Yes, indeed, apples contain essential potassium,' Ping replied. 'We'd prefer bananas, but we don't have the space for such trees, as they grow to a height we can't accommodate. Admittedly, plantain would suit more of the resident personnel, and we're trying to develop a true dwarf but without success as yet. Most of what we grow here serves a dual purpose, you see; oxygen purification as well as fresh produce for minimum dietary requirements. We must have cultivars in all the ranges that do not generally exceed forty centimetres. We even have wheat, a cultigen that's only twenty to twenty-four centimetres.'

'Wheat?' Dorotea exclaimed as Ping guided them around the balcony to the spiral stairs to the lower levels.

'Yes, wheat,' he said almost fondly. 'It's a great oxygen generator. Ten square metres grows enough for one person's oxygen; for two at full growth and, harvested, it's made into flour, of course.'

'That's *Ipomoea batatas*,' Amariyah said as she stepped onto the lower level and pointed to the tanks of thriving club-shaped leaves.

'Indeed they are sweet potatoes,' Ping said, grinning. 'We eat the tubers and use the foliage the same way we do spinach.'

'Which type? Ceylon *Basella alba* or *Spinacia oleracea*?' asked Amariyah.

Rhyssa and Dorotea were hanging behind the two, and exchanged understanding grins.

Your student is showing off, Rhyssa said.

So long as he doesn't require me to have the same encyclopedic memory. I've forgotten most of my Latin, Dorotea replied with a wistful sigh.

'We plant both types of spinach in cut-and-cut-again tanks,' Ping replied.

'I wouldn't have expected the Station to have *Brassica oleracea*,' Dorotea commented in a casual tone, as they made their way down the steps to the next level. *It's one of the few names I remember.*

Good on you!

'Oh, we couldn't get along without them. We've the Greensleeves, loose leaves that don't grow too tall. Spivoy and Spitfire are within the outer height limit, but it's mainly the loose leaves,' Ping went on.

'Is this unit limited to temperate-zone planting?' Amariyah asked.

Ping glanced back up at the older women, raising his eyebrows over her intelligent queries.

'Yes. We also have tropical, twelve-hour-day-length climates that the *Arachis hypogaea* and *Cocoyams* require.'

'Peanuts and taro root?' Amariyah said, with a lift of her own eyebrows.

'We try to produce the varieties that appeal to the various elements of our multi-ethnic population. Of course, the protein we use can be flavoured and shaped to be indistinguishable from what it imitates. Chicken, beef, seafood, even the more exotic venison, ostrich and kangaroo.'

'Ahhhh,' and Amariyah dropped his hand to stand in front of the quadrant sown with one crop, its lush green hiding the tank that had nourished it. *'Oryza!'* She could not resist touching the long stalks, carefully since the rice was close to being harvested.

Ping Yung pointed across the atrium. 'And our special cultigen of *Triticum*.'

What's that? Rhyssa asked Dorotea.

Wheat!

'*Above the wheaten plain*', Rhyssa quoted.

Wrong! Dorotea replied quickly. *It's fruited plain, not wheaten. It should be the fruited plane* above, *if you're referring to Padrugoi's crop! But 'amber waves of grain' are mentioned in the song,* she conceded.

I yield, Rhyssa countered.

Dorotea rolled her eyes.

During the rest of the tour, Rhyssa and Dorotea listened and watched; both were delighted by the rapport between Amariyah and the young hydroponics specialist. Once he realized how much the girl already knew, how well read she was, he was more than willing to expand and encourage her to access additional programs on the Teacher that would improve her chances of securing a hotly contested position on the Padrugoi CELSS.

He even showed her the special seedling chambers, small alcoves branching off the main facility. As was her fashion, she crooned over the young plants, stroking a tendril here, with delicate fingers righting a drooping sprout there.

'What is your success rate with seedlings?' Amariyah asked at her most scholarly.

Rhyssa sighed.

Dorotea shot her a look. *You don't suppose she'll try to increase his success factor, do you?*

If she does, will we know? Rhyssa asked in an equally rhetoric tone. *She might at that. Just look at her! She didn't touch Chester as gently when he was a baby.*

Is she making a benediction, or a pass of her as yet un-discovered Talent? I don't feel – wait a minute, and Dorotea held up her hand. Then she gave her head an exasperated shake. *Just like my mother.*

Amariyah is a micropsychic?

She is if I have any sensitivity at all. Dorotea now gave a snort of disgust. *And if we put an Incident net on her while she gardens, it'd only inhibit her. Your grandfather tried so hard to catch Mother at it . . .*

Knowing what her grandfather thought Ruth Horvath did in her microTalented way, Rhyssa stifled her giggle. Dorotea

281

glared at her, and then grinned like a mischievous female much younger than her actual age.

Well, your grandfather really had hoped that Mother would be able to develop the therapeutic-touch healing, Dorotea added.

Rhyssa was saved from an overdose of Latin, genetic selection, yield optimization and cultivation management by the appearance of Yeoman Nicola Nizukami, coming to guide them to their luncheon appointment with the Admiral.

Amariyah was loath to leave Ping Yung, but he finally terminated the occasion by reminding her, ever so gently, that this was his shift, and he must get back to his plants.

'I'll tell you how the seedlings do, Amariyah,' he said as a final promise to her.

No sooner were they in the lift to the Control level, than Amariyah heaved a great sigh.

'I will return,' she murmured.

Threat or promise? Dorotea asked.

Knowing the determination of that young lady, both. Let's do some discreet listening, shall we?

Since their visit had been so expeditiously arranged, it was unlikely that the presence of five parapsychics up-station had reached scuttlebutt. Rhyssa was of two minds on that discretion: she would have liked to sample reactions to their presence and perhaps catch other biases, but now she felt free, legitimately, to catch the prevailing mental climate of the Station. So she and Dorotea unshielded their minds, sampling the general tone of those passing them in the corridors.

Mostly people were concerned about their present duties, or wondering about rest-period entertainment. Neither telepath caught anything untoward, and only one officer was puzzled as to how the limo had arrived at First Base well before its estimated time of arrival. Had it been testing the long-awaited 'new drive'?

Who's thinking that? Dorotea asked.

A senior-grade lieutenant. Oh, it's Madlyn's crush – Dash, Rhyssa responded. *And he thinks of himself as 'Dash', too.*

He's a com officer, so he would probably know about it in the line of his duty.

He didn't hear about it from Maddie, did he? And Dorotea's tone was stern.

She doesn't come into his mind.

She'd be annoyed about that! Dorotea was most amused.

'This way, ladies,' Nicola said, palming open a door and stepping aside for them to enter.

'Ah, Rhyssa, Dorotea,' and the Admiral came towards them, arms wide in welcome. Behind him was a conference table – Rhyssa wondered if this was where Ms Leitao had collapsed during the history-making session with the Space Authority. 'Boris is on his way up, but his cohorts are on the prowl, or so he advised me. Come, come. What would you like as an aperitif? Barney there will get it.' Dirk Coetzer waved to the discreet appearance of his steward, who smiled at the ladies. 'By the time Boris arrives and we've had lunch, I think we'll be able to contact First Base so you can reassure yourselves that Peter Reidinger really is all right.'

'Madlyn did that,' Dorotea said, then she asked Barney for a Campari and soda with lemon if he had it, and took the comfortable chair the steward held out for her.

'If a contact is convenient,' Rhyssa murmured with no demur.

'It most certainly is,' Dirk said, seating her himself. 'What will you have to drink?'

Rhyssa asked for white wine, and then turned to Amariyah who had settled into a chair, smoothing out the aquamarine-blue tunic that Tirla insisted she have for this special trip. It emphasized the colour of her eyes.

'A fruit juice, if you please, Admiral, sir.'

'Did you like our hanging gardens?'

Amariyah blinked. 'I didn't see any *hanging* gardens, Admiral, sir.'

'Either Admiral or sir is correct, Amariyah Bantam. And, in point of fact, all the gardens up here might be called "hanging", because we are, as it were, hanging in space.'

Amariyah accepted the correction of the proper mode of

address and the interpretation of 'hanging gardens' with a slight attentive cock of her head.

'Which do you prefer? Sir or Admiral?'

Dirk Coetzer was obviously unaccustomed to precocious and self-confident children, no matter how polite.

'Sir will do for the Admiral, Amariyah. Are you an uncle of anyone?' Dorotea asked while he was digesting her ward's unusual manner.

'Yes, several, in fact.' Dirk cleared his throat and his voice. 'This is a new one on me.'

'We can see that,' Dorotea remarked. 'Life can be a very serious business, Dirk, as every adult has learned. Some of us older and some of us younger than others.'

'I see,' and the Admiral did.

Just as the drinks were served to the ladies, Boris arrived with Commander Bindra.

'Ottey's got a bee in his bonnet,' Boris said after civilities had been exchanged. Amariyah cast him a startled look. 'How did you like your tour of the hydroponics, Amariyah?'

'Very interesting, Uncle Boris. There are no bees up here. They have to pollinate by hand, as Ping Yung explained to me.'

'Uncle Boris spoke metaphorically,' Dorotea said gently, leaning towards the girl.

'Oh!' Amariyah accepted that, and took another sip of her drink.

'Lunch is served,' Barney said in butlerian tones, his glance falling last on Amariyah, who loved to eat. 'All has been produced here on Padrugoi, Miss Bantam,' he added.

Since they had brought good appetites with them, the guests concentrated on the first course of the meal, a green soup.

'Will I be able to talk to Peter, too?' Amariyah asked after lunch, when the plates had been removed and Barney had discreetly withdrawn.

'Of course, dear,' Rhyssa said. *She is the soul of discretion, Boris.*

'After that, Miss Bantam, perhaps you'd like to investigate our Mall. Yeoman Nizukami will escort you,' Coetzer said.

He addressed the girl as if she were indeed more adult than her ten years.

'Then you can discuss the important matters,' Amariyah said in her usual blunt fashion.

'Exactly, Miss Bantam.'

A rap on the door was followed by its swift opening, and Dash Sakai came in, followed closely by Nicola Nizukami. She stood discreetly to one side.

'Ah, Lieutenant. Dorotea, you may not have had a chance to meet Dash Sakai, one of Padrugoi's communications officers,' the Admiral said.

Dorotea held out her hand, smiling in an innocent, grand-maternal fashion.

'A pleasure, Lieutenant.'

He gave her a quizzical stare, bowing slightly as he took her hand, surprised at the strength of it. 'My pleasure, I assure you, Ms Horvath, since Madlyn has told me that you were her first contact with the Eastern Parapsychic Centre.'

'Has she, now?' Dorotea said, and smiled enigmatically.

'If the ladies will pardon, it's time to initiate the call to First Base,' Dash Sakai said, striding to the console.

Dirk gestured for his guests to pull their chairs closer together at the table, facing the wide screen. They had barely resettled themselves when the view cleared to the now familiar sight of Watari's office, and the usual occupants: Watari, Cyberal, Lance, Johnny and Peter.

'Oh, Peter,' and Amariyah leaped to her feet, holding out her hands as if she could bridge the tremendous distance between them.

'Hi, Maree, good to see you!' Peter Reidinger's face warmed with real affection. 'Didn't expect to. How's the garden?'

'Oh, Peter, have you seen the main hydroponics unit up here?' She had been so well behaved during luncheon that this sudden burst of enthusiasm took Dirk Coetzer by surprise, as Amariyah babbled on about all she had seen and learned. 'All you told me about were the decorative plants, not the *Triticum* and the *Lycopersicum esculentum* and the *Brassica oleracea* and two kinds of spinaches and . . .'

285

'This is not really the time to discuss the tour, Amariyah dear,' Dorotea said, gently putting a restraining hand on the girl's wildly gesturing arms.

'Look, Maree, I just saw the ones on First Base. We'll compare notes when I'm downside. OK?' Peter assured her. 'But we have other very important things to discuss now, honey.'

'Oh!' Amariyah could not miss the scowl on Watari's face and subsided instantly, looking almost – for her – frightened.

Dorotea pinned a far sterner look on the Colonel, and he cleared his face instantly.

'I'm sorry,' Amariyah murmured to everyone, and moved away from the table. 'Hello, General Greene, Mr Baden. I am to go to the Mall with the yeoman now.'

'Then you will see some of the small garden beds I told you about, Maree,' Peter said, encouraging her. 'Sorry we can't talk now. I'll be back home in another ten days. It's great to see you.' His gaze flicked from her to Rhyssa, Dorotea and Boris.

Amariyah looked back over her shoulder even as she held up her hand for Nicola to take to lead her out of the conference room. Dirk introduced his guests.

'Colonel,' Boris began with a glance at the Admiral, 'you have an offender on First Base known as Phanibal Shimaz.'

'Shimaz?' Watari stiffened, giving Cyberal a quick, almost accusatory look. The Major ducked his head, rubbing his forehead. 'That misbegotten son of a—' Watari gulped to a stop.

Peter gasped at both the mention of that name and Watari's uncharacteristically secular lapse. Johnny frowned with sudden understanding. Boris gestured with one hand, as if he could fill in whatever disparaging adjectives the Colonel had not spoken out loud.

'Small wonder we've felt a malign presence,' Johnny said, turning to Lance. 'I'd forgotten all about the kidnapping.'

'I hadn't,' Peter said softly, his lips twitching.

'I didn't know you'd met him,' Johnny said.

'I didn't. Just been his unwilling guest. In those days I couldn't have read him.' Peter swallowed at the very thought and gave his head several quick shakes, dismissing something baneful.

'Just as well you haven't,' Boris said.

'You were kidnapped by Shimaz?' Watari asked Peter, for once shocked out of his usual scowl. 'He was sent here for that. And you were one of them?'

Peter shook his head again. 'No, I escaped.'

'And freed a hundred others at the same time,' Rhyssa said, since Colonel Watari would not have known how bravely Peter had acted. 'As well as revealing that despicable commerce.'

'I had no reason to forewarn you, Peter,' Boris said apologetically, 'since I was unaware that you were going to First Base. However, as he is the only one incarcerated on the moon who might wish you harm . . .'

' "Harm" is a little mild for what we feel passing his block,' Johnny interrupted.

'There's absolutely no way Shimaz will encounter Mr Reidinger,' Watari said at his most emphatic. 'Even before I knew of any connection between Mr Reidinger and that felon, there was no chance of their meeting. Shimaz is currently restricted to his cell. His wristband prevents him from leaving the prison facility. I doubt Mr Reidinger needs to see it. As a matter of Base security, Mr Reidinger is accompanied everywhere by well-trained security personnel.'

Boris held up his hand. 'That's not at issue, Colonel. What we need to establish is what records you have of any contact between Shimaz and Earth, or Shimaz and Padrugoi.'

'He's not allowed any contact, Commissioner. Those are special privileges which he lost early on in his incarceration.'

'Not even mail from his relatives?' Boris asked.

Watari paused. 'We are required to deliver mail from bona fide relations on the authorized list accompanying the detention order.'

'Would you kindly copy us that list?' Boris asked.

A flick of Watari's fingers sent the Major to another console, where such a list was generated. A small screen appeared on the Padrugoi screen, and Dash Sakai was quick to trigger the copy icon.

'I can't believe that we forgot about Shimaz, Peter,' Rhyssa said, taking advantage of the lull to speak. She had been watching him intently, initially relieved by the glint of exhilaration in his thin face. He had come through a testing time, and had stood up well to the challenge. She was inwardly seething that that dreadful Malaysian prince had resurfaced.

'I'm not likely to see him, Rhyssa,' Peter said with a wry smile. 'The prison wing is not on my agenda. Anyway, I'm keeping my shields up.' He smiled reassuringly.

Rhyssa. She stared, and the little smile on Peter's face turned up in one corner. *Did you hear me speak your name? Just nod your head once.*

PETER! Rhyssa gripped the arms of her chair in shocked amazement. She managed to nod.

Don't worry, Dorotea was saying, evidently totally unaware that Peter was also 'pathing Rhyssa. Peter's 'voice' was clearer. *Shimaz can't get to Peter.*

No need to shout, Rhyssa. I can hear you perfectly. You know I can use gestalt with any generator, Peter went on.

WHY ARE YOU DOING IT NOW? She was aware that that was an inane question.

First, I wanted to thank you for that shout of yours. It saved our lives, you know. And second, I've just never had the occasion to try to link from this distance.

Rhyssa had difficulty coping with what he had said. Then she felt Dorotea's hand close on hers, the concern the older woman was feeling, and was severely disoriented. She agitatedly waved her hand to still Dorotea's voice in her mind so she could concentrate on hearing Peter, not quite digesting the fact that Peter's mental tone was much stronger than that of the woman sitting beside her.

I can hear you very, very clearly, Rhyssa. Peter modulated his voice as if encouraging her not to scream at him. *Now I know what Madlyn must have sounded like when she was just learning.*

PE-ter, and between one syllable and the next, Rhyssa exercised stern control and lowered her tone. She exhaled deeply. *Is it just me you're talking to?*

Yup! And he winked. *Dorotea knows you're upset. She thinks it's about Shimaz.*

You can read her all the way from First Base?

I can see her on the screen. But I shouldn't 'path more, or the engineering gauges here at First Base may just start spiking with my usage. Perhaps we should both concentrate on this meeting.

Peter, don't leave me.

Now we've made contact, I'm never more than a thought away. And the mental chuckle he sent her was mischievously self-satisfied.

Dorotea's elbow nudged Rhyssa's ribs. *Don't worry about that monster, Rhyssa. Watari's the last man in the world who would let that scuzzball near Peter.*

Rhyssa shook her head and smiled reassuringly at Dorotea.

'I know Peter's safe,' Rhyssa whispered, patting Dorotea's hand. She could not, however, keep her mind on the comments about the condition and readiness of Limo 34 being exhaustively discussed. She took surreptitious deep breaths to control her mental ferment. Not only had she been able to reach him in the limo, but also Peter had now been able to make telepathic contact with her when she was some four hundred thousand kilometres away from him? The ramifications of such a range boggled her mind. 'Pathing was not Peter's strongest parapsychic suit, so if he could do this . . . Oh, Lord! she thought, reeling slightly in the chair. How else had his range broadened when he'd had to save the limo? Was a dire circumstance the catalyst required to release Talent from inhibition? As Johnny Greene had saved himself from sure death in that etop crash? Would Peter *know* how he'd done it? asked another part of her brain. She shook her head. She'd had no real details about the extent of the sabotage, now being discussed. She must concentrate on *that*. She could think of this astonishing development later.

'The release clips of the escape pods had been epoxied shut,' Watari was saying, reading from his notepad. 'Only one airlock is functional: the tail assembly must be replaced.

289

The old Mylar has to be scraped off before a new coating can be applied. The sabotaged MPUs will be sent back to you so that you can compare our findings with yours.'

'So when,' Admiral Coetzer broke in, 'will the General and Peter be able to return here?'

Watari blinked. 'We do have two other limos at First Base,' he replied in a slightly injured tone, as if the Admiral should have known. 'As soon as Mr Reidinger has completed his survey,' and Watari turned to the young man in question; Rhyssa thought there was a respectful dimension in his manner towards Peter, 'we will have a totally secured shuttle in which to send him and General Greene back to Padrugoi.'

'The Colonel has expedited everything, Admiral,' Peter said, and was it only Rhyssa who noticed the subtly more mature expression on his face? 'Possibly to get rid of the hot cake I seem to be.'

'Mr Reidinger,' Watari protested.

This has been a learning experience for Peter, Dorotea remarked. *And little was on the original agenda about 'surveying'.*

'I should be finished "seeing",' and Peter inclined his head just perceptibly in Rhyssa's direction, 'everything I might need by tomorrow.'

Incredulous, she sank back in her chair, wondering why she hadn't ever considered the possibility that Peter, in gestalt with a generator – anywhere in the solar system – could 'path to her. Possibly, she told herself with rueful honesty, because she'd been able to 'path anyone she'd ever met on Earth, and had never needed to extend her range . . . until that moment when sheer terror struck at the thought of losing Peter. How limiting!

Why has your mouth dropped open, Rhyssa? It's not appropriate. Pay attention, child! Dorotea's tone reprimanded. *Ah. Boris has just received relevant information.*

Hastily Rhyssa redirected her attention to the LEO Commissioner. He had his notepad in hand.

'Two names of Shimaz's court-authorized approved relatives match those who have sent messages to Albert

Ponce,' the Commissioner was saying. 'I think we need files on those who have daily contact with Shimaz.'

'Only the guards, on a daily basis, Roznine,' Watari replied. 'He's been so obstreperous, he had to be placed in a separate cell. Even when we make him work he messes up, so he's really not worth the cost of the air he breathes. No one likes the man.'

'Liking and doing his bidding are two entirely different matters, Colonel. I can rule out nothing in this murder attempt that might possibly show us even the most remote connections between two convicted felons on widely separate satellites, both of whom have sufficient reason to wish to harm Peter Reidinger and/or any other parapsychic.'

'But surely they've known about General Greene, since he teleports supplies to Padrugoi?' Watari replied.

'Knowing, and having the materials to hand and the opportunity to use them appropriately, are also factors,' Boris said.

'The equipment needed, the highly specialized type of epoxy, the MPU circuits, would surely be beyond a convict's pittance—' Watari broke off.

Boris's smile stopped him. 'Not Ponce's. He consistently wins large sums of credit betting. Shimaz may provide for whatever he might lack – if we do indeed establish links between the two criminals – via his relatives. There is also the connection between Shimaz and Ludmilla Barchenka. He was involved in Padrugoi's construction, you know. I don't know how friendly they were. Be that as it may, the connection between Ponce and the prince was firmly established during their trial.'

'But technically—'

'Technically,' Boris continued, ignoring Watari's interruption, 'Ponce was a good enough technician to rig his own special effects. He has also, we noted from Station files, been accessing a variety of educational texts.' Boris's grin was ironic. 'From the titles, he has kept himself up to date.' The LEO Commissioner held up his hand to forestall any response from Watari. 'It is a facet of the penal code that a prisoner may have access to unclassified study materials to promote his rehabilitation.'

'Shimaz has no such access, nor demanded any.'

Boris nodded. 'He was accustomed to employing experts to advise him. There is a very active group on Earth that insists no man, or woman, is beyond rehabilitation.'

Watari struggled not to comment on that point. He had to cope with the prison facility that sequestered those who were psychologically unable, or unlikely, to accept rehabilitation.

'Your difficulties are appreciated, Colonel,' Dirk Coetzer said. 'Major Cyberal, as the executive officer of that facility, can you add anything that might link the two men?'

'The guards are, of course, all military. They are rotated frequently to avoid fraternization with the prisoners,' Cyberal said in a wry tone. 'Of course, in Shimaz's case that is unlikely, since he is thoroughly despised and treated completely by the book.' This appeared to be an instance when Cyberal agreed with 'the book'. 'It is, however, quite possible that we have overlooked the power Shimaz can exert on his relatives or those who work for them.'

'Really, Major,' Watari started to protest.

'I have mentioned it in my reports, Colonel,' Cyberal said in an aside. 'I have also had additional surveillance put on those who might be bribed or coerced. I have no recent,' he stressed the word, 'report of any.'

'It wouldn't necessarily be "recent",' Boris said.

'I'll send you all relevant files in a secured blip, sir,' the Major said, and swung his chair to the second console.

'Include everything since Shimaz was transferred to the First Base High-Security Facility at Oceanus Procellarum,' Boris said at his most formal and forbidding.

'Yes, sir.'

Admiral Coetzer spoke into the silence. 'Then the limo will begin its return to Padrugoi by Friday morning?'

'Yes, Admiral,' Watari said.

'With passengers?'

A flicker of relief crossed Watari's face.

'Who will have been monitored by me,' Johnny Greene said, straightening up from doodling on the paper in front of him.

Watari shot him a look.

'Oh,' and Johnny raised a hand, 'discreetly, Colonel, discreetly. While it is generally known that I teleport, it is not known that I 'path as well.' He shifted in his chair, watching Watari before he added mendaciously, 'Of course, I generally need to have established some sort of tactile contact to do so. In view of the problem we experienced on the way out, oblige me in this and give me a list of those who are scheduled to be on Limo Thirty-four this trip.'

'Of course,' Watari replied with a brisk nod of his head. 'If I might suggest it, Admiral,' and he continued when Coetzer gestured for him to do so, 'the tightest security at Padrugoi might be advisable.'

'Already in effect,' Coetzer said blandly.

'I have a legitimate excuse to remain on-station,' Boris said, his eyes glancing from Rhyssa to Dorotea. 'I will do so, with your permission, Admiral.'

'Granted.'

'I am reassured,' Dorotea said sardonically. She gave a sigh. 'It is too bad that the punishment does not fit the crime, isn't it, Colonel Watari?'

'Doro-te-a!' Rhyssa exclaimed, knowing exactly what her old friend and mentor meant.

Well, it would be fitting, and relieve the Colonel no end.

Boris caught the inference and regarded the silver-haired elderly Talent with a mildly reproving glance. 'The World Government does not sanction either capital punishment for offences or unusual and inhumane restraints, Dorotea Horvath.'

'And that speaks well of the current level of humanity,' Dorotea agreed wholeheartedly. 'Except,' she added in a very low voice, 'for one or two I could name.'

'A long file is coming through on the secured channel,' Dash Sakai said from his place at the conference-room console.

'My thanks, Major,' Boris said and rose. 'Bindra!' He motioned to the Padrugoi security officer, who had remained silent in the background during the conference. 'If you will take charge of that and initiate a review, I shall return to your office shortly.' Now he turned to Coetzer. 'That satisfies my immediate requirements, Admiral.'

'Mine, too. Ladies?' and Dirk gestured to Rhyssa and Dorotea.

Though there were many questions Rhyssa wished to ask Peter about his phenomenal telepathic range, this was not the time. The rogue had the audacity to grin at her as if he completely understood her dilemma. Which, considering his sudden spurt of Talent growth, he probably did.

'I'll see you when I see you then, Peter. Johnny, Colonel, Major,' Rhyssa rose.

Dorotea was on her feet, too. 'I'd best rescue that nice yeoman from Amariyah. Be sure Peter eats enough up there, John.'

'Oh, I will, Dorotea,' Johnny said. He and the others had risen as well, out of polite habit, even though the women were not in their immediate presence.

Watari leaned forward, fingers raised, and Cyberal broke the connection.

CHAPTER TWELVE

In the Colonel's office on First Base, Peter sat down again, elbows on the armrests and fingers lightly linked. He chuckled to himself at the memory of Rhyssa's stunned expression when he'd contacted her telepathically. He hadn't really been sure that he could 'path that lonely long distance to Padrugoi. Though why an ephemeral thought would be harder to 'send' than a solid mass escaped him.

What's funny, Pete? Johnny asked, and for all the General's ready humour and whimsical view of life, his present mood was quite serious.

Merely Dorotea's remark about punishment fitting the crime.

Oh? That cocoon thing you were stuck in?

Peter nodded.

'Watari, is that passenger list ready?' Johnny asked, holding his hand out. *I'll tell you one thing: Watari would love to have that bundle of depraved corruption totally immobilized. It's a wonder he hasn't fallen into a fault or run out of air.*

There aren't faults near First Base on Oceanus Procellarum. And according to what Vin Cyberal has told me, he's not allowed outside, Lance said, *though there are many who wouldn't think twice about pushing him naked out of an airlock.*

Lance rose from his chair. 'Pete, time for some tucker? I heard what Dorotea said. I'm not having her fault me. If you'll excuse us, Watari?'

Peter grinned, sneaking a glance at Vin Cyberal.

'Yes, yes, of course,' and Watari was busy at his console. 'You're dismissed, Major.'

Peter rolled his eyes.

He's really worried, Pete, after Boris's little sermon, Johnny said. *I'd be along as pointman if I didn't have to clear up a few things here with Hiroga. It's only another thirty-six hours, and then we'll be free as the birdies again.*

Outside the Colonel's office, Corporal Hinojosa awaited them, smiling as they emerged. She was such an anodyne to her Colonel.

'I gotta get some food in this bottomless pit, Nina,' Lance said, indicating Peter.

'I'll catch you after lunch, Peter,' Cyberal said. 'Got something to look into.' He walked swiftly into the main Control area.

'I didn't burn that many calories today, Lance,' Peter said in mild objection.

Lance gave him a wide-eyed look. 'You weren't saving any, either, the way you were bounding about the hydroponics unit, the back acres of Clemens and the main storage depot. That's the best place for one telepad.'

'Yes, it would be,' Peter agreed absently. It had been great to know that Maree had had a tour of Padrugoi's CELSS. If they were anything like the ones here at First Base, no wonder she had been all keyed up. Poor kid. She'd want to have a good yak with him when he got home. 'Do I go to the observatory this afternoon?'

'Yes, sir, you do,' the corporal replied as they boarded the elevator.

'I'm looking forward to that one,' Peter said. He would have liked to have seen that facility earlier, but had acquiesced to the tour Watari had planned of the *important* sites: the (correct) landing site; the main supply reception area; the parking fields; the sector where the containers of the REE, rare earth elements, that paid some of the costs of First Base were assembled; the emergency airlocks; and the secured holding area for sensitive deliveries. The table in Watari's office was also available for small parcels.

The elevator doors parted, and Nina gave a quick look back and forth before she stepped out and led Peter left, towards the officers' mess. She also looked inside the mess, her eyes darting about the room, before she allowed Peter past her.

It'll be a bloody relief to get out of all this hyper surveillance, Peter remarked, though he let nothing of his disgruntlement mar the smile he gave Nina as he passed her.

As it was well past noon, there were only four personnel in the facility, three female supply officers at one table and a male communications lieutenant at another. The mess sergeant himself took their orders, recommending the beef stew. By now Peter was aware, having seen those facilities, that First Base produced all its own foodstuffs, fresh from hydroponic tanks or the protein vats. So far the sergeant's recommendations had been spot on, so both he and Lance ordered it, plus green salads that would have been picked that morning from the tanks.

'Just what did Dorotea mean by "punishment fitting the crime", Pete?' Lance asked. 'She had a gleam in her eye that boded no good. Oops, sorry, lad. Caught that flicker.'

'It's all right, Lance. It isn't generally known that Shimaz abducted Tirla and me.'

Lance's expression echoed the shock in his mind. The capture and conviction of a royal Malaysian prince for child abuse and organ farming had been well publicized. But not how the criminals had been apprehended.

'We were nabbed just as we came out of the Old-fashioned Palace of Gastronomical Delights,' and Peter grinned wryly. 'Gassed and then incarcerated in foam cocoons so we'd have no tactile contact. Not even with our own bodies. The lack of sensation didn't affect me, but it sure terrified the little kids. Tirla got angry enough to 'path – first time she'd done that – to Dorotea and she broke herself free.'

297

'The cocoon wouldn't have stopped you long,' Lance said loyally.

'The anaesthetic did,' Peter said with a grimace. 'I have bad reactions to drugs. It was Tirla who got moving, got me out, and found out where we were so we could tell the Centre. Tirla managed to read enough of their aircraft IDs so that Boris could check who they belonged to.' Peter paused. 'One was Flimflam's, the other registered to the Malaysian Ambassador.' Peter let out a long breath before adding, 'It was Tirla they beat up. I passed out.'

'All the kids were released?' Lance asked.

Peter nodded. 'And that whole ring was busted wide open.'

'With Flimflam on Padrugoi and Shimaz here.' Lance shook his head in irony. 'Crazy universe, isn't it?'

The mess sergeant arrived with the individual stew pots and the salads.

Suddenly, remembering what Boris had said about Flimflam cooperating with Shimaz's relatives, Peter sniffed cautiously at the savoury steam rising from his meal. Was it just his imagination, or were his guts aching?

Shall I be taster as well, Pete? Lance asked.

God! I'm getting paranoid.

A little of that is usually called 'caution', Lance replied. *Mine tastes fine – full of capsicums, but that's the way I like it.*

Some stew juice spilled on the table as Lance 'ported it out of Peter's dish.

Clumsy, Peter chided, though he was quite happy to allow Lance the honour.

Hmmm. I've saved myself from some weird dysenteric episodes with my taste buds. Same as mine, and absolutely no aftertaste. Eat! 'However,' Lance went on aloud, 'it's another area to consider.' *Poisoning is always possible, but it's the contract cooks on duty right now, and I don't think they're likely suspects.*

Peter ate hungrily and had two big bowls of the fruit that was on the dessert menu. That seemed to quiet the unusual inner restlessness.

Are you coming back with us, Lance? he asked as he spooned up the last of the juice.

Naw. Got another month on this contract. Lance preferred short-term contracts, and time back at Adelaide.

Did me being here disrupt your schedule?

Not at all, Pete. Lance's smile was broad. *Gave me a nice break from some of the tedious stuff.*

Tell me, can you 'assemble' elements at a distance?

Lord no, Pete. That's your bailiwick, Lance said without a trace of resentment.

Why? Peter pressed against Lance's touch.

Lance shrugged without a hint of rancour. *Because it just is. I see things differently, I guess.*

Peter accepted that with a little smile. *See things differently? OK, Lance.* 'Well, here's Major Cyberal to take me walkabout,' Peter added.

Alvin Cyberal had been his guide, with the corporal shadowing them, to all the points he wanted to 'see'. Johnny usually accompanied them, fascinated by the facilities on First Base, exchanging information with Cyberal on posts where they had both served or visited. Peter did not reveal, or hint even to Johnny, what he now realized: that he could have 'ported accurately on the basis of a clear visual aid. But he'd only known *that* after he'd landed the limo between the two historic NASA markers, using a photo as his guide, a high-resolution image that he could 'see'. Of course, many of the security points he'd been taken to on First Base were not rendered in visuals, for security reasons. Having seen them, Peter could now 'port to them. Once seen, never forgotten – a facet of the telekinetic mind. Being *here*, at First Base, visiting sections that other civilians would have been denied, was a personal triumph for Peter – though he was responsible enough to have wished the flight had been trouble-free. Of course, if that had been the case, he might never have had such a remarkable insight.

Peter was delighted to be going to the observatory, especially with Cyberal, who had mentioned an interest in astronomy.

'Installing a telescope on the nearside wasn't very smart, but the early bureaucracy made some pretty stupid errors here that we're still trying to correct,' Vin said. 'You may have read about the panic early this century about possibly harmful asteroids, PHAs, and near-Earth objects, NEOs.' Peter nodded, since those had been mentioned on his astronomy course. 'A prime reason for a lunar base was to track them. Still is. Only now First Base has access to the far-side space telescopes.

'Dr Pienarr's ambition is three Darwin-type installations on the moon,' Vin continued as they walked down the corridor to the astronomy wing on the back of Akahiro Block, 'set at three different positions – to have complete observation.' He made a broad gesture with one arm, grinning at Peter for such ambition. 'Actually the first is started, dug into the top of Mount Hawking in the Poincaré Crater range on the far side, and accessed by video links from here. Meanwhile he has a director's use of the far-side scopes, so the old one – a Schmidt-Cassegrain catadioptric – is used more for instruction and tracking the NEOs and PHAs. However, we're supposed to be looking for a place where you can safely put packages for the doctor.'

'So I am,' Peter replied. He was impressed that he'd be seeing the facility that had linked with the telescope that had discovered the M-5 planet in Altair, sixteen light years away, the ultimate destination of the *Andre Norton*. He didn't need to look that far, not even beyond this system, to find where he'd have to stand to use his Talent to get colony ships quickly and safely to new worlds.

He chided himself for having such vaulting ambition. Rather grandiose of you, isn't it, Peter? Certainly it's a challenge. But he'd met others, hadn't he? And succeeded? You only need to stumble once, he reminded himself sternly. But that didn't mean he shouldn't *try*, did it?

'You've met Captain Opitz and Dr Pienarr before, haven't you, Peter?' Alvin Cyberal was saying.

The corporal took her usual stance before the main door to the astronomy office. There was a foyer to the actual workspace, and the telescope that was housed in a dome beyond, with the control station and an access airlock for any more radical adjustments and repairs required. These would have to be done in a space suit, so the more delicate manipulations were all handled inside. On the walls of the foyer were prints of views pertinent to First Base, including an old mural of the crew of the Apollo 12 and one of the Surveyor-type spacecraft. Cyberal pointed to the left of the main entrance, to the wall covered by a huge aerial shot.

'The Subaru telescope, the one Ajmal admires from the last century. He wants to develop a whole new generation of telescopes for use on moons, including this one,' he said in a low voice, grinning.

'Wasn't that operational at the beginning of this century?' Peter asked, lowering his tone.

'It first saw light in January 1999.'

Stepping into the main office, Peter saw that the walls were adorned by programmable screens, operated from the rectangle of small ergonomic workstations facing them. Under the screens were cabinets in which crystals storing huge quantities of data were carefully filed along with additional compact devices that he did not recognize, but took for astronomical data recorders. On the far wall, across from the entrance, was a wide window of dark glass; beneath it was an elaborate control panel with storage cabinets below. A clearly marked airlock facility undoubtedly gave access to the telescope chamber. A locker to the right of that was plainly labelled 'EMU'.

Only one station was occupied. Captain Opitz and Ajmal Pienarr looked up when Peter and the Major paused on the threshold.

'Ah, Major, Mr Reidinger,' the blonde Opitz said, quickly skirting the desk, while the astronomer moved more slowly to greet his guests. 'Let me give you the safety spiel all visitors get.' Mockingly she changed her voice to a fruity, low contralto. 'Emergency masks are situated at intervals,' and she pointed to Peter's right and the one nearest him, 'and there are two airlocks, right and left,' and she indicated them. 'Don't try the one on the far wall. That's the observatory. No air in there.' She had very blue eyes, like Amariyah's, Peter thought, which the slate-grey fatigues seemed to emphasize, rather than dull. Her uniform fitted her mature form very well.

On the other hand, Dr Pienarr looked as if he had grabbed the first coverall to hand that morning, evidently from under a pile of heavier objects that had left creases in it. There were coffee stains down the front and on the right cuff. He was balding, with wisps of dark hair across his skull and a thicker mass over each ear in need of trimming. But his hazel eyes were bright and his smile easy; one hand was extended.

'I am so very glad to have you in our facility, Mr Reidinger. Ooops, handshaking's bad manners with psychics, I'm told,' and he shoved his right hand into a pocket.

'Not at all, Dr Pienarr,' Peter said, holding his out. He was pleased with every chance he had to show a new digital dexterity.

'Oh, I say, thanks muchly.' Pienarr's grip was firm and quick. 'Afternoon, Vin. Thought you'd be the guide here. Got those spectroscopy images you wanted. I think,' and he patted the various pockets of his coverall.

'Here,' Simona Opitz said, handing him a thick white envelope.

'Oh, yes, thanks, See,' and the exchange was made with thanks from Cyberal. The Captain gave a little smile and executed an about-face, walking briskly to an arc of the workstations on the lower level where she began to slot crystal data cubes into a reader.

'Now,' and Pienarr rubbed his hands together, 'what would you like to see? We have several projects at the moment. We always do. The SPOT.'

'The what?' Peter asked politely, not recognizing the acronym.

'SPOT,' Pienarr repeated as if to an inattentive student, 'the Solar Polar Ozone-finding Telescope.'

'I didn't realize that it was operational,' Peter said, retreating from that gaffe. The Major hadn't mentioned that in his rundown of the observatory's connections.

302

'Oh, yes, five years now.' Pienarr's manner was as if he expected criticism. 'Well, with all the zodiacal dust, we had to do something to avoid the extinction that bollixed clear shots of some of the more interesting nebulae. Hubble did well enough in its day, with detail down to less than one hundred milliarcseconds across. YEAST improved on that, of course, but SPOT frees us from the interplanetary dust within our own system. But more importantly, it checks ozone layers of any likely planet for free oxygen in the atmosphere. It's a well-trained telescope.'

Peter struggled to translate the acronyms from his earlier Teacher astronomy studies. He saw Cyberal's lips twitch.

'SPOT's a sirius one, you see,' Cyberal murmured close to Peter's ear, and then turned back to Pienarr with a carefully attentive expression.

'Oh yes,' said Pienarr, 'we spent over a year investigating the Dog Star.'

Peter cleared his throat hastily to stifle a groan over the pun. He did recall scanning the technical arguments about where to place the newest generation of space telescopes after YEAST – just beyond the heliopause, or in an orbit around the sun, highly inclined to the plane of the ecliptic where all the planets lie? The solar orbit had won, since it was easier to achieve a polar orbit by sending the ferrying spacecraft to Jupiter, and use Jupiter's gravitational pull as a slingshot.

'We have several hours on SPOT today for our latest project,' Dr Pienarr said smugly, and pointed to the workstation to which Simona had returned. 'Simona is reducing our last spectrophotopolarimetric data of a likely star system within the constellation Aquila.' Columns of figures now came up on the wall screen facing Simona Opitz. 'Likely, in that the G-type primary might have satellites, so we'll also check ozone layers for free oxygen. We need a completely sampled coronographic image of the system. Now Far-side Number One is looking for space ice,' and he gestured to another workstation on the upper level.

'Space ice?'

'Yes, you know, frozen water, even possibly the water that

303

was once used by a higher life form than that which we found on Mars. One would have to purify such ice, but even if it is only good for irrigation, it's a very valuable commodity.' Dr Pienarr gave Peter a telling glance for his surprise at such basic husbandry in space. 'Well, that's what Far-side Number One is doing; you probably passed it to starboard?' He cocked his head enquiringly.

'We did,' Peter admitted, and diplomatically said nothing else.

'Far-side Number Two is doing a survey of the M-type asteroids of the Patroclus group,' Ajmal said, very pleased. 'The Space Authority has been nagging us for details so that they can begin mining operations. Certainly would increase resources.'

'Won't that cause problems?' Vin Cyberal asked.

'Not unless they had to be moved,' Ajmal said.

Moved, Peter echoed in his thoughts. 'You could move an asteroid?'

'Are you asking if *you* could, telekinetically?' Ajmal asked, his eyes twinkling.

Peter laughed, not only as an answer to the astronomer, but also to relieve his startled reaction to the very idea. Not that he thought he was likely to do so. Could he?

'Technically,' Pienarr continued, and Cyberal grinned at Peter, 'I suppose that could be done, with the newest rockets the SA has developed. Attach 'em, blast it out of its current orbit. God knows, there're enough asteroids.

'That's another problem we monitor – generally on FST Number Three,' and Ajmal waved towards the workstation diametrically opposite them. 'Then, on that scope,' and he gestured almost contemptuously to the rear wall, and the window that looked onto the Schmidt-Cassegrain, 'we constantly track NEOs and the PHAs. There were several close ones in the late twentieth century – 1989 CF, 1997 XF11 and, most particularly, 1999 AN10. Do you know what NEOs are?' His eyes fixed on Peter as a teacher's will on a student suspected of ignorance.

'Yes, I do,' Peter replied easily. 'Wasn't it First Base that identified the very close crossing of the1998 HH49 in 2028?'

'Yes, it was. The Station was just operational,' and a look of regret crossed Ajmal's round, mobile face, 'but I was not on-station then. Indeed, I hadn't even decided on astronomy as a career in 'twenty-eight.' He sighed. 'Well, that PHA was unusual, even for its whimsical type. I'm sure you understand that many small bodies cross Earth's orbit without incident. We certainly are extremely careful not to cry "wolf" to the SpaceForce. Any PHA is well documented and ephemerals constantly projected, so there's plenty of warning and no last-minute panic about Doomsday or Armageddon or Nemesis.' He raised his eyebrows and widened his eyes in despair of such dramatics. 'October, it was, the sixteenth, and although HH49 should have passed within five hundred and sixty thousand miles of Earth, its orbit was perturbed by the passage of the Comet Enzuka in 2027, so action had to be taken and the PHA was rather neatly disintegrated. Of course, with a united world government, the suspicions and paranoia of the late twentieth century simply can't recur.'

Peter sensed that Dr Pienarr was about to exercise one of his favourite hobby horses and interposed with his request.

'If it's possible, I really would like to see what you're looking at now in the Patroclus group,' Peter said eagerly.

Ajmal stepped agilely up to the nearest workstation, gesturing for them to follow him. 'What we've been focusing on isn't as spectacular as . . .'

'Oh, don't change it just for me,' Peter exclaimed, but Ajmal had already typed in an altering set of commands.

'Nonsense. Even I know you're not the usual visitor. I'll just bring up one of the more impressive ones in the Patroclus group. I've saved the coordinates of the search pattern, so it'll be no trouble at all to track back. Ah, here we are,' and with a grand flourish of one hand, he indicated the monitor that lit up with images.

Peter was awed to have such a sharp focus on the distant object whose orbit was following Jupiter. Seeing was required for believing as it hung in space, moving just perceptibly against its backdrop of asteroids and stars, Jupiter not visible in this frame.

'Tithonus,' Ajmal announced, tucking his hands under his biceps as he viewed the spectacle. Unnecessarily, the doctor repeated the information running along the bottom of the screen activated by his workstation. 'Number six-nine-nine-eight in IAU, inclination one point seven, eccentricity nought point nought six eight, with a twenty-eight-kilometre diameter. That'd be a handy one to move, at least, if you're really considering that, Vin,' and Ajmal gave Cyberal a sly look. 'Just fire the rockets in whichever direction you want to break it free from the L-5 point, and inject it into a new orbit.'

Peter could even make out what looked like 'dust' on the uneven surface of Tithonus. In his previous expeditions to observatories, the emphasis had been on the main planets of this solar system or observations from the faint object spectrographs of systems that were then the subjects of intense colonial interest.

'You seem fascinated, Pete,' Cyberal said in the sort of voice one used to break into intense concentration.

'Oh, sorry. Yes, I am fascinated. Thank you, Dr Pienarr.'

'Oh, not the title, please.' Ajmal gave a testy wave of his hand. 'Does get to you, though.' His attention had returned to the image.

'I wouldn't mind your going back to the M-asteroid. I would rather not interrupt your work any more than I have to,' Peter began politely. Then he pointed to the window and control panels of the telescope. 'May I have a look?'

'But of course, my dear boy, of course. Though,' and Ajmal's tone became almost derogatory, 'it's of a much earlier generation than the ones we now work with.' After a pause, he added, 'It was built in situ.'

Peter glided over. The wide partition window seemed to be one of those that would turn opaque at a touch. Yes, there was a toggle clearly marked 'window' on the control board. Accustomed to the usual dome protection, he was at first surprised to see the huge barrel, at least twelve metres long, just sitting out in the open. But there were no elements to guard against – only the full rays of the sun. Another control was marked 'deflector shield', and he would have looked further, but suddenly there was noise coming from the foyer.

Over Cyberal's shoulder – because the Major had stepped in front of him – Peter saw Corporal Hinojosa backing in a step ahead of several white-coated figures. Peter swallowed, getting a flashback of a scene during Barchenka's Mutiny.

'It's all right,' he told Vin when he felt the public minds of the newcomers and knew they were harmless. Hinojosa's doorkeeping was helpful, not deterrent.

'Just my staff, Vin,' Ajmal was saying, startled by the sudden defensive posture of the Major. 'Their shift is starting.' He turned to Peter as four men and a woman filed in. 'We keep very odd hours here, you see. Now, since she's making such a glorious transit, let me show you Callisto. As you may not know, once Mars Station is up and running, she's being considered for an advance Base.'

'She is?' Peter echoed, surprised. 'Really? Isn't she covered with craters? Isn't there supposed to be a salty ocean sloshing beneath all the ice? Wouldn't that make her ineligible for a permanent installation?'

Ajmal Pienarr beamed as if Peter were a precocious student. Vin Cyberal cleared his throat in discreet warning, and Ajmal shook his head.

'I thought this young man had total clearance,' he said almost testily.

'On First Base, but not necessarily to all of the Space Authority's future plans,' the Major said.

Peter forbore to find out more from a closer 'path at Ajmal's very open mind, but his interest was certainly piqued.

'The moon yesterday, Mars tomorrow and why not the universe next week?' Peter said expansively, to show he had taken no offence.

'Yes, yes, and here's Callisto. Splendid, isn't she?' Ajmal said, stepping back a pace and folding his arms on his chest, the better to admire the sight on the wall screen.

As fascinating as the asteroid had been, Peter was amazed at the size of Callisto, a brownish-orange marble in a sky dominated by Jupiter's formidable bulk to the left. He knew the moon had the oldest surface of the Jovian satellites, since it hadn't been constantly recycled by volcanic activity, like Io, so the moon hadn't had the chance to cover her crater scars. She had sustained multitudes of 'hits', to judge by the interlocking impact craters that riddled the surface she turned resolutely outward.

'Valhalla?' Peter asked, pointing to the largest of these features.

'Correct,' was Ajmal's response, nodding once again with pleasure at Peter's accurate identification.

'Aj, we need to alter the tracking on Number One now,' Simona Opitz said from her station, one of the white-coated men standing by her. 'Or did Mr Reidinger want to see the space ice?' She turned a very friendly but firm smile on Cyberal. 'Have you remembered to ask where you want him to 'port objects in here yet? After all, that's why he's here. We can't monopolize his time, you know.'

Which Peter had no trouble interpreting to mean 'monopolize *our* time'. Well, he could appreciate that, now he'd seen the staff arrive; they seemed to be waiting for their day's assignments.

'You were very good to give me so much of your time, Ajmal,' Peter said affably, glancing back at the astronomer who was actually pouting. 'Where would it be safe to 'port in here? I certainly wouldn't want to . . .'

'Over there.' Ajmal gestured negligently towards the window partition and the control panel, exasperated by the Captain, who merely smiled back. 'We don't use that area as much.'

Peter took good note of the angle of the partition window, the edge of the control panel, and the storage cabinet beneath it, looking very much like the corner of many other facilities. Then he saw the discoloration on the wall from the top of the window to the floor that resembled the southern tip of South America and Cape Horn. That and the window sill would make it an easily identifiable site for him to 'see'. Since deciding on such a place was the real reason he'd been brought to the observatory, his business here was over.

Saying all that was polite to Ajmal and then Simona, Peter left the observatory with Cyberal.

'Damned managing female,' Cyberal said without rancour when they were in the corridor and the corporal was once more their advance scout. The astronomy office was on the north end of Akahiro Block. 'Ajmal loves to talk, or had you noticed?'

Peter nodded with a little chuckle. 'But all of that,' he began as they retraced their steps, 'the mining and Callisto; they depend on getting the Mars Base started, don't they?'

'It is started, you know,' Vin Cyberal replied in a low voice. 'It's keeping it going that's the problem. It needs more personnel, supplies, material, instrumentation and air. Water's been found.' He shrugged at the immensity of the task involved. 'But we don't know if it's enough. That's how come the search for space ice.'

'Well, humans walked on the moon mid-twentieth century; they can now live comfortably and independently on it, so why not on Mars before this century is out?'

I should have asked to 'see' the Mars Base while I had the chance, Peter railed at himself. For that matter, there were plenty of coordinates he could use now that Airy was the Greenwich Meridian line of Mars, and there were enough high-resolution images to paper the walls of the old Pentagon Building.

Back on Padrugoi, Cass Cutler had disguised herself as yet another innocuous cleaner, complete with a service trundle-cart full of janitorial supplies. She had trudged the corridors of the lower levels, 'hunting' for Flimflam. She had found him late on the first day, innocently asleep in his proper quarters. The contact was enough to refresh her 'sense' of him, but she didn't like what he was dreaming about and balked at probing deep enough to wake him up and get him moving about, so she could see what he was doing and where he went.

The 'janitorial staff' was composed mainly of offenders sentenced off-Earth: offies, in the current slang. They wore double wristbands, which technically limited them to the lower levels of Padrugoi. Janitorial squads were brought above the permitted level by guards, especially when the open, public areas had to be cleaned up after special assemblies or brawls among freighter crews. They were searched before and after the work period. Cass observed to herself that brawls could be started. So it wouldn't be hard to 'leave' something behind where only the intended recipient could find it. There might indeed be a flourishing black market on Padrugoi, in spite of all the precautions. No anomalies had been brought to official notice since Barchenka's time. She didn't know if this was a reflection on Admiral Coetzer's more enlightened regime or not.

Until the sabotage of Limo 34. Only *that* had been arranged to be a space accident and no one, or no evidence, should have remained to explain the destruction. Had Flimflam, if indeed he was responsible, slipped out of a work party on the boat bay and sabotaged the spaceship? Not by himself.

The next shift started in two hours, so she cleaned the dormitory hall. Ironic, that the area janitorial staff lived in needed cleaning. She was accustomed, from work in the Linears, to filth, but those buildings were much older than Padrugoi. Finally, men and women emerged from their sleeping quarters to eat before going to work. No one noticed her, but then, part of her value was that she could blend nicely into any sort of background. Five men exited Flimflam's room, but he did not. The prospect of cleaning for another eight hours in this section of Padrugoi had no appeal whatsoever, even if the hallway hadn't been so clean since oxygen had first filtered into it.

She decided she'd better get some sleep. If she had to do any chasing of Flimflam, she'd need to be rested. Crowd control was easy compared to surveillance. She slipped into a nearby, almost empty female accommodation, ignoring the pong in the room and the thinness of the mattress. She tried to set her mind to wake her up if she felt Flimflam's mind moving away from her. But she discounted the depth of her fatigue.

She was awakened by another cleaner who indignantly

demanded why she thought she had the right to take some-one else's bunk. Meekly, Cass left with her trundle-cart and cast about her for Flimflam's mental signature. It was well into the afternoon before she sussed him suddenly at a distance – he might have come off an elevator. She couldn't 'path too far away without a partner, but it was him, coming her way. She whipped out a damp rag and began to scrub.

She could feel his mind seething as he neared. So chaotic with doubts that she automatically tried to broadcast reassurances. And stopped. The day she helped Flimflam would be a cold one in Hell. Out of the corner of her eye, she was surprised to note that he was wearing tailored fatigues and the insignia of a lieutenant junior grade in Communications. He passed her without so much as a glance, fretting over the lack of news. What news? she wondered. He was twitching inside and out, jiggling one hand as he strode, outwardly confident and wearing the sort of expression that would turn aside any casual enquiries. He inserted a metal strip into the slot of a door halfway down the corridor and went inside.

'Well, well, well and well,' Cass murmured, laying her hand on the plasteel wall. He was doing something. The moment his activities inside stopped, she bent over, and her hind end would be all he'd see of her. She did not make the mistake of working too industriously, since the cleaners she observed never used much energy on the job.

Flimflam, his mind disquieted by a variety of anxieties about the rewards of failure, which he still vehemently denied as he examined acceptable excuses, strode past her. He was no longer clad in tailored clothes. Trouser legs of regular issue flapped about his ankles, showing regular-issue ship shoes rather than the polished leather half-boots that an officer usually wore.

'Well, he always was a quick-change artist,' she mused. She let him get out of sight and then, trundling the cart to the door he had used, she got out the special strip Com-mander Ottey had warily entrusted to her – it allowed entry to any room up to CIC – and got in with a quiet snick.

One look inside and she hauled the cart in as well, closing

the door behind her. Staring about her, she whistled in surprise. In her haste to get in, she hadn't noticed the label on the door but whatever that said, it lied. Flimflam had converted it for his own use. Part of it was his changing room for a variety of uniforms and collar tabs, no rank higher than lieutenant commander, but every type of authorized apparel from fatigues to dress tunic hung from a rail. The other part was supplies. Drawers and shelves contained sundry items from instant sustenance packets to gourmet freeze-dried foods, bottles of wine and hard liquor, drawers packed with circuit boards and tools, manuals (two marked TOP SECRET), including the MPU one, odd-shaped vacuum packs, identified only by serial codes. Hanging on a nail were a half-dozen wrist IDs. How did he remove his distinctive double wristband so that he could use these? The fact that Flimflam possessed spares of anything was disturbing. She jammed the bands into her thigh pocket, patting them flat. Having had a good look round, she turned back to the door, looking for any surveillance device Flimflam might have planted. There was none, but there was a sketch of sorts on the back of the door, marked with squares, rectangles and circles, running vertically in a weird design. She stared at it, trying to comprehend its significance.

'How dense can you get, Cutler,' she said, slapping her forehead as it suddenly occurred to her that this was a rough diagram of the Station's levels.

She found her current location, a square, the shape of this room. Keeping the layout of Padrugoi in mind, she worked out that there were two more square repositories like this, one in the Mall, another in the non-commissioned officers' quarters. She fussed over the circles, which were so oddly placed, gave up on them and tried to suss out the rectangles. The largest one ought to be on the boat bay. That made a lot of sense. If Flimflam had been responsible for the sabotage of Limo 34, and she suspected that he had had a lot to do with it, he'd've had to have all his supplies for that job in one place, as well as additional help, to do it in the time available. What were the circles? OK, Cutler, what is circular on a space station? Glancing about the room, racking her brains, her eye caught the ventilation grill in the ceiling.

'Yes, stupid,' she murmured. 'Now did General Johnny give him that idea, when he secreted his troops in the conduits around the inauguration site before the Mutiny?'

There were nine circles on the rough map, ranging up and down Padrugoi's long stem. In her mind's eye, she slid a map of Padrugoi over the sketch and memorized the positions. She could hunt for the conduit and ventilation sites later. All would have to be large enough for a man of Flimflam's size, though he wasn't all that big really – medium height and weight – and that sort of cut down the options. She should check the boat-bay site next. But first for that evidence the boss always needed. She took out the print recorder and ran it over every surface. It would record all fingerprints, including her own, but would provide undeniable evidence of who frequented this room. Flimflam couldn't have done the sabotage on his own. He had to have had accomplices. Maybe never allowed in this room, but surely when he did that rush job on Limo 34?

Boat bay next! She removed a change of clothing and rank from her trundle-cart so that she could reach her destination without too many questions on the way.

Opening the door and checking to be sure the hall was vacant, she emerged as a CPO from Transport, and pushed the cart out. She closed the door, noting that it was labelled '7299A'. She wheeled the cart almost to the next intersection, where she left it and walked smartly away.

The boat bay was occupied when she got there: a maintenance team was working on another limo, but were too busy under the eyes of a CPO to notice her entry. Moving as if she were on an urgent errand, she strode to her target door and, slipping in the special key, was relieved when it opened. She entered, letting the door close on her as she palmed on lights. She whistled softly. Unlike 7299A, this room was a mess and was filled with an acrid smell. The grill had been removed from the ceiling ventilator; that was interesting. Improvised steps in the form of empty plastic frames suggested that someone or several someones had left via that route. More important to her search, however, were the circuit boards and crystals. Careful not to smear any fingerprints on what surface there was, she peered at the yellow printing on the boards.

'Hmm. For MPUs, huh? Like they use in limos. Very interesting.'

Tools were also scattered about an empty container clearly marked *EPOXY Type 34-AS-9, Fast-acting.* A large red label under that legend warned about using it without safety gloves and mask. She saw the cuff of one safety glove and several masks discarded in a corner.

'Let's see now, six, seven days? There might still be residual traces on skin and clothing that a sensor could pick up. Some of those grunts don't bother washing,' she reminded herself.

She took out the print recorder and slowly scanned the printable surfaces available, of which there were quite a few. She had a stitch in her back when she'd finished the circuit. Hopping up the steps, she flicked the recorder around the aperture. Prints might be smudged, but enough could be made of them to confirm that this had been used as an egress for those owning the prints. Then she hoisted herself up into the ventilation shaft, ducking her head as she perched on the edge. Light from other openings in both directions allowed her to see to intersections.

'Hmmm, Flimflam'd need to pick skinny grunts. He's not, even in tailor-mades.' She spread her hand, which she knew measured twenty centimetres from little finger to thumb, a reliable gauge, and decided that the opening was just wide enough for a man, not too broad in the shoulder. He'd've had to scrunch in his shoulders a bit. 'Wonder if he'll have old bruises or scrapes on his arms,' she mused. At least there was reason for the boss to do a thorough examination of him. She considered if continuing would be profitable. 'Maybe, but I'd get dirty and tired and someone else can do this sort of work,' she muttered. 'I'd better get back to the boss. I've found Flimflam, and I've found evidence that should stand up in a trial.'

She lowered herself back through the opening, holding

onto the edge to kick the crude steps out of the way before she dropped to the floor. Dusting off her hands and uniform, she exited the room, whistling merrily, and didn't bother to notice if the maintenance crew had seen her.

On her way back to the Commissioner's temporary office on the CIC level of Padrugoi, she realized one of the things that might be causing Flimflam anxiety: Limo 34 had landed safely at First Base, though the news had not been bruited about. So all his efforts to sabotage the flight had been in vain. Couldn't happen to a nicer sucker! She wondered who would be on his back because he'd failed. That was someone else's problem. She was here because she could recognize Flimflam's mind. The LEO Commissioner was loaning the Admiral appropriate, parapsychic staff in this investigation. Not that she could, or would, probe that scuzzball but she certainly could locate him, and she had. She found the appropriate lift, inserted the metal slip of her pass and continued on her way. As a crowd-control empath with a limited 'path range, she'd have to report in person. Besides, she wanted to see the expression on Boris Roznine's face. She also needed to get to a schematic of Padrugoi so that she could identify the locations of Flimflam's other depots. She rapped on the office door.

Ah, Cass, said Boris in his unmistakably deep mental voice. *Come in.*

She did, pausing in surprise at the disarray in the cabin. Roznine's office in Jerhattan was always tidy, but here he was surrounded by pencil files of all colours, hard copy, two monitors displaying graphs and curves, as well as a recent tray with half-eaten sandwiches. Boris looked tired; even his fingers wavered a little over his notepad.

'I got proof,' she said, waggling the print recorder before she passed it over to him. 'And do you have a schematic of the Station? I got some other locations I want to get down before I forget 'em.'

With no hesitation, Boris whisked a sheet from under some other hard copy on his desk, and flipped it to her.

'Been here,' and she grabbed a marker and circled the

315

point. 'Seven Deck, room 7299A, and it'd be interesting to know what it's officially used for because Flimflam made it a dressing room cum food stash, with liquor for bribes, tools and too many vacuum-packed gimmicks for me to identify.'

Boris let her make her notations. With a final flourish she marked the one at the boat bay. 'You'll want to send a security team up there *muy* pronto, boss. Ottey's going to love it. Mind you, the Epoxy 34-AS-9 container is empty but that was the one bit of alleged sabotage equipment I could recognize. Smell of the stuff might still make a sensor jump.' She pointed to her markings. 'These are places – as near as I can estimate – where he must have other drops. He put an aide memoire on the back of the door of room 7299A.' She grinned sardonically.

Boris leaned to one side of his worktop, flipped open the com and gave the number. When he had Ottey online, he gave crisp requests that were more orders than suggestions to search 7299A and the boat-bay storage locker. He paused, listening to a question that was probably just as crisp, if Cass knew Ottey, and turned back to her.

'D'you know where he is right now?'

She twitched a shoulder as she sprawled in a chair. 'He had assumed his lowly janitorial persona when he exited 7299A. Once I saw what was inside, I took prints and investigated the one location I was reasonably sure of finding – the boat bay. He's real worried.' She paused to grin maliciously and then sat forward abruptly. 'Oh, tell Ottey that the ventilator shaft in the boat-bay site was open, steps up to it and all. I took good prints before I had a look. Must have used small guys, or ones with narrow shoulders. Flimflam ain't that broad across the chest.'

'They're on their way,' Boris said, closing the connection.

'I felt it was wiser to report back to you once I'd ascertained the nature of the boat-bay location,' she went on, receiving a positive nod from her boss, 'rather than try to discover his current whereabouts. I also found these.' She withdrew the tangle of ID wristbands and let them casually fall from her fingers to the worktop.

Eyes widening with dismay, Boris grabbed the nearest one and popped it into the security clearance unit on one side of his desk. 'Lieutenant Schafer, Supply?' Even as he repeated the name of its wearer, the machine bleeped and flashed an error message. The printout informed Boris that Lieutenant Schafer had been transferred three years ago. He picked up another. 'Commander Uskar, Engineering?' For the past two years, Uskar had been teaching at Newport Naval Base.

'I wonder Flimflam ever bothered to sleep in that cell of his,' Cass observed wryly. 'Though I guess that once in a while he had to be where he was supposed to be. Those first two IDs would have given him access to wherever he wanted to be. From what I saw stashed away, he could change service branch and identity any time he needed to.'

Boris did not bother with the rest of the bands. He re-opened the com-link. 'Roznine again. Bindra? Ottey's already gone, has he? Excellent. Something else has come up, if you'd be so kind as to step down to my office?'

Cass grinned. When the LEO Commissioner spoke in that tone, 'be so kind' meant like, right now! Cass wondered just how Flimflam had acquired the wristbands in the first place, since such IDs were worn constantly – by their legitimate owners – and were hard to replicate; but perhaps not for a scam artist like Albert Ponce. Or had he just switched counterfeits for the originals?

'For someone supposed to be limited to one section of Padrugoi, he certainly had the freedom of the Station,' Boris remarked at his drollest.

'What else could you expect from someone like Flimflam?' Cass could objectively admire the man's ingenuity and resourcefulness.

'I do not care to speculate,' Boris said repressively, but Cass was not intimidated and grinned back. 'What I find somewhat surprising is that he didn't try to leave the Station.'

'Well paid to stay aboard until it was worth his while to leave?' Cass asked with an innocent expression on her face. 'He's been up here long enough to explore the indigenous opportunities to the fullest. And he was involved in the

317

White-Coat Mutiny, wasn't he?' She pointed to the secret caches she'd put on the schematic.

'He was, but only peripherally. Barchenka was no fool, and he lost privileges supporting her.' Boris frowned, fingering his lower lip thoughtfully. 'LEO is going to have to follow different avenues of investigation.'

Cass knew he was thinking about personnel. LEO was always short of the right kind of personnel, which was one reason she had drawn this duty.

'International LEO already has cooperated with surveillance on Shimaz's relatives; those who have been up here, at least, for one reason or another, including one Ahmin Duvachek, who demanded a formal Health and Welfare appointment to ascertain if our facility was according Mr Albert Ponce's human rights.' Boris's expression was ironic.

'Ah!' Cass drawled the syllable out. 'You do remember, don't you, boss, that Flimflam was not the brains behind the child-farming scheme.'

'All too true, but we haven't been able to establish if Shimaz is involved in this mess. Though I remind you that he did work with Barchenka.'

'Maybe he's bankrolling it?'

'Haven't traced credit transfers yet. Though Kibon does regularly transfer credits downside. He has relatives, too.'

Cass opened her eyes wide. 'All God's chillun got relatives.'

'Credit going out doesn't worry me as much as credit coming in, and we haven't found that yet. It'll be interesting to see what Flimflam has secreted away at these points.' Boris tapped Cass's marks.

'Nasty man, Shimaz, waiting so long to get back at Peter.'

'Not just Peter. They've been after General Greene a while, too, but he's slippery. And confidentially, Cass, this is not the first time Peter's been at risk since he became an official Centre employee.'

She was clearly startled by that admission. 'You mean, those clowns on his birthday?'

318

Boris nodded. 'The Faithful Brotherhood of whatever-it-was has now been traced back to one of Flimflam's Religious Interpretative Groups.'

'Has anyone tried for Tirla?' Cass asked, sitting bolt upright on the chair, half afraid, half resentful that the girl she had rescued nearly six years ago might be at risk again. Roznine's sister-in-law had been more involved with Flimflam and Shimaz than Peter was.

'Oh, that one,' and Boris's expression was affectionately droll. 'She suspects there have been quite a few attempts. She has a finely tuned sixth sense of survival.' A small smile of approval turned up the corners of Roznine's generous mouth. 'It's only recently that we have correlated those incidents as perhaps part of a larger plot for revenge.'

'Barchenka didn't know *her*,' Cass exclaimed, puzzled.

'We don't know that Construction Manager Barchenka is involved at all – bar having had brief visits from two of Shimaz's relations. We're trying to find out if Ahmin Duvachek is related, or connected in some way to her. Though it takes little imagination to see why she certainly would enjoy getting back at Peter and John Greene.'

'That's fer damned sure, boss.' Then she rose. 'How's Ranjit doing? I haven't caught even a twitch from him.'

Boris pursed his lips, but his light blue eyes were amused. 'He's following a different line of investigation, working undercover.'

She nodded acceptance of the tacit injunction. 'Then I'd better get back to turning over every slimy stone in the facility. I shouldn't want Flimflam to get word we were looking for him, and hide someplace he didn't mark on that door map.'

'Keep your mind wide open, Cass.'

'And my shields up.' She slipped out the door and was gone, moments before Bindra tapped on his door.

Ottey contacted Bindra in Roznine's office, and informed them that the boat-bay storage locker indeed contained items that could be identified as having been used in the sabotage of Limo 34. It was being cleared of the evidence. Surveillance equipment had been installed, as well as a

fast-acting, proximity-triggered gas device that would immobilize anyone who entered the locker from either the
ventilator shaft or the door. A second team was already
dealing with room 7299A and was installing similar arrangements.

Boris and Bindra then took the ID bands to Admiral
Coetzer. Controlling his consternation, the Admiral in-
structed Bindra to investigate possible safeguards against
future theft, and to initiate discreet ID spot checks. (Lieutenant Schafer and Commander Uskar had turned in the
bands they wore on the day of their departure downside, and
no one had thought to see if the bands were legitimate
before destroying them, as per regulations. The two officers
would have received new IDs on arriving at their new posts.)

The Admiral contacted a First Base com officer for a
secured line to General Greene, and was informed that he
was currently in conference with Colonel Watari.

'Put me through, please.'

When Johnny came on, Dirk Coetzer briefly reported
what had just been discovered.

'One thing's sure, Dirk, there's no way Shimaz can move
around First Base that easily,' Johnny said.

'He's under twenty-four-hour surveillance,' Watari said,
subtly criticizing Padrugoi's security. 'He's banded, so he
can't get out of his cell without setting off a general alarm.'

'That's reassuring,' Coetzer replied at his blandest.
'Johnny, get yourself and Pete back here as soon as possible.'

'Maybe we're safer here,' Johnny had the impudence to
remark.

'As you can well imagine, General,' the Admiral replied at
his most formal, 'we are going to review security measures
relating to convicts serving sentences on-station.' He glanced
over at Boris, who inclined his head, accepting that contingency. 'However,' the Admiral went on, 'I do appreciate that
Flimflam is an unusual operator. We've had no more than
minor disciplinary incidents with anyone else.'

'It only takes one,' Bindra remarked through gritted teeth.

'Do not, I repeat, General, do not advise anyone of your
ETA.'

'Gotcha, Admiral,' was Johnny's rejoinder, and First Base signed off.

'I shall have a word with the Attorney-General, Admiral,' Boris said. 'Meanwhile, Ms Cutler is trying to find Flimflam's current whereabouts.'

'When she does, I'll have him arrested,' Bindra said.

'No,' and the Admiral lifted one hand, 'if Ms Cutler can keep track of him, it might be more interesting to see what he'll do next.'

'Only if he doesn't try to revisit one of his depots,' Bindra said.

'A point, Admiral, Commander,' Boris began. 'Ms Cutler mentioned that he had been wearing Communications tabs. Let's run the CIC tapes and see if he turns up. Or a request for any information on Limo 34 by anyone on-station.'

'All contact with First Base has been on secured lines,' Dirk Coetzer said, and then began to smile. 'How about if we just leak some misinformation and see how Flimflam reacts?' He leaned back in his chair and steepled his fingers in anticipation.

Wake up, Pete, Johnny's voice interrupted Peter's dream of spinning asteroids and gibbous, leering planets that enlarged and diminished like balloons.

'Whaaat?' Peter found it hard to rouse himself. It seemed as if he'd only just got to bed.

That's right, and now you gotta be out of it, packed and ready when Nina knocks on your door.

Why? Peter demanded as he was levitating himself off the bed.

Because we're packing our tents like the Arabs and stealing away, Johnny said with mischief in his mental tone. *Get a move on. She's nearly there. You don't want Nina catching you in the altogether, do you?*

Peter drew in an indignant breath, suppressing the twinge to his chest. One didn't *feel* vanity; it was imagination.

Just kidding, and for once Johnny sounded repentant.

Peter did not dally, though he took the time to change his appliance, as it was full enough to be emptied. He was dressed and inserting the last pencil file into his carry-all when he heard a very light rap on the door.

'I'm coming,' he said, gliding to it and opening it to see the corporal looking unfairly wide awake and as pretty as ever, her brown eyes bright despite the hour. He envied her exuberance.

She pointed in the direction they were to go, and started off in a quiet jog trot, Peter increasing his forward motion and surreptitiously knuckling the sleep out of his eyes. He hadn't even had time to wash his face.

Where are we going, Johnny? She just pointed, Peter said in complaint.

Back to Padrugoi, with all possible steam and secretivity.

There's no such word. Why? How? I didn't think the limo was ready yet. It's two in the morning, Johnny.

There are other vehicles. Flimflam's been a heavy operator on Padrugoi, and there's now proof that he was involved in the sabotage of the Thirty-four. I'm taking no risks with you.

I am not, I repeat, I am not, Peter said in a fierce tone, *driving us back to Padrugoi.* Even if I think I could, he added very, very privately to himself. Perhaps it was just as well that they were going back to the Station. He doubted he could have talked Watari, or Opitz, into allowing him another look through the telescopes. Not that Padrugoi didn't have access to the far-side scopes. Now that he knew what he was looking for, he'd be able to have time on those FSTs more easily there than here. Watari would want to know why. He ran First Base by 'the book'.

I, on the other hand, Johnny continued, oblivious to Peter's private ruminations and responding to his emphatic statement of intent, *I do not wish that you should waste your valuable energy and any calories on this trip. I personally head-picked the passengers coming back on Limo Twenty-eight, since Watari wouldn't let me take it without any. I pulled rank and got Xiang Liu as pilot, though he wasn't next up on the roster. Watari conceded that choice because he wants us off First Base even faster than Dirk wants us back. Catch ya when you get here.*

Peter felt Johnny close the mental connection and, if they

were to be taking off shortly, noted that Johnny would be doing pre-flight checks with Xiang.

Nina Hinojosa was leading him through Babe Ruth Block – no angry pulse at this time of night, so even Shimaz slept. They encountered on-duty officers, nodding as they passed, but stayed on the lower level, moving towards the old, original Lunar Base building. Nina paused at the steel doors across the final segment and inserted her security pass. She motioned him to follow quickly through the irising portal as soon as there was space enough for her. She waited almost impatiently for him to catch her up. He'd had half a mind to levitate himself head first through it.

An arrow on the wall told him they were heading towards B-lock. The hallway which connected the Base to the airlock was empty, but he could smell sweat and other odours that indicated it had recently been occupied. They went up the steps of the accordion tunnel sealed to the open hatch of the 28. Nina stopped.

'Here you are, sir. It's been a pleasure to meet you,' she said with a salute. Then she smiled up at him, her dark eyes sparkling.

He had no right to return the salute. Surprising himself, he bent quickly and planted a kiss on her cheek before whirling himself on board. He nearly ran Johnny Greene over, and devoutly hoped that the General had not seen him kiss the corporal.

'In you git, lad,' Johnny said, hauling Peter in by a handful of the coverall. 'We're outta here.' With a farewell nod to Nina, he tapped the closing sequence of the hatch. 'OK, Xiang. He's aboard.'

Secure your stuff in bunk ten. Same one, but a different and much safer *bird. Then join me forward. I saved you a good seat.*

Peter did as he was bid, and murmured a greeting to Xiang Liu as he took his seat.

'Bad penny turns up,' he said.

Xiang smiled. 'Good penny to have on board.'

A red light flashed off into green on the control panel, the signal that Nina was safely inside the departure room and the airlock secured on the Base side. The retractable access tunnel was pulling away. Another red light switched to green and they were completely disconnected from the Base.

Without touching more than surface thoughts, Peter felt the anticipation of the passengers behind and beside him. One and all were delighted to be going 'home', although one and all were slightly annoyed by the unexpected hour of departure. Most were enlisted personnel or civilians, and the single officer was not one whom Peter had met in his whirlwind visit to First Base.

Peter couldn't feel much motion, but the view out the front window altered as the limo was taxied to the take-off site. Peter could feel the build-up of power, so different from the drop-off exit from Padrugoi.

He heard the formal exchanges between Lieutenant Xiang Liu and First Base, and only briefly wished himself in the engineer's position. He'd done it once, when it mattered the most, when Johnny was pilot. He was not entirely sure that he was glad to be just a passenger this time, but he was tired.

'Our status is go,' an unfamiliar voice said – whoever was engineer this trip. 'Mr Liu, are we scheduled for a standard lunar departure?'

'That is correct. First Base, are we green for go?'

'You are green for go on our computers, Limo Twenty-eight,' and Peter recognized Watari's voice.

'We have a green for go,' Xiang Liu reported, and Peter could hear the relief in the man's voice.

As the limo blasted off, Peter felt the pressure pushing him into the chair padding. He thought he preferred the easier take-off from Padrugoi, although the surge of the rockets was exciting. For the space of the ascent, he almost felt his bones pressing against the skin of his back. This trip to the moon had made him quite fanciful. He'd be glad to be back on solid Padrugoi.

CHAPTER THIRTEEN

Back on Padrugoi, Ranjit Youssef and Shandin Ross were patiently engaged in that most boring of investigative tasks: reviewing the entrance and exit tapes and cards of every visitor to Padrugoi since that security measure had been initiated under Barchenka, when the main stem of the Station had become operational. Thousands had belonged to grunts on work duty from the Linears and other over-crowded and underemployed urban areas around the world. Barchenka had not played favourites, at least at that level. Too many of the names the two men checked came up MIS, missing in space. That designation would alter – due to the Talents' vigilance – as they worked their way through to the inauguration. However, Ranjit and Shandin, sipping quantities of coffee and sugary substances, had not reached that far yet in their survey. They had had, for their purposes, to isolate the various ethnic groups by nationality, trying to find some lead to Shimaz and/or Albert Ponce and/or Barchenka. They had to establish who was still employed by the station and from which ethnicity. If Flimflam had waited six years to take revenge, others could have been planted, too.

They did have the few leads: relatives of Shimaz – Riz

Naztuk, Zehra bint Arrof, and Spaz Zenoun. The first was an uncle, actually ten years younger than the prince. Riz was a minor Embassy official, assigned to Jerhattan after Shimaz's conviction. Zehra was a first cousin, and had been implicated in some minor local government fraud, but her family connections had saved her from conviction. Spaz had a younger brother who had been sentenced to the Lunar Prison for terrorist activities and the massacre of over four hundred people in various bombings. Spaz had also worked on Padrugoi and was, by trade, an electrician. Padrugoi re-employed such technicians for short-term work, since they were already familiar with the Station. Spaz was one such. And the Ahmin Duvachek link.

Naztuk, bint Arrof and Zenoun had been logged on at the Station frequently, but, as Ranjit discovered, much more frequently in the last year. Duvachek had come only the once, but once might have been enough.

'D'you think Zenoun could have "arranged" good reasons each time he made "repairs"?' Ranjit asked Shandin.

The telepath gave a long sigh, leaning back in his chair and stretching until his joints popped.

'I get called down to Arrivals to check him, and I've never sensed anything in his public mind.' Shandin grimaced. 'Of course, I'm not allowed to go deeper, but I've also had no occasion to. Hello!' he added, jabbing at the hold button to stop the scroll. 'Zenoun was here five times last month and only one was for repairs.' He spun his chair over to Ranjit's station, where the LEO lieutenant was viewing entry tapes. 'Show us the passengers on March fifth, Ranjit.' Spaz was the third man through the security arch. He carried a pack that he languidly tossed to the security guard, who did the usual rummage through.

'Nothing illegal, or the guard would've spread the contents out,' Ranjit said.

'Guard knows him,' Shandin remarked, for the tape now showed Spaz's mouth moving. There was a pause, during which the guard made some remark before waving Spaz through.

'Who was on duty that day?' asked Ranjit, as the guard's

face was not visible. The surveillance unit was trained full on the faces of arrivals.

Shandin went back to his station and typed in a query. 'Corporal Ito Kuwahari.' Shandin entered another command. 'He's on leave.'

Ranjit pinched his lower lip between two fingers. 'Let me check.' He spoke a low command. 'Spaz stayed overnight, and whaddaya know! Look at his pack as he leaves: it's much flatter now.'

The two men exchanged smug glances.

'Good thinking, Ranjit. Let's just check Uncle Riz and Zehra and see if they brought anything with them, and maybe left some of it behind. Can we get prints of all three? Just in case they turn up where they oughtn't to have been?'

They smiled again at each other. The painstaking investigation had borne enough fruit to encourage them to look for more.

'Let's also go over the surveillance records at Barchenka's. Be very interesting to see if any of these mugs,' and Shandin waved his hand at the glossies of the three suspects, 'have ever been to tea with Barchenka.'

'Now, is it my office that checks with Corporal Kuwahari on leave, or yours?'

'I don't think we can. Where's Kuwahari's home? Osaka? On the off chance he happens to recall Spaz?' Ranjit asked.

Shandin twitched one shoulder. 'Be our guest. Osaka's out of my ball park. Kuwahari might recall the incident, though I can't fault him if he doesn't. Hundreds have come through since then.'

As soon as the rockets of Limo 28 shut down and they were in free fall, Johnny 'pathed to Peter details about the most recent developments at Padrugoi.

Flimflam? Peter was surprised. The only time he'd been anywhere near the man, he'd been unconscious. Anger flared in Peter as he remembered that Flimflam had beaten Tirla.

Ol' scuzzball himself, doing his usual thing. Caught him with his fingerprints all over some MPU components;

probably the originals he so kindly replaced for us. And more prints in the Epoxy he left behind. Whether or not it'll all be sorted out before we get back is doubtful. Meanwhile, connections are being made and evidence collected. Enjoy the next coupla days. They'll be the last peaceful ones either of us will have for a while.

Peter digested that information. *Is Flimflam,* he asked a moment later, *why we made such a precipitous dawn getaway?* He hadn't really had enough sleep last night – this morning.

Bingo! You are beginning to appreciate my devious mind. I'd planned this sort of getaway the moment you landed us. Even before Dirk told me about Flimflam's complicity.

But! But!

Never mind Watari. He is basically a good Commander, Johnny admitted. *Just doesn't like things that ain't according to the book, his book, and we sure as hell ain't according to any* book *yet written. Xiang went over this bird with every sensor known to man, with a maintenance crew I* personally *checked.* He weighted that word to imply that he had done some not totally 'legal' scanning.

Aren't we going from the frying pan into the fire?

There're a lot more 'paths available on Padrugoi than there were on First Base. Lance is getting some well-deserved sleep at last.

What? *Look, I don't* need *to be wrapped in cotton wool for the rest of my life,* Peter began angrily.

Cool it, Pete. You'll be working your butt off soon enough to pay for this luxury cruise. You'll bitch then, I suppose, about being out in the cold cruel world.

Wanna bet?

Johnny imagined a huge grin on his face.

Then Peter asked, *Was Flimflam the only one involved in this sabotage?*

Scarcely, Johnny replied with a snort. *Although,* he added quickly with a puzzled sigh, *I'm still trying to figure out who had the most to gain by offing us. Flimflam was just waiting for a chance, but he'd've had to have help. Fraga and Leitao?*

328

Them? Peter was dumbfounded. *I thought they were both Space Authority.*

I'd never heard of Fraga before. Though I have heard Leitao's name. Johnny mused. *He was sure babysitting her. Stayed with her in the sick bay until I was ready to 'port them down. And that collapse of hers – I'd like to know more about those two.*

She was scared stiff. Of me! Peter couldn't quite suppress the note of injured surprise in his voice.

Exactly. She was scared stiff of you, the psychic, although she must have known that you – and I – are teleports when she was drafted to come up to that meeting. 'Pressure of work'? 'Overwork'? I don't think so. What about scared of what she had on her mind? I want some answers from those two. Later: now you finish the night's sleep I so ruthlessly interrupted, Pete.

It took Peter a while, using limbics, to erase the angry indignation and get to sleep, secured in the netting. He woke to the sound of low voices in the corridor outside the privacy cubicles. He had slept himself out, and was much revived by the rest. With a touch of chagrin he thought of his outburst. He winced and felt the reaction – reminding himself sternly that he was in free fall and to move accordingly. He was also hungry, and needed to empty his appliance.

He gave himself a gentle shove out of his cubicle, using the head to empty his appliance before drifting towards the forward cabin. Xiang was on duty, talking to a man in a smart civilian coverall sitting in the other position. Xiang let one arm drift up as he saw Peter. Peter mimed eating and glided into the galley that was unoccupied, save for the lingering aroma of a savoury. Peter twisted the selection dial, stopping at fried chicken with rice and peas, and remembered the lunch he'd eaten with Ceara Scott. He chose that, not really caring if it was time for 'lunch' or not. Once again he could sense an odd clamp in his belly. Free fall was affecting him?

Thinking of Ceara made him wonder: had there been any investigation of Mai Leitao or Georg Fraga while they'd been here? He tried not to resent the woman's reaction to him. Had he remembered to tell Johnny about Fraga's unexpectedly opaque mind? How had Flimflam been involved? With Fraga or Leitao? Or Barchenka? She would surely have a crow to pluck with him and Johnny. But how could she be connected to Shimaz, who was very much incommunicado on First Base?

And, if Flimflam could finagle trouble on Padrugoi, was it safe to send such unreformable personalities to the Station to serve their sentences? Or cause the trouble Shimaz did at First Base? Not that it did him any good, since Hiroga Watari had a Japanese attitude towards criminals . . . that they were not to be cosseted.

As standard procedure required all persons eating at any of the mess halls on Padrugoi to run their hands through the ID box at the entrance, a secondary investigation by Commander Bindra was efficiently and expeditiously conducted. Five persons – three were offenders and the other two confessed that they were badly in debt to Flimflam (facts that Kibon corroborated) – were detained in the brig's isolation cells. Their fingerprints and traces of an epoxy on their skin and clothing verified their presence on a prohibited level of Padrugoi. A sixth man also had traces of the damning substance, but he was not detained at that point. Commander Bindra had specially chosen crews installing security devices in any ventilation shaft or conduit wider than fifty centimetres. Additional measures were being contemplated apropos a closer supervision of all offenders.

Peter did a lot of thinking on that return voyage, reviewing in his mind what he had seen on the telescopes and the ideas that the sights had generated. He itched to get time at Padrugoi's astronomy workstation. Then he sighed. Undoubtedly he'd have little free time when they got back. Vin Cyberal had passed the remark that Watari was hourly adding to his long list of urgently required items. At least Peter's contract with the Space Authority limited the number and mass of 'portations per day. He'd *make* time for use of the FST, and access the updates of astronomy texts from data files. There was so much he had to corroborate before he'd dare mention his notion to anyone, even Johnny. Maybe especially Johnny.

First he needed more visuals of the existing Mars facility before he'd attempt to 'port something that far. Would it be better to use Padrugoi as his base for such a heave? Or would he have to go back to First Base – when it was in a better conjunction with Mars, of course. Padrugoi constantly upgraded its own astronomy facility, and, if he could arrange time on the FSTs – he didn't really need the range and power of a SPOT – he doubted anyone would much question his request. He could just imagine Watari's outburst if Peter had asked for scope time on First Base.

Hearing what was officially being done with asteroids had given him another idea – bizarre to be sure – but was it any more bizarre than what he was able to do with a paralysed body? One did have to consider that Callisto's surface was icy, had no magnetic field and wisps of atmosphere and the crust covered a salty ocean. He regretted now that, once the Galileo programme had finished early this century, priorities had focused on firmly establishing a Lunar Base and preparatory work for a manned Mars Station. But you wouldn't want to site a facility on an unstable, icy envelope like Callisto's. An asteroid that could be terraformed. An M-type asteroid, one about twenty to thirty kilometres in diameter; might as well dream big, Peter, enough iron to mine *in situ* and sufficient magnetic force to secure the atmosphere dome to the surface.

Would Ganymede, or would Io, be better for his needs? Those two satellites were 'inner', and he wanted as broad a window for telekinetic thrusts as possible. Somehow Callisto appealed to him more. Named after a nymph beloved by Jupiter, if his memory served him. And changed into a bear by Juno. Suddenly the laughing face of Nina Hinojosa crossed his mind. Would she be what the ancients had called a 'nymph', small, supple, pretty, dark-eyed? And no Juno would have been able to turn *her* into a bear! He chuckled at such whimsy. Furthermore, Callisto's orbit was farther out from her primary than Ganymede.

Had he finally found the right place to stand?

Yes! And he must spend scope time on Callisto, learning all he could about that satellite. Some stray thought pinged in his head and he tried to hang onto it. He relaxed; trying hard *not* to think about the fleeting thought he wanted to grasp. He wished he'd been on those dratted sensors when he'd used gestalt on the First Base generators. They had had an entirely different feel. That was it! He froze. The generators! That's what had been nagging at him since Limo 34 had landed. Suddenly he realized that every single generator he had ever used in gestalt had its own special sort of 'noise', or perhaps 'feel' would be the better term. Over the past days, he'd gestalted with Padrugoi's solar-powered generators, the ship's fuel-powered one, the exceedingly easy-to-tap CERN generators, the far-side telescope's solar array and most recently, had had just a nibble at the nuclear/solar-power-augmented generators on the moon. All were different, some subtly so. The generators at Jerhattan Spaceport differed from the battery-powered ones he'd had to use in emergencies. How did he do it? He swore silently. He'd always known he 'felt' what he 'ported, but unconsciously, when he touched any new generator, he 'felt' it, too. And tuned his mind to it. Maybe that's why other people couldn't gestalt; they couldn't tune into the generator. Or maybe not the generator they were trying to use in gestalt!

How would he be able to express the subtlety he had only just realized existed? Ah! All those damned sensor readings, made to show generator use and burned calories! They were good for something after all. He exhaled and realized how tense he had become. Would such readings prove what he wanted them to prove, over and above usage and physical effort? First he had to have them to examine with this new interpretation of the data. Data! Data was everything! And he'd need a lot to do what he wanted to do now!

Peter was excited by these reflections. He could feel his fingers twitching for all those damned printouts. And chagrin that he had ever protested about the nuisance of being wired up to make them. Unable to sleep now, he examined the new premise, wondering exactly which sort of generators he should have on Callisto. What a prospect! His speculations wove between Callisto and the various types of generators as intricately as asteroids tumbled in their orbits.

If Peter was too excited to sleep, Johnny slept a good deal. Whenever Peter heard him snoring, he'd 'port him onto his side, so his thoughts were not interrupted by the noise.

'To make up for when he didn't sleep on First Base,' Xiang commented to Peter when he noticed Johnny's continued absence. 'Cameron's my official co-pilot.' Xiang cast a sly sideways look at Peter. 'The General said he'd done all the work on the way up.' The co-pilot grinned. 'I don't think so.' He went back to squeezing his dinner from the food pouch in his hand without waiting for Peter's denial or agreement.

Their unanticipated arrival at Padrugoi was the only problem they had on the trip. Going 'down' to Padrugoi struck Peter as an odd if accurate way of describing it: the moon was sort of 'up' from the Station, in an orbit above it. However, getting permission to land at Padrugoi made up for the quiet of the journey.

'Goddamn it, you're early here too, Liu, and where am I going to put you all of a sudden?' demanded the Portmaster who immediately came online when Xiang made contact. Desmond Honeybald was a civilian, formerly supervisor of Jerhattan International Airport. He'd been taken on to control Padrugoi's airspace when the project first got under way, a flamboyant but exceptionally capable personality.

'How come I wasn't warned? Least you could do. How come you're still supposed to be at First Base? No one bothers to keep me up to date, do they? And how come you're driving the Twenty-eight instead of the Thirty-four you went out on? Oxbridge and Auers're supposed to be piloting. Not Liu and Cameron. How am I expected to keep track of this port's traffic when no one tells me anything? And the Admiral has to give permission to any ship landing on the wheel. Like I'd send a pirate in there, or sumpin'. Ha! *Now* I'm supposed to secure this line.' There was a brief pause in the Portmaster's diatribe. 'All right. Secured. Now you gotta tell me who's on board. As if we were expecting some minor deity or sumpin'. At least you know how to dock, Liu. Yes, Liu, that's who's piloting. Now they don't want to know who's on board. Make up your mind, Admiral. Yes, they're coming in smooth and easy. Like all of 'em should! Sure, it can dock at Bay Three. It's a limo, isn't it?' Another pause. 'Yes, sir. Yes indeed, sir,' the Portmaster said in a far more respectful tone of voice. 'I understand, sir. No, I do not need a vacation. I just got back from one. I will, sir. Thank you, sir.' In yet another change of voice, gruff rather than aggravated, 'Did you hear that, Pilot Liu? Bay Three. Two of your passengers are to find their way immediately to Admiral Coetzer's ready room. The others may disembark in the normal fashion. I'm repeating verbatim, Pilot Liu. Do you read me?'

'Loud and clear, Mr Honeybald,' Xiang said, grinning fit to split his cheeks. 'Bay Three. The two passengers have heard your message. Proceeding to Bay Three as ordered.'

'Welcome, welcome, welcome!' Dirk Coetzer said when his yeoman announced the arrival of the wanderers. 'We didn't even dare warn Honeybald, though he himself is a rock of discretion, that you were due in, ETA unknown.' The Admiral gave Peter a long speculative look. 'Did you enjoy your look at First Base?'

'We both did,' Peter replied. He was feeling odd. Perhaps it was merely getting adjusted to gravity again. He certainly shouldn't get twitches in his extremities for *that*!

'So have you any news for *us*?' Johnny asked, settling himself in his chair.

'Yes, we've been rather busy here,' and Dirk turned an almost admonitory glance at the General, who seemed to be implying that they had not. 'Boris Roznine is continuing his investigations downside, but he left behind two Talents, both of whom have had mental contact with your old friend, Flimflam.'

'You haven't arrested him?'

Dirk Coetzer gave an unhumorous grin. 'We know exactly where he is at all times. We're waiting to see who will contact him. We have incontestable proof that Flimflam was involved in sabotaging Limo Thirty-four. His accomplices are incommunicado. I am reliably informed that he is currently in a state of very high anxiety. As he can't go anywhere that we can't find him, we might as well use him as bait.'

'Turnabout's fair play,' Johnny agreed. 'How long'll you play him?'

The Admiral appeared to consider this. 'I'd say not long after Peter begins working for us again?' He cocked his head, his blue eyes sparkling with anticipation.

'Really? Hmm.' Johnny turned to Peter with a wily expression on his face. 'You did take my advice and rest on the way down?'

'As much as you did,' Peter replied. 'I'm ready to go to work.' He grinned amiably at Johnny, wondering how soon he'd have a chance to 'work'.

'When?' asked Dirk Coetzer with such alacrity that Peter blinked. 'We have a very long list.'

'I expect so,' Peter said before the Admiral could elaborate. 'I wouldn't mind having a meal.'

Dirk immediately flourished a double-folded sheet at him. 'All the calories you want!'

Johnny intercepted the list. 'When did you get this?'

Dirk widened his eyes. 'It's what you didn't take with you on the Thirty-four.'

'Oh!' Johnny's irritated expression faded. 'In that case, let's compare it with the list the good Colonel gave me just before our precipitous departure.'

Dirk chuckled. 'Watari didn't like that, I should imagine.'

'Not at all according to his book,' Johnny said, removing a second strip from his thigh pocket. 'Ah, yes.' He laid both lists on the table so the others could see. 'Well, he *is* consistent, and we should repay his generous hospitality as soon as possible. Dirk, will you join us? It seems to be lunchtime here.'

'Nicola, two more for lunch,' the Admiral said, bending to his intercom.

Over the high-carbohydrate meal, Dirk brought them up to speed on other developments.

'We have reason to believe, and may shortly be able to prove, that Flimflam was supplied with tools and the MPU circuits by a contract electrician, Spaz Zenoun, who had worked on-station during Barchenka's time.'

'Has *she* been implicated in the sabotage?' Johnny asked.

'Circumstantially,' the Admiral admitted. 'Boris has a team reviewing the Barchenka surveillance tapes. He's got proof that an uncle of Shimaz's, Riz Naztuk, visited her on three occasions, one not long after you began working up here for the Space Authority, Pete,' the Admiral said.

'Not conclusive enough to do anything, is it?' Johnny said.

'Boris is working on that.'

'OK, how else is Shimaz involved? I can assure you that he's been under increasingly heavy observation at First Base,' Johnny said. 'For the past six months he hasn't even been allowed to mix with other offenders.'

'Boris and I had an interesting conversation about that,' Dirk said, using his napkin before continuing. 'I believe that, when he was sentenced to incarceration at the Lunar Prison facility, he made threats. I believe there are fanatics among his associates who would consider it an honour to implement them. Almost like a fatwa.'

'In this day and age?' Johnny exclaimed scornfully.

'Oh, you'd be surprised,' the Admiral said. 'Boris has discovered a link with the Faithful Brotherhood who attacked you in the restaurant, Peter.'

'*What?*' Both men stared at him.

'It was one of those splinter groups. They had attended Religious Interpretative Group meetings led by a certain Very Reverend Ponsit Prosit.'

'Flimflam?' Johnny's voice came close to a squeak. Peter stared at the Admiral, fork poised on the way to his mouth.

'The very man,' Dirk replied with a confirmatory nod of his head. 'Once again, inconclusive.'

Johnny rattled his fingers on the table, blinking in thought. 'Ah, yes, the guys who fell all over you at your birthday party would have finished their sentences by now.' He cocked his head significantly at the surprised telekinetic. *A valid reason for the cotton wool, Pete?*

'That's interesting. However, while offenders can't get down, neither can anyone with a LEO record get up,' Dirk said. A thought also occurred to him. 'Flimflam gave evidence once before to save his skin.'

'You said you were using him as bait?' Johnny said.

'If he attracts anything, that's an entirely separate issue,' the Admiral replied. 'If "they",' and he bracketed his fingers around the pronoun to indicate the 'unknown' quantity, 'fall for it, it's all to the good. Cass Cutler says he's in a sweat of fearful anticipation. He must be expecting a contact. And,' he raised his hand to forestall Johnny's interruption, 'we have tripled security measures in the Arrivals hall and on the Mall. Boris sent up two more empaths to listen, supporting Shandin, Ranjit and Cass. Closing the Station would defeat the purpose.' He grimaced. 'And we've all those quite legitimate freighter crews.'

'OK, OK, we get the message,' Johnny said with a grin at Peter. 'Are you stoked up enough, Pete?'

Peter had been eating an excellent dessert – two pieces of a very good apple pie – while the other two were discussing the situation. He was, however, very eager to get to their office and review all those previously detestable energy-use readings to see if all his ambitious reflections on the return trip were in any way valid. Maybe he should also contact CERN and Professor Gadriel. Abruptly then, Peter swallowed the last mouthful of apple pie and got out a question.

'Admiral, I wanted to know if you've heard anything from Professor Gadriel.'

'The Professor?' Dirk patted his lips with his napkin, concealing a small smile. 'Well, yes, Peter, I have.'

Peter braced himself.

'Admittedly he was considerably confused – and a trifle irritated – when the latest set of circuits in his gestalt

337

generator fried for no apparent reason.' The Admiral raised his hand to forestall Peter's chagrin. 'When Rhyssa gave him the answer, he was delighted. He said it was proof he was on the right track.' Dirk cleared his throat. 'He's busy reconstructing them and would like very much to have a chance to talk with you. Good man, Gadriel. I said you'd make time.'

'Oh, I will, sir, definitely,' Peter said, letting relief wash over him. He put down his fork and then noticed that the muscles on the back of his right hand were twitching.

'Pete?'

'Sorry, Johnny.'

'Dirk, we can work just as easily from the conference room as CIC, and get at least some of this stuff cleared,' Johnny rattled the lists, 'before we officially return.'

'Good notion. Most of the passengers on the Twenty-eight are in transit downside right now, in the regular shuttle,' Dirk said, tapping a code into his wristcom. 'Sakai, you will ignore any sudden fluctuations of the generators. Do you read me?' The Admiral gave a nod of satisfaction for the immediate and unquestioning confirmation. 'Do you need anything else in the conference room? Nicola can supply it.'

Johnny gave a sideways grin of mischief. 'Nothing we can't get ourselves, I suspect.'

'Especially since you made it to First Base.'

'Exactly. See you later, Dirk. C'mon, Pete. We'll earn our luxury holiday to the moon.'

They 'ported themselves into the conference room and turned up the lights. When Johnny 'ported in the recording equipment, Peter made his usual grimace. No need to alter his reaction to being recorded until he could prove his point.

'Look, we're doing *this* according to Mr Hoyle, and with tapes to prove it. I'm not going to have you overloaded,' he said as he began placing the sensors on Peter. '*I* need logged proof of what mass you 'ported and the energy you expended. To give CFO Taddesse the proper corroboration that you're working according to the terms of your contract.'

Peter submitted, hoping his suppressed excitement didn't

register as an energy reading. Then he spread out the list, beginning to check off the items, which included calculations of mass, descriptions of contents and the current location in the various cargo corrals. Johnny called up separate windows for each of the locations and gestured for Peter to settle himself comfortably.

'Watari doesn't want much, does he?' he grunted as he checked off individual units and tallied a total of their mass.

'A lot are lightweight,' Peter said, keeping his smile to himself. Once again he was diverted by the subcutaneous spasms on the back of his right hand. He didn't feel anything, of course, but he'd never noticed a visible twitching before.

'OK! This is the first batch. I'll assemble them in a pack.' He grinned at Peter. 'You can send them all to the main supply depot on First Base, now that we are both familiar with it!'

'That's right. We've both seen it.' But Peter amended to himself, it isn't that we need to *see* where we're going to dump shipments, though that's essential, too. It's that we don't put artificial limits on ourselves, like only to and fro between Jerhattan Spaceport and Padrugoi Station. That was the distance Johnny had limited himself to. Another requirement was to use the right sort of generator for each individual until he or she could learn to 'tune' into any kind. Like the CERN generators that he had tapped into to save Limo 34 in that critical moment. He was relieved that an official apology, and compensation for the fried circuits, had been given Professor Gadriel.

However, if he was to fool Johnny into an innocent 'port as far as the moon, where had he been on First Base that Johnny hadn't? Oh, and Peter felt a surge of amusement, the observatory! Were there visuals of that distinctive stain, the southern half of the South American continent? Or, using that as a design, could he render a good digital representation? The voice-address unit in his cabin was state of the art.

'I've got the first load assembled, Pete,' and Johnny

pointed to the lower left-hand window on the monitor. Station lights illuminated the mix of crates.

Peter 'felt' them. Then he put his mind to 'touching' Padrugoi's generators. They *were* different: lighter, crisper, easier to deal with than nuclear or fuel-powered ones. He chuckled. They were tuned to a C-major chord, the same as the CERN gestalt generators and the far-side telescope's solar array had been. Which would be best for his ultimate purpose? He wondered if his energy-use readings would mirror the light, crisp feeling, the C major. Did he have to draw on them less, or more, than other types?

He couldn't see the screen of the recorder from his angle. He could wait until the day's work was despatched. Back to the matter at hand; sending his bread-and-butter thank-you shipments to First Base.

The mass of the containers was not unwieldy; certainly nothing like the heavy mass of the 34, which he had 'heaved' towards First Base. He 'saw' the destination and the exact area on the depot floor against the north wall, which he and Johnny had designated. He caught up the mass, leaned just the right amount into the generators, and 'pushed'.

'Easy,' Peter said, taking a deep and satisfied breath when he'd finished.

'Now, let's see how long it takes them to realize they've got their order. How do you feel, kid?' Johnny cocked an eyebrow.

'Fine,' Peter said with a shrug.

'I'll get the next batch ready. Do you need anything?'

'Not yet. Hey, shouldn't we tell Rhyssa that we're back?'

'Not at three a.m.' Johnny pointed to the time-zone clocks. The face labelled 'Jerhattan' displayed the very early morning hour.

Peter now remembered the odd jerks of the muscles on his right hand. It was doing nothing right now, relaxed on the table top.

They did three more light 'portations in the next two hours. Johnny was separating a larger mass when the conference-room com beeped.

'Yes, sir,' Johnny answered without much courtesy. 'Oh,'

and his face brightened. 'Took them long enough to notice.'
He pressed the speaker button, and the Admiral's query was
audible to Peter.

'How many have you sent? How's Pete?'

'Four.' Johnny answered the first question.

'I'm fine, Admiral,' Peter replied for himself.

'Do you need any calories?' A faint hint of amusement
coloured the Admiral's voice.

'Not yet.'

'I had Barney order in some fruit and savouries for you.'
Then the connection was broken.

Peter could not stifle his groan. Did everyone on the
Station know exactly what he was supposed to eat? He saw
the muscles on the top of his left hand begin to jump. As
soon as he could, he wanted to ask Ceara about *that*! He
didn't want any physical problems cropping up right now to
postpone his analysis of the energy-use printout data.

'Time, kid,' Johnny said and Peter obediently 'saw' the
mass ready to 'port and despatched it.

'Now, I'll have some fruit,' he said.

At nine a.m., at the end of this shift, he 'pathed to Rhyssa,
who would now be in her office. *Rhyssa?*

Peter! Where are you?

*On-station, earning my keep. Is everyone all right down
there?*

Of course, and her mental tone implied that nothing ever
happened 'down there' that he should worry about. *But I
wasn't notified.*

No one was, Rhyssa. Not even the Admiral.

*You said you were earning your keep. When did you get
back to Padrugoi? Why haven't you contacted Madlyn? She
said you weren't to be back on-station for another two days
from the last report she had.*

You know how devious Johnny can be.

Indeed!

We're still not *here, which is why we didn't contact Madlyn.
Only Dirk.*

She paused. *Well, I suppose that's advisable with all that's*

*happening. Did he bring you up to date? Barchenka may be
implicated as well as that wretched Shimaz.* Peter felt her
mental revulsion for the man. A real scuzzball! He had never
forgotten the way the man had leered at Rhyssa that day
in her office. *And Flimflam. I can't believe they're able to
pull off such antics when they're supposed to be so closely
watched!*

Me neither! Peter tried to suppress the rancour he felt.

Peter! Rhyssa, catching it, sounded alarmed and critical.

Look, Barney's bringing in our order and I'm starved, he
said to change the subject. *When I've finished eating, I'm
going to bed – tucked in safely by the good General.*

Peter! There was now concern in her tone. Then she went
on more briskly. *We also need to talk about that long-distance
call you made me.*

He didn't want to talk about that now. Maybe he could
fob Rhyssa off until he had really good news to impart.

*I need to eat, Rhyssa, and I need to sleep. I'm real tired.
Catch ya later, as Johnny would say.* He managed to imbue
his mental tone with light-hearted amusement to reassure
Rhyssa. He really didn't want to lose her good opinion of
him. In fact, he was a bit surprised by what he'd said to
her.

Rhyssa wasn't naive. Surely she accepted the fact that
Barchenka and Shimaz would try to avenge themselves on
him and the General. That Flimflam would not have meekly
accepted his sentence; that it was in his nature to do all he
could to evade the restrictions set on him and seek to get
back in any way he could at those who had been at all
responsible for the curtailment of his preferred lifestyle.

'What'd you say to Rhyssa?' Johnny asked him when
Barney had left them alone.

'Why?'

'She says you've got cynical.'

Peter shrugged. 'I guess you do when you've been the
object of a . . . what did you call it, a fatwa?'

Johnny gave him a long look. 'Yeah, I guess.'

Peter noticed his left-hand muscles jumping. 'When are we
going to be officially back?'

'About the time someone notices the corrals are being mysteriously emptied.'

Ranjit! Cass said urgently, not wanting to use her wristcom in the midst of the crowd of men and women on their way to and from the level's mess hall. *Flimflam just went into Kibon's.*

Hear ya! He goes several times a day.

Not every hour on the hour, like he's done today. Besides, I caught a glimpse of someone else in there with him and Kibon. He never allows two in that room.

Right! Gotcha. Can Suzanne spin off to tail the other guy when he comes out?

The LEO Commissioner had insisted that the girls work paired, considering the fear Cass had reported emanating from Flimflam. If the man was cornered, there was no telling what he could do. Cass was strong and well trained in self-defence, but she was glad of Suzanne's company. She was able to get a good night's sleep, too, with Suzanne there to stand a watch on their quarry.

Can do. Wanted to warn you.

Keep on Flimflam's track, the LEO lieutenant replied.

Like epoxy!

I'm sending Chet down to your level. Just in case. Lemme know if you can suss out who's the third man at Kibon's.

Abruptly Suzanne swore an oath, hauled Cass to the side of the corridor and bent to fix her boot, loudly cursing the cheap junk that was given out as shoes. Cass bent over, pretending to help, able to cock her head sideways to keep Kibon's door in sight. She could 'hear' Flimflam's dominant emotions: his mental tone was shrill, like someone close to breaking, and coloured with righteous indignation and anger. She could sense Kibon's stillness, as if, by his silence, he would be unnoticed. The third man was in as much control of himself as Kibon, emanating condescension and amusement. Suddenly that evaporated and she felt a stab of pain, Flimflam's; then Kibon's flash of fury. The door was wrenched open and a swarthy-skinned man of medium height, wearing the sort of anonymous coverall that would permit him to blend into any group on-station, ducked out, and in one stride was part of the corridor traffic.

Got him, Suzanne said. *One real satisfied bastard.*

I'll check Flimflam.

Kibon had not even had time to get off his stool to close the door when Cass barged in. Flimflam was pressed against the far wall, dislodging pencil files as he began to slide to the floor, his eyes bulging out with pained incredulity. Foremost in his mind was the betrayal, after all he'd done for them.

Flimflam's down, Cass told Suzanne and Ranjit and, managing to get the door shut before anyone in the hall was aware of what was happening, repeated the mayday on her wristcom.

'Back on your stool, Kibon,' she ordered the bookie as she reached into a hip pocket for a shock-shot. Crouching down by Flimflam, she sprayed the emergency aid into his arm with one hand and with the other, examined the wound. 'You'll live. He missed anything vital. What're you wearing? It deflected the blade. He was aiming to gut you.'

A knife would have shown up on any one of the security arches, to keep offies from smuggling weapons into this level. Padrugoi might have to allow the working public to walk freely on the main levels, but that didn't mean precautions were not taken whenever possible.

Cass, Ranjit, he's heading up, said Suzanne. *I think he's freighter personnel. They got a certain way of walking when they're back in gravity. You know what I mean?*

A stir in the hallway outside, and Kibon's door opened again. Kibon groaned at the security and medical team that had materialized there.

'More won't fit,' he muttered. 'Get him outta here.'

'No sweat, Kibon,' Cass said, so sweetly that Kibon blinked in surprise. Beckoning to the first man to grab Flimflam's shoulders, she hoisted his feet and they hauled him out into a corridor occupied only by the emergency team and the backs of those hurrying from the vicinity.

Flimflam's dimming consciousness was coloured by shock, betrayal, fury, blooming pain and a determination to 'make them pay'.

344

'He'll live,' said the medic after a cursory examination, and he waved to the team to proceed to the nearest elevator.

Where are you, Suzie? Need help?

I got Ranjit and Chet with me.

Then I'll stay with my quarry. He's angry enough to think something useful. Maybe I'll just get him thinking that perhaps confession would be very good for his soul.

He has one? Just get him to talk out loud, Cass. It doesn't count in court if he just thinks *it!*

Tell me about it.

Commander Ottey, Shandin Ross and two other security officers Cass didn't know were already in the infirmary two levels up. All the way there, while Cass pumped the injured man with thoughts of 'confess', 'make 'em pay', 'get 'em good' and similar provocative mental directions, she managed to stay out of his direct line of vision as much as possible. Flimflam's thoughts continued to revolve about retaliation and how much pain he was in. That was all he voiced.

'Something for the pain. I'm hurt. I'm in pain. Gimme something for the pain!'

'We did. It'll kick in in a minute,' one of the medics snapped to shut him up.

Has he said anything useful, Cass? Shandin asked. He and the others also stayed out of Flimflam's immediate line of vision.

He's full of revenge. Then she caught the reason. *But he's too damned scared of 'them' even to think names or faces.*

Maybe he doesn't know any, Shandin Ross suggested.

That's always possible. But today he's been in and out of Kibon's like a yo-yo. So I figure he was expecting to meet someone there. And he did. Has Ranjit caught up with his assailant yet?

Closing. Man doesn't realize he's being followed either. Arrogant bastard. Shandin raised an eyebrow in distaste, then grinned. *Got him! In possession of a very sharp, plastic, bloody spike.*

345

'Damn!' the medic examining Flimflam exclaimed, reaching for a stimulant.

He's dying, 'He's dying,' Cass said telepathically as well as out loud. 'Tell them to watch that spike, Shandin. It must have been poisoned. The wound was superficial.'

Medics closed in on Flimflam, trying to resuscitate him. Cass stepped back, leaning against the wall, trying to catch something useful from the man's receding consciousness. The need for revenge remained dominant until he was totally mindless.

'Cass? Cass!' Shandin caught her shock at the death and reached her before her knees gave way.

'I hate it. I hate it when minds wink out like that,' she whispered, grateful for the lieutenant's support.

'I need help,' Shandin began, looking around for a medic.

'I'm here with it,' and Cass tried to focus on the red-haired woman pressing a hypospray against her arm. The woman grinned up at Cass. 'Let's get you out of here.'

Cass felt the surge of sympathy and understanding from her as Shandin carried her out of that cubicle and into the adjacent one where she was lifted onto the narrow bed.

Ceara's an empath, Cass, Shandin said. He, too, was broadcasting reassurance.

That's my job, Cass replied.

Not right now, it isn't, Shandin said as Ceara attached a monitor to Cass's finger.

Cass agreed.

Peter did not feel the least remorse when he and Johnny were informed that Flimflam had died of a poisoned knife-thrust. He was struggling with his analysis of the data he needed from the reams of energy-use printouts, both for himself and Johnny. He wasn't nearly as tired as he had made out after the second day of scheduled 'ports to First Base. But he used that excuse. He wasn't exactly sure what data he hoped to extract, and gave up after two hours. There were two jobs he needed to do; the analysis was only one. Equally important in his mind was recreating the 'South

America' discoloration with which he would fool Johnny into 'porting all the way to First Base.

'Let's rid him of his self-imposed limitations,' Peter muttered to himself as he accessed the draw program on his worktop. Gradually he worked up the sketch of the discoloration in the observatory in the corner of the partition window with the control worktop, the cabinet beneath, got the colour tones as well, including the opaque smokiness of the window. The general image resembled facilities that Johnny probably 'ported to many times; save for that distinctive splotch and the angle of window and worktop. Making the visual wasn't anywhere near as easy as he thought it would be. He could hold a light-pen but he didn't have the fine muscle control needed for minute changes, although he seemed to have finally got the hang of using the device. Possibly he was inspired by this means to the end he desired. He grinned. He stared at the visual, adjusting proportions, adjusting colours, adjusting until his eyes watered. The image had to be perfect so that Johnny would 'see' it distinctly enough to 'port to it. After all, there was only one spot in this solar system that was identical; in the observatory office on First Base.

Yawning several times in succession made him check the time, and he found that he'd spent nearly three hours on the project. But he was reasonably satisfied with it. He'd check his imaging again in the morning. The muscle between his last two fingers on his right hand was twitching again. It didn't hurt. Of course, it couldn't. He had no feeling in his hands, even if the skin was jumping about from some sort of a tic. Perhaps he'd better see a medic. Maybe he could see Ceara. He could call her to his room. No, he couldn't call a woman to his cabin even if she was a qualified doctor. Seeing her in a professional capacity was permissible, wasn't it? He yawned again. And put himself to bed.

He was up, had changed his appliance, showered and dressed before he felt Johnny's mind touch his.

I'm up, I'm up, he said.

You sound revoltingly chipper.

Peter grinned. Johnny sounded as if he were hung-over.

Had breakfast?

Shut up and eat yours now so I don't have to smell it. Barney's waiting for you in the conference room. Tell him I'll need plenty of fresh coffee. And stress the 'fresh'. A pause. *Please.*

Sure thing!

Johnny arrived well after Peter had finished his meal. Peter had had time to transfer the image of 'South America' to the conference-room files, securing it with his personal code. The moment Johnny arrived, Barney appeared, ready with the coffee, which he placed before the General, as well as hard copy of the day's teleportation list.

'You know,' Peter said casually, 'we could go into business for ourselves. T and T.'

'Huh?'

Peter waited until Johnny had had a few sips of the hot, fresh coffee. It even smelled good to Peter.

'Telepaths and Teleporters Incorporated, or Limited, because there's really only three of us strong kinetics. I include Lance.'

'Good of you,' Johnny mumbled, both hands on the cup, elbows on the table. He wasn't really hearing anything yet.

Peter 'reached' for the day's schedule and unfolded the sheet, laying the hard copy flat. 'Did we hear confirmation of receipt from First Base?'

Johnny nodded and then clutched at his head. 'Yeah.'

'And they've cleared the telepad?'

'Yeah.'

'I wouldn't want to dump some of today's heavy stuff on yesterday's fragile shipments.'

'You won't.'

Peter checked the items a second time, looking at the mass and descriptions. 'Not a bad day's work. I think I'll start with some heavy stuff.'

'Be my guest.'

'Who did this to you? The Admiral?'

'Who else, considering we're not here to anyone else,' Johnny said, and took another swallow. 'Great coffee, Barney.'

'Thank you, sir. If I am no longer required?'

'Bring Pete a high-calorie snack about ten, would you, Barney?'

'Of course, sir. And please secure the door behind me, General,' he added apologetically.

'Yeah, 's OK, Barney.'

As soon as the door closed behind the quiet steward, Peter threw on the lock.

'I'll just assemble the first stuff,' Peter said. 'Oh, and there're a few things for us to shift downside, too. Shall I save them for you?' If he set a pattern today, it would be easier to slip in the one he wanted Johnny to do. But not when he had a hangover.

'I'll get to them later, Pete.' Johnny cleared his throat and finished that cup of coffee.

'I'll fill, Johnny. You might burn yourself,' Peter said kindly. Johnny shot him a caustic glance but held his cup out. Peter 'ported the carafe over and filled the cup.

'Thanks. Don't ever drink, kid. Not really worth it.'

'I'll remember that.'

Johnny slumped over his coffee while Peter organized the first send. He would have to be patient for his Great Experiment. He wanted Johnny in his full senses, as much to do the 'port as to appreciate what *was* possible! First the moon, then Mars, and then? Peter's heart leaped within his chest with excitement.

'Don't forget the sensors, Pete,' Johnny had enough presence of mind to say.

As well he hadn't already put them on, Peter thought, or maybe palpitations of anticipation didn't register on monitors. He could attach the pads to himself but it took time. And once again he saw his hand muscles spasm and had an odd sensation in his fingertips. From residual electricity in the pads? He really must resume his Reeve board exercises. With Flimflam dead, and undoubtedly some sort of confession from the assassin, surely their return could be officially announced! And he could arrange for some telescope time. He had to know if his notion was feasible.

'I'm wired,' he announced to Johnny and, setting his mind to the gestalt, made the day's first transfer to the main depot at First Base. 'That was almost easy,' he added, though it hadn't been all that easy. He just wanted to imply that, preparing the ground for Johnny.

'Don't sound so cheerful.'

'Why shouldn't I? Flimflam's dead, and they'll find out more from his assassin.'

'No, they won't,' Johnny said. 'Like all well-programmed assassins, he suicided.'

'Oh!' That was too bad. It also meant that this whole sorry mess of intrigue and revenge wasn't cleared up.

'However, the good Admiral's security guys are picking the brains of the freighter crew. Not literally, that isn't legal. But the good ship *Elise* has been moored on-station for the past eight days.' Johnny frowned. 'Indeed, since our limo left. So perhaps Idi ibn Sorkut – at least that's the name on his papers – might have let drop some titbits in the Mall while awaiting the news that Limo Thirty-four was MIS.'

'You sound better.'

'I'm not really.'

'Could all this really be – what did you call it – a fatwa?'

'More than likely, though a fatwa was a religious punishment, for blasphemy. This is for plain revenge.'

'Plain?' Peter exclaimed.

'No, I guess there's nothing plain about this at all.' Johnny raised bloodshot eyes and managed a grim smile. He pulled the list over to him. 'You've done the first?'

'I'll organize the second, too. You haven't had enough coffee yet.'

Peter laid his hand on the list to draw it back to him, aware that his fingers were twitching.

Johnny saw it and blinked to clear his eyes. 'Is that new?'

'Seems to be. Doesn't hurt. I don't feel it.'

'That's nerve action. You're not supposed to have working nerves.'

'A fringe benefit of free fall?' Then Peter suggested slyly, 'Maybe all the hard work I did landing us?'

Johnny reached for the com-unit and gave an address. 'Is Dr Scott available? Good. Will she please report to Admiral Coetzer's conference room? This is not an emergency.'

Suddenly Johnny thrust his coffee mug into Peter's left hand, curved where he had laid it to hold down the schedule list. Peter jerked his hand away from heat.

'I felt that!' Peter stared down at his hand.

Johnny moved the mug to Peter's right hand, slowly pressing the thumb up against it.

'And that?' Johnny's voice had dropped to a whisper.

'Yes.'

Slowly, as if he would almost rather not be disappointed, Peter kinetically fitted both hands around the hot coffee mug. He swallowed hard.

'I can feel heat in all my fingers and in the palms of my hands.'

He raised his eyes to Johnny's. A slow and incredulous smile spread over the General's face, and his eyes were shining with extra moisture. He slid his hands lightly over Peter's.

'D'you feel that?'

'Just a slight pressure.' Peter wanted to cry. For the first time since Dorotea had found him in the hospital, he wanted to cry. He blinked very hard. He couldn't cry in front of Johnny Greene.

'If you do, I will,' Johnny murmured, and gently embraced him. *Can you feel this?*

Peter gave his head a little shake, his head resting against Johnny's broad shoulder. *Just a sort of pressure. But even to have the use of my fingers again! I haven't been able to move them since that damned body brace shorted out, with me in it.* He didn't shake with sobs – that was probably beyond his new capability – but he did feel his chest move and let the tears roll down his face. Until they heard the tentative rap on the door.

'Admiral?' The muffled voice was female. Mentally Peter reached out and recognized Ceara Scott.

Johnny opened the lock and, as she pulled the door forward, she took a quick look at the occupants and hurried inside, her eyes focused on Peter. She closed the door quickly.

'What's wrong?' She hurried to his side and Johnny released his hold.

'I don't think nerves spontaneously regenerate,' Johnny said, his lips twisted to one side.

'I feel heat,' and Peter demonstrated by clasping the coffee mug in both hands.

'But you can't,' she exclaimed. Then, shaking her head in a double denial, she altered her remark. 'You shouldn't be able to! I saw your medical files, the spinal trauma.'

'I can feel heat,' Peter repeated, holding the cup up in both hands towards her. Johnny instantly extended the flat of his hand to support the mug.

'That coffee's hot, you know.' The General's tone was gruff, but his eyes remained very shiny. 'I don't want you splattered and burned because you're showing off.'

'Let's just see what we've got here,' Ceara said, deftly removing the hot cup from Peter's hands and noting its heat. 'Undoubtedly hot.'

She took Peter's left hand and turned it over, noting the redness. She pressed one fingertip.

'I felt that, too,' and there was delighted amazement in Peter's voice.

'I didn't quite feel that,' he said with less delight when she pressed the skin of the next knuckle of the finger. She dug her fingernail into his skin and he felt the sharper prod. 'That I felt,' and he looked at the mark her nail had left on the skin.

Ceara eased herself into the nearest chair. 'You should see a proper neurologist as soon as possible. And there isn't one on-station. We've got to find out if you really could have had some regeneration. We do have an MRI in the sick bay.' She broke off, eyes blinking in confusion. Peter could feel her mind blazing alternately with optimism and denial. Miracles didn't happen any more. She gave her head a sharp shake. 'I didn't realize you were back on Padrugoi.' Her glance took in Johnny.

'I'll see if Dirk will admit we're here. Especially if we have to get Peter down to the sick bay. First order of business.'

Johnny reached for the com-unit as briskly as if he were no longer suffering from a hangover.

'Second order of business is this,' Peter said, tapping a fingertip – and feeling it – on the day's list.

'Would he be endangering himself?' Johnny asked Ceara anxiously, pausing on the com keypad.

'How?' Peter demanded. *After all that's happened to me in the last two weeks?*

CHAPTER FOURTEEN

Upon hearing that Peter needed to go to the sick bay, Dirk Coetzer was concerned.

'What has to be done?' Peter asked Ceara warily. He'd had more than enough physical examinations, even if he hadn't 'felt' them.

'We've a good MRI, though no EMG.'

'What's that?' Johnny demanded, far more alarmed than either Coetzer or Peter.

'Electroneuromyograph, but it's done with sensor pads, much like that equipment,' and she nodded to the unit to which Peter was already attached. 'Used to be much more intrusive. Anyway the sick bay doesn't have one. You'd've had to go downside. I'd recommend Finn Markstein. He's a neurologist. I trained with him at Mountainside Hospital.'

'Will the MRI be conclusive?' Johnny asked. 'Will we see what's going on?'

Peter turned to regard Johnny with some amusement. Johnny sounded so anxious, while Peter was being far more objective. Catching the look, Johnny flushed and gripped Peter's shoulder, then remembered Peter might feel it and threw both hands up in the air in bewilderment.

'General Greene, if I haven't collapsed by now, I won't. But let's just get the second shipment off.' He looked at Ceara. 'Then I'm all yours.' It was his turn to blush.

She covered her mouth with her hand to hide a grin before giving him a more professional look.

'An MRI doesn't take that long, but it will reassure everyone about your present condition.'

'He's worried about a shipment.' Johnny ignored her reassurance and waved his hands over his head, rolling his eyes. 'He's not worried about "feeling" for the first time in, what is it, six years?'

Peter grinned at Johnny's histrionics.

'Look, Peter, don't concern yourself over 'porting,' Dirk Coetzer began placatingly.

'Admiral, *that* is my job here. I made it to First Base so I could 'port more efficiently. I'm not about to malinger when General Greene cannot undertake such assignments on his own.' Peter swallowed hard, hoping that his agitated response would not put Johnny on guard. Hurriedly he said, 'I'll send the second shipment, go down to the sick bay, get this MRI and be back in time to send number three.'

Ceara gave him a long look that said clearly 'only if the MRI is good'.

Johnny had to be persuaded regarding Peter's return to work after the MRI, but Dirk was clearly pleased at Peter's diligence. Johnny even added his mental push to Peter's on the second shipment. Peter kept his pleasure over that to himself. It would be so easy for him just to duck out at the last moment, and leave all the 'port to Johnny. *Then* he'd tell him the destination and prove to doubting Johnny Greene that his gift did not have limits.

Johnny did suggest that they 'port themselves and Ceara down to the sick bay, preferably right into the room with the MRI equipment.

'I also don't want anyone thinking you've got a medical problem,' Johnny said, to justify that manoeuvre.

'Assassins don't just fall out of convenient lockers, Johnny,' Peter replied, but he didn't object.

There was enough space in the MRI chamber to accommodate all three of them. The main sick bay was more than adequate for normal problems: a special section dealt with anoxia and other space accidents.

Only when Peter levitated himself to the required supine posture on the MRI bed did he feel the least bit apprehensive. He'd had numerous MRIs, but this time it was different.

Ceara took a set of goggles from the hook near the programmable screen on the wall, which was out of Peter's line of sight.

'These are virtual reality glasses. I can see the anatomic structures of your body, Peter.'

The shell of the MRI passed over his body and the results slowly began to scroll down the screen on the wall. There was complete silence once the shell was back in the ready position.

'Well, I'd like to have Commander de Aruya verify this,' Ceara finally said, removing the glasses.

'Why, what's wrong?' Johnny demanded before Peter could.

'Because the MRI shows me extensive neo-neurogenesis.'

'What does that mean?' Johnny asked.

Peter smiled. He knew.

'The nerve endings are bonding. There's an apparent reconnection of severed nerve endings, neurofilaments, nerves and sheaths.' Ceara swallowed audibly. 'No, I'm wrong. They have bonded! I can see the original insult to the spinal column. The severed microbundles are fused together. In the human body, the individual neuropils grow much like the roots of a plant.'

Peter's mind stopped with that explanation. Grow? Like a plant? *Amariyah!* He was only peripherally aware of Ceara and Johnny discussing his original injury and paralysis, and the recent fractures. Ceara was saying she wanted to compare this scan with all his previous MRI files. Would the Centre release them to her? And bring up a specialist, like Dr Markstein? Could she now ask Commander de Aruya to give a second opinion?

'Does that mean Peter is no longer . . .' Johnny stopped,

unable to voice a word he had scrupulously avoided using in Peter's presence.

'From this MRI, the original injury has been healed. The nerves have rejoined: the spinal column is no longer severed.' She paused, and took a deep breath. 'Technically, he's whole again. But that doesn't mean it won't take considerable time and effort for him to rehabilitate his muscles.' Ceara spoke slowly but with a tinge of awe in her voice. 'He's overcome so much already.'

'I think,' Peter began, unable to curb his irritation at being demoted to a pronoun – especially by Ceara – 'that I would like to *feel* again!'

'Oh, Peter, I do apologize,' she said, bending down to look into his eyes where he still lay on the MRI pad. Her face was red with embarrassment. 'How unprofessional of me. Here. Sit up.'

Even through his irritation, he 'felt' her keenly mortified chagrin.

'Do you mind if I ask for Commander de Aruya's opinion? This is out of my area of expertise.'

'Yes, of course,' Peter said, raising himself to a sitting position. He wondered what it would be like to make such a simple everyday movement *physically*. The shining fact was that possibly *now* he would have the choice! But more than that, he added very privately to himself, I would like to pee and crap like any other male. He'd managed to ignore the necessary presence of the waste-bag, but he would be so glad to be rid of the damned appliance *for ever*!

A wiry, fit man, Commander de Aruya kept his thick white hair trimmed like a skullcap, and his dark eyes dominated a mature countenance. He gave a professional smile that faded the instant he saw the MRI screen. He shot Peter a startled look and another at Ceara. He donned the goggles and peered intently at the MRI image.

'Yes, I see.' He regarded the screen intently, an index finger tracing the image of Peter's spinal column until he came to the old damage. 'Mr Reidinger, if you wouldn't mind, may I do a second scan?' When Peter assented and

357

resumed the supine position, he added, 'Save this one, Dr Scott.'

Peter, head in the chin rest, closed his eyes and fervently prayed with all his soul that the second reading would mirror the first. Dear, dear Amariyah! He couldn't wait to hold her! Yes, *hold* her in his arms and *feel* her dear body. Rhyssa and Dorotea would be over the moon. And he smiled at the phrase. He'd been there, too.

'Thank you, Mr Reidinger,' said the smooth, baritone voice of the Commander. 'You may sit up now.'

Ceara was empathing him very strong, positive, joyful, encouraging thoughts.

Hey, Pete. Looks the same to me! Boy, *are Rhyssa and Dorotea going to rejoice!* Johnny said triumphantly.

'Have you any idea how this neo-neurotropism occurred?' De Aruya's eyes were sparkling in his eagerness to hear Peter's answer. 'Somehow – and I'd give a lot to *know* how – your body has re-formed the vast network of nerve tendrils that comprise the nervous system in your spinal column.'

'I think,' and Peter considered his words, still awed by the miracle, 'my friend, Amariyah, is a microkinetic. Only she doesn't know it.'

'A microkinetic?' De Aruya was obviously having trouble crediting such a source.

Ceara did not. 'Oh, my word, like Ruth Horvath was?'

'I can't think of any other explanation, Commander,' Peter said, feeling his heart lift within him as he stared at the second MRI image on the screen. 'It is a unique Talent, and I know of no other person who is so gifted. She does have an extraordinary skill with plants. Nerves are, as Ceara just mentioned, filaments the way roots in a plant are.'

'Hmmm,' and Commander de Aruya made the appropriate contemplative noise as he stood, left hand supporting his right arm as he rubbed his chin, eyes intent on the MRI.

The buzz of the com-unit startled them all.

'Well?' asked Admiral Coetzer.

'He's OK, Dirk. More than OK,' Johnny said, the nearest to the unit. 'Much more than OK. And,' Johnny turned back to Ceara and the Commander, 'quite able to get on with his job. Aren't you, Pete?'

Peter didn't wait for permission but stood erect. 'I am fit to continue the day's schedule, am I not, Commander?'

'Well, yes, ah, I see no reason why not. May I access your records?' The Commander recovered his poise sufficiently to be completely professional. 'Whom do I ask?'

'Martin McNulty at the Eastern Parapsychic Centre,' Peter politely supplied. 'Coulson was the SA orthopaedist who vetted me for my current duties.'

'Coulson, yes. Good man,' the Commander said in an absent tone, obviously still trying to correlate the information on the MRI and his knowledge that Peter Reidinger had been paralysed for nearly half of his life.

'So, shall we get back to work, Pete?' Johnny asked, laying an affectionate hand on his arm.

Peter did feel that as the slightest pressure, closed his eyes and smiled.

'You're all right?' Johnny asked, increasing the pressure.

Peter opened his eyes and smiled. 'I'll need some calories when we've finished.'

'Any damn old thing you want,' Johnny said, separating the words in ardent assurance. *Let's go, and let the good doctor tell the Commander all about us unique parapsychics.*

They 'ported back to the conference room.

And let us break the great news to Rhyssa and Dorotea before McNulty gives them coronaries by asking what the hell I've done to you. We've got a bit of time – enough for that – before we ship number three.

AMARIYAH! The telepathed shrieks were not only in unison but also in a volume that conveyed the complex emotions of Rhyssa Lehardt and Dorotea Horvath: surprise, astonishment, incredulity and consummate relief.

That's Amariyah's gift, Dorotea said, moderating her tone. *Peter? You're on the Station and able to talk to me directly? Rhyssa, you didn't say anything . . .*

Later, dear heart. Let's digest this momentous news, Rhyssa said.

D'you think it was the massages she gave you, Peter? Dorotea's query was nearly simultaneous.

Can you think of any other agency that would bond – regrow – nerve fibres? Bundles, filaments, sheaths? The whole nervous system? Remember her garden when the basketball smeared it? She regrew *those plants, root, stem, branch and leaf.*

That's right. She did, Dorotea said.

So she is, like your mother, a microTalent, Rhyssa added.

I don't think we'd better tell her yet, Dorotea said in a very thoughtful tone.

That Peter's healed? Rhyssa was confounded.

Of course not. But if she doesn't know what *she does, let's not inhibit her.* To which Peter agreed thoroughly. Dorotea went on, *She's got to mature into her Talent. And now we know what it is, we can direct and strengthen it. Oh, Peter, you'll be able to* feel *again!* There was no doubt about Dorotea's jubilation on that score.

It's going to take time, Johnny reminded them.

You may even wish you hadn't, Dorotea remarked in a very dry tone. *But it* will *be worth the effort, my dear, dear boy! Oh, it will!*

Peter could almost visualize Dorotea standing there, fists clenched in triumph over this news.

When will you be downside? she asked.

Unless I'm grounded by a higher authority, Peter replied slyly, *I have two more weeks of this contract work period, long enough to make our First Base trip worthwhile.*

You'll have no trouble doing that, Peter, Rhyssa said at her drollest. *Don't you skimp on calories when you're doing such long 'ports.*

Commander de Aruya up here would like my file from Dr McNulty.

Yes, yes, of course.

And Ceara recommended a neurologist, Finn Markstein.

Martin McNulty will undoubtedly know who to consult with best, Rhyssa said.

Peter almost resented that tone of 'we know best'. He reminded himself that Rhyssa did have his best interests at heart. And she might be recovering from the shock of the disclosure.

In Padrugoi's security offices, Ensign Liz Predush was still matching surveillance tapes with the images of those who had visited the Station during the critical time when Limo 34 could have been sabotaged. She was comparing faces of arrivals with those taken at other locations on every level.

Suddenly a match sharpened her attention as the two screens blinked out a *bingo!* A match. One didn't need a full-face image to make a match: the state-of-the-art imaging program analysed not only the face, but also body type, height, mass and any unusual characteristics. On arrival, a visitor's image was taken full-face and then in profile as she or he moved through the security section. The program had enough data to provide positive identification.

'Georg Fraga,' she murmured to herself, noting the arrival data, and then the fact that he had been on the boat deck where Flimflam had had his workshop: where Limo 34 had been moored, awaiting her passengers. The person nearest him had his back to the surveillance lens. Her fingers flew over the pressure-sensitive keys, enlarging the figure, hitting the 'match' command.

'Well, lookit this,' Liz said, and no longer resented the long hours that now culminated in this moment. 'Commander Bindra? I got something to show you.'

'Georg Fraga?' Bindra leaned over her shoulder, eyes bugged out at the double match. 'He's Space Authority. He was supposed to be in the sick bay with Mai Leitao until General Greene was ready to 'port them down.'

'And that's Albert Ponce, sir. Can't see his face, but this guy matches him physically.' Liz enlarged the figure once again, sharpened the focus. 'He's wearing Engineering tabs on his collar. Can just make 'em out. We can check with what was found in 7299A.'

Bindra straightened, slowly letting his breath out, feeling sharp triumph.

'Good work, Liz. I'd never have thought it of Fraga, though.'

361

'Everyone has a weakness, sir. Just as you keep telling me.'

'Yes, but what is Fraga's?'

Ensign Predush sat back in her chair. It wasn't up to her to comment about people at Fraga's level.

'Document this, Liz, and I think we'd better give the data to Commissioner Roznine. It'll be his baby downside.'

Boris Roznine, in his official capacity, was paying a discreet visit to the Jerhattan headquarters of the Space Authority. As he approached the security barrier, he was rehearsing several approaches, so it was a distinct surprise when a large hand stopped him.

'Where might you be going, sir?' said the large, muscled man who had halted his progress.

'I'm LEO,' Boris began, holding out his wrist.

'You don't look it,' was the reply.

'What do you mean by that?' Boris was astonished by the response.

'Well, you don't.'

Boris pushed forward, thrusting his wrist towards the reader to establish his identity.

'Oh, you're the LEO Commissioner,' the guard said with a slight accent on the LEO, his expression amiable as he read the panel on the narrow decoder screen, steadily green in 'identity confirmed' mode.

'I told you that.' Could the guard possibly be detaining him on purpose, in order to give warning? 'What did you think LEO meant?'

'It could be your astrological sign,' the guard suggested with an indolent shrug followed by a grin, 'but you certainly aren't a Low Earth Orbit.'

'Oh.' Boris was surprised. He'd never realized that there was an alternate version of the acronym: one that would certainly be in common currency at the Space Authority.

'To each his own,' the guard said, blithely waving him through the security arch and into the building.

Without further hindrance, Boris made his way to the elevator banks, cutting through the visitors in the huge, vaulted lobby, glancing only briefly at the model of Padrugoi suspended from the ceiling. He reached the level he required and told the attentive security woman at the desk that he wished to see Secretary Abubakar immediately. Impassively she gestured to the wrist reader inset in the desk, and her manner became considerably more cordial as it clarified his rank and identity. She leaned over the com-unit and announced his presence. Obviously the answer was positive, for she escorted him to the end of the hall and, opening the door, gestured for him to enter.

Secretary Abubakar was on his feet and coming forward to welcome his visitor, however unexpected.

Boris held up a pencil file. 'I came straight to you with this information, Secretary.'

'Information?' Abubakar accepted the file and put it in the reader. The information came on the screen on his desk. 'Georg? But he was with Mai the whole time.'

'Notice the time of the encounter, Secretary. There was sufficient time for Fraga to reach the boat bay, speak to the man we have positively identified as Albert Ponce, aka Flimflam, and return to his vigil beside Mai. As she was sedated, he has no one to vouch for his so exemplary vigil.'

'But Georg Fraga? I can't believe it.' Abubakar sat down heavily, his handsome face showing sincere disbelief and astonishment. 'He passed the highest security checks. His work has been above reproach.'

'What is his connection with Mai Leitao?'

'Colleagues. Colleagues only. He's married to a research executive and they have two children. Leitao's never been the least bit interested in men. She's still on holiday. But I can't see any other connection.'

'Then let us ask ourselves what might tempt a man like Georg Fraga to liaise with an offender like Ponce, and risk his job with the SA. Why was Mai Leitao so terrified of Peter Reidinger? Because he's psychic? Is it possible that she's religiously inclined? Might have encountered Ponce in one of his Religious Interpretative Group activities?' Abubakar looked shocked at the questions Boris fired at him. 'In strictest confidence, there already has been a totally

363

unexpected connection with Ponce's spurious RIGs. Is there any way that Ponce or Shimaz could have coerced Fraga? Would either of them have had contact with Shimaz? Or been in Malaysia?'

Abubakar took one more baffled moment. He shook himself and, waving Boris to the comfortable chair beside his workstation, regained his legendary composure. 'We shall certainly find out, Commissioner. We shall certainly find out. We have too much at stake at the Space Authority right now, especially now that young Reidinger is online.' He asked for the confidential personnel files.

Three hours later, they found the connection. Georg Fraga's oldest child had had bladder, liver and pancreas replacements. The organs had been supplied to the hospital.

'Shimaz!' Boris said, running his fingers through his blond hair in a moment of rare agitation. 'He farmed children for organ transplants in the hills of Sabah!'

'But that transplant operation was nine years ago,' Abubakar exclaimed.

'Since you have such faith in Fraga's integrity, perhaps you would not object if I were to ask him a few questions?'

Abubakar hesitated only briefly and then nodded. He opened the com-link and requested Georg Fraga to come to his office. 'I don't see how Mai could be involved. She lives only for work,' and the Secretary's little smile was rueful.

Fraga appeared, and Roznine saw no apprehension in his posture until the Secretary introduced him as the LEO Commissioner.

'How may I help you, Commissioner?' His manner remained smooth, and quite possibly he wasn't aware that Boris was a strong telepath, though most people at Fraga's level knew that LEO used parapsychics.

'I must ask you a few questions in line with an ongoing investigation,' Boris said.

'But of course,' Fraga replied, his mien still betraying no trace of guilt or apprehension as he took the chair the Secretary had indicated.

Boris crossed his right leg over his left knee, outwardly

totally at ease. 'Would the name Shimaz mean anything to you?'

'No.'

That was true enough. 'Listening' for truth or falsehood was not illegal so long as listening went no further than public thoughts.

'From what source did you obtain organ transplants for your son?' Boris snapped the query off.

Fraga went into shock, the colour draining from his face and his mind hardening. It would now be more difficult for Boris to tell truth from fiction, but there were other betraying signs of guilt or anxiety.

'Oooh!' Fraga seemed to fold in on himself. 'I *had* to. I *had* to. I've repaid every single credit. Mai took it out of my salary. She said she had a discretionary fund. She was willing to *loan* me credit from it. I have repaid it.'

'Mai Leitao was involved?' The Secretary was astonished, and glanced covertly at Boris.

'I certainly didn't have that amount of credit at my disposal. I was desperate. I asked her would the SA see their way clear to give me an advance. I had to tell her why. There wasn't much time, you see, if Josef was to live. The credit had to be sent to the special account number I was given.'

That also was the truth. Fraga was willing for that to be seen in his eyes, his manner, his agitated hand gestures.

'Do you remember where the credit was sent?' Boris asked.

'A bank in Sandakan.' Fraga swallowed and clasped his hands. Possibly, Boris thought, to control their shaking.

'An organ farm was situated in the nearby mountains,' Boris said in a neutral voice.

Fraga visibly shuddered and closed his eyes. 'I didn't know.' He opened his eyes. 'I didn't care.' He made an effort to master himself. 'My son was dying.'

Boris waited a moment before he asked the next question. He disliked harassing people who had acted for the best of personal reasons, but Law Enforcement was as necessary to this complex world as whatever order could be achieved. Organ replacement from unauthorized sources was illegal.

Almost as dangerous to the recipients, who might pay exorbitant prices; possibly paying again when the organs failed or bequeathed other diseases on the patients. In some respects, Shimaz's operation had been well organized; the transplants did match the recipient's blood type and tissue sample, and in most cases the organs were healthy, the transplants successful.

'Did you make contact with a person on Padrugoi during your visit there on the fifth of January?' Boris fired the important query before Fraga could recover.

Fraga dropped his head into his hands.

'Did you bring him a message or some item?'

Fraga was close to collapse. Boris waited. Abubakar's face was a study of sympathy and consternation, his eyes sad. Fraga's reply was jerky; it was obviously an effort to speak.

'I brought a message. I was made to, or the illegal organ purchase would become public knowledge. And Mai would be implicated, since the credit note could be traced back to her office.'

'Tell me how, and when, you were asked to be a messenger? In person?'

'No, a com message. Out of the blue. Eight years after the operation.'

'Precisely when?' Boris asked ruthlessly.

Georg Fraga raised his tormented eyes. 'The day before the meeting up at Padrugoi.' He gave a mirthless sound. 'I kept a voice print. In case there was another attempt at blackmail. I'd've gone to you then.'

That was, Boris was pleased to 'hear', the truth. He suppressed the flare of pleasure that Fraga had had the forethought to take a print. It would be a valuable piece of evidence. Since Fraga had been honest, Boris would see what he could do to mitigate the charges against the man. Honesty was the best policy.

'It's regrettable that you didn't come to us in the first instance,' he said sternly.

'And be charged with an illegal organ transplant?' Fraga asked ironically.

366

'Did you tell Mai Leitao?' Abubakar asked gently.

'I had to find out if she'd been contacted, too. I had to warn her.'

The Secretary nodded. Now he turned to the LEO Commissioner.

'May I enquire what happened as a result of Georg's delivering that message?' he asked in a bleak tone.

'Fortunately the consequences were not as serious as they might have been,' Boris replied. He turned to the dispirited Fraga. 'The voice print will be a crucial piece of evidence, Mr Fraga.'

'I'll get it for you.'

'I'll come with you, Mr Fraga, as I have taken entirely too much of the Secretary's time.'

Fraga rose stiffly.

'Come back here directly, Georg,' Abubakar said in a colourless voice.

Fraga gave a slight bow and then led the way out of the office.

The next two weeks did not give Peter a single opportunity to put in for time on Padrugoi's link with the far-side telescopes. But he did make time for one thing: a call to Professor Gadriel to make his own personal apologies. Checking the time in Geneva, Peter placed a person-to-person call on a secured line to Professor Tomas Gadriel at CERN. High time, too. Apologies should be made sooner rather than later. He knew that Rhyssa, as head of the Eastern Parapsychic Centre, had been in touch with Gadriel, but Peter had been responsible for the ruination of those new circuits, not Rhyssa. It should be just after the lunch break at the research facility.

'*Bonjour, Conseil Européen pour la Recherche Nucléaire,*' a pleasant-sounding receptionist answered.

'*Bonjour,*' Peter replied in his best French, '*ici Peter Reidinger de la station d'espace Padrugoi. Je veux parler avec Professeur Tomas Gadriel, s'il vous plaît.*'

'You are calling from Padrugoi?' The receptionist switched to flawless English, making it clear to Peter that his accent needed a lot of work. 'May I tell the Professor the purpose of your call?'

Peter felt himself growing hot. 'I wanted to discuss his latest parapsychic experiment with him.'

'Very well,' the receptionist said, 'one moment please.' The line went dead for some seconds. 'I am transferring you to the Professor now; good day.'

'Hello?' The voice that replaced the receptionist's was baritone. 'Mr Reidinger?' There was a distinct note of pleased surprise in the tone.

'Professor Gadriel, thank you for accepting my call,' Peter began.

'Ah, it is yourself who calls me,' and the Professor switched on the visual, showing himself to be totally unlike Peter's original mental image of the telekinetic physicist. A tall, burly man who looked more like an alpine climber than scientist, beamed at him. With both hands he smoothed back thick brown hair from his forehead in what was a characteristic gesture, as he leaned eagerly towards the screen and planted muscled forearms on the worktop. 'I must thank you for all that you have done.'

Peter was surprised. 'Thank me? But your generators!'

'But the science!' Professor Gadriel responded with a Gallic twist of his shoulders. 'I am so glad that my generators were available when you needed them, and flattered that you would think of them at a time when you were quite obviously under a lot of stress—'

'Professor, what were you told?' Peter broke in.

'I was told nothing,' Tomas Gadriel laughed. 'But I am a man of science, and if you work at CERN, you learn to think quickly. My instruments were on and tracking that day, young man. I know exactly when you dumped power into my generators and exactly how much power you dumped. The explosion in space – the so-called "fire in the sky" – was on every newsvid. It took me less than an hour to sort through the maths, you know.'

'I see,' Peter replied slowly, wondering who else would be able to do the maths. 'Wait a minute, you say "dumped"?'

'*Mais oui!*' Professor Gadriel said. 'You dumped over

ninety-eight gigawatts of power through my circuitry. It held up rather well, too. It did not take me long to realize that that figure represented an orbital translation – and a lunar one at that. You see, you had to compensate for the difference in specific energy.'

Peter slumped in his chair. 'Professor, I don't understand. What specific energy?'

Professor Gadriel pursed his lips in thought. 'Young man, has not Madame Lehardt insisted that you are well rounded in all the sciences?'

'Well, she has tried,' Peter said in a rueful tone.

'And do I not understand that you have a keen interest in space flight and space travel?'

'I do,' Peter admitted.

'Then I would expect you to understand that for every kilogram of mass you put in an orbit, you must have increased the body's energy – both kinetic and potential – by a certain amount.'

Peter nodded in comprehension. 'I'm sorry, I follow you now. In translating an object from Earth's orbit to rest on the moon, I had to change the total energy per kilogram for every kilogram I lifted.'

'If by "lifted", you mean teleported, then yes, exactly,' Professor Gadriel agreed. 'But there is more energy per kilogram in an object orbiting the Earth at an altitude of two hundred kilometres than there is in an object at rest on the moon. So the energy had to go somewhere, n'est-ce pas?'

'Naturally,' Peter responded automatically. 'But how did your generators cope with such an influx of power?'

Professor Gadriel shrugged. 'They did not, of course. But my gestalt circuitry took the power, and when the couplings fused, the power grounded to Earth. Which is a pity, because otherwise CERN would have sold a very tidy sum of electricity to the European Power Grid.' The Professor grinned. 'Next time, we will handle that. In another six months, please feel free to repeat your performance.'

Peter grinned back. 'It's not a performance I want to *have* to repeat, thank you.'

'And why not?'

'Because I have never felt so drained,' Peter replied. 'But why, if I received so much power, should I feel drained?'

'You should ask my fuse the same question, young man,' Professor Gadriel replied with a hearty guffaw. 'It's not the direction the power flows in which matters – it's the total amount of power.'

Peter nodded thoughtfully. 'I can see why there would be a power surplus in this case, but if we are only teleporting objects from place to place on Earth, why do we need gestalt generators?'

'Well, of course,' the Professor replied, 'you don't – or we would never have discovered psychic powers. Over short distances, for small masses, the power requirements are such that the psychic's own power is sufficient. It is only over long distances or with large masses that we require additional help.

'Of course, even over relatively short distances, we telekinetics require more power than we use – and that is a mystery,' Professor Gadriel continued. 'It is a mystery which I am trying to solve.'

Peter laughed. 'I thought the biggest mystery was how psychic powers worked at all.'

Professor Gadriel threw up a dismissive hand. 'That problem was solved long ago. *Mon dieu*, what Teacher program have you been using? You have heard of Heisenberg, correct? And Schrödinger? You understand quantum mechanics, don't you?'

Peter found himself nodding decisively to all three questions. 'I certainly do, Professor. At least, I thought I did. I did pretty well on Teacher exams in physics, and general applications of quantum mechanics and string theory. But I'm afraid I don't precisely appreciate what quantum mechanics has to do with telekinetics.'

'You do not? But I thought that everyone knew—' the Professor broke off and slapped his forehead in disgust. 'Ah, idiot! I cannot *believe*—'

'Professor, I'm very sorry to have distressed you. Maybe I

should let you get back to your work,' Peter said, dismayed at the Professor's temper.

'No, not you – me!' The Professor slapped his forehead again for good measure. 'Perhaps you haven't had time lately to read the technical journals from CERN.' When Peter shook his head, unwilling to admit that he didn't have time to read any technical journals, just manifest lists and where to send what, Gadriel nodded his head sympathetically. 'Then you did not know that we, here at CERN, now know how telekinetics and all the psi powers work.'

'You do?' Peter was shocked. 'That is excellent news. With that knowledge we should be able to build gestalt generators to take us to the stars!'

'Ah, but it is not so easy, Mr Reidinger,' the Professor said sadly. 'Knowing how psi powers work is the easy part; making them work better – that is very difficult.'

'How do they work, Professor?'

'Our psychic powers utilize the quantum mechanical effects of an observer on a macroscopic scale,' the Professor said simply. Peter looked confused. 'You know that in the realm of quantum mechanics, simply observing a particle changes its state, correct? Professor Heisenberg embodied this in his Uncertainty Principle.'

'Yes,' Peter replied, 'the Heisenberg Uncertainty Principle states that with subatomic particles it is not possible to observe their state without the energy used to make the observation causing a change in that state – if you shine a light on an electron, it will either change its speed or its orbit.'

'Correct,' the Professor said. 'The effect of the observer is more profund, even. In the case of Schrödinger – and his poor unfortunate imaginary cat – an observer is *required* before an observation can be made.'

'Like Schrödinger's cat – no one can know if the cat is dead or alive without actually opening the airtight box and looking,' Peter agreed.

'Exactly,' the Professor replied enthusiastically. 'And we Talented people are very special observers. While nothing

371

can be said to have really happened without an observer, we, with our Talents, can make things happen the way we want them.'

'So I teleport objects by *wanting* them to be where they need to go.'

'Very good. But I would have said, we move objects by *observing* them to be in their new location,' the Professor corrected, nodding furiously.

'And telepathy?' Peter asked.

'Telepathy is even easier. It is purely a quantum-mechanical effect,' the Professor said. 'Telepaths think they are talking with someone, and that that someone hears them – neural stimulation at the quantum-mechanical level.'

Peter's face lit up with understanding as he absorbed the Professor's explanation. 'Our Talents work because we *want* them to!'

'Exactly.'

'And the gestalt generators?'

'They increase our ability to realize quantum-mechanical effects on a greater scale, as well as handling any specific energy concerns.'

Peter frowned. 'That doesn't explain why I get better results with some generators than others.'

'To understand that, I would need to see your telemetry – some measurements,' the Professor replied.

Peter grinned. 'I understand that you've been looking into this, and we have collected quite a lot of telemetry from our work up here on Padrugoi. I can download it to you now.'

The Professor glanced at his watch. 'For you, Peter, I will make time to analyse this data. Let me clear my schedule while you commence the download.'

Fifteen minutes later, Peter and Professor Gadriel were elbow-deep in their accumulated data.

'I see what you mean here, Peter, about the various loads,' Professor Gadriel agreed, highlighting one section of a graph. 'It certainly looks like everyone goes through a period of adjustment when they first join into gestalt with a generator.'

372

'What I've been trying to understand, Professor, is why I can't get a correlation between the graphs for different generators,' Peter said.

'Please, Peter, it would be easier for me if you called me Tomas,' Professor Gadriel said, smiling. 'We are friends now, *non*?'

Peter swallowed. Professor Gadriel was easily twenty years his senior – but his ready smile was infectious. 'Very well, Prof— Tomas. But if you look here,' and Peter brought up multiple graphs in the lower window, 'there seems to be no correlation. And without correlation—'

'We are missing something,' Tomas interrupted. He stroked his chin thoughtfully. 'Some piece of data is not in our picture. Let's look at the data for General Greene.'

'Very well,' Peter agreed, rapidly graphing that data and displaying the results.

'Ha! I see something,' Tomas said. He pointed to the graphs. 'Look at how much longer it takes General Greene to come into gestalt with these generators. Always he takes longer.' Tomas tapped rapidly on his keyboard. 'Here are my traces from my older gestalt circuitry. I am quicker, even than you,' he noted. 'Now why is that?'

'Some of these installations are newer than others,' Peter noted. Quickly he ran up graphs of gestalt against installation date.

'Hmm, the correlation is not exact,' Tomas said. He frowned thoughtfully, then brightened. 'But some of these would have received newer circuitry. Where are the records?' and his fingers flew over his keyboard again. 'Ah, here. Let's see now.' Peter's graph was rearranged on the screen. 'Hmm, still not quite a perfect fit.'

'Would all the newer circuitry be the same?' Peter asked.

Tomas shook his head. 'No, almost every circuit is custom-built, an experiment. I've been working with smaller circuit paths, aiming for higher efficiencies. Your Padrugoi equipment is three or four generations old. And some of these other installations – pah!' He waved a dismissive hand. 'Why, this one in Australia is ancient.'

Peter groaned. 'I got a headache every time I used it.'

Tomas shot him a startled look. 'Really? Headaches. This is something else we must consider. I recall a headache once, way back . . .' His voice faded away. 'No, I cannot remember. Let me consult my notes.' Again his fingers tapped on his keyboard. 'You wouldn't believe the amount of silliness I am willing to record, Peter,' Tomas said, shaking his head. 'By the way, I am recording our work together now, is that a problem? I should have mentioned it earlier, but most of my colleagues already know my penchant for recording everything.'

Peter shook his head. 'No, sir. In fact, it makes quite a lot of sense.'

Tomas grinned. 'Good, I am glad you agree. I get someone else to deal with the words that the silly speech-to-text software still can't handle. Mostly, it's very good. But not as good as a . . .' His voice trailed off. 'Ah, here it is. Yes, I had some trouble with your Australian generators, too. But my charts . . . hmm. I was still faster than you or General Greene, with those machines.'

'Perhaps you are more powerful or—'

'Nonsense! I know my limitations,' Tomas cut him off. 'There is no time for false modesty or bragging. We are dealing with science, Peter. There is a reason – probably a good one – why it is easier for me to form a gestalt than you.' Realization dawned in Professor Gadriel's eyes. 'Of course! I designed the circuitry, and tested it. Why would I bother to give myself a headache when I could avoid it! Hmm, somehow the circuitry works best for me . . .' Tomas's words trailed away again as he lapsed into thought once more.

'Maybe you tuned it—' Peter began.

'*Voilà!*' Tomas shouted. 'Or perhaps I should say, eureka! You are right, Peter. I most certainly did tune those circuits. How was I to know that I had tuned them best for me?'

'Would that explain the different times to achieve gestalt?' Peter asked.

Tomas shrugged. 'Perhaps. Or the headaches. I would imagine that both are aspects of how well a particular telekinetic is in tune with the gestalt circuitry – but I imagine that some telekinetics are better at entering into gestalt than others, no matter how well the circuitry is tuned. We shall have to experiment.'

'Great,' Peter said. 'When do we start?'

Tomas threw up his hands. 'Peter, you are unquenchable. We have been at this now for – *zut alors!* – seven hours and you want to start running experiments?'

Peter looked abashed. 'Sorry, Professor, it's just that—'

'I know, my young friend, youth has no patience,' Tomas said. 'But I will need some time to think this over and build new circuitry.'

'I'm sorry,' Peter once again felt obliged to apologize.

'You should not be!' Professor Gadriel responded hotly. 'We have made great strides this day, you and I. When we are done . . . who knows? But now I must report this to my superiors – I will need to draw a lot of new equipment.' When Peter made to speak again, Tomas cut him off. 'Do not worry – I shall have no problem getting it. Let me have some time to sort things through – I shall contact you again as soon as I have more.'

Peter caught Johnny showering, too excited to wait a single minute before sharing that incredible conversation and its rewards for them.

Well, one thing's sure, Gadriel's not all wet the way I am right now.

Sorry, Johnny.

He caught Johnny's tolerant sigh.

Don't be. I'd heard something about Gadriel before our interesting trip to First Base, but I didn't actually connect quantum mechanics with what we do. Didn't anyone think to tell us?

There's some sort of Murphy's Law, isn't there, that says that people who do the work are the last ones to know?

If there isn't, there should be. OK, you recorded too, didn't you? Send it to my workstation and I'll review it. And don't let's tell Dirk right now. We should see if it works for us, and then organize a new contract.

Is that all you ever think of, contracts? Peter was both amused and irritated by the General's practicality. Being able to work more efficiently shouldn't be translated into more credit. Or should it, especially if it benefited the Centre, as well as the kinetics involved?

And don't tell Rhyssa just yet, Johnny added. *I don't want to get her hopes up until we're sure Gadriel's right.*

Peter grumbled but obeyed. And had another diversion for his spare time when he wasn't 'porting shipments to First Base. Commander de Aruya had forwarded his MRI readings and Peter's incredible neo-neurogenesis to Mountainside Hospital.

Neuro-specialist Finn Markstein wanted very much to examine Peter Reidinger in person, and arranged to come immediately to Padrugoi for this purpose.

A man in his early thirties, with a face that looked much younger than his years and experience, he had a confident and optimistic manner. His field of concentration was spinal injuries, including bypass operations that provided some limited mobility. Although Peter sensed that Markstein was highly sceptical that the source of the miraculous neurogenesis was an eleven-year-old girl, Dr Markstein did not argue the point, murmuring about gift horses. Markstein discussed Peter's case with Commander de Aruya, and on video link with Martin McNulty. The station physiotherapist, Mike Malaj, was briefed to restore Peter's body to full working condition. He had to gain strength gradually and the resilience to perform gross motor movements. As Ceara had suggested, the fine motor skills would take longer. Finn Markstein was willing to advance the opinion that full recovery from the paralysis was possible, with dedicated hard work on Peter's part. A hydrotherapy tank was already part of the sick bay's equipment, and Peter was scheduled to spend a good deal of time in it between 'portations and the exercise facility.

'You're not really in bad shape, Pete,' Mike told him on the second day. 'Smart of you to keep working out on the Reeve board. I won't kid you, though. It's going to be rough at times. I gotta work you hard. Nothing personal, you realize.'

Though intellectually Peter did realize that, it was hard not to think that Mike was a despot, putting him through strenuous exercises, demanding more and more at each session. If Sue, his original therapist, had seemed strict, she was a pussycat in comparison to Mike.

'Gotta get those quadriceps moving,' Mike used a litany of those muscles in a sort of chant as he worked Peter through his body: arms, chest, abdomen, pelvis, back and legs. '*Think* into the tissue of pectoralis major. And don't forget the minor. Let's get these arms working – deltoid, biceps, triceps, the flexors. Your belly, sir, and its latissimus dorsi, the rectus abdominus. Your good ol' gluteus maximus, medius and minimus. Get 'em working. Make your muscles remember what they once did. Quadriceps, rectus femoris. They will remember, you know, if you *make* them. You're a psychic. Make your mind work for you.'

'I was,' Peter gasped, sweating to move inches when a half-hour before he had 'ported hundredweights to the moon, 'doing just fine that way. This is different.'

And, oh, how different it was! It almost defeated him. Sternly he reminded himself that getting rid of that damned appliance would be worth an ocean of sweat. Markstein reassured him that the diversion could be reversed and that he would be able to control his bodily functions. That was an ambition devoutly to be wished. The operation had been done – without his realizing what it meant – after the consultants regretfully announced that his paralysis was incurable.

When telekinesis had given Peter mobility, he had pleaded with Dr McNulty to reconnect him, but the doctor had regretfully replied that Peter did not have the sympathetic nervous system to control voluntary actions, no matter how clever he had been at counterfeiting movement in his limbs.

'If I have to wait for voluntary muscle control to develop, how will I know when it does?' Peter asked Finn.

The doctor twitched his lips, cleared his throat and his eyes gleamed. 'You'll know. The man in you will stand up and be noticed.'

It took Peter a moment to realize what Markstein meant, and then he felt the blood rush to his face. He remembered, all too vividly, the three a.m. bath!

'You'll know, Peter,' the doctor repeated gently.

It took nearly ten days of designing, testing and refining – and some very serious headaches – before Professor Gadriel, Peter and Johnny Greene were satisfied with their results.

'Look at this, we have a hundred per cent decrease in power consumption when the circuits are tuned,' Professor Gadriel chortled happily to himself. 'And you were so right, Peter, to think of using musical notes for tuning – very efficient. I also notice that your friend Lance Baden is tone deaf, which probably explains why he cannot achieve the gestalt. It is also true that some telekinetics take longer to achieve a gestalt, but those times decrease significantly when the generators are tuned to their pitch.'

'It's as though a telekinetic has a particular range of ability – and the peak efficiency is at a particular frequency,' Peter observed.

'I agree,' said Johnny Greene, who at first had been rather dubious. He rubbed the back of his neck in a vain attempt to rid himself of his latest headache. 'And now I know why I like songs in G major more than those in C.'

Peter's best key was C major.

'I also see that our efficiencies increase with the greater efficiency of the gestalt circuitry – the point-one-micron circuits are much easier to work with,' Johnny noted. 'Professor, when do you think we can push down to finer circuitry?'

Tomas frowned and shook his head. 'We are dealing with a great deal of power, General Greene. It is very hard to design such fine traces to handle such high loads.'

Johnny sighed and nodded. 'But it is obvious that the closer we are to the quantum-mechanical limit, the easier it is for us to enter into the gestalt.'

'Ah, but we must be careful not to let other quantum-mechanical effects overwhelm our circuitry,' Tomas countered.

'I think the really important question, Tomas, is when can we get this new circuitry installed up here on Padrugoi,' Peter said.

Tomas perked up. 'Oh, didn't I mention?' Across the link, the other two shook their heads. 'Ah, well – today, if you can stand the headache of picking it up.'

'Can we!' Peter and Johnny chorused.

The several crates of ultra-sensitive circuitry were deposited with the delicacy of a butterfly into the high-security storage on Engineering deck.

From such sublimity, Peter reported for another very physical session with Mike. And sweated, had his muscles galvanically stimulated, ate the special diet – which included the complex carbohydrates he needed – despite the extra loads that had to be emptied more regularly from the waste-bag. He also reinstituted the limbic exercises Sue had taught him. In a way, that was following Mike's advice about thinking into his tissue. And deadening the pain! It was almost good to *feel* pain, to stretch and compress. Almost!

Peter was almost sorry to have the next week off because Lieutenant Temuri Bergkamp was quite willing to install the CERN circuits, to improve the performance of his generators in gestalt. He said it would take at least the week to get them integrated. He grinned at both Johnny and Peter; the twinkle in his eye indicated that he must have been on the list of those who needed to know how Limo 34 had been able to make it to First Base.

A week off from telekinesis did not however mean a week off from physiotherapy, because Martin McNulty made provisions for him to continue the relentless exercises.

He and Johnny gratefully 'ported downside to the Jerhattan terminal. For the first time, Peter noticed the expanse of low land that had once been a nice urban area, until a compulsory government acquisition had transferred the residents to other, quieter habitations. Jerhattan Transport Complex had grown but not outstripped the available area. The telepad was east and south of the main buildings and the grid of concrete take-off and taxiing strips.

379

Even the airbus hotels needed room to manoeuvre and make their vertical landings. Small craft used auxiliary fields.

Here, there would be space for a suitable 'headquarters', Peter decided, near enough Jerhattan proper for access – especially by telekinetics – and cargo space for the containers. Johnny had never referred to Peter's mention of a commercial amalgamation of telekinetics and long-distance telepaths. Peter was not going to rush the idea. Simply because Johnny hadn't taken him up on that casual reference didn't mean that the General had not heard it. There had been so many exciting and unexpected developments, especially the talks with Tomas Gadriel. The Professor had also offered the new circuitry to Rhyssa. She and Sascha were excitedly discussing how this would alter the training of any new kinetics. This could well be the most important breakthrough for parapsychic research since Henry Darrow had invented the Goosegg that could record brainwaves and prove genuine incidents of psychic activity.

Maybe, Peter mused, when they got back to work, the Gadriel gestalt would make it easier to trick Johnny into sending to 'South America.' He would try when they reported back on duty. He'd get on with the analyses and he'd also make time to star-gaze, or rather, asteroid-gaze.

Now, he was just a step away from Amariyah.

Both Rhyssa and Dorotea told him in no uncertain terms and so frequently that he wondered if they thought he'd lost his wits as he regained his limbs. He, of all people, knew he must be adroit. How he was going to also impress on Amariyah *not* to inhibit her talent – which she didn't yet know she had – was another matter. He had read all he could about Dorotea's mother, Ruth Horvath, who had been able to manipulate cells, but could never consciously tap into her microkinetic talent. He read how deftly Daffyd op Owen, Rhyssa's grandfather, had dealt with Ruth: subtly inspiring her innate maternal sympathies for persons he wished her to 'heal' and 'alter'. Sometimes this had been successful: it was not an easy Talent to have, use or direct.

According to most parapsychic experts, a person did not come 'into' his or her Talent until puberty, or until a trauma

380

forced them to use alternate skills, as had happened to him. Instinct had governed Amariyah's abilities – the instinct to heal, nourish, protect. Some latent Talents, like Ceara Scott's empathy, were not apparent even at puberty, emerging later gradually, almost unnoticed.

Peter tarried at the Jerhattan telepad. Long after Johnny had taken himself off to his home in Virginia, finally realizing that he was ridiculously postponing his reunion with Amariyah, he 'ported himself to the Henner estate, the trees around the perimeter beginning to bud out. Why did that surprise him? Objectively, only four weeks had elapsed since he had said goodbye to Dorotea and Maree. Subjectively, a very great deal had happened.

He would have given much to be able to stride smartly down the path to Dorotea's neat house. That was in the future. He didn't yet have the physical strength to relinquish kinesis. Also, he wasn't sure how often he *would*. It was such an effort. Only the reward of removing the waste-bag was worth the struggle. And a longer, healthier life. Markstein had been eloquent on that topic. Long-term paralysis had devastating effects on the body of the skeleteam. Peter grinned. While there was a trickle of people heading towards the transport tube and their day's work, they were there, in the distance.

Amariyah! Dorotea! Rhyssa! His mental tone was not quite a shout, since all three were nearby.

PETER! Rhyssa's response was a second faster than Dorotea's. Both rang with joy.

I'll meet you at Dorotea's, Rhyssa said. *You sound so good!*

Amariyah doesn't 'hear', Peter, but we're just having breakfast.

I ate above. Padrugoi's day is ahead of Earth's right now, but I could certainly use another cup of tea.

He 'ported himself into the hallway outside the kitchen. He sensed Amariyah in her bedroom.

'Maree? I'm home,' he called, and opened the door to the kitchen.

Quickly wiping her hands on her apron, Dorotea opened

her arms to him. He couldn't step fast enough to get to her, but he could close his arms tightly around her body, and 'feel' her frailty. Fortunately, he only had so much muscle in his arms, so 'tight' wasn't bone-crushing.

'Oh, Peter, you *have* improved,' she cried, and he could feel the pressure of her arms about his waist as she hugged him enthusiastically. Then she pushed him away, to stare into his eyes, trying to assess the less obvious alterations in him. 'In so *many* ways, my dear, dear boy!'

Amariyah charged into the kitchen, shouting with joy. If he hadn't instinctively braced himself, she would have propelled them against the sink unit.

'Peter, Peter, Peter, Peter, *Peter*!' she carolled in a litany of welcome, flinging her arms about his waist.

'Ama-*ree*-yah,' Dorotea exclaimed in automatic protest. 'Have some manners!'

Peter embraced her slender frame, so much more vibrant than Dorotea's, wriggling as if to bore inside him to display her joy at his homecoming. A swift, impetuous hug, and then she released him, grabbing his hand, not even noticing that he could close his fingers about hers.

'Come see, come see. I've so much to show you,' and the wiry little girl tried to haul him after her.

'Amariyah Bantam,' Dorotea said firmly, gripping a fold of her tunic top and pulling her back. 'Breakfast is ready and the garden will not disappear.' *Though at times I wish it did,* she added with an exasperated sigh. *No, I take that back,* and her face mirrored guilty dismay. 'Peter, sit down at the table. The kettle is about to boil for your tea, and you will surely eat some of the Danish rolls I made for you.' *If you sit, she will.*

Peter sat. Heaving the most dramatic of sighs and rolling her eyes in pique, Amariyah reluctantly settled to her place.

'Did Ping Yung tell you if those plants thrived?' was the first question she asked after a long drink of orange juice.

'Yes, he did, and they did, and he wants you to come more often.'

Amariyah flung a see-I-told-you look at Dorotea, who smiled tolerantly.

'Does the hydroponics unit at First Base use Triticum, too?' Amariyah continued to fire questions at him throughout the meal. But only, Peter thought affectionately, because she wasn't guiding him around her gardens and explaining which plants had done the best this winter and what she'd accomplished during his absence. After all he had survived and been part of and victim to, her chatter was a relief; the restorative touch of a different kind of reality.

Rhyssa joined them for coffee and one of Dorotea's Danish pastries. The three Talents began one of those lightning mental exchanges for the details that Amariyah did not need to know. Both Rhyssa and Dorotea were eager to hear all about Peter's physical progress.

'You're not taking a vacation from your exercises, Peter m'dear,' Rhyssa said as she dunked her pastry in her coffee.

As if I'd have the chance with Martin, Mark and Mike – three formidable Ms – choreographing my 'week off', Peter said with some asperity.

'Helping me in the garden is exercise,' Amariyah said. 'And I will massage you.'

Peter grinned. 'I've missed it, dear.' He laid his right hand on hers and squeezed.

'That's much stronger,' the girl said, with all the solemn approval of an adult.

Very privately Peter wondered that, these days, people only felt free to mention his paralysis because it was being reversed.

Definitely I felt more heft in you, Peter, Dorotea added, then her eyes filmed briefly. *Just as Amariyah did. Even squeezing for a hug. So telling, so reassuring.*

Dorotea, Peter exclaimed, hiding what he had discovered about her body.

'I suppose there's no indication yet how long it will take you?' Dorotea went on more briskly.

Peter replied meekly. 'I must work hard and not shirk my exercises, no matter how painful.' *And if I'm a good boy, I should be fit for the marathon in October.*

MARATHON? the two women exclaimed together.

383

'I will see that you do, Peter,' Amariyah said.

You both know what I want the most, he said on an entirely sober note.

Dorotea nodded. *Daily teleporting to the moon has not been a strain on you, with all that strenuous physical exercise?*

A snap, Peter said, accepting the change of subject. *If I can tune myself into the available generator, I can 'port it.* Opening his perceptions wide, he watched Rhyssa's face to see her reaction to that very broad, if accurate, statement. He was surprised that she didn't take him up on it. She probably had more urgent problems. Just as well, since he hadn't completed his theory. He really would have to get back to those reports.

Would that it were true for more psychics, she said with a rueful expression in her eyes and a lift of one shoulder. *Remember the basketball incident?*

Yes, and Peter couldn't think why she would remind him.

One of the villains of the occasion, and then she spoke out loud, 'Scott Gates is demonstrating a strong kinetic ability.'

HE IS?

No need to shout, Peter, Rhyssa said, wincing.

Sascha will be training him on the Gadriel gestalt, won't he?

Of course, and Rhyssa sounded surprised that he needed to ask.

Just how much, Peter wondered, would tuning into the Gadriel circuits affect telekinesis along the range of such abilities? Certainly it would alter the limits that he had to believe were self-imposed. Certainly he had proved that he could both 'port and 'path further than anyone – including himself – had suspected. And Scott Gates would receive training on the Gadriel gestalt. Good!

'Scott helps me in the garden,' Amariyah said. Then she frowned a bit. 'I don't know why he volunteered, but I think he's coming to like it.'

'He's only fourteen,' Rhyssa said with a grin. 'Sascha's got a lot of basic training to do with him before he can specialize. With all you have to do right now, Peter, you don't have time to take on a trainee.'

'That's true,' Peter admitted, but he didn't want to miss an opportunity to catch a Talent early enough.

'I'm training him, too,' Amariyah put in.

'And doing a good job of it, I'm sure,' Peter said, smiling at her.

'What are you up to, Peter Reidinger?' Dorotea asked, as blunt as ever.

'Yes, what?' Rhyssa reinforced the query.

He grinned at them both. 'My prime directive from you, Rhyssa, has always been to find other kinetics who can make a gestalt.' *Remember that I was not quite Scott's age when I discovered it.*

That is a good point, Rhyssa agreed. 'You could certainly meet him, get his mettle, as it were. That would do no harm.'

'No, it wouldn't.' To himself Peter added, and quite possibly a lot of good.

Rhyssa then cocked her head at him. *What else did you learn between here and First Base, Peter?*

Peter smiled for an answer and, when he felt her unmistakable push at his mind, he raised one hand and slowly made his index finger move in admonition. *Tsk, tsk, Rhyssa. Wasn't it you who taught me never to peek?*

Both women were so impressed by that gesture that they were distracted.

Speaking of peeking, he went on to keep the advantage, *Johnny told me about Georg Fraga and Mai Leitao.*

That's sad, though, Rhyssa said, then her mental tone oozed distaste. *So, Shimaz is implicated?*

Peripherally at least, Peter replied. *Johnny said that they traced the voice print Fraga took when he was blackmailed. It identified a Riz Naztuk, who is Shimaz's uncle. Of whom he has many, as well as cousins by the dozens,* he said, trying to lighten the revulsion both Rhyssa and Dorotea felt at the mention of the Malaysian. *Riz Naztuk's face appears on Barchenka's surveillance tapes as a visitor but their conversation, while undoubtedly ambiguous, doesn't implicate them. Yet.*

How wide did Shimaz's connections spread? Dorotea

asked, appalled that the wretched pervert still figured in their lives.

That's going to take time to discover, Peter said. *There are only so many psychics available for that kind of work.*

Rhyssa's expression was full of regret.

'I have finished breakfast,' Amariyah announced. 'All of it,' she added, glancing sideways at Dorotea. 'You may now see my gardens, Peter.' She got down from her chair and held her hand out to him in unspoken command.

Obediently, Peter got to his feet and took it, grinning sheepishly at the two women.

Come for dinner at our place, Rhyssa said. *Dorotea may not hog you to herself. The boys are demanding a share of your company.*

When Dorotea nodded her head in agreement, he accepted, and then allowed Amariyah to haul him outside. He found the tour oddly relaxing, and was able to answer almost all her questions about the gardens on First Base.

'I've got to do my physio now, Maree,' he said almost regretfully.

'I'll come with you. I will do massage after. I do very good massage. You said so yourself.' She gave him a level adult stare, waiting for his affirmative response.

He ruffled her blue-black hair. He'd done that before, of course, but had never been able to feel its silkiness on the palm of his hand.

'You do the best massage in the world, Maree dear,' he assured her. Peter had wondered just how he could avail himself of her Talent without drawing undue attention to it. He'd talk the physio into agreeing. 'I know you have Teacher this morning.'

She made a face, reverting to a child's annoyance. 'Do I have to?'

'If you want to do hydroponic gardening in space, you have to.'

'Oh, very well,' she said with a long-suffering sigh. 'But you come right back.'

Don't you dare try to probe, Peter Reidinger, Dorotea said at her sternest.

I wouldn't dream of it.

Amariyah was an entirely different facet of potential Talent from Scott Gates. Scott already *knew* he could teleport. Maree's unique ability must be nourished as tenderly as she would her most delicate plants. Would she, too, *grow* into her Talent?

CHAPTER FIFTEEN

Peter was making his way back to Dorotea's, and Amariyah's promised massage, for which he was literally aching, when he saw Cass Cutler ambling on a course parallel to his.

Hi, Cass! Here to see Rhyssa?

Nope, she replied and swerved across the lawn to join him. *I'm here on special assignment.*

'Oh, really?' he said aloud. Her gamine grin answered his next question. 'Why me?'

'Cos they ain't caught all the perps yet, and you're a lot more at risk on your own home ground than upside.

Peter halted his glide and stared at her.

'But there're psychics all around me . . .'

Cass shook her head. 'They won't be looking out for *you,* Pete. I got orders from the boss,' she ticked off on her fingers, 'the General *and* the Admiral, and that's too much rank for me to buck.' She grinned again, her eyes sparkling. 'Not that I would, seeing as how I have your welfare at heart, anyhow.' *Now don't get all fussed, Pete,* she admonished.

He seethed with indignation. *Don't try wheedling me, Cass. I'm well able to take care of myself and I have, goddammit, proved* that.

Cass nodded in agreement. *It's as much for the others that I'm here.*

That stopped his complaint and cooled his anger. Dorotea had felt so frail in his arms. Amariyah was so precious. Abruptly he had a sense of how Rhyssa felt about him and his Talent. It was a sobering reflection.

All right. You're not here on your own, are you?

No. Some of 'em you don't know and shouldn't see, and we'll all try not to intrude. You're supposed to be on R and R down here. I'm listening for a lot of reasons, Pete. She appealed to him with her eyes and body language. *Ignore us, will ya?*

He smiled and continued on, Cass beside him. *Sure. But who should I listen for?*

Any mind you can't identify. Any person you've never seen around here. And don't, promise me, go near that ice-cream parlour on the mall! 'Port a treat in for Amariyah if she frets, but don't leave the grounds.

He nodded compliance, resenting it but having to admit candidly that he understood the rationale. Hell, he and Tirla had been kidnapped once before when they had slipped to the mall without anyone knowing they'd gone. He was not about to have that happen to him again, or most particularly to Amariyah.

What else is new? And he could mentally imply that he wanted news of Boris's investigations.

You probably know more than I do, Pete, she said with a detached shrug. *I'm just the gal on the beat.* 'Nice catching you like this, Pete,' she added out loud, and took the left-hand path at the Y-junction.

Amariyah had not lost her knack of massage. Relaxing as her hands gently soothed muscles and tendons, Peter wondered idly how long it was going to take him to move physically, rather than telekinetically. He mocked himself. Amariyah had already performed one miracle. It was up to *him* to make his way forward.

She extracted payment from him in the form of another tour of her gardens, the ones they'd missed after breakfast.

389

He wondered what Ted and the other groundsmen had left to do.

Peter, Dorotea and Amariyah appeared at Rhyssa's home in time for him to spend half an hour with Eoin and Chester, and gave them a suitably edited account of his trip to the moon.

Over dinner, Peter was able to tell Rhyssa and an attentive Dave more of what had been done. He tried not to wax too excited about seeing the asteroid on the far-side telescope, or the conversations that had ensued. Rhyssa knew that he had taken an astronomy course and would have been interested in that facet of First Base. Nothing more was said about Shimaz, Flimflam and the 'problem' with Limo 34. Dave did mention that all the Parapsychic Centres were actively recruiting; he was in charge of the publicity campaign.

On the way home that night, Peter wondered if Dorotea was aware that they were being 'followed'.

I'm not that *feeble in the wits by any means, Peter Reidinger. Thank God, Amariyah already has her hair stranded. They've put her in the 'at risk' category, you know. There will be no way she can be removed from these premises, I assure you.*

He used the excuse of fatigue when Amariyah tried to cajole him into a trip to the mall, to the Old-fashioned Parlour of Gastronomical Delights.

'But I got a new dress just to wear there with you. I'll give you another massage. A better one.'

Peter chuckled. 'I'm also on a strict diet, to build muscle and strengthen bones, and it doesn't include chocolate sundaes with every topping known to gourmets. I'll bring one in for you, if you like, and you may eat it in your room so I'm not tempted.'

That was not quite what Amariyah had in mind, but Peter could be as stubborn as she could. They compromised. She could wear the dress and he'd watch her eat the sundae.

The dress was blue, beautifully cut, another example of Tirla's elegant taste. Maree would soon be eleven. He must be back down here for her birthday. No, better still, he'd invite her up to Padrugoi. No use taking chances.

She had heard the physio recommend to Peter that he exercise his fingers to increase their dexterity, and improve finer motor control. Although the physio thought he should try playing the piano or a stringed instrument or sketching, Amariyah thought that weeding would be equally therapeutic and more useful. He said he wanted to learn how to draw. She said he could use her light-pen – she had the very best one on the market, which she used to plan her garden beds – if he'd help her weed. He agreed.

In fact, he spent a lot of time using the light-pen, clumsily at first, but gradually with more finesse. Eventually he was able to sketch 'South America' rather deftly. Then he doodled, as Johnny Greene did; only he doodled asteroids tumbling or spinning through space on their axes, or atmosphere domes and generator units. For instance, his own 60MHz generator, with Gadriel gestalt circuits tuned to C major.

Six days later, Peter was at least refreshed when he 'ported himself to the Jerhattan telepad after Cass duly escorted him to the Centre's pad. He'd kept to the Centre's grounds, chatted with the young people who had just started training, played with Rhyssa's children, and Tirla's, for she came three times. 'Checking on you,' she said, radiating approval of his physical breakthrough.

He waited for Johnny by the personnel carrier. The General arrived, his skin ruddy with new colour, his nose peeling, and his whole manner bursting with renewed vigour.

'You obviously had a great time,' Peter said, almost grudgingly.

'Sally wasn't campaigning anywhere,' Johnny said, his eyes sparkling. 'My sons remembered that I was their father, and I got rid of my Padrugoi pallor. Now I can take another four weeks of lifting bales and toting barges.' He looked Peter up and down. 'How'd you get on?'

'I got seven more massages from Amariyah!' And those were actually the high points of Peter's week home.

'You didn't tell Maree your suspicions?' Johnny raised his eyebrows in query. Peter shook his head.

'No, nothing was even whispered in her vicinity. We're to let her develop at her own pace.'

'And how's your forward pace?'

Peter's shrug was a looser, more natural movement than his previous imitations of the gesture. 'We'll see what this week's SSEP reveals, if anything, and Mike's assessment of my muscular strength.'

'Our chariot awaits,' Johnny said, gesturing to the shell. 'I dare you to *walk* that far.'

'Oh, no. You're going to have to wait like all the others for my—'

'Formal muscle-power debut?' Johnny asked when Peter stalled for the right words.

Back on Padrugoi, Ensign Patterson was once again on duty on the boat bay, and greeted them with a salute. He delivered the message that Admiral Coetzer would be pleased if they made their way to the conference room when they were settled in their quarters.

'They're going to work us hard today, I know it,' Johnny said with a glance at the clock and a groan. 'Maybe we should have timed our arrival for a more civilized hour.'

'You picked it,' Peter said.

'Then let us go about our daily occasions,' Johnny said in a pompous tone. 'Meetcha in the conference room in five.' Johnny 'ported himself away.

With a nod to the ensign who was trying to act nonchalant about the General's disappearance, Peter left as well. His quarters looked exactly the same, and, although the cabin was tidy – he was never quite that neat – it also had an unused feel to it. Would he have a shadow on-station, too? He dropped his gear on the bunk and 'ported to the conference room.

The monitor displayed the day's schedule with a brief note of welcome back from Dirk Coetzer; and confirmation from Lieutenant Bergkamp that the Gadriel circuits had been added to the Padrugoi generators, tuned to both C major and G major. Peter was glad to be first in. He could take

392

advantage of the time to see if he could set up his 'South America' scam. He scanned the list and found the very one – only ten kilos. He'd have to change the destination to . . . where? On Earth . . . someplace Johnny didn't know and would have to get a visual of. He couldn't think of a target, so he invented one: a new customer – Calco Laboratory – a lab facility would have features much like 'South America'. Calco would be 'situated' in Jerhattan. God knows, there were enough small companies like that in the industrial perimeter of Jerhattan, which was well within Johnny's acknowledged 'limit'. Speaking quietly, Peter did the necessary editing. Since he was familiar with Johnny's preference for hard copy, he touched the print button, feeling the moment of contact in the tip of his finger. He chuckled to himself. If Johnny liked to hold hard copy, Peter liked to touch keys, now that he could.

'Ho there, you beat me to it,' Johnny said, arriving in the room. 'Barney?'

For a single moment, Peter froze, having forgotten that the steward might be waiting in the serving alcove. He told himself firmly that Barney could not have seen, been interested in, much less suspicious of anything Peter had just done. Just then, the door from the hall opened and Barney entered, carrying a tray of supplies.

'Had to collect fresh coffee, General. Good morning, Mr Reidinger.'

Peter let go a relieved breath. He really wasn't up to deception. Although maybe that's why he'd get away with this.

'Got our day's work organized, Pete?' Johnny asked and, with an offhand motion, Peter passed him the paper copy. 'I'll just get rid of the downside junk.' He whistled. 'Boy, First Base ought to pay off its mortgage with these shipments of rare earths.' He paused, running his finger down the side of the sheet. 'Only destination I don't know is the Calco lab.'

'They sent a visual,' Peter said, bringing 'South America' up onscreen.

'Humph. Well, there can't be two stains like that in the

393

world,' Johnny said, settling into his chair preparatory to leaning into the generators.

'Easy to see,' Peter remarked, clamping down on his inner tension. 'I'll just assemble the first load to the moon.' Should he wait and give Johnny a hand if he 'felt' any difference, 'porting that far? He didn't dare mess with Johnny at the outset. Better wait! Johnny must realize that he had the kinetic strength to 'port to any place he could 'see'. *You go first, Johnny.* He was really pleased with how casual he sounded, despite the way his gut was acting. How had he forgotten that aspect of sensation?

'Remember to tune into your G major circuit,' he said casually to Johnny.

'I certainly will. This'll make 'porting a snap.'

Peter let himself 'feel' Johnny get tuned to the new configuration, and the General smiled at the ease of contact. Then he started his 'port, frowning slightly as the gauge on the generator panel swung over at his usage.

'And it was only to Jerhattan,' Johnny exclaimed, baffled. 'Boy, that sun must have scrambled my brains. What happened? Gadriel's gimmick was supposed to make this easier.'

'Well, no,' Peter said blithely, grinning fit to crack his face, 'actually, General Greene, you just pushed ten kilos to the astronomy laboratory at First Base. Congratulations!'

Johnny's jaw dropped and his dark brows met across the bridge of his nose.

'I *what*? Say again!' There was 'General' in that command.

'I said, actually, General Greene—'

Johnny flicked an impatient hand, his glare deepening. 'I know what you said. Tuning into a generator makes that much difference to my range?'

Peter gestured to the monitor. 'Tuning does make a difference, I'm sure, but you ought to be able to 'port to wherever you can "see", Johnny. As I did to the bollard in the parking lot, and to the table in Watari's office.'

For a very long moment, Johnny stared at 'South America', jutted his jaw, cocked his head to glower sideways at Peter, then back at 'South America'.

394

'Ten kilos?' he asked in an all-too-quiet voice.

'Ten kilos of storage crystals that Dr Pienarr ordered.' Peter waited. He knew Johnny Greene well enough to see the tension building in his body, and he awaited the explosion with considerable anxiety. 'I changed the—'

'NEVER EXPLAIN!' The General propelled himself out of the chair and Peter backed away. Then Johnny threw his head back and howled with laughter, doubling over and slapping his hands on his thighs. 'Kid, you're amazing.' He took a step forward and gave Peter a buffet on his shoulder, which would have knocked Peter off balance if Johnny hadn't also grabbed his arm to steady him.

'I never thought you a devious type, Pete,' Johnny said through gasps of laughter, his eyes tearing with mirth. 'Hoisted me on my own petard, you did.'

'About time, don't you think?' Peter asked sardonically, cocking his head and regarding the older man.

Barney emerged from his alcove, for once baffled by their antics.

'It's too early in the morning,' Johnny said, controlling hilarity with an effort, 'for champagne, and Peter doesn't drink. Coffee please, Barney? And whatever Pete wants to celebrate his connivery. Good one, Pete! Caught me fair and square.'

He wiped his eyes and dropped limply into his chair until Barney put a coffee mug in front of him and a teacup for Peter, steam from the herbal brew sending off a spiced aroma.

'I caught you, Johnny?' Peter asked, noting the odd turn of phrase.

'Yes, caught me, Pete.' Johnny's eyes twinkled over the rim of his cup as he took a judicious sip of the hot coffee.

'You mean, you knew you could 'port farther?'

Johnny nodded, with a rascally expression on his face.

'I suspected, but I also knew damned well that if I admitted I could, I'd be made to. Never volunteer.'

'You volunteered *me*,' Peter exclaimed with some indignation.

'True, true, but if you'd shown the least sign of strain,

kid,' and the General turned quite solemn, 'I'd've called a halt, like right then.' He brought his hand down edgewise on the table in a firm blow. 'Lance was sure you could do it too, so we arranged that little bit of foolery from the Adelaide Centre. I never thought you'd play the same trick on me.' He gave his head an admiring shake and chuckled again.

'Lance? What about *his* true range?'

'Ah,' and Johnny rocked his spread fingers in a gesture of doubt. 'Gadriel says he's tone deaf. He can't "tune", so he can't access the circuitry, Peter.' Johnny let go an understandable sigh of satisfaction that *he* could. 'He's fine over short distances with the strength that's in him. But I don't think he could make it for a long haul. Too bad – he'd be an asset.'

'To "see" is to 'port,' Peter murmured.

'For you, and you've proved that's right for me, too. But until we do find someone else with that extra little something . . .' In one of Johnny's volatile changes, pure mischief gleamed in his green-flecked amber eyes. 'What were you telling me the other morning, about a company of telepaths and teleports?'

Peter smoothed his face of all expression. Johnny had been so hung-over. From now on, Peter would be more cautious about what he said.

'Just testing the water.'

'How?'

Peter pointed to the clocks on the wall. 'Tell you later. We've got stuff to move.'

Johnny nodded. 'You're right there. Only, kid,' and he touched Peter's elbow, 'next time you give me something to 'port to First Base, warn me, will ya? I nearly ran out of "tune"!'

They finished the first session in complete accord, and organized cargoes for the second hour's work.

'Why didn't you come with me to the observatory?' Peter asked. 'Mind you, I'm glad you didn't, or I wouldn't have been able to fool you.'

'While you were there, I was busy talking Watari into the necessity for our abrupt and stealthy departure. Vin Cyberal was reviewing the surveillance tapes on Shimaz to make sure he'd had no contact with anyone since the limo got there. He'd been on restriction for the last month, so there had been no contact with anyone.'

'Restriction?' Peter asked.

'Yeah, well, complete isolation. If an offie gets real obstreperous – and that's Shimaz's middle name – he's totally secluded. Not quite cocooned as you and Tirla were, but the next best thing. Food, water and surveillance are on automatic. Not even a moon mite could get in. And none did.'

'So then he wasn't involved?'

Johnny made a grimace. 'Certainly not directly. The theory is developing that this fatwa-type operation is also on automatic. Someone, or several someones, is following his original orders to take revenge on you, and me, for the indignities heaped on his very worthy soul.' Johnny flicked his fingers restlessly. 'He was, of course, working up at Padrugoi on the Josephson Junctions, so Barchenka knew him. Maybe too well. But he was convicted, sentenced, and in the Lunar Prison before she plotted her little Mutiny. Uncle Riz made visits to her, so if she had opted for revenge . . .' his eyebrows twitched, 'and she would have loved to get back at both of us for defusing her Mutiny, that would explain how Flimflam got around so handily on Padrugoi. Fortunately for all concerned, it's doubtful that he ever passed on this information.' Johnny paused thoughtfully. 'Maybe that's why he was assassinated.' Abruptly, Johnny slapped both hands on his thighs. 'Enough of such maudlin speculation. By the way, Lance should be passing through Padrugoi this week on his way home. He's finished the current construction contract, and he wants to renew his acquaintance with full gravity.' Johnny winked broadly. 'On your way, kid. Surprise him with your physical prowess.'

As resolutely as Johnny, Peter put Barchenka, Shimaz, Flimflam and vengeance out of his mind and turned to more profitable thoughts. Once again, he wished he could find, or

397

train, more people to use the Gadriel gestalt. Especially since Johnny had remembered Peter's grandiose Telepaths and Teleporters scheme. Either way, two out of three was a step towards that goal. Maybe not this year, or next. Perhaps not for another decade.

You're only twenty, Peter told himself firmly to dampen his enthusiasm.

That twenty-year-old self felt like cartwheeling down the corridor.

That evening, when Peter tried to book time on the Station's link with the far-side telescope, he was politely told that even officers had to submit a summary of why they should have use of telescope time, what constellation they intended to focus on and what conclusion they hoped to draw. The request could take as much as a year to be granted. For all Peter's bravado about prerogatives, he did not quite have the confidence to force the issue.

'However, Mr Reidinger, you may not realize how much is available on file. All use of the telescopes is recorded. You might review the sessions and see if any of them correspond with the stars you're interested in seeing.'

'Actually, I wanted to have a look around our own system,' Peter said.

'Then you'll find all you need to know in storage,' the ensign told him fatuously. Peter doubted that. No one had ever needed to know what he did. Or why. 'Shall I register you for the first available space? Would you take a cancellation?'

Peter said yes to both suggestions. He wished he could have asked Johnny how to proceed. If General Greene had wanted time, it would have been made available. As Peter hadn't even formulated what he envisioned of T&T to tell Johnny, he certainly didn't want to muddy that idea with another half-ass concept, like breaking Tithonus free of the Patroclus group and moving it to an orbit around Callisto and using *that* as his place to stand. As strong a teleporter as Peter was, he doubted he was up to 'porting an asteroid. Of course, he'd need Johnny's clout and authority to obtain

398

the new rocket drives to install on Tithonus. But that was another problem.

Meanwhile, the *Arrakis* was nearing completion, and recruitment for colonists had begun. In another year and a half, she would be launched. Even with Johnny, Lance and the aid of all known kinetics on Earth, the 'portation of a colony ship to its destination – even tuned into Gadriel's gestalt – was just a mote in his eye. Right now.

When he checked the archives, he found that thousands of hours had been devoted to the solar system and the individual planets and their satellites, going back to the Voyager, Pathfinder, Galileo, Soho and Cassini, all well before Padrugoi's link with the far-side telescopes was initiated. The more he read about Callisto, the more he realized that Tithonus was the better solution for a base. He wondered if there were any bollards at the temporary Mars polar facility. He could imagine the expressions on the faces of Admiral Coetzer and Secretary Abubakar when he told them he'd consider supplying Mars, too.

Meanwhile he had a lot of work to do, proving his worth to both gentlemen and improving his muscular development. Peter could hardly wait until Lance got to Padrugoi on Friday. During the week he happened to be in the officers' mess at the same time Ceara was. He enjoyed talking with her, and felt more relaxed when he went back to the conference room. But then, she was an empath, and undoubtedly she automatically responded with a soothing aura. He didn't mind. He found her company excellent. On Wednesday he met Ping Yung in the corridor, and listened to the hydroponics expert going on about Amariyah's rescue of the delicate seedlings.

'She really has a knack,' Ping Yung said enthusiastically.

'Undeniably.'

'I hope she's being encouraged.'

'You may be sure of that.'

Tentatively, the man added, 'She may be too young. I mean chronologically,' and he flashed an apologetic smile at Peter, 'but there is a work-experience course up here on Padrugoi. I'd be glad to sponsor her.'

'She'd love nothing better. I'll mention it.'

Then they separated. Peter did tell Dorotea about the offer the next time he spoke to her. He contacted her now and then, to 'practise'.

A little young is right, she replied but he could tell she was pleased and was considering the notion. *It's a distinct possibility.*

No trouble there? Peter asked anxiously.

I can't even garden without someone lurking behind the nearest shrubbery. And, she paused, *I think Amariyah's noticed – as much as she notices anything else when she's gardening – but she hasn't* said *a word. Do thank Ping Yung when you see him again.*

I will.

That Dorotea and Amariyah were still being guarded bothered Peter, so he broached the subject with Johnny that afternoon.

'No real news,' Johnny said. 'And no real proof either, even though the theory of a fatwa is still valid according to Dirk. Cimprich has been briefed.'

'President Cimprich?' Peter was astonished.

'Yeah, the World President himself,' Johnny drawled. 'You constitute a valuable natural resource, Pete, and the good ecologically minded President is not about to have it wasted.'

'That's still a possibility?'

'Naw, naw,' and Johnny waved his hand in curt dismissal. 'Not with the new security measures Dirk put into effect.'

'You didn't tell me,' Peter accused him.

'You didn't ask.' Johnny returned his stare without a blink. 'Effectively, there are new surveillance units in every conduit and ventilator shaft big enough for a rat. In fact, there's talk of training rats to do the patrols.'

'You're kidding me.'

'Not as much as you think, Pete. All offenders' wristbands have been reprogrammed. They can't so much as close a locker door but they're logged into it. All visitations are thoroughly investigated, even Teacher groups. A lot more are denied as trivial. So many folks decided to come because,' and his voice turned whiny, ' "it *is* a public facility, built by world funds, and everyone else on our floor in the Linear has gone up".' He gave a derisive snort, in his inimitable fashion.

PETERRRRRR! PETER! DIDA!

Peter clamped his hands on his ears, though the sound was not aural but mental.

'JAYSUS CHRIST!' Johnny said, shaking his head, his eyes rolling. *Cool it, Madlyn.*

It's not Madlyn. It's Amariyah!

Peter 'ported himself to the personnel carrier on the transit deck. A hand on his arm as he inserted himself told him that Johnny was not going to be left behind.

Peter? He heard Madlyn's startled query but ignored it, as he and Johnny 'ported the carrier to the telepad at the Centre. They instantly homed in on Amariyah, kneeling beside Dorotea's body sprawled on the lawn.

From other parts of the estate, people were converging on them. Scott Gates was the first to arrive, looking startled, but Peter didn't recall that until later. He was on his knees beside Dorotea, noting her pallor, the utter limpness of a usually vigorous person.

I can't feel her. I've always felt Dida Tea, Amariyah was saying, her hands stroking Dorotea's arms, and then moving, almost tentatively, to Dorotea's temples. *It's here. It's clogged. The blood!*

Peter 'felt' with Amariyah.

A blood clot, Johnny? Panic gripped him. *What do we do about a blood clot?*

I don't the hell know! I'm a telekinetic! I NEED A MEDIC, A CARDIAC ARREST UNIT AND GODDAMN FAST, Johnny broadcast, seeking a pulse in Dorotea's wrist. *God, she's got frail. Pulse is very erratic!*

I feel it, Amariyah repeated. *If I can just—* With the utmost delicacy, Amariyah's dirt-stained fingers were dowsing for the fine veins over the ear. *Here. It's here. I can feel it. It's blocking. It's so small.* She sounded surprised.

Peter had taken basic first aid. He knew what to do with fractures, heart attacks, trauma, even drowning. He knew that blood clots meant a stroke, but he'd never heard what to do besides call for medical assistance. He did not even know if Dorotea, to whom he owed so much, was *having* a stroke. So what was Amariyah talking about?

Couldn't we just 'port her to the infirmary? Peter asked desperately, watching for any sign in Dorotea's beloved face.

It's just *an infirmary. It doesn't have what's needed!*

What about Jerhattan General? Peter had once sworn never to return to that institution. But he hadn't been conscious when he'd been in the emergency facility in the Henry Hudson, so he couldn't 'see' it. *Where's Dr McNulty?* Frantically Peter cast his mind about the grounds, trying to sense where the doctor was.

'Give us room here.'

In a daze Peter heard someone giving orders. A blanket was 'ported to cover Dorotea's limp body. Yes, warm; keep her warm, Peter thought. No one knew anything more therapeutic to do.

Except Amariyah. Suddenly, she smiled, and with a final caress of Dorotea's dishevelled white hair, sat back.

'There,' she said softly and with great satisfaction. 'Just like Ping Yung's plants. There was a blockage. It's gone now. I smoothed it away.'

Peter blinked. The pallor had gone from Dorotea's face and a little breath escaped her lips. Her eyelids fluttered, opened.

Lie still, Dorotea, Johnny said authoritatively.

What on earth? The mental voice was weak, confused.

Don't move, dear, Rhyssa said. Her mental voice was calm and reassuring, although she was panting from having raced down from the main house.

'Well, I'm certainly not going to lie here on the ground.' Dorotea's voice was thin, breathy, with just a hint of testiness. 'Whatever happened?'

'What happened is gone,' said Amariyah, pressing the blanket tight against Dorotea's shoulders when she tried to move.

'I felt sort of faint there for a moment,' she admitted in a feeble voice.

'Let me through, let me through,' cried an urgent baritone voice, and Martin McNulty appeared, swinging his emergency pack to the ground beside Dorotea and opening his hand scanner. Johnny and Rhyssa made room for him while Peter lifted a reluctant Amariyah out of the way.

'But I did it,' Amariyah said, squirming in Peter's grip. 'I soothed it away.' Then she stopped twisting. 'How did *you* get here, Peter? Are you home from the Station again?'

'You called for me, Maree,' Peter said softly, cuddling her against him. 'You called.' His eyes met Rhyssa's; hers were huge, her face pale as she swallowed against a dry throat.

'I can't tell without a full scan,' McNulty said, rising to his feet. 'Probably a slight stroke. Heart and pulse are irregular. I don't like the blood-pressure reading. The medicopter's on its way.'

The thrump-thrump of the blades was audible, coming closer.

Don't, Rhyssa said, looking at Peter, who was thinking about 'porting Dorotea to the 'copter or 'assisting' it to a speedier landing. *She's all right now. I can feel it. Let them do what else is required now. You two come with me back to the house. We need to talk.* She nodded down at Amariyah, still held in Peter's arms.

'Dorotea's stable right now,' McNulty continued. 'I think the immediate danger has passed.' Then the doctor frowned at Peter, suddenly realizing that he was present. 'I didn't know you were back from Padrugoi. No one told me to make arrangements for more physio while you're here.'

'A flying visit, Martin,' Johnny answered. 'Officially we're still on Padrugoi.' Though the General was still pale from the shock of Dorotea's seizure, his sense of humour was irrepressible.

PETER!

He winced at his name. He wished Madlyn wouldn't do that.

It's all right, Maddie. Rhyssa answered for him. *Dorotea's had a slight stroke. Martin says she'll be all right. Peter and Johnny will be back shortly. Cover for them if you can.*

Oh, I can, if they promise to tell me everything when they get back.

A stray perception crossed Peter's errant mind: maybe Madlyn had no limitations to *her* telepathic range. Could she learn to 'tune' into the Gadriel gestalt? Or was that limited in application to kinetics? She'd be as distinct an asset to T&T as she had been to Padrugoi. The medic team raced in, pushing past the concerned residents waiting to know about Dorotea. McNulty supervised Dorotea's removal, while Rhyssa and Johnny spoke to the others who had come in answer to the psychic summons. Peter took the opportunity to glide to Scott Gates.

'I know you live on the other side of the estate, Scott. How did you get here so fast?' Peter asked. Scott was getting tall and filling out, though at the moment his colour was pasty. 'Were you just in the basketball court?'

Scott gulped, grey eyes showing a trace of panic and astonishment.

'No, I was at home, at Teacher. I heard Amariyah scream. I just got here.'

'You just got here. I certainly appreciate your quick response, Scott. And I know Amariyah does. Thanks.'

'No problem. We're all supposed to keep an eye out for them, you know.'

And, thrusting his hands in his pockets, Scott slouched away. He turned back once, when the medicopter could be heard lifting off.

They all watched it go. If Peter had had any idea of 'where' it was supposed to go, he would have sent it.

That wouldn't be a good idea, Pete, Johnny said, squinting up at the sky through the leafing trees. *Too much casual air traffic. It'll get there fast enough.*

And 'pathing Dorotea might just upset her, Rhyssa said. *Not that we're all not upset.* Then she held out her hand to Amariyah. 'I need a cup of tea, Maree. Dorotea will be fine with Dr McNulty to care for her.'

'I know she's fine,' Amariyah said blithely, but it was Peter's hand she took as they walked back to the house. 'Did you really hear me, Peter?'

'Loud and clear.' He stared hard at Rhyssa, because he wouldn't equivocate and betray Maree's trust in him. *Just don't call 'wolf'*. He paused, but Amariyah didn't ask what he meant. If she'd 'heard' him, she would have wanted him to explain.

'Can you stay?' she asked, pushing open the kitchen door.

'For a cup, yes.'

'I've the tea you like, Peter. Will Dorotea's blend be all right for you, Rhyssa?' Moving about the kitchen with complete poise, Amariyah flicked on the kettle, took milk from the fridge and cups from the cupboard. 'I believe you prefer coffee, don't you, General?'

'Yes, I'd prefer that, Amariyah.'

The adults settled at the kitchen table.

Did you hear her too, Rhyssa? Johnny asked. 'Cookies would go nicely with coffee, Maree.'

'There are always cookies in this house,' Amariyah said firmly, with a prideful tilt of her square young chin.

Her voice lifted me right out of my chair, Rhyssa replied, glancing sideways at the General.

And she lifted us right down here, Johnny replied. 'I take two sugars.'

'Too much sugar is bad for you!' Amariyah replied disapprovingly.

'I need sweetening.'

Peter damned near tripped over his feet to get into the carrier, Johnny said.

You were holding me back, was Peter's reply.

But she didn't hear your remark about crying 'wolf', did she? Rhyssa went on. 'Oh, thank you, dear. Coconut and shortbread.' Rhyssa took a nicely browned coconut cookie and passed the plate to Peter. *What a range!* She sighed with melancholy.

Teamed up with Madlyn, who knows how far they would be heard? Peter thought very, very privately.

She's awful young, Johnny said, selecting shortbread. *She may not be able to 'path as a normal way of communicating.*

She's got a little while longer to go, I think, before she hits puberty. Rhyssa sighed again, taking a sip of the tea Amariyah had served her.

Let's not make Amariyah a damned pronoun, Peter said.

Peter! Rhyssa gave him a stern look.

You know how I hate being a pronoun. And we're talking behind her back.

And over her head, Johnny said, eyeing Peter with a calm-down stare.

Peter subsided.

'Would you mind staying with me and the boys, Maree, while Dorotea's in the hospital?'

'Will she have to stay as long as Peter did? May I bake her her favourite pie?' Having served everyone, Amariyah sat down with a glass of milk. Noticing the adults' positions, she put her arms on the table, too.

'We'll see, dear,' Rhyssa said reassuringly.

We'll see, Peter said in a very droll tone, reaching out his hand to ruffle Amariyah's hair.

Won't we just! Johnny put in. *Rather pinpoints her psychic ability.*

Not precisely, and Rhyssa spoke slowly, thoughtfully. *She may well be an example of a microTalent that is so instinctive she won't be able to access it.*

Well, she accessed it damned cleverly for Dorotea, dissolving that blood clot before it could do any damage.

That's what we think *it did,* Rhyssa corrected Johnny.

Whatever. Did the trick.

'When may I see Dorotea at the hospital?' Amariyah asked, using a paper napkin to wipe her mouth of a milk moustache.

'As soon as Dr McNulty says we may,' Rhyssa replied.

They finished their tea, coffee and milk, and then cleared up the dishes. Rhyssa and Peter helped Amariyah pack a few things for her stay at Rhyssa's, and lock up the house. Amariyah insisted that she walk with Peter and Johnny to the personnel carrier because she wanted to see one, having slept through the trip from Bangladesh on Carmen's lap.

In all, Peter and Johnny were gone less than an hour. Only Madlyn had any inkling they had ever been absent.

CHAPTER SIXTEEN

They returned to Padrugoi, and almost immediately had a call from Dirk Coetzer, who asked could he interrupt them now for a few minutes?

'Interrupt?' Johnny exclaimed. He looked guiltily at Peter. 'I thought Madlyn was going to cover us.'

I did. But you're back now, and the Admiral is very anxious to see you. I had Nicola tell him you had some very heavy 'ports on this morning's schedule.

'Dirk sounds smug,' Johnny said after a moment's thought. He no longer looked guilty. Peter tried to emulate him. 'At least he's not Watari, who'd snoop at our 'ported list while he's here.'

The Admiral did seem extremely pleased with himself as he entered the conference room. He did look around it. The two kinetics exchanged nervous glances, and Johnny pulled a scowl that looked very like Watari's.

Counting the silver? Johnny said.

Peter agreed that the Admiral looked as if he was inspecting the premises.

No white gloves, he remarked.

'Dirk?' Johnny got to his feet, straightening his tunic. 'To what do we owe this visit?'

'Come see,' Dirk said.

What canary has our dear Admiral swallowed? Johnny asked.

Dirk made hurry-up motions with his hands, and, since speed seemed to be called for, Peter decided to glide instead of walk. It was faster. He did notice the smell of fresh emulsion, and wondered if a door was missing on the corridor. Most peculiar. The Admiral stopped, ran his card into the security slot at the next door and gestured for them to enter.

I see a few feathers on his lips, Peter said, and then stopped so quickly Johnny almost ran him down.

Warn me which power you're flying under, pal. Wow! Johnny repeated the last word aloud as he glanced slowly around the room.

'Well?' Dirk asked impatiently.

Both men were slowly and appreciatively absorbing the contents and layout of the spacious room. Obviously two smaller units on the CIC floor had been thrown together. This first section contained a suite of couch, chairs, table and to the right, two doors: one probably the head and the other a service alcove. To the left was the larger room, programmable screens on three sides, storage cabinets underneath and four ergonomic stations set in a U-shape with worktops between them.

'The office we've been promising you,' Dirk said at his most genial, and eager to point out the amenities. He gestured to the screens. 'You'll now be able to screen cargo corrals, lists, engineering readiness and any destination visuals you need to see.' He held up a branch of sensor pads. 'All you need to record your 'ports.' He replaced them carefully and slapped at the padded chair next to him. 'Ergonomically comformable chairs, the latest in worktops, extra chairs and another station for visitors.'

'Like Lance Baden, no doubt,' Johnny said, with a cynical lift to one eyebrow.

'Yes, he'll be here Friday, won't he?' Dirk rattled on. 'The left-hand one is a special link to Engineering. A serving alcove off the main room,' he pointed to the door on the left wall. 'Coffee, Pete's favourite tea, and high-calorie snacks already stored. Your own head and shower. And a couch long enough for anyone who needs a catnap.'

'Indispensable,' Johnny said.

'General Greene,' Peter said, glaring at his friend, 'how can you be so ungrateful? You've been complaining every day since we got back about our need for proper office space and dedicated equipment.'

Dirk laughed and dismissed Johnny's pose. 'If he affects that attitude, I know he's well pleased.'

'Am I now?' and Johnny set one of the ergonomic chairs spinning. Then he relented and grinned broadly. 'It's perfect, Dirk. Even paper for me to doodle on.' He touched the pristine pad prominently displayed by the keypanel. 'It'll suit us both, to the ground, as it were. Won't it, Pete?' He stopped the chair's rotation and sat in it, immediately stretching his legs out under the workstation, before reaching out to align the pad straight with the edge. 'Perfect. Nearly as good as the stuff we've been shipping to First Base,' he added with a sly glance at the Admiral.

'You are some tulip, Greene,' Dirk said, shaking his head.

'Really, Admiral, it's so comfortable-looking,' Peter said, imbuing his voice with unreserved approval. 'I mean, and the colours are great.'

'At least they're not AirForce blue or First Base slate,' Johnny remarked, though his glance about the newly fitted room was admiring.

'Oh, do shut up, Johnny,' Peter said. 'It's exactly what we wanted and what we need.'

'I like green,' Johnny said meekly. In a single fluid motion that Peter would give anything to be able to perform when he had control of his physical movements, Johnny rose and clapped an arm over Dirk's shoulders. 'To tell the truth, I didn't expect anything quite this elegant.' He eased Dirk to the door. 'We'll transfer our files and let you get back to work.'

Sensing that Johnny particularly did not want the Admiral to know about the Gadriel circuits just yet, Peter flowed forward, quite willing to speed their guest on his way.

'You'll need these,' and Dirk handed out two security cards. 'Only Barney and I can get in.' He assumed a humble mien. 'I hope you don't object to me.'

'Never,' Johnny said warmly, and clapped Dirk on the back once more before he left. 'C'mon, Pete, we'd better get moving or our landlord might just evict us for failure to perform.' He paused for another moment, though, looking around the well-appointed room, and exhaled in total satisfaction.

With ease, they 'tuned' into their individually tuned Gadriel circuits and 'lifted' all their files from the conference room, including Johnny's latest doodle pad.

In the next few days, Peter experienced considerable frustration when skills he had struggled so to perform telekinetically, now had to be discarded in order to retrain himself to do them 'normally'. He particularly wanted to show Lance how he had progressed, but he seemed to get his signals switched.

'What *is* normal for me, Ceara?' he asked, throwing down the light-pen he had been using. 'I can *do* so much kinetically that it's almost more of an effort to do it the way everyone else does. And I'm not good enough yet to do what I want to do.'

'Even world-class artists had to learn to control their tools,' she replied.

'You saw me drop the fork at lunch today?'

'Anyone could. A lot of people do,' she replied, soothing him with her thoughts. 'They think nothing of such a slip.'

'Ahhhh, Ceara, don't try to empathize me,' he said, eyeing her fiercely.

She blinked and tried to assume an innocent expression. Then gave a sigh. 'Sorry, Peter, it's second nature to me.'

That shut off his gripe, because it *was* second nature to them both to use their parapsychic talents. That was what annoyed him, but the paradox existed.

She touched his arm, knowing he liked to be touched now because he had so much more sensation in his limbs.

'Remember what you're making progress *towards*,' she said with a significant nod.

Peter struggled not to blush. She was a physician, but she was also a very pretty woman, and he didn't really feel comfortable with that reference to regaining 'normal functions'. In her professional capacity, Ceara was up to date on his progress and encouraged him when, as now, he lost patience.

'It won't be long, Peter. Now, shake your hand to relax all the muscles. You've been trying too hard again. I think the image is coming on fine.'

'Well,' Peter said with a sigh, 'I'll try again.' He was copying the print of an ancient clipper ship. The sails were very difficult to sketch, with lines and braces. With his free hand, he ran his fingers through his hair in an unconscious gesture of frustration. And froze with surprise when he realized what he'd done. Ceara caught that gesture, too! The pen slipped from his right hand, across the worktop.

'Oh, Peter! You did it! Without thinking. See, your muscles do remember,' and she threw her arms about his neck and kissed him on the lips.

Suddenly, he knew what Finn had meant – that the man within him would stand up and be noticed. This was not the bath-giving Nurse Roche. This was Ceara Scott, for whom he felt more than empathy at this moment. He caught her arms and held them about his neck, levitating out of his chair and pulling her against him. She returned the embrace enthusiastically. Her eyes widened as she became aware that not only were his muscles remembering, but that also certain glands were in working order.

'Oh, Peter, how marvellous!'

'Ceara,' he began. Her mind opened to his completely, filling him with her willingness, an urgency of her own and an intense desire for intimacy. He was even able to lift her into his arms and carry her to the bed. 'Porting would have been faster, but there were some things a man didn't hurry.

*   *   *

411

On Friday, while they were waiting for Lance to arrive, Peter wanted to level with the Australian about the Gadriel circuitry.

'It isn't as if he didn't know I tapped into the CERN generators to save us,' Peter said.

'Yeah, but do you want to tell him he can't because he's tone deaf? That's sorta mean, isn't it? Let it be for now. We're not really sure what we're doing, anyhow.'

Peter reluctantly accepted the argument. Lance arrived and was suitably impressed with the office. 'No names on the door,' he remarked, jerking his thumb over his shoulder. Then he put his hands on his belt and took a slow look around, nodding as he catalogued the various amenities.

'Hmm, nice digs you've got here.' Stepping farther into the room, he rotated one of the comformable chairs. 'Bang on.'

'Coffee, Lance? Tea?' Peter said, making himself physically walk to the serving alcove.

'Hey, lookit you! On your own two! That's great, mate. Real great. Couldn't happen to a nicer bloke!' Lance beamed, his eyes crinkling up.

'Coffee? Tea?'

'Tea's fine. Haven't had a proper cuppa since I left First Base.' He settled into the chair and exclaimed again as he appreciated its contours supporting his long frame. 'How's Dorotea? Special sort of woman.'

'She's fine,' Johnny said. 'They conclude that she had a pin stroke, TIA, and she's on medication to prevent a repeat.'

'With Amariyah watching her like a hawk.'

Lance chuckled. 'Heard that little bit of nothing rousted everyone out of their skins. Talented, is she?'

Johnny held up both hands. '*She* has to find that out for herself.'

Peter wished that he could broadcast to the world that Amariyah's special Talent had worked a miracle on his body, but he perfectly understood the necessity for silence on the subject. In that same instant, he realized not only that he wouldn't want Amariyah to be burdened with trying to heal all the sick of the world – she'd be killed trying, and she would try – but also how Rhyssa and Johnny had protected him until he was mature enough to handle his potent abilities. Very few, even those who knew him well, would have noticed his physical changes. And even fewer knew how he had extended his telekinetic and telepathic range.

'What about,' Lance paused, rethinking the adjectives he was about to use, 'Shimaz, and that lot?'

'Wal,' Johnny drawled, sitting back and smiling with malice, 'InterLEO has been busy tagging anyone and everyone once connected with either Shimaz or Flimflam, or the other suspected accomplices.'

'Reprogrammed their ID bands?' Lance asked, idly twisting his own. 'Thought they were having a good look at mine, when I said I was heading up here.'

Johnny nodded. 'There are enough regular checks, even on an international basis, to complete the process.'

'And the Henner estate is prickly with sensors – wall, tube, gardens, shrubs, trees and helipads,' Peter said. 'Everyone's safe there.'

Lance made a rueful noise. 'Don't like to think that such precautions had to be taken for us psychics. We should be able to fend for ourselves.'

Johnny flicked his fingers. 'Sharpen our wits a bit, put us on the qui vive. No harm done, and no harm *can* be done.'

'Did we ever find out who was cheating the Station on fuel?' Peter asked.

Johnny swivelled about to stare at him a moment. 'Yes,' he said, recalling a conclusion that had obviously slipped his mind during other crises. 'Pota Chatham solved it. Every single one of the Station's suppliers was shorting tank refills.' He gave his shark's grin. 'She thinks that the bean counter at SpaceShifters started the scam. He's far worse than Taddesse as a CFO. The other suppliers got suspicious, saw a good thing working and started pumping measures, too. The freighter captains were bribed, or scared, into not reporting the problem until Honeybald started noticing the fall-short dockings. *Now* all the tanks are filled while one of Dirk's finest watches and guarantees the tank full. The

suppliers all had to pay stiff fines for short weights. Thanks.'
He took the fresh cup of coffee Peter handed him.

'Now,' and Johnny rubbed his hands together, 'what have
we got for today? You get a special demonstration, Lance.
We got some heavy stuff,' and he asked for the list on one of
the programmable screens. 'And number one is heavy. Pete,
you take that.'

'Hey, they're both on First Base,' Lance said, sitting up
straight.

'Yeah, ain't they?' Johnny replied, grinning at him.

'You?' and Lance pointed at the General, 'can make First
Base?'

'Yup, with a little help from my friend here.'

'Remember that bollard on the parking field?' Peter
asked, thinking that this was an appropriate time to mention
the Gadriel circuits.

No. Not yet, said Johnny very tightly. He went on out loud.
'It was "South America" in the astronomy office for me.' He
paused, enjoying Lance's look of awe. 'Pete conned me into
sending ten kilos to the astronomy office at First Base. South
America,' he added in voice command, and Peter's carefully
detailed image came up on the screen.

'Well I never,' Lance began. 'How much can you shift?' he
asked, professionally intrigued.

'I don't want to make him run before he can walk,' Peter
replied, mimicking Johnny's drawl.

'Wish I could get the hang of the gestalt,' Lance said
ruefully, shaking his head.

'You're not the only one,' Johnny remarked, cocking his
head significantly at Peter. 'Still, we won't hold that against
you, will we, Pete?'

Abruptly the main screen lit up with the head and
shoulders of a very worried Dirk Coetzer. His eyes took in
the three men in the office.

'Good, you're all there.' He took a deep breath as he
turned to Peter. 'I know this may be totally impossible, Pete,
but we've just had a mayday from Mars polar. They've had
an equipment failure. The humidifier's conked out. Has been
for days, and now other sensitive equipment is showing the

effects. So are their tempers. If we don't get replacement parts to them in the next two days, there'll be major systems failures.' He paused.

'You know, Dirk,' Johnny drawled, 'the three of us might just be able to make it that far. If the spares aren't heavy.'

Are you out of your tree? Lance exclaimed.

No, just out on a limb.

'We'll need the clearest visuals of Mars polar you have, Dirk,' Peter said. 'Do you have replacement parts on hand up here?'

'In the priority cargo net, ready for the supply ship due to go next week. Next week'll arrive too late,' he said grimly. He looked to one side. 'Thanks, Nicola. Waybill AF 44MPS8276.'

'I copy,' Peter said.

'I fetch,' Johnny said, and the vacuum-sealed units appeared on the table in the lounge of the office suite, covering it. Lance whistled.

Thank God for Tomas Gadriel. That would make all the difference to this 'port, said Peter.

I'm getting very good at this, Johnny said. 'Doesn't mass much, Pete.'

This time, General Greene, you do the 'port with me!

You bet!

'Where's my visual, Dirk?'

'Surely they have a table to eat off,' Peter said. His mind was humming as he anticipated the demand on his abilities.

'Yes, but I don't have any visual of the catering area.'

'A workstation?' Peter was getting anxious. It was inconceivable that there wasn't anything available to 'see'. 'Surely there've been tapes of their accommodation, their work spaces, the hydroponics unit?'

'The *Amazon* craft they came in would be empty,' Johnny suggested, and called up a visual of the interior of the Mars ship. 'Enough space there. I got the VIP tour when it was up on the gantries.'

'Might be a tight fit,' Peter said.

'Plenty of floor space right now.' Johnny added the dimensions of the main cabin at the base of the visual.

'They went to Mars in *that*?' Lance was incredulous, his eyes flicking around the much larger office. 'No wonder they don't have spares.'

'Used parachute drones to land supplies. Tedious work.' Johnny shot Peter a look.

'We'll give it our best shot, Dirk,' Peter said, physically and clumsily moving to the chair at the engineering station. He didn't want to waste an ounce of mental energy before this crucial long 'port.

I'm with you all the way, Pete, Johnny said, skidding his chair over to Peter's and gripping his arm. Lance pushed in on the other side, taking Peter's free hand in a firm clasp.

The generators sang the most beautiful C-major chord Peter had ever heard. Then Peter grinned. He'd been quicker than Johnny in establishing that 'port. It had gone out in his key.

Peter got 'hold' of the cargo net.

Take the biggest breath you can, kid.

Out of the corner of his eye, Peter saw Johnny's chest rising. He inhaled, thinking firmly of the net and its life-saving units sitting in the centre of the *Amazon*'s cabin space. As he 'ported, he felt Johnny's wide-open mind pushing with him, and a second reinforcement – nowhere near as strong but steady. Lance! He might not be able to initiate the gestalt, but he sure could give it a shove, his grasp warm and firm on Peter's.

Then, like running into a wall in the dark, Peter felt a psychic stop. God! Had he missed? Had he reached his limit somewhere out there between Earth and Mars? Would men and women die because he was overconfident?

Breathe, kid.

Peter felt the elbow in his ribs. Opening his eyes, he exhaled, sparkles of imminent anoxia dancing before his eyes. He let himself collapse in the chair.

'Have you done it yet?' Dirk asked anxiously, his eyes dark with concern. Someone loomed beside him on the screen. 'Shandin said the generators went off the gauge.'

'We can't be certain, Dirk,' Johnny said, panting. 'But we sure did give it a damned good try, the three of us.' *Tone deaf he may be, but he's an asset. We'll tell him how and why later.* He grinned at Lance. 'Knew you'd be a help.' He returned his attention to the Admiral. 'Tell Captain Vartry to look in their ship. Only space we knew wouldn't be occupied.'

'Yes, of course – the ship would be a logical telepad.' Dirk Coetzer took a deep breath, his eyes unfocusing briefly.

'Now don't get any ideas, Dirk,' Johnny cautioned him, quickly raising one hand in restraint.

'No, no, of course not,' he said, but there was just that little curl of his mouth that suggested he was not above thinking ahead. 'There's a communications lag, you know.'

'I know,' Johnny said. 'It's only thirty-seven million miles from here. Takes exactly a hundred and ninety-eight point six seconds – three minutes and eighteen point six seconds.'

'That long?' Peter said, desperately wanting it all to have happened simultaneously.

'And to come back,' Johnny said, with admirable sang-froid.

'Drink this,' Lance said, putting a glass of orange juice in front of Peter, who was leaning limply back in his chair, and fresh coffee in front of Johnny.

Do you realize what we just did? Peter asked.

We shipped a package all the way to Mars, that's what we just did, Johnny replied.

We hope, Peter said with a gulp. *We also just merged our minds.*

We did what? Johnny leaned forward so quickly that he nearly knocked the cup off the surface.

Lance stared at Peter, his mouth dropping.

I felt you, and Peter pointed at the General, *and then you,* his finger went to Lance, *come in to help me push. We were all in on that one! Oh, we've talked together over distance, but we've never* combined *to 'port anything. This, my friends, is a major breakthrough!* With that declaration, Peter lifted his glass and toasted them both.

'But, *if* you did,' Coetzer went on, unaware of that tele-pathic exchange.

417

'If we did,' Johnny said, winking at Peter and Lance, 'there'd be a new contract. And there would be a new organization for you to deal with.'

'What?' The Admiral didn't quite absorb that.

Johnny! Peter protested.

'Let's just bide our time,' Johnny said smoothly. 'It ain't over till the fat lady sings. And we sure want to hear her.'

In his office, Dirk was fiddling with a pencil file, turning it over and over in one hand, glancing to his left.

Johnny sipped his coffee. Peter drank his juice. Then, resorting to physical means, he walked himself to the serving alcove and found apples, carrots and some pecan pie. He clumped back to his station, aware of Lance watching him. He wished he were a little more graceful, but that would come. He hadn't quite the muscular strength in his thighs to sit smoothly and flopped down, the pie nearly slipping from his plate.

Johnny doodled.

Lance tapped his fingers.

Dirk Coetzer kept running the file through his fingers.

The com bleeped.

Everyone jumped.

'They got the message,' Shandin's voice said. 'Vartry's going out to the ship.'

Johnny's doodles got wilder.

Lance went to the head.

The tension in the office was thick enough to cut.

Peter finished an apple, and thought seriously about a carrot. He looked at the records for generator use. He hadn't had the pads on, so he didn't know how many calories he had burned in that 'port. He wished now that he had, since that data would be necessary, he fervently hoped, in the future.

Dirk was now swinging back and forth in his chair, looking anywhere but into the screen and at the three telekinetics. He rubbed his face.

Peter rubbed his face, prickly with short bristles of beard that he was finally growing.

More time elapsed.

We could 'port some of these, Peter suggested, wanting to do something. There were some downside 'ports he felt up to doing.

You're a glutton for punishment, Johnny said.

Are you OK, Johnny? Peter reached out to close his fingers about his friend's arm.

Well, I did take a deep breath – but if there was another piece of that pie?

I'll get it, Lance said, rising.

'You're eating, aren't you, Pete?' Dirk asked.

THEY GOT IT! Madlyn Luvaro's loud voice was never welcomer. *DASH SAYS CAPTAIN VARTRY HAS IT! IT'S THERE! YOU DID IT! YOU DID IT!*

Johnny shouted the message out loud.

Dirk Coetzer leaped from his chair, arms flung out, face split with the joy of success. The next moment the screen showed him dancing about his office with Nicola as a startled partner.

Peter stared at the sight, for a moment weak with relief before exultation flooded his mind, soul and body. Johnny was yodelling like a drunken cowboy, clapping his hands over his head, folding them into the victory sign. Lance was doing some sort of stamping dance around the room.

A pounding on the door reached Peter first. Dirk Coetzer was still in his office, so who was at the door, wanting to come in so urgently? It took Peter a little effort to sense it was Ceara on the other side. He hurried across the room, making his legs stride, grateful that he could make such a physical effort because his mind was still reeling from that thrust. Not something they could do on a regular basis. Yet!

'Oh, Peter,' Ceara cried, throwing her arms about his neck. 'I've the most wonderful news for you.'

Peter hugged her tightly, chuckling.

'What's happened?' she exclaimed, suddenly aware of the antics in the room and on the screen. 'I've never seen the Admiral like that before.'

Peter whirled her about in his own excess of joy, their movements automatically operating the door closure. This was *his* moment, to share with his closest friends.

419

'What's happened? You're glowing with it, Peter. Oh, please tell me.'

'Mars, Ceara!' Johnny said, crowing. 'We 'ported to Mars!'

She clung to Peter's arms for support as she assimilated the information. Her face mirrored the feelings that engulfed Peter. He'd thought 'porting to First Base, to prove to Taddesse, Leitao and Abubakar that he *could*, had been triumphant. *This* was an even greater achievement – a merge of minds.

'Oh, it is indeed your day,' Ceara said, grinning like a fool at Johnny and Lance, and still in Peter's arms. She took a deep breath and Peter could sense she had something important to tell him. 'Finn and the Commander just okayed the reversal.' She pointed to the side on which he carried the appliance. 'You won't need that any more.'

He was stunned. Now it was Ceara who supported *him*.

Sometimes one could have too much joy, Peter thought, as she helped him back to his chair. Johnny thrust a slice of chocolate cake at his face. Lance held out orange juice in one hand and a shot glass of brandy in the other.

'Shock!' Ceara was saying. 'He's in shock.'

'He and the rest of us,' said Dirk Coetzer, swinging into the room, a bottle of champagne in each hand, his face reflecting the morning's glorious achievement. Shandin, Nicola, Madlyn and Dash Sakai followed him into the office, each as euphoric as the Admiral.

Let us not, in our euphoria, mention to Dirk anything about merging minds right now. And we have some good news for you, Lance, when we've a break in all this excitement. Then Johnny went on out loud. 'Now, Dirk, this isn't something we can do on an everyday basis.' He gestured for Nicola to fill his glass to the brim.

'You delivered the goods where it was needed most,' and Dirk thumped Johnny on the back. Less vigorously, but every bit as enthusiastically, he clapped Peter on the shoulder. 'A toast, now everyone has a glass.' He held his up. 'First the moon, now Mars.' Everyone repeated the toast. 'My God, I'm proud of you!'

'We're not unpleased ourselves,' Johnny allowed, beaming as broadly as the Admiral did.

In a flash, Peter reviewed what had begun as a simple wish to leave a hospital environment and be freed of his invalid restrictions. He had learned to manage kinetically a seemingly helpless body. He'd been able to send material and supplies to help complete Padrugoi. He had been at the Space Station's inauguration and prevented a mutiny. He had learned to hack the black and help build the *Andre Norton*. He had reached out to the moon and made First Base. There, he had found that Callisto was the place for him to stand to 'port colony ships to the distant stars. Amariyah's gift had completed the healing process of his once useless body, and he, who had never expected to be whole, had reached full manhood. How much further could he go now, with all the possibilities of the Gadriel tuning, and now the mind-merge which he, Johnny and Lance had discovered?

With a slightly possessive and very loverly arm about Ceara's shoulders, Peter lifted his glass.

'A man's reach must exceed his grasp,' he grinned at everyone in the room.

EPILOGUE
Fourteen years later

The bottles of champagne, carefully imported from Earth, were chilling in buckets full of Callisto's ice; undrinkable, of course, but capable of cooling wine.

The same cast of characters was present with a few important additions, Peter thought, glancing around those standing and sitting in the control tower of the Federated Telepath and Teleport installation on Tithonus, now a satellite of Jupiter's tenth moon, Callisto. He was even getting accustomed to the great mottled orange Jovian bulk that was seldom missing from the thick wraparound windows.

Callisto Tower, as the Tithonus installation was called, was ready for this historic moment. Admiral Dirk Coetzer, silver-haired and bursting with pride, was seated at one console. He was to have the honour of issuing the command to the tower team to begin the *ISS Bradbury*'s historic teleportation to its destination, Capella.

For this great endeavour, Lance was tuning the great tower's Gadriel generators, buried deep in the core of Tithonus. Peter could hear them singing in his favourite key, C major.

On one screen, former Commander Dash Sakai had the massive bulk of the *Bradbury* at her mooring off Padrugoi. On the other, he was getting the highest possible resolution on the visual of the M-5 planet in the Capella system. Madlyn, his wife of many years, sat beside him, beaming proudly at him.

Among the spectators specially invited for this occasion were Rhyssa and Dave Lehardt, though their teenage sons, Eoin and Chester, were beginning to fidget. Also present were Sascha and Tirla Roznine, Shandin Ross, the Admiral's long-time aide and telepath, and Nicola Nizukami, now a chief petty officer. To one side was Amariyah Bantam, chief hydroponics engineer and emergency medic, with an imperious tilt to her determined chin, at the fore of the rest of the tower staff. More than half of the forty men and women had some psychic ability. Only Dorotea Horvath and Professor Gadriel were missing from those whom Peter had assembled for this occasion. Peter smiled in sad remembrance of how proud Dorotea had been when he had placed Tithonus perfectly at its Lagrange point above Callisto.

'And now you have the right place to stand, don't you, Peter?' Dorotea had murmured for his ears alone.

How ecstatic the Professor had been on that same occasion, because his gestalt generators had provided the telekinetics with the kind of power they could tune into so effortlessly.

Peter shook himself loose from the memories, and concentrated on the task to hand. Johnny Greene, in the informal AirForce blue coverall he preferred, occupied one of the three comfortable couches. Sally, his wife, stood proudly beside him. On the second couch was Scott Gates, looking just a trifle nervous about his part in the imminent ceremony. Peter would occupy the third, and now his wife, Ceara, smilingly beckoned for him to take his place.

The com-unit bleeped.

'Callisto Tower, this is Captain Gale Johnson of the colony ship *Bradbury*. All systems are green for lift.' The Captain used the new term Peter had selected to replace 'teleportation', a lengthy and somewhat daunting word.

423

'Very good, Captain Johnson,' Admiral Coetzer said, nodding significantly to Peter, who stretched out on the third couch. 'Are you ready, Tower Prime?'

Peter took a deep breath, looked over at Johnny's wicked expression and Scott's rather apprehensive one.

'We are indeed, Admiral,' he said, closing his eyes and 'feeling' for the support of the other two minds. 'Initiating the merge.' He reached out for Johnny's mind, suddenly as professionally alert as Scott Gates's. 'Admiral Coetzer, do the honours!'

'*Bradbury*, this is Callisto Tower, initiating lift.'

The generators peaked, keening under the strain as Peter Reidinger, John Greene and Scott Gates hurled the million-tonne ship out to the stars. Everyone inhaled sharply as the *Bradbury* disappeared from the Padrugoi screen.

'Well,' Admiral Coetzer said with a tight smile, 'that's that.'

Johnny Greene looked sharply at him, but it was Peter who spoke. 'Admiral, I think we need to talk about our contract.'

Dirk laughed. 'It seems we're always talking contracts!' But he shook his head, pointing to the monitor showing where the *Bradbury* had been. 'You've proved that you can send the *Bradbury* somewhere – but it'll be another forty years before even that pet SPOT of yours will see the light of that starship shining back from Capella.'

Peter's eyes gleamed. 'So you're saying, Admiral, that until we can prove that we have lifted the *Bradbury* the forty-five light years to Capella, we will have a hard time revising your contract with FT&T?'

Dirk Coetzer nodded. 'I'm afraid so. I *know* you can do it, but others are going to want to see proof.'

'I told you so,' Johnny muttered smugly to himself.

'Well, how about we step over here,' Peter said, motioning the Admiral towards Dash's monitors, 'so we can discuss proof more objectively.'

Dirk sighed. 'Peter, I don't think there's much more to—'
His eyes latched onto the telescope's image of Capella's M-5

planet. 'What's that?' The Admiral pointed to the glittering speck now visible.

'That's the *Bradbury* orbiting Capella,' Dash Sakai said, somehow managing to keep his voice steady as if he was reporting no more than a normal arrival.

Dirk's jaw dropped, and he turned first to Johnny, then to Peter, raising a finger accusingly. 'You knew! You lifted it back in time. Why didn't you tell me? Do you know what that means? Do you know how this will speed up our explorations? How did you do it?'

It was Peter who answered him. 'In order, yes, we did know – or at least we were pretty sure. We didn't tell you because we only had the one lift to Mars to go by, and there was enough time between our lift and their getting those critical replacement units that it could have been a normal space translation. We know that without this sort of timely transportation, all the colony worlds will be doomed to lag technically behind Earth – because it will take at least as many years as they are light years distant for news and inventions to travel to them.

'And how did we do it?' Peter finished with a smile. 'We do it naturally.'

Dirk quirked his eyebrows at this confident and oh so powerful young man.

'Remember,' Peter said softly, 'we have to "see" what we're lifting – at both ends. Then we "tune" ourselves to do the job.'

'Peter – no, Mr Reidinger,' Dirk's face burst into a huge grin and he grabbed Peter's hand, pumping it fiercely, 'you'll get that new contract. Hell, you'll get 'em all.' He dropped Peter's hand, shook his head in awe and thrust his big fist upward in triumph. 'Yes! The stars are ours!'

Peter felt his heart about to burst, felt Ceara's reassuring hand on his shoulder, gripping it hard, for her empathic bond told her how deeply he felt this moment.

He had so wanted to be a part of Earth's space programme. Now he *was* that space programme.

Softly to himself, he said: ' "Or what's a heaven for?" '

425

HISTORICAL NOTES

2082 The second A-ship, the *Arrakis*, was launched from Padrugoi with a complement of four thousand colonists and crew, bound for a 'likely' planet in Procyon, eleven light years away. As with the *Andre Norton*, most of the passengers would remain in cryogenic suspension.

The keel for the third projected A-ship, the *Avalon*, was laid in the construction facility at Padrugoi Space Station.

2084 The first Mars colony was established at the former Space Authority Mars polar site near the southern pole where sufficient water had been discovered to sustain a colony. This installation would also supply and assist Asteroid Mining, a branch of the Space Authority, which started 'claiming' the suitably named and numbered asteroids they would use. If the person named on the IAU files was still alive, they received royalties. There is no record of any such transactions in the last decade of the twenty-first century.

2086 Using the highly specialized Gadriel gestalt generators, the asteroid Tithonus was moved from the Patroclus cluster to a new orbit around Callisto, by kind permission of the

426

Space Authority, and with a deed of grant in perpetuity, for services rendered by an organization known as Federated Telepath and Teleport. FT&T was registered with a board of directors including Managing Directors Peter Reidinger and John Greene (retired US SpaceForce). Also listed were Lance Baden, Madlyn Luvaro Sakai, Amariyah Bantam and Scott Gates. Rhyssa Owen Lehardt, David Lehardt, Professor Tomas Gadriel and Sascha Roznine were listed as consultants.

2088 Construction began for an atmosphere dome on the former asteroid Tithonus, now Callisto's satellite in a stable orbit about its adopted primary. Immense generators were buried deep in the asteroid, while a blunt structure rose above its surface. Miners seeking supplies, or just a change of scenery, called it the 'tower' – or Callisto Tower.

2090 Federated Telepath and Teleport was licensed by the World Congress and the Space Authority to become formally chartered as communicators and transporters on a first-come, first-served basis. FT&T guaranteed the training and supervision of all its parapsychic Talents who were graded from Talent 1, or Prime, since the recipient of that title had to be both a strong telepath and telekinetic, down to minor abilities at Talent 12.

2100 The first B-type ship, the *Bradbury*, was teleported by Callisto Tower forty-five light years away, guided by the time-resolved imaging spectrophotopolarimetric of their destination in Capella.